Manshare

Manshare

A Novel by
Maxine Paetro

M. Evans and Company, Inc.

NEW YORK

To Madeline and Sam, my parents,
and in memory of my grandmother, Hannah Ellis

Library of Congress Cataloging-in-Publication Data

Paetro, Maxine.
  Manshare.

  I. Title.
PS3566.A332M36   1986   813'.54   86-2093

ISBN 0-87131-472-X

M. Evans and Company, Inc.
216 East 49 Street
New York, New York 10017

Design by Diane Gedymin

Manufactured in the United States of America

9 8 7 6 5 4 3 2 1

1

THE CLOCK PRESIDING OVER THE ENTRANCE TO GRAND CENTRAL
station declared the time to be 8:27. Hanna Coleman winced. She did
a fast calculation as she half-sprinted, half-wove through the morning
mass of several hundred thousand commuters and subway passengers
onto the escalator. She was on her way to the Pan Am Building, the
34th floor conference room and the monthly editorial meeting at *Urban
Life Magazine.*

She figured it would take her five minutes if the elevator was waiting,
seven if it wasn't. She'd have to dump her coat somewhere and she
wouldn't have time to change out of her running shoes, so she was
going to be late. There was a death penalty for lateness. "Go, go,
go," she urged the escalator. "Come on, will ya," she threatened the
revolving doors at the top. " 'Scuse me, 'scuse me," she murmured,
her long auburn hair swinging as she shoved past the line of people
on the second flight of escalators. "Open," she commanded the elevator, and it did. "Hey, Rose, save my life," she blurted to the
receptionist on 34, as she wadded up her coat and tossed it under
Rose's feet, out of sight.

She paused one breath's worth to look in the mirrored surface of a
bronze award plaque. Her cheeks were flushed from exertion. Had she
combed her hair? Had her lipstick smudged? She had. It hadn't. Go
calmly now, she cautioned herself. Face death as though you are above
it.

Waiting for the ether of silence and the dual blades of Stein's eyes to pierce her chest, Hanna quietly opened the conference room door. But instead of silence, there was noise. Wonderfully buzzy noise. David Stein, the Editor-in-Chief, was not among the twenty-five writers and editors lounging in their chairs, smoking, doodling, gossiping, pouring coffee from the urn at the far end of the room. The meeting had not started. Oh, God, thank you, Hanna breathed. Today was not the day to be late.

Mahelly Colucci, Hanna's best pal, sister almost, waggled a hand frantically signaling that she had saved Hanna a seat, then bowed her fluffy blond head over her notes. Mahelly was always nervous at editorial meetings, excessively nervous for a person who couldn't lose her job. Her monthly column, "Fitness First," was free-lanced. Her copy was generally mailed in or dropped off, with any changes made on the phone. But the December issue, the annual holiday gift issue, was one of the year's most important issues and Mahelly was there to present an idea for a special winter fitness article. Mahelly hated public speaking.

Hanna had to smile. Mahelly was nervous, but she had nothing to worry about. For a moment Hanna wished she could exchange places with her friend of fifteen years. God! If only she were going to get up in a few minutes and propose a comprehensive report on massage techniques or something. Lucky Mel. I'm glad you're here, Mel, Hanna thought to herself. She waved back and walked toward the coffee urn. As she walked past the long conference table, she continued the thoughts that absorbed her so thoroughly that she had missed her subway stop this morning and yesterday had lost her too-expensive, electric blue cashmere scarf in a telephone booth. The same thoughts had been with her nearly every minute for the last three weeks, imprinted on what Hanna imagined was a tiny videotape loop in her brain.

Hanna envisioned herself at this meeting seated next to David Stein. He would gift her with a smile (a faint smile but a real one), or maybe a private look, as some less lucky co-worker choked on badly prepared remarks. Perhaps he would scrawl a note in thick cobalt blue script with his fat fountain pen and turn the note for her to see. Then he would say, "Coleman," sternly, no favors now, and she would smile confidently, rise, and without a rustle of paper she would smoothly, logically, oh so brilliantly, present her idea, which was so sensational, so winning, that Stein would not be able to help himself. He would turn in his chair and not merely say, "Very good, Coleman," his highest accolade, but, "Very good, Coleman. That's the kind of editorial thinking I want to hear from the rest of you." And he would direct that remark right across the inky black conference table square into the greasy face of Brian Atkins, who would mumble incoherently. Hanna filled a styrofoam cup with coffee and smiled.

Naturally, this charming vision had a reverse side. Hanna's smile faded as she imagined Atkins sitting next to Stein. Atkins would add his spidery green annotation to Stein's thick blue script. They would laugh together. Atkins would rise to his full five foot, five and a half-inch height and casually reveal a feature story idea so blindingly brilliant that the room would actually shake a little in awe. Stein would say, "Well people, I guess I don't have to look any farther for our next Features Editor," and Atkins would smile smugly before sitting.

"Coleman," Stein would announce and she would stand, big round patches of sweat growing unimpeded under her arms. She would present her formerly brilliant idea which even to her ears would sound sophomoric, girlish, dumb. Stein would turn to Atkins and say with ill-disguised contempt, "What do you think of Coleman's idea, Atkins?" and before he could reply, Hanna would knock over her coffee cup. As the milky brown fluid streamed smoothly across the table toward Stein's cobalt blue pin-striped lap, she would vaporize herself into the smoky air.

"I wouldn't buy it, Hanna," a friendly voice intruded into her reverie.

"Huh," she started, and found herself staring into the wide, benign face of Design Editor Kathy Broome.

"You've been standing in front of that coffee urn for so long, I thought you were thinking of buying it," Kathy said with a smile, "but I didn't think cafeteria contemporary was your style."

"No, of course not," Hanna smiled back, grateful to be out of her daydream. She allowed Kathy to get past her to the urn, added a packet of Sweet'n Low to the styrofoam cup, and took a deep breath followed by a sweet sip, and surveyed the room.

Every bit of luxury that had been spared in the egg-cartonlike cubicles at *Urban Life* had been poured into the main conference room, and Hanna was always amazed by the contrast.

Outside the conference room were worn linoleum floors, gray steel desks, bright green lights on computer faces, cold white lights in the overhead fluorescent bulbs, and the fluctuating cacophony of office sounds: voices, electronic phone rings, heels clacking on lino, the labored groaning of the copier, the wheeze of the printers dragging the printing wheels across the connected pages of computer paper again and endless again.

To Hanna, the polished metal door leading to the conference room was a vacuum seal. Entering the conference room from a narrow side of its rectangular shape, and stepping over the threshold, Hanna often got the sensation she expected (but disappointedly never received), while straddling the state line between, say, New York and New Jersey. Here a foot planted on cold, scarred linoleum. Here a foot gently impressing wool carpeting the color of rain clouds and twice as dense.

The long walls to the right and left were covered in pale gray, padded panels that when opened revealed video equipment, light boxes, charts, liquor in cut-crystal decanters, but Hanna imagined more exotic things were hidden there: red telephones, cosmic telescopes, dancing girls or even a door to another dimension. Almost anything was possible where David Stein was concerned.

Indirect lighting slipped silently from recesses in the ceiling, causing the conference room table, black, smooth and large enough to seat thirty, to gleam like a garden pool in the middle of a moonlit night. Thirty rounded black matte metal chairs, padded and covered with soft yellow leather, squatted on wheeled feet, were clustered around the table. Beyond the table was the magnificent far wall, made entirely of glass the width and height of the room, positioned to face straight down the majestic corridor of Park Avenue to the south.

This was the place where it would happen for Hanna: Dodge City, New York.

As Fashion Editor for *Urban Life*, Hanna had a very cushy territory, hers after four years in retail advertising, four years in cosmetic sales promotion and four tough years proving herself in *U.L.* Her column, UrbanWear, was, in Stein's words, a "profit center." Her three to five flashy pages, carefully conceived, expertly written and beautifully shot, attracted advertisers to the magazine, and the owner and publisher of *U.L.* sure loved Hanna for that. The manufacturers of the fashions she selected for her editorials loved her too. They pushed sample clothes into her hands and tickets to fashion shows and parties. The work was easy for Hanna, too easy. Fashion editorials, no matter how deliciously they were crafted, were advertising copy. It was ad copy, despite the challenges she forced on herself to find new words, new designers, discover threads of trends that weren't yet trends. After a dozen years of professional life, Hanna had had fashion every way there was. She'd done it and done it, and now she wanted something more.

Urban Life was a glossy book with a $3.00 cover price, directed to the affluent city dweller, neatly tabbed in sections—art, music, the theater, the home. But beyond the notices of special events, the splashy photos, the theatrical criticism and the predictions of the next new thing or place, *U.L.* had a serious journalistic presence. Although it would be going too far to say it shamed the newsmagazines, it would certainly be fair to credit it with unusual and interesting perspective and uncanny almost precognitive timing of stories soon to be in the general news.

David Stein was the talent in features. He had been hired away from a top-rated news weekly and brought to *U.L.* to make it the best-selling high-ticket consumer book in the country. And David Stein was doing just that. He had fired the sweet and charming former Features Editor, and never replaced her. He held the job of Features Editor in his left hand, Editor-in-Chief in his right. It was unclear if he ever intended to install a new Features Editor beneath him, but there were at least two in that noisy conference room who wanted that job.

One was Brian Atkins, who wrote UrbanBeat. Atkins was a real reporter. He had crossed over to *Urban Life* from ABS Broadcast News. He despised the broadcast news machine, he said; hated "writing pap for dorks to read on camera." He wanted back into journalism, he said. Three months ago he had written the cover story, "Ripping Off the Landlord," after Stein had okayed the idea at the editorial meeting. The issue sold out after two days, and they had to go back to press. Stein had sent around a memo congratulating him.

The other contender was Hanna. Hanna wanted to be Features Editor the way a goose wants to honk. She was a writer and she wanted to write. Being Features Editor would be the best job she could imagine even with her considerable imagination. As Features Editor, she could choose subjects that interested her. (God, wouldn't it be great not to have the Perry Ellis Fall Season Show be the highlight of her working years?) Her stories would be trumpeted on *Urban Life*'s cover. Through the sheer process of working she would be exposed to new people, events, ideas. She would learn something new every day. And then there was the money, and the prestige.

Once a month at the editorial meeting, after all the editors reported the completion of their sections for the upcoming issue and reported their progress on the next two issues, after questions had been answered, pieces moved around, charts updated; after Stein had detailed the success or failure of the last issue, he would open up the meeting for a discussion of new feature ideas. Subjects were presented, cases made. Some ideas were scornfully rejected, some were noted and filed, some were given immediate approval.

Hanna's fashion background was almost a handicap, but she had asserted herself, volunteered when Stein had thrown an idea needing development on the conference table, conceived ideas of her own. As a result, some of her feature stories had been published and two of them had been cover stories. "Nice going, Coleman," Stein had said, when having read her submissions, he approved them, but smiles and pats on top of the head were not enough to raise Hanna Coleman, "the fashion lady," out of suede coats and turkey leather boots into features for good.

Hanna thought again about Stein. Magnificent in his elegantly draped, double-breasted, blue-black Giorgio Armani suits. Stein, with his thick black hair, his strong nose flaring at the nostrils, his evil, sexy eyes; one blue, one green, and his narrow-lipped mouth capable of bestowing blessings or curses as easily as the time of day. David Stein, Editor-in-Chief of *Urban Life Magazine*. He was the man Hanna had to please.

Last month in the middle of a starry late summer night (Ariel Potamkin, *U.L.*'s undercover astrologist, would tell Hanna that Mars moved into Gemini), Hanna had an idea for a new section.

Certainly Stein's memo lauding Brian Atkins had provided the stimulus. Was it insomnia that brought about the idea or the idea that brought about the insomnia? Hanna didn't know. She just knew that she was awake, and that while one part of her brain was seemingly absorbed in watching Late Night with David Letterman, another, slightly rabid part of her brain was bloodhounding around in her head looking for an exit.

Hanna locked her brown eyes on stare, twirled a clump of auburn hair. How, how, how to dump UrbanWear. How to shift safe, boring, day-after-day into overdrive. She was, she thought, intelligent, ambitious, dedicated, well-trained. She was *the* 1980's New York City contemporary woman. If she couldn't figure out how to get promoted into the real job . . . wait, contemporary woman. Wait a minute. She was an *urban* woman. Urban woman. God. She was working in the center of the fastest, smartest field in the citiest of cities, New York,

New York. Fashion was just a piece of what was interesting to women. If she could just figure out how to package it, she could find a way to relate almost everything to how it affects urban women: the law, economics, advertising, network programming, world issues. OK, even fashion.

What if she could write a new column every month under her by-line. Maybe she could call it UrbanWoman. Yeah, that was great. Imagine, bona fide reporter's access to everything. That would do it. Real writing, impactful and noteworthy and God, the opportunities. The cover stories. Yup, that would give her a clear shot at Features Editor.

But she'd need a start. She couldn't simply present UrbanWoman as a rough concept to David Stein. Right now the UrbanWoman idea was just good enough for him to give it to a known pro. Sure, he'd say, "Thanks, Coleman," and give the column to Nora Ephron or Judith Viorst or someone. She would need a nuclear warhead of a story idea to get David Stein to let her write her own column. What could she write about?

Guy Spencer, Hanna's man, lover, paramour, was as usual gently snoring through Late Night with David Letterman, but it was OK, she felt, to ask him to be a guest star on Late Night with Hanna Coleman.

Hanna shifted a little under the satin quilt to look at the back of the curly head of her lover, tucking the quilt around his shoulders with her free hand. The steady sound of Guy's breathing quieted her own pulse. Guy would know what to do. He was so smart, so clever at seeing the big idea. Hanna could have a million ideas a second, ranging from puny to gigantic, and sometimes they all seemed the same size. Guy would have no idea or one idea. If it was one, it would be the right one.

"Guy. Honey." Hanna moved the quilt an inch down on Guy's shoulder and dipped her head to touch her tongue to that warm spot.

No response.

"Guy," Hanna very softly kissed his shoulder twice.

"Hanna. Not now."

"Honey, I just want to talk."

"Wuhh timeizit?"

"Ten-thirty," she fibbed.

"Oh. Mus've dropped off."

Hanna sat up quickly and shut off the TV and turned on her lamp. Guy raised his head from the pillow, fluffed it, put his head back down, still facing away from the purring, racing, kissing machine who was his bedmate.

"Guy, I just had an idea. Listen to this."

"Lis'ning."

"What do you think about this? A new section. Get this. Urban (slow beat) Woman."

"Great. G'night."

"Guy. Wake up. Pay attention."

Guy turned over, opened his brown eyes, ran his hand hard over his mouth a few times, put both arms on top of the quilt with a soft fumph.

"OK, Lois Lane. Get talking."

"Mmm mmm mmm," Hanna kissed him on each eye and then the mouth. "This is it. A new section called UrbanWoman, about and for urban women. I write it. It's mine. The Urban Woman writing about the things that affect today's city women and the beauty is, I write about anything I want to write about. Like maybe I want to interview David Letterman and have him tell me what he finds sexy in women. Wrong, wrong. That's dull. That's been done. Wait. Maybe like I'll interview top women execs and have them tell me truthfully how to use sex in business. That's closer. But it's still not right. It needs to be more important than interviews, deeper, you know what I mean? The stories should change reader perceptions, make them mad or smarter. Maybe I could write about what it's like to be a New York City woman who works at the phone company and supports her three children alone. Something like that. I don't know," she gently bit one of Guy's biceps. "I don't think I have my lead story yet, but I think there's an idea here. What do you think?"

"Mmm hmm," Guy said after he yawned. "You do a few columns and then Stein makes you Features Editor, right?"

Hanna grinned broadly, licked a wide swath on Guy's neck, ending in a kiss on his earhole. "You're so smart, Guy."

"Not smart enough to get you to stop doing that," Guy said twisting a forefinger in his ear.

Hanna laughed. "Do you like it, huh, huh, huh?" She bounced on her knees shaking the bed and Guy.

"Uh-huh, I think it's good, Nan."

"Goody. I need a story idea. Help."

"How about this?" Guy put a curly forearm over his eyes to block out the light. "Write about this new kind of single urban woman—

MBA's, lawyers, like that, who've got these great jobs and no boyfriends.''

"You mean because they can't find guys as good as they are?" Hanna asked holding her breath.

"I don't know. Maybe there aren't enough men."

"That's great, Guy," Hanna said slowly. "That's great. Thanks."

"Do you owe me one, Nan?"

"Mmm hmm."

"Good. How 'bout telling me what time it is? Really."

"Gosh, I owe you more than that," Hanna said. "Want me to fix you something to eat? Do you want a massage? Wanna take a bath together?"

"Listen, you banana," Guy said, reaching over Hanna's body and turning off the lamp. "You haven't fooled me. I know it's two o'clock in the morning. I've got an 8:30 meeting tomorrow."

"Sure, honey," she said, disappointed. Guy found her face in the dark, kissed her mouth, rolled over and resumed the position he had occupied a few minutes before.

Hanna lay quietly and listened to Guy's breathing and the inaudible clank of her unmeshed thoughts. She knew that twisty night-brain noise wouldn't dwindle to a hum until the problem was solved. She burrowed into the nest of cotton sheets, soft downy pillows and comforter. She turned over on her side and put an arm around her lover's waist, wedged some sheet between her face and his back and closed her eyes. She thought again about Brian Atkins and David Stein and about urban women. She opened her eyes. She rolled onto her back. Onto her stomach. Guy groaned in protest. "Sorry, honey," she whispered, and she sat up.

There was an extra blanket in the trunk at the foot of her bed. The hinges squeaked and Hanna winced at the sound. She lifted out the camphor-smelling folds of wool and went out to the living room. Moving carefully in the dark, she found the hard-seated, hard-backed Victorian sofa she loved unreasonably, and tucked herself in. She squirmed on the slippery velvet sofa, which was only the length of a medium-size teenage girl and tried to trap her 98.6 degrees under a lap throw smelling of mothballs. How could she sleep? Everything inside her head was grinding. She felt as if she had almost conceived. Her idea, inseminated by Guy's words, nourished by ambition and frustration, needed only recollection to give it form. She turned a light on in her head and began to think and remember.

A clock would have said the night lasted the standard number of hours, but in Hanna's mind the night was longer than any arctic night. It was fifteen years long, by twenty stories high, by one wall's distance, by right this minute. When Guy found her and gently shook her awake the next morning, Hanna couldn't remember having fallen asleep at all.

And now as she took her seat next to Mahelly in the conference room, Hanna knew she was ready. She was wearing her blue pin-striped suit (would Stein notice?), her best hundred-dollar cream silk blouse and her running shoes, which were a nice, if accidental, touch. Her thick mahogany hair was gleaming as it hung to her shoulders. She turned to smile at her friend, to give her encouragement. Mahelly. It had all begun with Mahelly.

2

"LOOK! THAT ONE, THE ONE IN THE GREEN SWEATSHIRT," HANNA HAD squealed, poking her forefinger through the slatted blinds of their dormitory room. Mahelly widened the space between the slats for a better look.

"That's Bruce? That's the guy you've been raving about all week?" Mahelly asked, shock in her voice. "He's a midget. He's in my Western Civ class. He's dumb. And he limps!"

"God, Mel, this is 1971, not 1371! Are you living in the dark ages, or what?" Hanna sputtered, annoyed. "How can you be so superficial?" Hanna gave Mahelly a supercilious stare before continuing. "I know he's not book-smart but he's brilliant about the land and about ecology. I knew the first thing you'd say is that he limps," Hanna muttered. "He hurt his leg trying to dismantle an illegal bear trap, you'll be interested to know."

The girls left the window and clambered onto their facing beds.

"OK," conceded Mahelly, "I'm sorry I said he limps. I really am. But seriously, would you ever marry that guy? What in the world would you ever do with him? Move to a log cabin in Montana, or what?"

"Marry? Who said marry? For the millionth time, Mahelly. I'm not dating these guys to marry them. I'm dating to date. It's fun, and if I'm going to be a writer I've got to know lots of different kinds of people." Hanna pulled a bucket out from under the bed and began unwinding a length of her mahogany hair from a fat pink roller. "And boy, can he ever kiss." She sighed, unclipped another roller from the top of her head and unrolled it.

Mahelly didn't say anything. She turned onto her back, and looked at the ceiling. She was frowning.

"I've got lots of time to get married," Hanna continued. "I wouldn't marry anyone I know at this place, anyway. Here's where I'm going to get experience and then when I move to New York, I'll be ready for real men . . ."

Mahelly went to her closet and pulled a suitcase from the top shelf. She opened the drawer to her dresser and started placing neat stacks of white cotton things in the case. "Yeah, I've heard the story," she said collecting a group of bottles from the dresser top and sliding them into a plastic cosmetic bag. "You're going to get a fantastic job, meet a ton of handsome successful men, dangle them around for a little while and when you are good and ready, you'll marry one."

"So what's wrong with that?" Hanna paused in her unrolling to stare.

"I don't know. Maybe it's too casual for me. Last week you were in love with Bobby. And before that it was Ricky and before that it was Roy."

"Ray."

"It was Roy."

"You're right. It was Roy. I was thinking of Ray from last term. Anyway, so what?" Hanna glared. "You act as if I'm sleeping with these guys. Or using them."

"I'm not saying that." Mahelly paused, and folded a sweater into the case. "It's just, how can you be so in love and then not? It's like they're really not quite real to you. It's just experimenting."

"Well, Mel," Hanna had said, lips thinned and white, "I guess I think I don't know what kind of man I should marry like you do."

"Meaning?"

"Meaning, you think the perfect man is going to appear out of the sky-blue sky on Pegasus I suppose, like heroes in those trashy novels of yours, and carry you off to Happy Ever After Land. You aren't going to have to do a thing but show up in a white dress."

"Nice, Hanna."

There was a pause. "Not very. I'm sorry. But you did start it."

"I know I did. I'm sorry too." Mahelly glanced down at her white dress. "But you are right, you know. I do think it's going to happen something like that. I'll know him instantly. He'll know me."

"And then what?"

"Shit, Hanna, I don't know. Could you please lay off? Could we change the subject?" Mahelly zipped up her bag and sat back down on the bed. Hanna pulled out the last pink stick from the backmost roller, shook out her newly made curls, and grabbed a bottle of nail polish from a shoe box on her pillow. Shiny bronze lacquer flowed onto a lengthy nail.

"You know, Mel, instead of going home to your parents' house every weekend, you really ought to hang around once in a while. It's fun here on the weekends. And tonight there's a DJ at 'The Saloon.' "

"It's not fun for me, Hanna."

"Please, stay for the game tomorrow. Bruce has this friend coming up from NYU . . ."

"Uh-uh. No."

"Please. You'll like him. He's on the debate team. I saw his picture and he's a doll."

"Oh, that'll cinch it. A debater. He'll love me."

"Mel. He will."

"I'm going home," Mahelly said. "Look, can't we both be right? Does it have to happen the same way to both of us?"

"Guess not," Hanna said dubiously. "Well, I promised I'd meet Bruce at his room." Mindful of her nails, she gingerly kissed Mahelly good-bye. "Have fun this weekend. Maybe you'll meet someone on the train."

"You have a good weekend too," Mahelly said. Hanna scooped up a sweater from the back of a chair, winked at Mahelly, and breezed down the hallway.

It was pretty crummy of Hanna to take such a low swipe, Mahelly thought to herself as she swung her suitcase off the bed. Who said being a party girl was so great anyway? Just because Hanna had a skillion dates didn't mean *she* had to. Or wanted to. Was she supposed to give her virginity away to one of those idiot, loudmouthed chimpanzees? It was a disgusting idea. When she made love for the first time it would be with a man.

Standing before the small mirror over the dresser she shared with Hanna, Mahelly pulled the rubber band from the end of her long yellow braid and ran her fingers through the thick hair. Her scalp ached now that her hair was released and she held her head for relief. Then she slowly moved her fingers away and looked at her face. Plain, she thought. Nice blue eyes, OK, but no lashes and my nose is a bore, and that mouth looks like it's never been kissed. And how about the hair, huh? She sighed. Look at that. What she wanted to see was a seamless sheet of blond sunlight hanging straight to the middle of her back. What she saw was a fan of ridges set by the tight plait, spraying away from her tiny face. The bride of Frankenstein, she thought, her nose and eyes pinking up at the thought.

I don't have to go to that stupid party, she thought. She'd been waiting all day to get back to that novel that she was halfway through. The cover of the silver-foiled, brightly embossed paperback beckoned. The title, *Those Fair Eyes*, gleaming in metallic purple script, swirled behind the drawing of a blond woman swooning in the arms of a dark-haired man. The book straddled an arm of Mahelly's desk chair, its spine cracked at midpoint. The book was a pace away, then it was in her hand. Mahelly gazed at the two figures illustrated on the cover. They were Raimundo, the ruthless ghetto attorney, and Sondra, the shy librarian who was compelled at last to reveal her secret desires. Mahelly dog-eared a page and put the book down on her desk. She sighed. What did she expect? That Raimundo was going to come crashing into room 203 of Dougherty Hall, pin her to the bed, and teach her about ecstasy? Hanna was right. She took her long white cashmere cardigan out of her suitcase and put it on. She flicked mascara on each set of lashes, braided her hair once more, licked both palms with her tongue, then slicked down the ruff of short fuzzy hair forming a halo around her face. She stuffed her feet into her Capezio slippers and without looking in the mirror again, walked out and slammed the door shut.

"The Saloon" was suffocatingly stuffed with people. By day, the cafeteria/lounge was sparsely populated by lunchers and readers, quietly lunching or reading. By night, especially weekend nights, the lounge was transformed into a plebian discotheque. Beer and wine was brought by the students, furniture pushed back, music brought in. The professorial staff was absent, and the party was sanctioned by the administrative staff on the theory that it was better to keep the students on campus where they were safe, than have them wander around the town of Cobleskill. And of course, at curfew, "The Saloon" was closed.

Tonight at "The Saloon" there was something special going on. WKIX, the local radio station, was throwing a party for the students of Cobleskill College of Fine Arts. It was a promotion and a thank you. Courtesy of WKIX, "The Saloon" had a free bar, free music, and on the dais built by WKIX amidst the jumble of wires and equipment was the *pièce de rèsistance*—a live, actual disc jockey.

And not just any disc jockey. The disc jockey was Frank Colucci. Even Cobleskill's cultural elite, many of whom deplored rock and roll as antithink, recognized Frank Colucci. He'd been photographed with the Beatles and with Little Richard, and by plugging and playing the songs of a little-known local group called the "Blacktops" he had pushed them to some national acclaim and the top forty charts for a few weeks last summer. In Cobleskill, New York, this was stardom.

Sound bombarded Mahelly as she wedged herself reluctantly into the overheated room. She looked for Hanna but could scarcely see over the heads of the writhing swarm before her. The bar was to one side of the dim space and she pushed a path to it. When she turned back to face the room, she saw the platform and she saw Frank. Frank was all she saw. It was as if the sound had been turned off and a tunnel of light had been carved through the dark just long enough to reach from Mahelly to Frank.

Frank was sitting on the plywood platform, bent over stereo and microphone gear, headphones clasping his thick dark hair. His muscles bulged when he bent his arms to "spin the wax." His strong features blurred when he lost himself in the lyrics of a song, and focused intensely, personally, when he joked with those who clustered around him, hoping to catch a little of his sparkle, a little of his fame.

Mahelly hung back and gaped at him. He was so self-confident, and masculine and alive, and something else. Something about his age maybe. He had to be at least six or seven years older than she. He was a man. He was a man like Raimundo.

Mahelly shook her head and laughed at herself. Imagine even thinking that Frank Colucci and she . . . what would it be like? That thick lower lip of his in her mouth, her hands pulling at that too tight WKIX T-shirt stretched now over his wide chest, putting her hands into that thick, dark hair . . . She shook her head again. Too much. He would never even notice her. As she watched, a platinum blond with a tight blue sweater threw her shoulders back, advanced her breastline, and elbowed a smaller girl out of Frank's vision. Mahelly could never do anything like that, never. She separated herself from the wall she clung to, pushed her way through the crowd moist with beer and exuberance, found the bar and ordered a ginger ale. She'd stay long enough to finish her drink, just so Hanna wouldn't give her such a hard time, and then she'd leave.

Turning into the room Mahelly noticed the music had stopped. Heading straight toward the bar was Frank Colucci. Mahelly froze. Her brain said, let's go, but her feet had forgotten where the gas pedal was located. She stared full into his face. Although she would have been prepared for him either to say "excuse me," and walk past her, or speak unfathomable phrases in ancient tongues, she was unprepared for what he did say. He said, "Hi."

Frank didn't know Mahelly was frozen by panic. He saw not a brassy, cheeky cheerleader like those who moments ago were pressing their breasts into his body and cocking their shiny heads for him to admire. Instead, here was a fair-haired, wan little beauty about the size of a buttercup, miserably clutching a can of ginger ale with both hands. She looked as if she needed someone to take care of her. He hoped it would be him.

"Hi," he said.

"Hi," she replied. He was huge. He looked a couple of stories tall. His face was broad and darkskinned. His nose was straight from between the eyes to midpoint, then took a slight turn to the right. His lips were full, a hint of Elvis there, and the same was true of his heavily lidded eyes. There was a thin white line of a scar crossing his right eyebrow and in Mahelly's survey of his face, her eyes locked on the scar. To Frank it looked like eye contact.

"What's your name, Buttercup?" he asked.

"Mahelly," she said.

"Ma-whatty?"

"Ma-hell-y," and then she spelled it. "It's short for Mary Helen. Sullivan. That's my last name." A long pause followed. Long to Mahelly, anyway. She could not think of a thing to say. Gee, you look like Elvis. No, that would be dumb. "How'd you get that scar?" she blurted.

Frank laughed. "I was caught in the middle of a disagreement between a motorcycle and a tree," he said. "I'd tell you about it but I still have to work and it's a long story. Will you have coffee with me after the dance?"

Frank elicited a yes response to his invitation. Because he was so "on" from the evening's excitement, he couldn't really see that what appeared to be quiet reserve in the buttercup of his dreams was actually awe, a cottony mouth and restrained lust. Still able to move her neck muscles, Mahelly nodded her head yes, and yes again later to Frank's dinner invitation for next Saturday night.

From then on, Mahelly thought of nothing but Frank.

Dating was difficult simply from a logistics point of view. Frank worked nights six days a week including weekends, from 8:00 at night until 2:00 the next morning. Mahelly was of course bound by a more conventional schedule during the day, but there were curfews at night. The rules demanded she be inside the dormitory by 10:00 P.M. on week nights, by 12:00 midnight on weekend nights. Their dates commonly went like this: Frank would pick Mahelly up in his prized 1957 Mercury sedan at 5:00 P.M. They would drive to Ralph's Pizzeria situated a block from WKIX. At five minutes before 8:00 air time, they would drop everything, even if it had anchovies on it, and race to the studio. Inside the studio, Frank would vault into the cracked leather swivel seat before the control panel, slide his earphones over his head, and with no discernible break in the program Frank would be on the air. Mahelly would sit in the small gray control room until moments before curfew, then she would dash outside, catch a taxi, and be back in the dorm by the time the dormitory clock struck the hour.

At first it was fun. Frank loved his work. He loved the music and the attention from the fans. The buttons on Frank's phone blinked steadily all night, and Frank swung easily from the phone to the mike and back again, the expressions on his large, handsome face changing, liquid, from intense concentration to laughter, to rapture when a favorite song caused the very steel of the control panel to vibrate in time with the rhythm.

Mahelly was impressed. It wasn't just her imagination—everyone said he looked like Elvis. Frank said his looks came from the two quarts of Cherokee blood he got from his great maternal grandmother, mixed with the marinara sauce flowing through his veins. When Frank sang along with the records he could sound just like Chuck Berry or James Taylor or John Lennon. Sometimes between records, he'd punch all the phone lines on hold and leave his fans to busy signals. Then he'd swing around in his chair, pluck Mahelly from her seat behind him, and whisk her onto his lap. "Come here, Bird," he'd say, "my hummingbird."

In Frank's lap, arms around his neck, Mahelly felt engulfed in his love. He seemed to surround every part of her, and even with the music bouncing from the sides of the room or buzzing tinnily through the headset, Mahelly could hear only the sound of her own breathing against Frank's neck. "I love you, Frank," she whispered once before she realized what she had said. "I love you too, Bird," he replied before jerkily swinging back to the microphone to pull a toggle and plug the varsity shop.

All love and no sex made Mahelly bold. The roommates were in their dormitory room. Hanna's red bedspread was crumpled at the foot of the bed. A carton bristling with hair curlers, sewing implements, packets of letters, filled the chair in front of the desk, which itself was completely buried in books, old flowers dried more by neglect than by intention, and hastily folded laundry. Hanna sat in the middle of her unmade bed swaddled in a red flannel bathrobe. A notebook was in her lap. The gooseneck lamp on the desk had been stretched at its neck to its limit and was now throwing a harsh 100-watt glare on Hanna's round face. She squinted her large brown eyes against the glare, added a word to the paper she was composing, scratched a paragraph out with a growl, ripped the rubber band from the thick ponytail of brown-red hair, and threw herself face down onto the bed.

"I hate Browning. I always will. I can't write this paper. I'm going to take a nap. Wake me if Bruce calls. Good-night."

Mahelly didn't comment. She sat, back erect, ankles crossed, in her chair in front of her tidy Formica desk. Her jeans were clean, her blue Oxford-cloth shirt was starched, her pale yellow hair was long and plaited into a braid that hung down her back. Her brow was knit in concentration.

"Does this look like Mother's handwriting?" she asked Hanna, holding out a pink sheet of stationery embellished with a few lines of fountain-penned script.

"Let me see. What is this? 'Dear Mrs. Wilkes, Mary Helen will be spending the weekend with us. Cordially, Kate Sullivan.' What are you doing, Mel?" Hanna held the pink tissue-y paper with an outstretched hand and shook it. "Frank? Finally? Are you going to spend the weekend with Frank?"

Mahelly nodded. She turned a glowing face to Hanna. "Do you think he'll like this?" She opened a flat box lying on her bed, brushed aside some tissue, and held up a nightgown of white cotton batiste, so thin Hanna could read the price tag through the fabric. A tracery of pale pink roses was embroidered on the bodice, the short sleeves were puffed and edged with pink lace.

"Melly, he'll love it, I swear," Hanna breathed. "Are you scared?"

"Uh-uh, no," she said putting her hands in her lap. "I know what it will be like."

Hanna grinned. "You call me if you want to."

Mahelly nodded, hugged herself, hugged Hanna, folded the pink note and addressed it to the dorm mother.

"It" wasn't exactly what Mahelly expected. It was better. It was worse. It was real. For one thing, lovemaking with Frank wasn't gauzy. No rose petals, no scent of jasmine, no slow motion embraces. For another thing, it hurt. He was so big, everywhere, and freed after months of constraint, he couldn't wait for nightgowns and wooing. Exhausted from his shift at the station, Frank could manage only a burger, a beer, a shower, and then, still damp, could tuck his darling under his huge form, plunge into her and shortly thereafter fall asleep.

Mahelly had been unprepared for the tenderness of her body and she hadn't known how vulnerable a man was during the act of love. Her big strong man nearly wept with his orgasm and Mahelly felt ennobled by this blessing, and maternal too. By being that vulnerable, Frank was in her charge.

The forged letter trick worked without fail. Most weekends were now spent not in the luxury of a colonial house in a Boston suburb, but in a studio apartment built with all the charm and substance of a cardboard box.

But there was a certain comfort in her new weekend routine. Six hours of sitting in a gray metal and glass studio reverberating with rock and roll until two in the morning, a stop at a hamburger drive-in, and a drive home to Frank's lovemaking, a leisurely Saturday morning, a repeat of the night before. Frank would sing that day's appropriate top of the pops smash,

Bet-ter than money, honey
Much better than money, honey
Much sweeter than money, hon-e-e-e-y—
We got love . . .

Hanna thought Frank too rough for Mahelly, too coarse, but she was so happy that Mahelly was happy, she could not tell Mahelly her thoughts. Mahelly was entranced by Frank's swarthy good looks, his charm. His pizza pie tastes gave her visions of the ways she would enrich his life with culture and art. Frank thought Mahelly was a princess. It was no surprise when he dedicated "Truly" to Mahelly on WKIX one night and announced to the entire Cobleskill to Poughkeepsie listening audience his intention to marry her.

But as in love as Mahelly was, she had reservations. She knew she could not be a DJ's wife and she told him so. "Frank, the hours are disgusting. The pay is awful. Do you really think we can live like this?"

"We could move, Bird. We don't have to live in Cobleskill. We could live anywhere. I'm a mobile music man."

"Where Frank? Some other little town where we can live two blocks from the station?"

"You want to live in New York City, don't you, Bird?"

Mahelly nodded solemnly.

"Then I'll have to get a gig in New York."

"I'll move there and wait for you," she said, and then she and Hanna graduated.

Hanna and Mahelly moved to New York, clean, pink, and hot from the greenhouse environment of Cobleskill College of Fine Arts. Hanna expected a career and love. Mahelly expected Frank.

Having had all their dreams come true so far, they had hardly thought it remarkable when a bare week after graduation, before they had hardly creased the classified ad section of the *Village Voice*, they found a truly great one-bedroom apartment with everything. Everything was an eat-in kitchen with south-facing French windows, a white-tiled bathroom, a bedroom with a closet that could hold a piano, a living room with an air conditioner, all in a classy 1930s high-rise building on 94th and Central Park West. Anything less would have surprised them more.

There they were in Manhattan. New York, New York. Roommates still, but no more pencils, no more books. Instead there was Lincoln Center just down the road. They were nearly next door to the Metropolitan Museum! They were two miles from midtown! The subway was so close, if had been closer it would have rattled the spoons. Life was perfect.

Hanna's plans had been so clear. She would land a job at *Vogue Magazine* and she would have those few affairs, just for experience, and then she would marry a handsome, successful man, when she was ready, who would make her happy in every way.

But Hanna was more wishful than she was precognizant. *Vogue Magazine* was full up. Their personnel office held over a hundred résumés on file from June's graduating class of the New York City schools alone, and countless applications from other young writers "willing to do anything" from colleges all over the country.

Cosmopolitan Magazine wrote Hanna a nice "no openings, thank you" letter as did *Mademoiselle, Redbook, Viva,* and *Better Homes and Gardens.* A rather spectacularly written cover letter to *Esquire* (Dear Sirs, I'm a woman who thinks like a man . . .) brought her an interview with an amused fashion editor but no job.

As the magazines rejected her offers to work, Hanna changed her list of prospects, enlarging the number and kind of possible place of employment. At last, her résumé, an interview, followed by another interview produced success. Macy's department store hired her to write copy for $226.00 a week. She was a real writer now, a professional. She sold the green Citroën her father had given her for her high-school graduation present, the car that apart from Mahelly was her best friend through college, so she could afford her share of the rent for the apartment she and Mahelly shared. She was genuinely grateful to Macy's copy chief for giving her this mercilessly grinding day and night job, a job that depended upon the sales results of her daily ad (or so Hanna believed). Between that and some freelance work, at the age of twenty-two Hanna was earning $18,000.00 a year. Not enough to shop casually on Fifth Avenue, but enough to pay the entire rent on her one-bedroom apartment, which she would very soon occupy alone.

Mahelly had needed to be in New York for different reasons. She wanted a life saturated with culture—art, music, and especially the dance.

While Hanna had been studying Journalism and English Literature, Mahelly had been studying dance. Growing up, if she could have had one thing she wanted in life and been forced to forgo every other kind of pleasure, Mary Helen Sullivan would have given up cashmere socks, her romance novel addiction, maple-walnut sundaes and her tiger-striped cat Willie, if only she could have professionally embraced the rigor and freedom of the ballet.

But Mahelly did not come to New York to become a ballerina. She had known it would be impossible since preteen dance class, where it was slowly revealed against her will, that her ankles were weak, her ligaments too short. When the other girls gained height and grace, becoming the swans they always knew they would become, Mahelly reached five foot one and a half inches and stopped growing for good.

Yet, living in New York for Mahelly meant if not a career in ballet, at least the opportunity to be near the New York City Ballet, the Joffrey Ballet, the Alvin Ailey Dance Company. It meant the Metropolitan Opera and the Museum of Modern Art. It meant Broadway and off-Broadway. Of course Mahelly would move to New York. How could she live anywhere else?

Money to Mahelly was as dependable as the full moon. At the first of every month, a beautiful blue check came from Chase Manhattan in the amount of $1,000, her allowance from home. It paid the rent and kept the roommates in food.

For the first three months in Manhattan, Mahelly took dance classes, read, shopped, doused herself in museums, but mostly she waited for Frank to move to New York and for them to be married.

A superstar in Cobleskill, Frank found to his initial disbelief and eventual acceptance that he didn't sound the same in NYC. His tapes were returned with rejection notes, the few interviews he had were fruitless. The general manager at ABC leveled with him. "Frank, there's too much talent trying to get in, and your sound is still a little small town. With a little luck I could maybe get you a slot with our O&O in Albany. . . ."

Taking a big psychological breath, Frank realized what Mahelly had said was true. Life as a disc jockey would be a life of $20,000 a year small-town jobs with bad hours, and late-night phone friends. He would give up being a thirty-year-old teenager and get a real job with real prospects. When he got an offer in New York as a radio advertising salesman with a pretty good firm, he accepted it.

Dazed, Frank moved in with Hanna and Mahelly for a few months. Hanna moved out to the living room. "Frank," Hanna had thrown her arms around him, "it's gonna be nice to have a man around the house." Mahelly was blissful. She was up at six every morning making fresh croissants, grinding coffee beans for her two roommates. Soon another one-bedroom apartment opened up on the 20th floor and Frank and Mahelly moved upstairs.

The wedding was held on her parents' lawn. Mahelly outbeamed the sunbeams as she floated down the path beneath the wisteria-entwined pergola to a patch of sunlit clover where Mahelly, who had never slept with another man, and Frank, who said he would never look at another woman, promised to love one another forever.

That Mahelly's improbable scenario had come true seemed to Hanna a miracle of the same magnitude as airplanes staying up in the sky. But it *had* come true. Mahelly became a housewife.

3

FOR HANNA AND MAHELLY, LIVING EIGHT FLOORS APART IN THE SAME
building was like being roommates without the bother. Mahelly didn't
have to choose between nagging and suppressing her anger that Hanna
was such a slob. Hanna didn't have to hang her clothes in the closet
according to length and color to satisfy Mahelly's sense of order, nor
did she have to clean out the refrigerator until the milk had turned to
a cross between butter and sour cream.

Instead, they had their own places with keys to the others. They
spoke not once but at least twice a day. A morning conversation would
find Mahelly in white silk pajamas, perched on the window seat at the
window overlooking the park, clear black coffee in a flowered Spode
china cup, newspaper laid over a bath towel to protect the pale fabric
of the window seat, window cracked open to allow the entrance of a
sycamore-scented breeze from the sea of treetops across the street.

"Did you sleep all right?" Mahelly asked over the white princess
phone connected by wire and electricity to the black standard clunker
on Hanna's gray metal desk at Macy's.

"Nope," Hanna answered, eyes restlessly scanning the copy she
was painfully eking out of the typewriter. Sleep? She had been writing
a loungewear headline in her head half the night.

"Did you drink the chamomile tea as I told you to?"

"Uh-uh, I forgot. I gulped about a glass of wine, though, and that
seemed to help for a little while."

"Oh, sure. You went right to sleep. But you woke up a couple of hours later, right?"

"Yeah."

"Hanna. Do me a favor. Drink the tea."

"Melly, if I had your job, I wouldn't need chamomile tea or anything. I'd sleep like a stone."

"You'd kill yourself if you had my job," Mahelly laughed. "I can see you now, cleaning out the cabinet under the sink, scrubbing Wisk into your husband's collar, going to white sales . . ." Mahelly trailed off with a snigger.

"Sitting around all day eating bonbons, taking a little walk in the park . . ." Hanna added in sugary tones.

"Hah, Snotface," Mahelly hooted. "That's what you think."

"OK. What are you doing today?"

"A lot, actually. I'm taking Frank's shoes in to be heeled, dance class at 11:00, return the salad bowls to Macy's, pick up the dry cleaning, and there's a sale at Saks," Mahelly said while gingerly turning the pages of the *Times*. "I want to get Frank a new robe. Dark blue, don't you think?"

"Mmm," Hanna said, turning the platen of the typewriter forward a few clicks, then back. She spilled a cracked cup of paper clips onto the vinyl-coated desk top, found a nice big one, unfolded it, stuck an end in her mouth. "You know, Frank would look good in red."

"Red? Wow, I never thought of Frank in red. Maybe. Although I think red will clash in here." She surveyed the white-painted and carpeted room, subtly punctuated with pastel cushions and pale watercolors. Not that Frank would notice whether the robe clashed or not. Frank didn't notice much when it came to things like colors, textures, feelings. Honestly, blue would be fine. "Should I stop in to see you when I'm at Macy's?" she asked.

"I don't think so, Mel. Not today. Claire is out and I have to do her ad too. Today is going to be awful." Hanna spread a small stack of yellow pages across her desk top and stared in despair at the dozens of headlines she'd created and rejected.

"Do you want to eat with us tonight?" Mahelly asked, a hopeful note in her voice.

"Can't," said Hanna. "Have a date. But I'll call you later."

"OK. Bye."

"Bye."

Mahelly put the phone down carefully and went into the next room. The bed was rumpled. The T-shirt Frank slept in was on the floor. She picked it up and pressed it to her nose. She loved the smell of him. His was a scent that was very special, she thought. It was something more than oil, and skin, and the lemon balm she bought for him at the pricey apothecary shop on the upper East Side. She thought of the scent as "Husband," and it connected her to him even when he wasn't there. She loved creating and caring for this place, her home. Tending these four rooms and providing a clean, efficient, attractive home for Frank was a real job and she was good at it. But she didn't feel quite full. For one thing, it was awfully quiet here during the day. An infant thought, a flicker of one really, pinched her consciousness. Should she get a job? She had tried talking it over with Frank, about doing something else with her time, but she had no real idea of what she should do. And Frank had said, "Bird, you don't have to work. I'm making plenty. I like having you home." Hell, she wasn't qualified to do anything anyway.

Mahelly turned the bedside stereo on and flute notes pranced into the baby-blue room. Ahhh, that was better. She opened the closet door. What should she wear today? Pants? Yes. Jeans? No. The khakis would be good. With what? White shirt? No. The collar was frayed. White T-shirt under the pink cotton cardigan. Yes. White socks and sneakers. Perfect. She stood in front of the mirrored closet door and unbuttoned her pajamas. She shrugged off the top and unhooked the waist of the bottoms feeling the dampness in the silken crotch as the pants slid down her legs. Her mind paused as the dampness registered its meaning. She looked at her body. How could she ever have been ashamed of this body? She was beautiful. Frank had made her see that. She ran her hands over her small breasts and across her tight belly. In the mirror she could see the heap of bedclothes behind her; the place where Frank had plumped a pillow under her buttocks this morning before entering and shortly afterward climaxing with a cry inside of her. She touched tender places, still thick and wet from unrelieved arousal. A spasm of lingering desire went through her.

Mahelly moved to the bed. She slipped between the sheets and the top sheet settled, almost floated, over her. Was she imagining it, or were the sheets still warm from their bodies? The gentle touch of the cotton cloth on her bare skin was so faint, so tentative, tiny hairs all over her body lifted to meet it. The tingling between her thighs turned to heat. Clasping one pillow with her arms and another with her thighs, Mahelly rolled on to her side and then she rocked. Slow minutes rode by on flutes and oboes, and then Mahelly could hear no sound but the thrumming sound inside her as she succumbed to the rhythm of her orgasm.

While Mahelly showered, straightened the bed and selected dance tights and leotards from a drawer filled with a rainbow assortment of these articles, Hanna splashed cold water on her face, poured herself another cup of coffee from the communal pot in the ladies' lounge and started her second ad of the day.

Hanna thought her life was like bouillabaisse—savory, unpredictable, nourishing, and full of sharp little bones.

Every morning started with a terror that her previous day's ad hadn't "pulled." By the end of the day, it probably had, her new ad had been submitted, and she could begin to worry about the next day's ad. Was "Frothy Flounces" too cute? Yes. Was "Next to Nothing Nighties" a winner? Maybe. Would "Shearling, Darling?" attract enough customers to clean off the rack of sheepskin mistakes?

But the real chaos for Hanna was not in the job section of her life. She was a good writer, a trained writer, and the pressure she put upon herself to do great ads only made her better and more secure in her chosen career. Any actual job insecurity was offset by the standing offer from Gimbels and the tangible proceeds of her nighttime free-lance work. The real chaos surrounded the part of her life concerned with romance. With all of her experience, optimism and willingness to learn, Hanna was finding that every year of her life brought her less rather than more knowledge of how to find her suitable mate.

At first dating held no expectations for Hanna. She wanted to be surprised. Each date was like reaching down into a bottomless Christmas stocking and pulling out a brightly wrapped and tied present and waiting with anticipation as the contents were revealed.

"Melly," Hanna would purr, licking her lips, as good as wrapping her tail around her legs. "I was out tonight with that gorgeous man from the bank."

"How was it?" Mahelly would ask eagerly, closing the bedroom door to protect Frank's solid sleep. A banker. Good. Hanna should marry a nice sound banker. Mahelly would put on a kettle, brew some

fresh peppermint tea, arrange the homemade cookies on a Limoges
platter, arrange Frank's huge robe around her small form, and wait.
"Tell me," she'd say, her face propped up in her two hands.

"Well," Hanna would begin, and then she would tell the story.
"I'm in love," she might say and then Mahelly would hear about the
banker's twin Burmese cats, his collection of gold coins, his blue TR3,
and then suddenly, the relationship would be over. He'd be labeled
"boring, boring, boring" and then Hanna would forget whom Mahelly
meant when she asked, "How's it going with George?" Or Hanna
would be fascinated for weeks with the banker's cats, and how he tied
his scarf, and his infuriating habit of forgetting to call when he said
he would and just when Hanna was composing a drop dead letter,
flowers would come to the office and lights would go on behind Hanna's
clear brown eyes. Then, eventually, the flowers wouldn't arrive but
Hanna's drop dead letter would, and then Mahelly would console
Hanna.

Or it would be about the married buyer in menswear.

"Mahelly, guess where I'm calling from?"

"Who is this?" Frank honked sleepily into the phone.

"Frank, it's me Hanna."

"Han?" Mahelly croaked, taking the phone away from Frank.

"Melly, guess where I'm calling from?"

"I give up, Hanna, where *are* you calling from at three thirteen in
the morning?"

"I'm in Paris, do you believe it?" Hanna shrieked. "With Sandy.
Remember the married man in menswear?"

Mahelly made an appropriate noise.

"He wouldn't let me go home tonight."

"What?"

"He stashed me in a limo and kidnapped me out to the airport. He
already had a ticket for me, can you believe this, and nobody knows
from the store. He's here for the Cardin show, and listen, I'll be back
Friday night."

"Han."

"Yeah, Mel."

"I'm jealous. Have a really great time."

By the time Hanna was twenty-four, almost twenty-five, and had
learned from the cabdriver how sexy she was, and from the married

man how beautifully she moved, and from the banker how pretty she was in the morning, she began to long for more than three months with the same man. Then she met Robin, and it was love at·first sight.

Robin was tall and thin, had curly hair and had gone to Dartmouth. He played the violin on weekends and the stock market during the week. He was an account executive with Merrill Lynch and trying hard to make good. He read the trade papers and knew all a young trader should know about Wall·Street;·he just wasn't·sure he was meant to be a salesman. He favored politeness over push. Should he be in this business? He couldn't even relate to the people he worked with. The men were all hustle, and he liked the women less. They wore suits and ties and tried hard not to laugh or flirt, as if they would get penalized if they appeared to be female.

Hanna's life was thrilling to Robin—the discos, the parties where he met people in the costumes they wore as normal attire; they were more real than the people he knew. He'd never met anyone as free as Hanna, so independent. Her decisions were based on her feelings of the moment and she would ride with her whims; a drive to Brooklyn to try out a new Hungarian restaurant, a sudden desire to see a hot film in Times Square, popcorn with milk for breakfast, an aubergine fox boa with rhinestone eyes. Around Hanna, he was in a constant state of arousal.

Their lovemaking touched Hanna in a new way. It was sexy but scary too. Sometimes Robin seemed intense enough to devour her. Other times, he seemed very far away. Hanna was entirely alert when she was making love with Robin, sensitive to his every breath and sigh. On occasion Hanna would cry after her orgasm. She was too happy, too scared, too full, not to surrender to all her feelings, and she told him so. Hanna learned how to play backgammon. Robin started wearing plaids. Hanna fell in love. So did Robin.

But Robin had a dark side, a secret part that he couldn't share. A good day was followed by one that was bad. A bottle of pills in his medicine chest frightened Hanna and she threw them away. A new bottle replaced the old. Sometimes Hanna had to shake Robin out of his gloom. Didn't he know how terrific he was?

After an especially wonderful day and night, a breakfast at a special new place, a concert in the park, an exchange of gifts, a movie with Mahelly and Frank, historic lovemaking, Robin would wake up in the middle of the night in terror.

"It's too much. It's too much, too soon," he'd say.

Hanna would go liquid with fear. "What's the matter, Robby?"

"I can't do this yet."

"Can't do what?"

"Feel like this."

Hanna would try not to panic. "Is it me? Am I doing something?"

"No. It's not you. It's me."

"I love you, Robby-Rob," Hanna would say.

When Robin wouldn't say, "I love you" back, Hanna would shake. Later in the night, Robin would wake her up. "I love you too," he'd say at 5 A.M.

One morning almost three months to the day since their first date, Robin woke up ashen-faced.

"What, darling?"

"It's just . . ."

"Tell me."

"It's just. I have to stop seeing you, or I have to give you my life."

"Why must it be one or the other? Can't we date?" Hanna asked, tears flowing down her face. Apparently not. Robin packed his Brooks Brothers shirts and blue cotton boxer shorts in a canvas duffel from L. L. Bean, tossed it into the trunk of his Rabbit, and drove away.

It took Hanna longer to get over Robin than the time they spent together. No amount of chocolate fudge, no number of sick days spent immobile in bed staring at a blank wall, no quantity of howling with her head in the lap of her best friend, could warm the cold, achy place that was simply devoid of Robin. It was time that did it after all. A good day, two bad days. A good week, a bad day. Immersing herself in ad copy as she was doing now, helped. And after six months had passed, she only thought of Robin when she saw a tall, curly-haired man in a Brooks Brothers suit.

The months of being with Hanna through her heartbreak and confusion produced a strange longing in Mahelly. How could she be envious of pain? Yet Hanna was living. Could she say the same? "Have a baby," her mother had said for the hundredth time when she phoned this morning to wish her only daughter a happy twenty-sixth birthday. "Let's make a baby," Frank had said this morning, walking into the bedroom from the bathroom, a towel draped over his hard-on. "Not this minute, OK?" Mahelly had laughed before deftly inserting her diaphragm. Have a baby? They had to be kidding. She wasn't ready. She was still a baby herself.

That evening she glanced down at the baby-pink linen suit Frank had bought her for this occasion, a birthday dinner for his "birthday Bird." The table in the expensive Italian restaurant was set for six. The two other couples were business friends of Frank's, one a man, one a woman, and their spouses. The crisp black and white room was almost empty. Mahelly could see the tall palms in the corners that had been almost invisible through the crowds hours before. The tablecloth was littered with crumbs and glasses of Champagne. A rummy Italian cheesecake, in its frowsy half-eaten state, dominated the table. Mahelly wondered again how long this dinner would go on. When would they finally leave? It looked to her like never. Or else it would take eviction by the suave tuxedoed restaurateur who was now counting the cash in the register.

The conversational grouping at their table had divided early on into a clump of four and a clump of two. The clump of four—Frank, Bob-from-the-office, Andrea-from-the-office, and Andrea's husband Joe, a financial executive from an insurance company, looked fresh and ready to order a few more courses. The clump of two—Mahelly and Dotty, wife of Bob-from-the-office—looked as if they had been painted onto the wall.

Andrea, a prize exhibit of women's lib in action, was dazzling in bright blue silk. Of course the men wanted to talk to her. She was smart and she could match words and wits with them all. Sure, she admitted to her rapt audience, she used sex appeal to sell radio time. But sex appeal cut both ways. The female media buyers couldn't be flirted with, and she felt they would buy from the competition to prove their power over her. An argument followed. Mahelly felt like a paper doll, an angry paper doll. She had nothing to add. She smoothed down the pink linen of her skirt, flattened a crumb with her finger and transferred it to her mouth. She smiled stiffly at Dotty, who smiled back.

Dotty was plump, dowdy, and twenty years older than Mahelly. She had raised four children. Although she certainly had nothing in common with Andrea, or Frank, or Joe, she had just as little in common with Mahelly. "You'll be happier once you start your family, dear," Dotty had said, patting Mahelly's arm. The woman's a cliché, thought Mahelly savagely. Why did a woman have to have children in order to be happy? Did Andrea have children, she wondered. She looked pretty damned happy. The bitch.

Mahelly watched the animated faces around Andrea, responding to her, playing to her and with her. Did any man, anybody look at her that way? Frank for instance. He loved her, sure, but did he ever bend his head just that way to hear what she had to say? Did she have anything to say?

With a chill, Mahelly fit pieces together. If Dotty was an anachronism, and Andrea was today, what was she? What was that song Frank used to sing? It was about a nowhere man, sitting in a nowhere land. That was her—a nowhere woman. A nowhere woman about to cry at her own birthday party. Hers? It wasn't hers. It was a business dinner for Frank. She sniffed and blinked her eyes hard, willing herself to feel anger instead of self-pity. She'd work out who she was angry at later.

A waiter materialized at the table, asked if anything else was wanted, and left a break in the conversation as he departed.

"And what are you up to, Mahelly?" Andrea asked, leaning forward, pearls swinging on her ample, blue silk bosom.

"Oh, not that much," Mahelly answered truthfully, flattered by the sudden attention.

"Come on, don't be modest," Andrea pursued. "You haven't said a word all evening."

"Well, I read a lot," she began (her mind searching frantically— what *do* I do all day?) "and I take care of Frank," she leaned against his arm, "and I dance."

"Oh? What kind of dancing do you do?" Bob inquired, out of politeness Mahelly was sure.

"It's sort of modern dance. At the health club." There was a chorus of "oh, how nice," and then Frank reached for the check, and Bob protested, and Joe stood to go to the men's room. In indignation, Mahelly reacted to the loss of her stage. She heard herself say, "I start teaching modern dance at the club next week."

"What's that, Buttercup?" Frank asked. "A job?"

"Yes," she said. "They've asked me to teach a class every morning. I think I should do it."

"Just one class? In the morning?"

"Mmm-hmm." She was shaking inside. What would he say? Do? If he dared to deny her this moment after staring down that bitch's cleavage all night, she'd bite his arm.

"OK, Bird. But don't turn into a working wife on me, will you?"

"Course not, Frank," she said through clenched teeth, unnoticed by anyone but her. She wondered if that job that she had been offered would still be open. And if so, how she would do at it. But mostly she wondered how soon could she start.

The answer was immediately. That week. She was handed a stack of short white skirts to wear over her leotards and tights, and a stack of insurance forms to fill out. She filled out her full name. Mary Helen Sullivan Colucci. She was given a locker and a key to the front door. It was true. She was a member of the work force. She cleaned the apartment with new speed and vigor, lingering less to admire her chosen colors and textures. She sang with Frank in the shower. She cut her hair to pixie-cut length so it would be out of her way when she danced and so it would dry quickly. Frank stormed. "You could have asked me, Mary Helen. I loved your hair."

"It'll grow back, Frank." She fluffed it with her fingers and smiled. She loved it short.

Mahelly's early-morning modern-dance class was soon followed by her late-morning jazz class, and then Mahelly was leaving in the morning right behind Frank and getting home moments before. Muscles formed where none had been. The best ones were those right under her shoulder blades, the ones that supported her new wings.

In September, at the end of her fourth year in New York, Hanna accepted the copy chief job at Piquant Cosmetics, Inc., and left retail, she hoped, forever. The difference between Macy's and Piquant felt as big as an elephant. She gladly exchanged the fluorescent lights and gray steel desked "bullpen" for a clean white office, black leather sofa and swivel chair, two windows, an electric typewriter and a secretary named Bonnie. The people who worked at Piquant were well-spoken, elegantly dressed and ninety-five percent women. The atmosphere was chatty, clubby, and when it came to clothing, competitive. Who would be the first to wear culottes, floor-length skirts, belted pants, see-through linen? Hanna, that's who.

She joined the health club and met Lefty. Lefty Lefkowitz was the blond, artificially tanned but really beautiful, perfectly built, Nautilus machine instructor. When he offered to show Hanna the ropes and hinted at more, she cautioned herself: this is just another form of exercise, Hanna. Don't let yourself feel anything above the waist. She learned the ropes and that Lefty got his nickname not because he was left-handed as she'd supposed, but because at the final moment, as he was poised between her legs, he had asked, "Do you want me to do this, because I can't spend the night." And she had said yes, because in her moist and panting state it was too late to say no. Immediately after, Lefty left. With Hanna he even left in the middle of the blizzard of '76. Each of the four women who saw her in the gym looking after Lefty in a certain stunned way, came into the sauna to warn her too late. "Latent queer," said one. "Hates women," said another. "Did he ask you if he should do it, because he couldn't stay the night?" asked the third. "Well at least he's consistent," she harrumphed. "Sorry, kiddo," said the fourth. "Men are savages."

"Not until I'm in love," she told Tony, a sleek young art director that summer.

"Please Hanna. You're screwing up my analysis," he pleaded.

"No," she said.

"I want to be in love first," she said to Greg, a football player, that fall.

"Hanna, you tease. If you mean no, don't be wearing low-cut black dresses," he said angrily before going back to Seattle with the team.

"I want to wait," she said to Anton on their third date. "Wait by yourself, sweetie," he said, dropping her off at the curb for the last time. She stuck her tongue out.

Hanna spent Christmas with her parents, trying to convince them she was happier without a man than with one. Really, she was fine, not to worry. How could they not believe her? It was true.

By her twenty-seventh birthday, Hanna had had affairs with blonds, brunettes, redheads, older men, younger men, shorter men, tough guys and softies. She'd felt love and pain and joy and fear and she knew what she was like as a woman to a man. She knew her auburn hair looked wild against black. She knew how to arouse a man over dinner by touching herself at the hollow of her throat, or by drawing her spoon s-l-o-w-l-y out of her mouth. She knew how to hail a cab or pick up a tab with ease and grace. She knew how to say no to a man when it was over and she could do it in a nice way. She knew when and how to be alone. Hanna knew how to do everything with a man but find the right one to love and marry, and this was what she was ready to do.

Oscar was Piquant's legal counsel. He had noticed Hanna several times as he walked past her office to his weekly meeting with Piquant's president.

On a day in March, when Hanna's office was filled with a rare mahogany shade of lilacs that matched her hair, and the air was scented to the ceiling, Oscar hesitatingly dipped his head into her office and introduced himself. Hanna said "Hi," and forgot about this silvery-haired man in his gray suit until she saw him again. The next time he said "Hi," he was no longer hesitating. He was smitten. In this state, he invited Hanna to lunch in a salmon-colored-marble room with white tablecloths and amaryllis stuck in crystal bowls.

At their third lunch, Oscar told Hanna he was married. Not past tense, present. He said his marriage had failed years before. He was currently negotiating a separation from his wife, Lois, but that with fifteen years between them and three children, it was something to be delicately done. "It isn't really fair, is it, the way men leave their wives," he asked Hanna rhetorically. "When two people marry there isn't a codicil in the contract that says, 'When the husband gets tired of his dull, sexless wife, he can give her a house and some money and leave for a gorgeous, sophisticated, crazy copy chief and think nothing of it.' "

Without meaning to, Hanna saw his point of view and admired his honesty and his morality. She adored lunches in beautiful restaurants, occasional bliss-blessed days off, drives into the country in Oscar's silver Mercedes, the "Magic Mobile."

"Clutch! Clutch! Depress the clutch," Oscar squawked as the Mercedes hopped down the road, Hanna at the wheel. "I forget where it is," she squealed falling into hysterics as the car coughed to a stop.

"Now's the time to ask for a raise," Oscar counseled when Hanna's eye-color campaign was the talk of the industry. "And tell them you want stock."

Luckily for Hanna, Piquant required half the energy Macy's had demanded. Luckily for Piquant, love inspired Hanna's vision and vocabulary. Words and colors were gilded with her passion for Oscar. Her package copy sang products off the shelves. Her ad writing won awards.

At twenty-eight, she spent masses of time with Frank and Mahelly When she wasn't staring at them with a fixed expression that belied her pretense of following the conversation, she was talking, talking, talking about Oscar. Mahelly wanted to be happy for Hanna; it had been so long since she'd been in love, but how could she be happy for the obsessed girl who was so manic or blue?

"He will leave her, you'll see," Hanna said.

"Of course he will," Mahelly said doubtfully.

"A married man cheating on his wife is by definition weak and dishonest," growled Frank.

"You don't understand," said Hanna. "You don't know him."

By her thirtieth birthday, Oscar was still married and Hanna was no longer satisfied. The "nooners" and blue-moon nights left her raw and wanting for more. She was no longer able to enjoy the time they spent together. She started to feel abandoned before Oscar ever entered the room. The more love Oscar felt for Hanna, the more guilt he seemed to feel about Lois. The more depressed Lois became, the less Oscar saw of Hanna. The less he saw of Hanna, the tighter she became when she was with him. Finally, Oscar told Hanna he "couldn't handle it any more," and good-bye.

For a long sunless, airless, soundless day, Hanna felt severance and relief. She felt as if a limb had been removed by a sharp blade. When the pain struck a few days later, she mobilized. She took a two-week vacation and a two-week leave of absence from Piquant and went to a weight-reducing spa in the Berkshire Mountains. For one month she fasted and exercised Oscar out of her body. She had no appetite, so three ounces of lettuce and two pieces of Melba toast seemed the most appropriate meal in the world. Sometimes she couldn't get it all down. She couldn't bear to think, so she jogged many miles a day. She knew there was nothing so therapeutic for her bruised soul as physical pain and exhaustion. The beauty of the mountains, the freedom from all mental stress, the purity of the very air buoyed her. Running away to the spa was such a perfect thing to do, it seemed like a prescription from God. Hanna called Mahelly every night and spoke with her parents every weekend but she called Oscar not once.

When she came back to work, she put together her portfolio of ads from Macy's and Piquant and applied for a job at *Urban Life Magazine*.

One day Oscar got up enough nerve to walk by Hanna's old office, but by the time that had happened a drab little brunette was sitting in Hanna's black swivel chair, and Hanna, having taken a $5,000.00 pay cut, was Assistant Fashion Editor at *U.L.*

Urban Life was in some ways more like Macy's than like Piquant. The space was airy and light because the Pan Am Building shot high into blue unobstructed sky. But the space was limited, so only senior editors had window offices. Hanna and other lower level staff had cubicles with natural light drifting over the six-foot-high plastic walls only after lunch. The group hum and the imminent deadlines created pressure but Hanna welcomed it. She didn't care that her box at *U.L.* was aesthetically deprived. She was with the smartest magazine in town. She was working for an ambitious woman who was being groomed to manage the West Coast office of *Urban Life* and couldn't leave New York until her replacement in fashion had been hired, trained, and secured.

Polly Thomas liked Hanna from the moment they met. And Polly's liking for Hanna grew with each day. Polly admired the intensity Hanna applied to her work, watched her pore over competitive magazines, prowl through the stores, visit the garment center showrooms on her lunch hours. In a big-sisterly way, Polly was concerned about Hanna's workaholism. It was an odd evening when Hanna signed out with the security guard earlier than 8:00 at night. The sign-in sheets showed Hanna working Saturdays and Sundays too. Doesn't this child think about anything but work, Polly wondered. When she inquired, Hanna answered with a smile, "It feels good to work this hard. Don't worry about me, honest."

And it did feel good to Hanna. She hoped time would pass quickly and that she'd never have another thought about Oscar. While waiting, she crammed her days with reptile skin shoes, silk jumpsuits, beaded jogging suits, all in a soon-to-be-successful attempt to stem the flow of psychic blood from her terrible injury.

Mahelly's days were chopped into one-hour pieces. Nine o'clock class to ten o'clock class. Ten o'clock class to eleven. Early lunch from eleven to noon. Lunch would be less about food than about collecting things she needed for home. She'd throw jeans on over tights, a sweatshirt over, appropriately enough, a sweat-soaked leotard.

"Taxi," she'd yell while still in the act of pushing the door open, and then she'd leap into the backseat of the cab.

"First stop, the deli on 49th and Second, southwest corner," she'd bleat through the partition. And then she'd tell the driver to wait, pay for the preordered cold cuts and ground coffee, jump back into the cab. "Next we're going to the tailor shop on 51st."

"Wait a minute, lady. I'm not a chauffeur, you know. I'm losing the start-up fare on the meter. I can't make a living this way."

"Please," Mahelly would plead. "I'm a good tipper."

At five minutes before noon, the groceries, dry cleaning, cobbled shoes, would be stowed in a locker and Mahelly would be in front of the lunchtime executive crowd of aerobic dancers. At five, she'd be home. At six Frank would walk in, add his sweaty clothes to the pile of her sweaty clothes and retire to his closet.

Frank didn't call it a closet. He called it WPOM. W-Peace-of-Mind. In a fit of something, Mahelly didn't know what, Frank had padded the large walk-in hall closet, installed a professional level turntable and cassette deck with earphones, added a graphic equalizer, a swivel stool and a fan. The *pièce de résistance* was affixed with the zest and joy of a younger Frank.

"Look here, Bird," he crowed, flipping on a switch from inside the closet. The sign hanging from the ceiling glowed red. ON THE AIR, it said with the confidence of a permanent fact of life.

Not so bad, Mahelly thought after she got used to the idea. Now from six to something like eight, Frank disappeared into the bosom of WPOM. He played his music and did whatever else he did in there. Mahelly stacked the bedroom stereo with Beethoven, turned the sound up to high, and took a long, hot, jasmine-scented bath. Then she'd put on one of Frank's T-shirts, make dinner, and if Frank didn't emerge naturally, she'd beat on the closet door until he heard her and come out.

Sometimes at night, they could both find the energy to make love. More often the energy of one would have to suffice for both.

Dinners with Hanna were rare. Frank seemed to disapprove of Hanna in some way.

"Gee, you were mean to Hanna," Mahelly would say.

"I wasn't mean to her."

"Well, you didn't say anything to her all night. It was embarrassing."

"Well, I find her embarrassing."

"What do you mean embarrassing?"

"It's sex, sex, sex with her, or men, or even when she's talking about her job—I don't know. She sounds like a guy half the time."

"Frank, you're crazy. I think she's an incredible woman, and I'm not just saying that because she's my friend. She's brave. She does things. She has a full life. I love listening to the stuff she does. It makes me nervous that you don't like her."

"I like her," he'd say. "I just don't really have anything to say to her."

So Mahelly would take the elevator down to Hanna's apartment after a quiet dinner with Frank, and the two would climb into Hanna's bed and talk.

When Hanna was thirty-one, Polly Thomas had moved to L.A. and Hanna had a window office and a promotion to Fashion Editor. She was gaining recognition as a talented, resourceful professional. She felt competent. A few lines on her face were visible in hard light, and she didn't wear such short skirts as she had, but her face had found its bones. She was no longer cute. She was striking.

The amount of insight Hanna had about fashion seemed to have an inverse correlation to the amount of insight she had gained about the ways of men and women. She was getting edgy about her marital status. People, men mostly, asked her questions generally beginning, "There's something about you I just don't understand," followed by "You are so smart and beautiful and talented, why hasn't someone married you by now?" This question always hurt and infuriated Hanna. After she deflected the questions with "I guess I just haven't found the right man" (weak excuse even in her own eyes), she felt depressed. What was wrong with her? What in the world was she going to do? She wished she had an answer she could live with or a problem she could solve.

One night, hers the only desk lamp burning at 9:35 P.M., Hanna swept a pile of metal-studded ostrich-skin neckerchiefs off her desk, thought about her dating history and composed a list of commandments for herself.

She typed:

Don't fall in love on the second date.

Don't sleep with men in your beachhouse.

Don't play sex therapist to the chronically impotent.

Don't fall for a man who is trying to determine his sexual identity.

Don't go out with men under twenty-five.

Don't go out with men who live with their mothers.

Don't go out with men who are more concerned with how well their pink shirt goes with their navy pants than you would be.

Don't go out with men who keep a lethal dose of sleeping pills in their medicine chest "just in case."

Don't screw around at the office.

Don't ever, ever, ever, fall in love with a married man.

Don't go out with a man who has just been dumped. He will dump you.

Don't go out with men who tell you after taking your clothes off, you really ought to work out with weights.

Don't go out with guys named Lefty.

Don't go out with men who call you "baby."

Hanna started to add, "Don't go out with men who are afraid of intimacy," but she didn't know how to test for this condition and typed instead:

Don't go out with men who say they don't want to get involved. They don't.

She leaned back in her chair under the hard light thrown by her desk lamp in the otherwise dark office, and examined her list. She realized every man she had dated had gotten a "don't" of his own and that it seemed likely that every man she would ever date for the rest of her life, would get his own spot on the list. I can't go out with every man in the world, I just can't, she thought with dread. The surprise package sensation of meeting a new man had been edged by the experience that each little package would engage her to a greater or lesser degree, and then would explode in a burst of colored flame in the palm of her hand.

The list wasn't very useful, but she thought she would share it anyway. She addressed an envelope to *Cosmopolitan Magazine*, inserted the list with a note, licked it shut, stamped it, and turned off her light. She stood and stared out for a very long time at the tiny headlights making their way up and down Park Avenue. Then she dropped the letter in the mail chute on the way out the door and home.

It was during this mood, this sure and certain feeling she would never meet a man she could love who could love her, when in the elevator of her apartment building of all places, she met Guy.

4

WHEN GUY FIRST SAW HANNA, SHE WAS SQUEEZING INTO THE CROWDED elevator filled with a nanny, two children (one in a carriage) and a matched pair of noisily panting Samoyed dogs. From his vantage point in the rear, he felt an almost uncontrollable urge to sweep her under his arm and claim her. She looked like a woman designed to be his. He couldn't see the curves of her body through the coat she wore, but he could sense them, and there was something soft and tremendously appealing in her expression. It looked as if her mind were slightly, charmingly, out of focus. She bent to pat one of the dogs, and her hair sluiced down the sides of her face like an auburn waterfall.

"Pretty," he breathed.

" 'Scuse me?" she queried, turning slightly, protectively, suspicious of him.

"That's pretty," he said quickly, pointing to her purple fox boa which was clasping its own hind leg and, turned to the back of her neck, was staring at Guy with twinkling rhinestone eyes. "Is it real?"

"Oh, yes, it's real," she laughed as they left the elevator and walked out through the lobby together. "It's a Norwegian fox and it's completely empty of fox, but everything it had on the outside is still here. See," she asked, turning the fox face forward. "It's still got its little noseholes and toenails."

"Yucckk," said Guy, wrinkling his face comically, holding the door open for her as they walked out onto 94th Street. "That may be more than I wanted to know about the poor critter."

46

"Look, he was on *sale*," she said and grinned as she walked backwards away from him. "I wouldn't have killed him, I swear." And with that, she waved the fox's tail good-bye, and disappeared. For days afterward, Guy saw Hanna walking backwards in his mind, waving that purple foxtail good-bye.

Guy asked the doorman who she was, found out her name and that she was living in the apartment under his, but he still had to hope for coincidence to bring them together. When he saw her next, he was with Barbra, a spiky-haired blond with smudgy black eyes. He smiled at her and turned away.

Barbra was an unpredictable, one-of-a-kind experience. She was twenty. She was fun. She sang, she joked, she slung breakable objects. (Sometimes she went too damned far.) She could make him laugh, she could make him mad, and he was never bored with Barbra. When she was sweet, she was very, very sweet, but when she was in a mood, she was dangerous. "Emote, goddamn it," she frequently shrilled at him, changing in seconds from a Persian kitten curled up on his lap to an automatic baseball pitching machine loaded with his dishware. Hey. It was his apartment she was throwing fits in, and she was breaking up his things! Emote? What did she want from him? He'd never hit a woman and he wasn't going to start at the age of thirty-six. But sometimes, with this little firecracker, he was tempted.

Up until four years before, Guy's world had been civilized. He was raised in Westport, went to school in Princeton, had married Joanne Wooten right after he had collected his MBA from Columbia.

Joanne was a nice girl. She was clean, sweet, and the daughter of family friends. Everyone said they made a terrific couple. Guy's mother had taken Joanne into their home almost before Guy had had a chance to think about what that might mean. "Bring Joanne home for dinner this Sunday, Guy," she said nearly every week. Marriage was more an assumption than a proposition. The sweet sex the two had together was a commitment to each other that seemed to require no verbal confirmation.

"A wedding present from us," his parents had announced, beaming, as they drove the pair to the front door of a small, white-framed, green-shuttered house on a nice street in Westport.

"Consider it a part of your inheritance, Guy," they had said.

"We're so happy we can enjoy seeing you use it while we are alive."

"Advertising has done right by me," Stuart Spencer had said to his son as they sat in the backyard swing of the new house. "In a capitalist country, the money is in the hands of the consumer. It's a good business, Guy. Listen to me." Guy listened and saw a future existence as sound and as classic as the planes of his clapboard colonial.

So why had he panicked at the ceremony? Moments before Guy said, "I do," he knew the promise he was about to make was a mistake. "Guy," the minister had said, "all you are and have belongs to Joanne. . . . Joanne, all you are and have belongs to Guy." Where had that come from? Guy had wondered wildly. Had they rehearsed that? He was penned in on all sides by white flowers, men he used to know but now barely recognized, and women in blurry green dresses nodding at him like orchid buds suspended over suspicious foliage. He glanced at Jo who smiled angelically at him. He smiled nervously back and twisted the ring onto her finger. I love her, he reassured himself. I'm doing the right thing, he reminded himself, I'm just nervous, and he kissed the bride.

Guy had gotten the right first job, assistant account executive at Reardon, Smiley and Hayes, a big packaged goods advertising agency in New York. At the age of twenty-four Guy became a commuter with a wife in the suburbs.

Joanne painted, furnished, and personalized the white house. Chintz-covered sofas and early American maplewood claimed the living room. A white iron and brass rail bed planted dainty feet in his bedroom and squeezed Guy's head between the bars when he tried to read at night. A flurry of hand-knitted babywear preceded Joanne's miscarriage. Another pregnancy was planned to assuage her grief. Jo *needs* a baby, Guy often thought as he entered his wife's body with determination. Planned sex, methodical sex, purposeful sexual intent with a woman he had once found comfortably arousing, steadily dampened his ardor. Anyone would be turned off by programmed sex, Guy thought. No conception occurred.

Guy's promotion to account executive came in the first year. Hard work and late nights at the office contributed to his promotion to account supervisor three years later. Joanne served elaborate warmed-over suppers and stared at him mournfully.

"I never see you anymore," Joanne said one day, uncurling clenched hands, plaintively exposing pale palms.

"I know," Guy said. "But it's so competitive in this business. If I don't put in more hours than the pack at my level, I'll be left behind. It'll affect the future of my career." I have nothing to say to you, he thought, sadly. "Jo, find something to do. It makes me crazy thinking about you waiting for me all day to come home."

"You're right. I'm bored and boring," she'd said, meeting him at the late train.

"I didn't say that . . ."

She waved his words away. "It's nuts for me to stay home all day and vacuum." Joanne became a sales assistant in a real estate firm. Good, thought Guy. The conflict of doing right by his job and wrong by Joanne was resolved.

A management consultant plucked Guy out of the R S & H talent pool and dropped him under a bright spotlight at Hastings and Goode, a competitive firm. By the time he was thirty, Guy was promoted to Vice President, Account Supervisor.

Joanne passed her salesperson's exam and began selling houses. Her work week began on Wednesday, jogged lightly through Friday, and broke into a full gallop on the weekends.

"I'm showing a million houses this weekend," she said blotting her lipstick carefully, fluffing her fine brown hair.

Guy opened a weary eye, placed a cupped hand over his erection. "So early?"

"The early bird gets the worm," Joanne trilled gaily. "I'll be home late."

The Spencers bought a new car, priced sailboats. Their kitchen gave birth to a sunroom with six sets of French doors and a brick floor. Guy calculated they would eat into their savings if they didn't increase their combined $70,000 a year. One of Guy's accounts became troubled and kept him at the office after hours four nights out of five. On the odd night he was home for dinner, the phone rang with the discretion of a jackhammer; Joanne's clients and co-workers. As their combined responsibilities and income grew, so did the space between Guy and Joanne.

It was a bright autumn afternoon. The air was sharp enough to sting his nostrils as Guy raked leaves in the slanting sunlight. He wished Jo was in the sunroom watching him. He felt suddenly romantic and husband-y in his red plaid jacket. He wished she would come out and sit in the swing and share this day with him. He glanced wistfully at the high-backed porch seat hanging by ropes from the sturdy limb of the old maple. He leaned the rake against the tree and sat in the swing himself. It had been years since they had sat together in the swing. He mobilized the slatted seat by pushing off with the rake. Then he leaned his head back and stared into the swooping canopy of thinning maple leaves. What was happening to his marriage? he wondered. He and Joanne had accommodated each other's schedule so efficiently, they no longer spent time together. They shared the same space, ate from the same dishes, used the same linens, combined their paychecks, but when was the last time they had talked?

Guy stared into the mottled blur above him. The cool air lifted his hair and while doing so, gently pulled his tangled thread of thoughts into a clean, straight line. They did talk, Guy decided, but they talked *at* each other. It seemed to him Joanne listened to him with an invisible stopwatch in her hand. She listened, all the while waiting for him to stop talking, so she could claim equal time to talk about her day. As for his part, he wasn't seeking her advice, he was just venting. If Joanne was in the house when he started talking, that was enough for him. He knew she paid enough attention to keep up with the movements of his business life, but she thought advertising, like football, was a silly man's game.

Hey, in a certain light, advertising *was* pretty silly. Certainly it was if it was your whole life. He loved it, though. Anyhow, now that she was so involved in real estate she could understand how thrilling it was to be electrified by one's work. But why couldn't they communicate that excitement to each other? Honestly, he wasn't any more fascinated by real estate than she was with advertising. He couldn't keep her clients and houses differentiated in his head. How many times in a conversation had he found his attention had drifted away and by the time he pulled it back, he had lost the sense of her story. Were the stories he told as dull as the stories she told? He hoped not.

The swing slowed and Guy shoved off with the rake again. He listened attentively to the pleasant sound of the ropes rubbing above him. It was a rhythmic, mesmerizing sound; rub-b-b, rub-b-b-b, rub-b-b-b, rub-b-b-b-b. As the swing slowed, the sound stretched out, attenuated. He kicked hard against the ground, feeling the first renewed rush of wind against his face. He found he was thinking about sex. What had happened to sex? It had never been exotic, that was for sure, but after the baby push had ended, it had still been cozy, connecting, touching. Joanne's now common response to an amorous advance was,

"Could we just cuddle tonight, Guy? I just want to cuddle." He pretended it didn't hurt, but it did. They weren't kids anymore, but still, he was a man. Lately, the bed seemed an acre big and the two of them could easily sleep never touching.

The swing stopped. Guy stood and walked to the house. He tried to remember. Had there ever been any passion in their marriage? When had this numbness taken over? Had it ever been otherwise? It seemed to him he and Joanne were less man and wife than . . . roommates!

Guy put together a cup of instant coffee and took it out to the sunroom. He sighed. Could they find a way to inject romance into their marriage? Could they create a passion they had never had? They should talk about it, not avoid it. They loved one another in a solid familial way and this love was rooted in mutual trust and knowledge of each other. They had drifted apart, but if they both wanted to, they could patch things up. They had both grown and grown up. The two of them really ought to spend more time together. It would be good for them. If they did more things together, they would have more common interests. That made sense, didn't it? They needed to dedicate themselves to making their marriage a success. He could catch the 6:08 instead of the 8:19. Jo could take the phone off the hook at night. They could spend Saturdays together. Days like today.

Where was Jo anyway? Guy looked at his watch. It was 1:45. The temperature was in the sixties. It was a perfect day to spend outdoors with his wife. If she were home, they could take a drive together; see something new. He turned on the TV and watched football. He didn't care who was winning. He restlessly stabbed the remote control channel changer. Joanne had said she'd be home by 6:00. They could start something new with a special evening tonight. He'd surprise her— take her to Bianca's down by the water. He tapped out numbers, made the reservation. This was good. But how was he to spend the next four hours?

The book chosen to kill time, killed his attention span instead. He oiled a squeaky hinge, glued a broken platter. He cleaned out his toolbox. He bagged leaves. He waited for Joanne. God, he felt alone. He wanted to see her, smell her, talk to her, touch her, make things right.

Joanne's voice on the phone at 6:00 was blithe. "I just got a call about the Tatum house," she said, "and while I'm at it I think I'll show him that contemp on Main . . ."

"Oh," he said. "When do you think you'll be home?"

"No later than eight."

"OK," Guy said. The reservation could be moved. He could find something to do for two more hours. But it was irritating. Didn't people have any sense of propriety? Weren't brokers entitled to the same nine-to-five workday enjoyed by every other damned person in America?

At nine-fifteen Joanne stood in the doorway. "I think I've got a fish on the line," she shouted into the sunroom. She stepped out of her shoes, walked into the small glassed room and stared at Guy sitting before a dark TV tube. "Miss me?" she asked with a wry smile.

"MISS YOU?" Guy bellowed. "MISS YOU? I've been waiting for you to get home all day and half the night! I've been lonely. I wanted to talk to you."

"Welcome to the club," she said turning away from him and walking to the refrigerator.

"Have you eaten?" she asked minutes later, harpooning a chunk of tuna fish in its Tupperware barrel and forking it into her mouth.

"I don't know what you mean," she said sleepily over her shoulder in bed that night. She brushed Guy's hand gently from her breast and replaced the strap of her nightgown. Her damp hair curled against his nose and she smelled soapy and clean. "I'm happy. I've never been happier in my life."

"You're happy?" Guy asked still throbbing from his lonely day. "Jo, how can you be so happy? We don't see each other except in passing." He dropped his voice so his erect penis wouldn't hear him. "We don't make love any more."

"Please, Guy," Joanne retorted, her voice tinged with sarcasm. "Let's drop this. I'm not in the mood."

"No, I don't want to drop it," he said, angered. "It's time we talked. Turn over," he said gripping her shoulders with iron fingers and turning her to him. The bedroom was bright with moonlight. He stared into her face. Her features were contorted with fury! Why?

"Jo, what is it?"

"It's amazing, that's what it is. We've been married for eight years. You've never liked making love to me and *now*, because you want to get laid tonight, you want to *talk* about it."

"Joanne. That's not true. I love making love to you." He leaned on one elbow and reached for her hand. That's a lie, he thought to himself. Don't lie to her. "It was our schedules . . ."

"Crap. Don't lie to me, you bastard," she said, slapping his hand away. "You have the same expression on your face when you're screwing me as you have when you're taking a piss." She reached over to the night table, found her cigarettes, and after four failed matches, lit one, inhaled, and exhaled loudly. "Do you think I don't know about you and your schedules? Do you think I don't care?" Her cheeks were wet and her nose was running. She put the cigarette down carefully in the ashtray and blew her nose.

"Jo, what's brought this on? Why are you so upset?"

"Guy! Stop it. Don't insult me. I'm tired. Let me be." She covered her face and took in great shuddering breaths.

"How can I? Look at you. You look as if you want to kill me! Will you talk to me?"

She shook her head fiercely, stubbed out the cigarette, and flung herself back down on the pillows, facing away from him. She covered herself to her eyes with the blanket and took several deep breaths before her breathing evened out.

Guy lay on his back and blinked at the air. What was she so incredibly angry about? What did she mean, "Don't insult me?" What was he supposed to know? If she was a different woman, he would think she was having an affair. No. She wouldn't. Never.

Having had the thought, Guy tried to blink it away. Joanne? Sleeping with someone else? Yet . . . where had she been tonight? How could it take three hours to show two houses? If she'd had dinner out, why had she eaten when she came home? Having an affair would explain the showers she took before she kissed him hello, the late nights, the all-day-long weekends. Guy felt cold. He pulled the blanket up to his chin.

"Jo." He touched her rump with the back of his hand.

"Mm."

"Jo, are you having an affair?"

Her breathing stopped. She moved her legs under the sheet, but she didn't answer.

"Answer me. Are you?"

Joanne rolled onto her back and put her hands out over the blanket. She reached over to the night table and moved things around. Guy heard the crackle of cellophane, the sound of a match striking. He witnessed the brief burst of light. He inhaled sulfuric air. The cigarette ritual was a silent preamble, a foreshadowing with the range and dimension of a Coppola film. He sensed that whatever followed was going to be bad. Very bad.

"Yes, Guy," she said evenly, "I am."

Guy sat up in bed. "You're making it up," he said. He wanted to rip the sheet off her body, grab her by her stringy hair and heave her through the window. "I don't believe it," he said. And then, *"Why? Tell me why. Talk to me."*

"Fine," she said, struggling for composure. "You want to talk? Do you want to hear how *rejected* I've felt all these years? How undesirable?" Her voice broke. She stubbed out her cigarette. She paused for long beats before speaking again. "Do you have any idea how I've felt swallowing your stories; your unexpected weekends in Chicago and your late nights at the office? No, don't pity me," she said, straightening her shoulders and glaring at her husband. "I meant what I said. I'm *happy*," she spit the last word into his startled face. "I'm taking care of myself just the way you do."

"Joanne. Make sense!" He reached for her. "I don't know what you're talking about!"

"Take your hands off me," she growled. "I don't want you to touch me. You must think I'm a real dope, but I've known what you've been up to for years. 'I have to work late, Jo. New business pitch, Jo,' " she said, mimicking his voice. "Do you think I'm stupid? *You* have weekend affairs. *I* have weekend affairs. You have late nights. So do I. You get your kicks in hotel rooms. I get mine in empty houses. I don't want to get *laid* tonight, because I've already *gotten* laid tonight—by a man who doesn't make me feel like an old *bathrobe*. Don't look so shocked, Guy. I told you. I'm *happy*." Joanne ripped a sheaf of tissue from the box, wiped her face, and stared at him indignantly. "Aren't *you*? Isn't this what you *wanted*?"

Guy stared at Joanne, at her pinched eyes, at her shaking hands as she clasped tissues to her collarbone and waited for him to speak. He tried to take in what she had said, but it was hard to do. The room was fading in and out. Guy could hear her breath rasping in her swollen throat. He could hear the old schoolroom clock ticking. Very slowly. He could see and hear, but the only thing he could feel was a prickling sensation on the surface of his skin. It felt like little stars burning on his cheeks, his chest, his hands. He couldn't feel anything inside, anything toward Joanne. What he was hearing couldn't be true. His wife, the woman he had lived with for eight years, would never sleep with another man. Who was this vicious, sobbing person in bed beside him? Guy had never seen this woman before.

"I thought you wanted to *talk*, Guy," Joanne said primly. "So why don't you talk? You don't like tit for tat?"

Guy worked his mouth, swallowed, blinked at her before he spoke. "I didn't sleep with anyone," he said dully.

"What? What did you say?"

"I didn't sleep with anyone, Joanne. I was working. That was all." A laugh burst from his throat surprising him. That grotesque guffaw was overwhelmed by a wave of hilarity so huge and senseless and unstoppable, Guy had to cover his head with a pillow. He doubled up on his side and pushed the pillow into his face, but he couldn't stop the sounds streaming out of his unbelieving mouth.

"Stop it, you liar!" he heard her shouting. He held onto the pillow as she tried to wrestle it from him and when that failed she pounded him hard with her fists. "Liar, liar, liar!" she shouted, flailing at him. He rolled over, grabbed her, and pinned her arms to the bed.

They stared, faces inches apart, and panted. Guy gripped her arms through to the bones. When their breathing slowed, Guy said, "That was the truth."

"*No!*"

"*Yes!*" He pressed her arms hard into the yielding mattress, and then released her. He rolled over onto his back and put his hands to his temples. The room seemed to vibrate around him.

"Dear God," Joanne was saying in a voice so thin, only the absence of any other sound allowed it to be heard. "What have I done?"

The unanswerable question went unanswered. Guy stared at the air in front of his eyes. He could almost make out the ceiling, but little flecks of light arcing like miniature comets distracted him. A thin trail of tears had slipped silently out of the outside corners of his eyes and had wet the pillow next to his ears. He felt cold inside. His marriage was disintegrating. This was what disintegration felt like. Beside him, Joanne began taking in deep, hoarse breaths. She sounded like a dying animal. He turned his head to look at her. The muscles in her face had slackened. Water rolled down her face in sheets. How had all this happened. Joanne wasn't a cruel person, yet she'd attempted murder tonight. All the anger, the fear, the secrets had exploded. If he hadn't forced her to talk tonight, how much longer would this have gone on? How could he have been so totally unaware? Had he truly lain next to Joanne all these years and never known she had slept with other men? Was he deaf? Blind? Off? That was it. He had turned himself off. Uh! The pain was incredible. Not that she had been with other men, but that for all this time, he hadn't known, hadn't had any sense at all. Why had she ever said anything to him? Why not? She'd been believing a lie and because of that had betrayed them both. He could strangle her for doing this to them.

"Why didn't you say something to me, Joanne?" he asked in an unsteady voice. "If you thought I was having affairs, why didn't you *ask* me?"

Joanne didn't speak.

"Answer me, damn it. Why did you find it easier to . . ." Guy paused forming the next words with distaste, "to sleep around, than to tell me how unhappy you were?"

Joanne rolled over onto her belly and burying her face in the pillow, wept. Her sobs flowed from some deep, bottomless place like the tears of a child left home alone. They conveyed helplessness and hopelessness and utter despair. Had he done this to her? He had. This woman whom he had married had pleaded with him to spend time with her and he had pushed her away, ignored her, talked down to her, shut her out of the vital part of his life. His anger turned to remorse. God, look what he had done. He stroked her heaving back, moving her hair away from her face. He had to know.

"Why didn't you ask me?"

"I was uh, uh, fraid," she said through tearful spasms. "I was uh, fraid if I asked you, oo, where you were, you would tell, ell me and our marriage would be oh, oh, ver." Saying this sent new spasms through her and Joanne pushed her face farther into the pillows.

Guy felt bitter fluid back up in his throat. He forced himself to swallow, went to the bathroom sink, and scooped cold water into his mouth. Please stop crying, Joanne, he thought. He pitied her. Thinking about what she'd told him made him furious and disgusted with them both. What a waste this marriage had been. He had been a bad husband and a fool. She'd been . . . worse. They'd both been cheated by settling for what they thought was mediocrity and was instead something much more terrible. What in God's name was he going to do now? There was no way this was going to be repaired. It would be nice though, if they could restore their humanity. Guy sat down heavily on the bed and turned to face her. He touched her shoulder and when Joanne looked up at him he opened his arms to her. She crawled into his embrace. He smoothed her hair and kissed her temple. She moaned in his arms; a shattered, battered thing.

"I want to die, Guy," she said. "This is so awful, I want to die. I'm so sorry," she whispered.

"Me too. I'm sorry too. It wasn't your fault. What you did—I don't blame you. You were just doing what you said. Taking care of yourself." It was true. He really didn't care that Joanne had slept with other men. He didn't want to know how many or when. He had no desire to punish her. The only relevant thing was that their marriage was dead. Had been dead. All the questions he had had about their marriage had been answered.

"How come, Guy?" Joanne asked. "How come you didn't sleep with anyone else?"

He pressed his cheek to her hair. "Shh," he said.

"Why? Please."

Guy sighed. "I'm a married man, Jo. That's why."

She whimpered.

"No, stop. Don't hurt yourself anymore. We've talked enough."

"Is it, Guy? Is it over?"

He kissed her brow. "Jo. It's been over for a long time. We just didn't know it." She nodded against his chest and letting out a great long sigh, clasped her arms around his back. They lay together listening to the other's breathing.

"We could try . . ." she said, the words falling drowsily out of her mouth.

"No, Jo. Please don't. I don't want this, what we have. I want more. You should have more too," Guy said breathing deeply. "It will be all right. It will be better for both of us. You'll see," he said, hoping he was right.

"Oh, God," she said in a feeble voice. "Are you leaving? When?"

"Not yet. I'll be here for a little while."

He rocked her then, and that night they slept wrapped tightly in each other's arms. In the morning when they made love, they did so with great tenderness, knowing they were not coming together but comforting each other against coming apart.

Three weeks later Guy found a reasonable one-bedroom apartment in Greenwich Village, and with cartons of household appliances, books and his favorite chair, he moved in.

Being "single" in New York was like living a completely different person's life. Guy never felt really at home on MacDougal Street, but how could he? Greenwich Village, Manhattan, was to Westport, Connecticut, as New England clam chowder is to *scungilli Fra Diavolo*. He adjusted though, put some comfortable secondhand furniture in his two rooms, then found the best restaurant, the best dry cleaners, the best singles' bar in the Village.

Guy finally broke his eight-year fidelity to Joanne with Margot, a sexy management consultant with a dresser drawer full of black lace underthings. She had salt and pepper hair and a personality to match: at forty-two, Margot knew what was right for her and when. When the relationship was over for her, she gently told Guy it was time to part, she hoped as friends. Guy was stunned. He spent evening and weekend time with Bo Henry, a college friend who helped Guy understand that going through the pain was preferable to giving in to it and returning to his marriage.

Guy was assigned to a new and larger account at the agency, and he plunged in. He frazzled everyone else on the account with his twelve-hour workdays.

Guy had in quick succession an affair with a professor at NYU, a policewoman he charmed out of giving him a parking ticket, a script girl, a violinist, a representative from the electric company. Then, with the shock of an adrenaline overload, he found something that felt better than love with Courtney Rand.

Courtney Rand was an account executive at Hastings and Goode and the most beautiful woman Guy had ever seen in real life. She looked like nothing so much as a lioness. She was lithe, she was gently tanned, she had pale green eyes and a mane of wavy caramel hair that she wore parted to one side and down to the middle of her back. Her clothing straddled dress-for-success and fuck-me-hard. Guy had never seen or imagined anything like her cigarette-thin herringbone suits complemented and contradicted by four-inch heels, seamed stockings and gleaming silk blouses all bows and collars and soft lights. And Guy had never been stalked before. Her approach began with ambiguous arm touching in meetings, whispery leg crossing in shared taxis to the client, and when Guy approached directly with a knock on the door, an invitation to lunch, Courtney would toss her hair, swivel in her chair, "Not this week, Guy," she'd say, "May I have a rain check?" And in this way Courtney teased him, and played with him, and when she had him stammering in her presence, she put a ring in his nose by blowing him in his office without locking the door.

This single act scared Guy and enraptured him, and for the next mostly exhilarating year and a half, Courtney and Guy were a known and admired "item" at the office. "I'm still wet from last night," would be typed on the interoffice memo Guy would open with his coffee in the morning. "Anything you want from me is yours," would say his note attached to the roses delivered to her office. "Do you like this?" he had asked raising her skirt, lowering her panties and gently probing her sex with his as she bent over the sink in the airplane washroom on their way to Chicago. Watching her flushed face in the stainless-steel mirror, he had silently roared.

Working with Courtney was a pleasure. Years younger than he and less experienced in advertising, she was nearly as highly regarded, but she didn't have as much knowledge. Guy felt tall, broad and very wise as he spread marketing data in a fan across her desk, underscoring key facts, watching her grasp concepts he'd indicate with a few words.

Sleeping with Courtney had gone dimensions beyond any sex Guy had ever known. Being inside her was like being pulled into a sensual vortex and he was powerless to do anything but concede, relinquish himself. Afterward he could hardly move. The powerless feeling was terrible, but he couldn't wait to feel that powerless again.

"I love you," he'd say, stroking a perfect thigh with his palm, shaking his head in wonder.

"I love you, too," she'd reply, smiling up into his face, running a tapered finger up the cleft of his buttocks, licking his nipples with a rasping tongue.

It was at the stockholders' meeting where Guy got the first intimation that there was more to Court's feeling for him than passion. They were standing together too close for good business sense (but since everyone knew about them, what difference did it make?), when Charlie Jackson, their immediate superior approached.

"Well, I must say, you look wonderful together, you two," Charlie said. "Court tells me you're going to be married." Guy blinked, surprised. "You know of course, that married couples can't work at H & G. I would hate to lose either one of you."

"Don't worry, Charlie," Guy said vaguely.

Married? Guy thought in disbelief. He was sitting on a metal chair with Courtney's incredible thigh lined up against his. He'd only just gotten divorced! Oh. The divorce must have meant something to Courtney. But even if he meant to get married right away, could he marry her? My God, he thought, the sexual acrobatics were extraordinary, but love? There was only one part of him that Courtney touched and right now it was far from his mind and feelings.

Telling Courtney was going to be hard. She liked to have what she wanted and she had a vindictive streak. He had never worried about it before.

"Court, what was Charlie talking about?" he asked that evening in her apartment.

"Oh, I don't know, Guy. I didn't really say we were getting married. He was just being provocative."

"You're sure."

"Mmmmm," she said stirring a drink and handing it to him. "He asked me if we were getting married and I said something like, 'eventually,' or 'naturally,' or something like that. What's the matter, lover? You do want to marry me, don't you?"

"Court, this is all news to me. Don't you think you ought to have discussed it with me before you said anything to Jackson?"

Courtney didn't say anything.

Guy continued, "I'm not ready for marriage again. I don't know if or when I will be."

Courtney's face stiffened. "I thought you said you love me."

"I, uh, do."

"You, uh, do? If you, uh, do, what do you mean to do about it?"

"Wait a minute. We were doing fine."

"Guy we've been out with my *parents*. We've been *sleeping together* for a year and a half. What do you suppose? That this could go on forever, just this way?"

"I don't like what you're saying, Court."

'Ditto."

"I don't want to get married," Guy said flatly. "Now what?"

"Fuck you, Guy." She walked to the door of her apartment, opened it, took the glass out of his hand, and as he walked through the doorway, slammed the door behind him.

"She slammed the door so hard behind me, she bruised the back of my head," Guy was telling Bo. The two friends were hunched over the bar. Bo, balding and bespectacled, was dwarfed by Guy's comparatively larger size. He laughed appreciatively.

"The old hell-hath-no-fury syndrome," Bo commented dryly.

"You said it! Then do you know what she did? Twenty-four hours later I see her licking her chops and sliding gracefully into a taxi with Jackson. Going somewhere for 'drinks,' I'll bet." Guy gave

Bo an astonished look. "Do you think she'd start an affair with Jackson to get back at me? Don't answer that. You don't know this woman."

Bo whistled through his teeth. Then he took the end of his necktie in his hand and held it over his head. He stuck his tongue out of the corner of his mouth and made a choking sound.

"What?" Guy asked. "What's that?"

"Narrow escape, buddy. That's what that was. A narrow escape."

"You mean if I were to marry her?"

"Mmmm," Bo said meaningfully. "Tough lady." He tossed a peanut in the air and caught it in his mouth.

"But I do want to get married again," Guy said quietly, addressing his beer.

"Hell, I'm for that," said Bo. He took off his glasses and polished them ineffectually with his tie. "I'm getting married next week, am I not? To my beautiful Sari. She's never slammed the door on my head."

"To Sari," Guy said, clinking his glass with Bo's. They drank. "You know, there was a lot I liked about Court," Guy said reflectively. "The thrills . . ."

"The chills . . ." Bo added.

"Yeah. I don't think I paid enough attention to those pointy teeth of hers." Guy took a swallow of his drink. "Bo, do you think you can have passion and homeyness with the same woman?"

"Mmmm. You sure can. That's how I feel about Sari. A different girl every night, and wants to have my babies."

"Lucky you," Guy said sincerely.

"It'll happen to you," Bo said before downing his beer. He looked at his watch. "Hey, I gotta go. Sari's waiting up for me. By the way, do you want my apartment? We'll be moving soon."

"Are you kidding? Move uptown? Of course I want it!"

"I thought you would. I've already spoken to the managing agent." Bo grinned at his friend. "Ready to go?"

"Thanks," said Guy tossing money on the bar. "What a guy."

Guy moved into Bo's swell former bachelor studio on 94th and Central Park West. He bought a car. He dated. He worked. He healed.

Luck and timing arranged a meeting for Guy with a spiky-haired and very volatile entertainer named Barbra, who sang at Michael

O'Rourke's Cabaret, a singles' bar up the block from Guy's new apartment.

Some nights after work, Guy sat in the front row of the cabaret and enjoyed the envy of other patrons—Barbra sang crazy songs to him. She was so wild, she made him feel like he was from another generation. Actually, he was. He let his hair grow a little, he bought orange-colored cords and a handsome brown leather flight jacket, added herringbones and tweeds to his formerly all pinstriped suit office wardrobe, and started walking to work every morning. God, when Barbra wasn't pissing the hell out of him, she made him feel young.

Barbra, with her ten-minute attention span, demanded no commitment from Guy. She thought straight-and-true Guy a novel adventure; their almost live-in dating, as close to suburbia as she was ever likely to come. She liked Guy for his warmth and his normalcy, but after a time normalcy paled and irritation roared. She couldn't stop fighting with him. He was a bore and that made her mad. How could a human being be such a slug? He was in bed by 11:00 at night when she was still hanging out at the club. He watched TV. While he was straight! He couldn't handle a good fight, and on his days off, he liked to read! Not for her, this superstraight man.

Barbra saw that being with Guy was bringing out the blackest side of her nature and she regretted it. She liked Guy, liked the security he represented, but they were a bad match. The old cow she kept running into in the elevator with the purple fox around her neck, who was probably pretend crazy but truly conventional, was the kind of broad this slug needed. Poor Guy thought he was a swinger. He didn't know it, but he was made to be married.

Barbra looked around the studio for any odd pieces of hers she might have overlooked, found a few, and stuffed them into a black leather bag. She wrote Guy a note, and then Barbra Werner split.

Guy noticed that Barbra's belongings were no longer in his apartment, registering this fact first with surprise, then with relief. There had been too much fighting between them lately. It looked as if Barbra had seen it first, but it seemed clear to Guy as he stood in his now strangely quiet apartment that they had had as much relating as they were meant to have. Guy exhaled a breath he'd been holding. Barbra's abrupt departure eliminated a break-up fight that might have left him entirely dishless.

Looking around the room, he saw a note lying on his pillow. Barbra had printed words with a marker pen in her childish hand on a scrap of grocery bag. "Sorry I didnt get 2 say good by. It was time. Take care. B." Guy smiled. He studied the note for a while, then tossed it into the top drawer of his dresser. He went to the kitchen and poured himself a beer. Then he washed his face, brushed his teeth, and put on his luckily clean, best blue shirt. After a self-inspection, which he passed, in front of the mirror, Guy opened the fire door, swung down one flight of stairs, walked decisively down the hallway to Hanna's apartment and rang the doorbell.

As soon as Guy put his finger on the button, he thought to himself, this is reckless. Nothing casual about going downstairs and ringing the damned bell. What if she opens the door and says, "Yes. May I help you?" She'll think I'm from Jehovah's Witnesses or something.

Guy was saved. Hanna was at that moment having a bologna omelet at Milo's. She was staring at the heading on the menu—"Milo's, Where We Never Compromise On Quality." This on a cracked acetate menu propped up by a grease-smudged sugar jar and a black-necked catsup bottle.

Milo was telling her again about his little village in Greece and how much she would enjoy tending the goats once they were married and he had saved enough money to buy a little house and a herd. This time Hanna just nodded, not having enough spunk on this solitary Saturday night to play along with their oft-repeated little game. If she could do it all over again, she thought, she would not do it as Milo-the-goat-herder's wife.

Guy's Saturday night was no less solitary. He walked over to the east side of town and caught the 6 o'clock Buster Keaton double feature at the Loews theater, ate Chinese food in the walk-up restaurant near Bloomingdale's, and went to bed and sleep missing Barbra for the few moments it took him to leave consciousness.

On Sunday morning, Guy took his sack of laundry down to the laundry room and there sitting on the floor, her back up against the warm, vibrating clothes dryer, was Hanna.

"Hi," he said presently, thinking wildly about the clothes he was wearing: the lime green pants one shouldn't wear over the Connecticut state line and the Danbury High School football jersey. "I'm Guy Spencer. Come here often?"

Hanna laughed. "Hi yourself. I'm Hanna Coleman. As infrequently as I can get away with."

"What?" Guy asked.

"I come here as infrequently as I can get away with. Never mind," she shook her head. Calm down, she said to herself. "I hate to do the laundry is what I was trying to say."

"Me too," said Guy pushing his plaid sheets and rumpled jeans in one machine, a big orange bedspread in the other.

"Cute pants," said Hanna with a sideways grin.

"I got them on *sale*," he said. "I wouldn't have killed them, I swear." They both laughed.

Hanna thought, he's cute. Very cute. I wonder if he's still living with the mean blonde. She ran her eyes over his body and liked what she saw. She liked his broad shoulders and his curly hair. She liked the way his face crinkled up when he laughed. She liked his brown eyes. She liked the little paunch that showed itself when he was bent over the washer. She liked his small rounded buttocks in those silly green pants. From the way he dressed it looked as if he wasn't living with a woman. She liked that he wasn't wearing a ring on his ring finger.

"Have you lived here long?" Hanna asked.

"Not very," said Guy. "I guess three or four months. Since September. You?"

"Ages," said Hanna. "I think about nine years. It's a wonderful building, don't you think?"

"Uh-huh," said Guy putting quarters into the machines. "Especially compared to the place I lived in before I moved here. You know, I think I live in the apartment right over yours." What a doll, Guy thought. She's gorgeous. Those breasts. She can't hide them even in that big sweater she's wearing. And those eyes. And so clean looking. No makeup. Will you fall in love with me? Will you marry me?

"Do you? Are you in the C line?" Hanna asked. Oh God, she thought, Is that him with the heavy feet over my bedroom?

"No," said Guy. "I'm in the B line. The studio apartment. My hallway overlaps your linen closet."

"Oh," said Hanna. He found out where I live, she thought with excitement. "You mean, if I stand in my linen closet and tap on the ceiling, you can hear me?"

"Yes," Guy answered staring her full in the eyes. "Will you?"

"Any time," said Hanna with a grin, and they both laughed again, the essential question answered; does he/she like me? Yes.

Hanna stood up from the comforting vibration and warmth of the dryer, which had stopped. She looked dreadful, she knew. She had laughed at his clothes, but how about hers? How about this stretched-out navy blue fisherman's sweater and the worn-out jeans? She folded her laundry, put it in a basket and stopped at the door.

"Well," she said tentatively. Is this it? She thought. Do I have to run into him in the elevator before I see him again?

"Wait," said Guy. Shit, he thought. Am I going to have to wait until I run into her in the elevator again? "Want to have brunch?" he blurted.

"OK, sure," she said. Goody, she thought.

"I'm going to leave this stuff in the wash here," Guy said. "Why not leave yours? Do you ever eat at Boomers'?"

"Sure," she said. And the two of them walked almost hand-in-hand, although both knew it was too soon for that, and had breakfast in a semitrendy coffee shop on Columbus Avenue. Liking what they found in one another over bagels and coffee but ending the morning before noon, both hastily invented a busy day. Guy invented his because he was so excited he was afraid his excitement would leak out and ruin things. Hanna invented hers because she had to finish the copy she'd put off writing yesterday in favor of a good mope.

From the beginning Hanna and Guy felt good together. The first night Guy picked Hanna up at her apartment and they went for dinner and a movie was as comfortable as if they had been going to dinner together for years. Their conversation was easy and so was the space between the conversation.

Hanna loved how solid Guy was. So sexy and normal. His nice meaty hands unfolding his napkin, helping her on with her coat, lifting her hair in back and holding it over her collar. She liked the nice possessive way he steered her away from a hole in the sidewalk, the way he protected her from walking out into traffic, the way he listened to everything she said.

Guy wanted to grab Hanna and hug her. She was adorable. She seemed so in charge of her life, but he could see this tender person inside holding up a sign saying, "Won't someone come and take care of me?'' She walked into holes and cars, couldn't keep a napkin on her lap. She phrased her words in such a complex way, he had to pay a lot of attention or he'd miss the sense of what she was saying. He couldn't take his eyes away from her. He wanted to put his hands through that red-brown hair of hers and cover her delicious body with his.

When Guy brought Hanna home to 12C, kissed her good-night, and reluctantly turned her loose, he did it with sadness that he was leaving her. Hanna said good-night and thought, that was a good kiss. I want more. Soon. I wonder when he'll call. She kicked off her shoes, pulled off her clothes, and went into the linen closet for a nightgown. As she did, she heard footsteps above her. She reached into the broom closet and tapped on the ceiling with the mop.

She waited no more than a few seconds when the tap was returned. She climbed into her clean white sheets swaddled in her white flannel gown with blue stripes on the bib. Some time between one and two A.M., Guy put on his terry-cloth robe and, risking everything, pushed Hanna's buzzer. Hanna ran to the door in her nightgown and, risking everything, let Guy in. No words were spoken. Her arms went around his neck. He put his arms around her waist and after some indeterminate time spent holding one another and swaying in the open doorway, Hanna closed and chained the door. Then she led Guy by the hand, into her bed, into her body, and into her worn and warm little heart which was now swelling with hope.

When they woke up the next morning before the sun, everything was still fine. Making love without toothpaste was fine. Kissing endless and gluey kisses was fine. Separating was hard and they made a date for that evening before they parted.

Hanna went to work reborn. She called Mahelly before she took off her coat. Mahelly said, ''Oh, Hanna, this sounds great!'' I hope this is it, they thought as one.

5

THE GYM WAS EMPTY AT THE END OF THE DAY. THIS WAS HOW MAHELLY loved it. Paul was straightening up the chairs by the pool, dunking used towels into the laundry bin, adding chemicals to the warm blue water. Donna, the office manager and Mahelly's good friend, and Mike, the sales manager, were in the front office going over the list of clients who needed to be reminded to renew and sorting through the bills that needed to be paid.

All of the sadly unfit had gone home with their bulges and flabby muscles and their sweat glands which poured perspiration down their dimpled fat. Mahelly could drop the cheerful smile, which required an arrangement of twenty-four small facial muscles and were the only muscles in her body she would exercise less if she could. She worked hard to help the club members get fit and she thought sometimes that the diplomacy the staff rules required got in the way. If she could really yell at them, show them where their fat creased up and bulged out, maybe they would work harder. God knew she was working hard enough.

With the absence of other people, the red-carpeted, mirrored room was pleasantly cool. Mahelly lay on the floor, giving in to her back's urgent pleas for rest. She felt her spine relax and after taking a few good breaths, her other muscles relaxed too. She still didn't feel right. What was wrong? Oh. Then she remembered the dark, tightly wound knot, which was still sitting somewhere under her rib cage. It was the size, shape and approximate composition of a ball of rubber bands. It was her anger at Frank. With surprise and disappointment she realized that eight hours of constant exercise hadn't budged or diminished it. Frank's flip good-bye this morning, "Have fun, Bird," was wound onto the fight they had last night, and that was wrapped around a hard core of past misunderstandings.

Working at the club was brutal, goddamn it. Why couldn't Frank see it? Sure she was working because she wanted to, but did that mean that it wasn't work or that it wasn't important work? The money she made here had paid for a lot of things they took for granted now, things they hadn't been able to afford on Frank's earnings alone. Soon a thick pile of money was going to pay for her new business; money she had earned herself. If Frank understood how important this was to her, he sure didn't let her know about it. He had about three minutes of tolerance a night for a story about her day. The lug. She knew he couldn't be different from the way he was, but could he bend a little bit, make a little try, was that asking too much?

"Miz Colucci. Are you there?" boomed Mike's sarcastic voice through the public address system and her mood. "Time to go home." Mahelly blinked in the fluorescent-lit present. God damn that son-of-a-bitch. She rose to her feet reluctantly and stuck her head out of the gym door. She called to him.

"Mike. Can you hear me?"

"Yeah," he shouted back, slamming a file cabinet closed. "Ready to go?"

"No, not yet. Mind if I lock up tonight?"

"Will you be long?" he walked up to the gym door, standing a little too close, Mahelly thought.

"No. But I want to take my time in the steam," she said, stepping a half-step back through the swinging door.

"Want company?" he asked with a smirk, knowing the answer would be no.

Mahelly glared at him before letting the door swing shut in his face. I'd rather be dead, you ape, than have you in the same room with naked me, she thought. Soon she'd have her own gym and she'd never have to see him again. But she'd miss Paul who gently guarded lives at the pool as he studied French and the humanities between infrequent drownings. Sweet Paul was so shy, he could hardly look at her, giving Mahelly the luxury of staring at his beautifully muscled chest and legs and at the tender bulge in his swimsuit.

Stripping the tights and skirt and leotard from her body in one motion, Mahelly stood and appraised her reflection in the mirrors paneling the walls of the bright changing room. Being nude in a setting that made other women flinch before quickly wrapping themselves in a towel, made Mahelly preen. Her body was flawless. Even her doctor said so. "Mrs. Colucci, you have the muscle tone of a woman a dozen years your junior," her doctor had said last week at her annual physical checkup, confirming what she already knew. She blushed now, remembering how hard she'd fought her vaginal muscles against contracting as Dr. Kramer had inserted slick gloved fingers into her pelvic cavity. Was Frank right, she wondered as she soaped herself quickly in the shower? Was she turning into a sex maniac?

She did think about sex a lot. She had never felt so physically alive in her life. During all those years of being plain Mary Helen, Mommy and Daddy's little girl and then Frank's little wife, she had channeled her sexual desire into romance novels with pretend heroes and heroines. Anyone could see that. Why couldn't Frank see that she had changed, had become a real woman with a real life, a real career and real sexual needs?

She let the warm water wash down her body as she remembered how just last night, moments away from her orgasm, split seconds away from his, she'd begged Frank breathlessly to wait for her.

"Damn it, Mary Helen," he had spat at her, pulling out of and off her body, getting to his feet. "I'm not a goddamned stud for hire." Mahelly had stared at him. His face was twisted with anger. His penis was hard, glistening, and pointed at her accusingly. "You're not some bimbo! You're my wife!" He slammed the bathroom door on her pleas to talk. When he returned to bed, he hugged her, she cried, they kissed and fell together into troubled sleep. But nothing had changed.

Mahelly took a rough white towel from a stack on a bench and then opened the steam room door. She gratefully inhaled the cloudy mass of moist air and stretched out full length on the warm, wet tile ledge. She rolled the towel into a pillow and placed it under her neck. She sucked in great lungsful of humidity and felt the steam bathe the inside of her body, opening it, releasing the tension in her muscles. She felt moisture beading up on her skin and running in little streams off her face and through her hair.

The water felt like light touches of gentle hands. She thought of Paul. If he were here with me, she thought, he wouldn't rush me like Frank does. He would touch me like this, and like this, and as she thought of Paul, she ran her hands slowly over the muscles she had shaped hour by blissfully painful hour. She imagined Paul's mouth on hers until her thoughts drifted dizzily into a space in her head as cloudy and as infinite as the vaporous room in which she lay.

Frank felt the bar more than he saw it. It was Mahelly's late night at the gym and on this and every Wednesday night, Frank had dinner at Rizzo's. This was his night to do what he wanted to do. There wasn't a client in the world he would take out for drinks or dinner on his Wednesday night.

They knew him at Rizzo's. Dom always broke into a big grin when he walked in and said, as he did tonight, "I've got your table all ready, Mr. Colucci. Pete, bring Mr. Colucci his drink." And then Frank would settle in at his table overlooking the garden in the rear and begin his meal with an antipasto salad swimming with anchovies, slick with oil, spiked with little green peperoncini peppers. The entrée would be a gut-busting portion of pasta, accompanied by garlic bread and a bottle of warm red wine. He'd finish dinner with a cannoli stuffed with either chocolate or vanilla filling, depending on how he felt that night. After dinner, he moved up to the bar.

Frank liked to sit at the stool nearest the wall where he would blend in with the shadows. There he would sit with his Sambuca and his cigarettes watching the colored lights on the revolving beer sign until he knew Mahelly would be home, and then he would go there too.

Tonight he was brooding. A newspaper article ripped from the front page of *Broadcast News* lay crumpled in his briefcase. "Murdock to G.M./WKIX" the headline read. Murdock. General Manager of WKIX. That turkey. Barney hadn't been half the DJ he'd been and now here he was, king of Frank's old mountain. Christ, he felt his full forty years. He'd been busting his hump for Blake Spot Sales for how long now? A decade. Ten years and what did he have to show for it? A few grand in the bank, a thirty-four-year-old sales manager, and a cold thick feeling in his stomach every morning as he dressed for work.

The fight last night with Mahelly still clung to his skin like a spiderweb accidentally breached in the dark. What had happened to her? She was changing in ways that he didn't understand. That damned health club was doing something to her and it didn't feel fair. She could always count on him to come home with a paycheck and do his husbandly duties in every way. Her part of the deal was to be a terrific wife. True, she did cook and clean and all that but she seemed to do it with a quick flick of a dustrag, and they were eating a lot of cold-cut, shortcut meals these days.

And now Mahelly wanted him to be some sort of sexual whiz. It was embarrassing. He didn't want to be embarrassed in bed with his wife. You weren't supposed to have to think about sex with your wife. Marital sex was supposed to be home. Where did she get off being demanding, anyway? Did she even appreciate him? Sure, she told him how wonderful he was and all that, but what did she know really? Did she know what it was like to go in every day and get your quotas handed to you by that fat ass Pete Peterson, and then spend your day lunching and smiling and selling to a raft of under-thirty media princesses who had the power of life and death over your sales record at the end of each quarter? No. How could she understand? Mahelly was like a little yellow bird in a white little cage that he just about paid the rent on every month. He paid it off in brown nose and bright white teeth, while she jumped around for a few hours a day in an air-conditioned gym with a swimming pool, for Christ's sake. She did that and straightened up around the house and that was it. His mother had four kids when she was thirty-two; four kids and not too damned much else.

Even though the restaurant his parents owned had been torn down and replaced by a car wash, even though his parents lived in a condominium in Florida, Frank could still recall every tile, every pot, every drawer in the kitchen of that old place. Colucci's Restaurant, "Authentic Italian Cuisine Our Specialty," had been his home. He remembered coming home for dinner long after school, coming in through the kitchen's back door. His father would be out front, drinking with the patrons. His mother would be cooking, always cooking, chopping, supervising in the kitchen. He could almost smell the garlic and the orégano and the sweat even now. He remembered sitting at the big wooden table by the window—fighting with Lennie and Rocco and Bobbie for the veal shank or the last stuffed mushroom, tossing the bread to one another, pulling the chairs out from one another, horsing around until suddenly there would be a real fight. He remembered his mother taking just so much before she'd grab one of them by the hair, slap one of them in the face if he didn't stop, and banish them all to the street.

Mahelly didn't want kids and Frank guessed maybe he was grateful. What would he do with kids anyway? He let the thought trail off. Did he mean that? His dad had been happy. He shook his head. There was something really wrong going on here but what? This wasn't getting him anywhere. He ordered another Sambuca, touched a match to its surface, and as he stared into the blue flame, he thought about holding up a bank. A small bank. Just one. Get a big bag of money and then what? Fly away.

Frank drank his drink, crunched on the coffee bean left stranded on his tongue, and set the glass down on the bar. He paid the check with his credit card, slapped a five dollar tip on the bar for Pete, folded a ten into Dom's hand. "Good-night, sir," said Pete. "See you next week, Mr. Colucci," said Dom, opening the front door.

"G'night, Dom," said Frank. Then he carefully navigated his way out the door, into a cab and home.

6

THE PARTY WAS IN HANNA'S APARTMENT. THE INVITATIONS HAD BEEN exuberant valentines—hearts dressed in lace, inscribed in chocolate-brown ink, "I love you. Come to my party," they said, and everyone came. Polly Thomas was in from the coast, striking in silver lamé and red sequins. Bo and Sari Henry were there, and Kathy Broome and her husband, Mike. Neal and Bobby, lovers living down the hall, were in an intense conversation with Frank. About what? Oh, if the building goes co-op, what to do.

Hanna swung through the ballooned and festooned, big-windowed living room, ablaze in her tight red leather pants and swirling big jacket in the same leather, with a cream camisole underneath.

The photographer, Arly Beauchamp, his white silk shirt opened to the waist of his jeans, his blond hair caressing his shoulders, lounged against the door frame. Under his arm, almost hidden by his comparative height, Mahelly, fresh as a freesia in white satin, was thinking what would it be like to do it with him? Was he a gentle lover? She thought so. Would he take pictures of her? "Would you take a picture of me sometime?" she asked.

"Sure," Arly replied, staring down into her blue eyes as if she were the only woman he would ever want to know. "What kind of pictures do you have in mind?"

"Mmmmmm," said Mahelly. Naked she thought. Naked on my bedspread, by the window with air going through my hair and you climbing out of your jeans, not being able to resist me. I'd like a picture of that. "You're the photographer," she said. "How do you see me?"

In a bathtub, thought Arly, with your eyes closed and my fingers up your snatch. "I see you in water, somehow," he said.

"Hey, you two," said Hanna. "Arly, let me borrow Mahelly. I need her for a second."

To Mahelly she said, "Are you crazy? Are you trying to make Frank nuts?"

"What are you talking about?" Mahelly asked innocently.

"What am I talking about? Did you ask 'What am I talking about?' " Hanna was incredulous. "Arly looks as if he's going to eat you any second."

"Really? Is he interested in me?"

"Mahelly?! Come on. Help me put some cookies out."

"No, really. Does he look interested in me?"

"You're a moron, you know that? Guy, Guy, will you get that bag of ice out of the fridge and chip it up? And will you keep this girl out of trouble?"

"What's she doing?" Guy asked, munching a stalk of celery.

"She's flirting with Arly, that's what, and in a minute Frank is going to catch on and break up the place." She shot Mahelly a warning glance and breezed out to the living room with the cookies.

"OK, I was flirting," Mahelly hissed sotto voce. "But I don't know what the big deal is. I'm certainly not going to do anything," she said defiantly.

"It's OK with me, cute stuff," said Guy thinking she *was* pretty cute stuff. Wow, with her color high in her cheeks like that and her eyes flashing, she looked hot. Guy smiled at her appreciatively. "I didn't say a word. Come and tell me what's going on in your life." He handed her a glass of wine, and Mahelly sat on the kitchen stool. Her expression cooled down. She slumped her shoulders and sighed. "Guy, you've known a lot of women. Do you think it's possible? Can a person just *become* oversexed?"

"Mel, what are you talking about? A little flirtation?"

"No, not just that. I seem to be thinking about sex a lot lately." She sighed again and looked up at him sadly.

Guy laughed. "First of all, everyone thinks about sex a lot. Secondly, it's almost spring."

"Spring? I don't get it."

"Sap's rising." He leaned over and kissed her on the cheek. He slipped her off the stool and put his arm around her. "Let's go to the party," he said.

I wonder what Guy's like in bed, Mahelly wondered, fielding his scent with her keen nostrils. I wonder.

The party made up to Hanna for ten years of deprived Valentine's Days. It was perfect. She actually had to say, "The bar is closed," when the time was quarter till two. Not one thing was broken or burned.

Mahelly *had* made Frank nuts. He got a headache and left with his reluctant wife at half past eleven. When they got home to the twentieth floor, he didn't accuse her of anything. He just stamped up and down on the white carpeting and smoked furiously. Mahelly Alka-Seltzered Frank and massaged his back, hung up her clothes and his, and with pictures of a lanky, blond photographer in her head, Mahelly seduced Frank, then submitted to his rough embrace.

For hours after his wife was asleep, Frank lay awake. He moved to the left. He turned to the right. He went to the kitchen and drank some water. He made himself a gin and tonic and drank that. He went out to the living room and sat in a delicate white chair and looked out over the park and smoked. He pulverized an imaginary Pete Peterson. He shook an imaginary Mahelly. Be my good Bird, he said in his head. His eyes got wet. He worked at the snarls inside him and then the alcohol soothed him. Wondering what he was doing up at 2:30 A.M., Frank climbed back into a bed just a little small for his frame, gathered his wife into his arms, and put his face in her hair.

"I love you, Frank," she murmured. "Me too, Bird," he said.

Hanna and Guy piled platters into the sink. They bunched forks and spoons into the fork and spoon holder in the dishwasher. They impaled the glasses on dishwasher prongs.

Hanna respected her red leather suit enough to hang it all up, but the camisole and knee-high stockings and red patent leather shoes fell in small drifts, here by the couch, there on the bathroom floor.

Guy stood in one place by the foot of the bed pulling and discarding until he stood bearlike, furry and huge, licking his chops. "Come and get me," she said, plump in the middle of her bed, lush in the center of the gray satin goose-down comforter. And he sailed in. They wrestled and grappled and pulled one another's hair, and bit into the other's mouth like fruit, until wet and soft and sleek and hard found all the right places, and they merged, stopping sometimes to revel in the excitement, separating completely, panting, and then pulling together, together, together, until spent and one, they slept.

On Valentine's Day, having known Hanna for a month, Guy thought, I love her. At two months, on the first day of spring, he told her so. "A lot of flowers," he had said to the florist. "Big ones. Lilacs."

"Anything else?" asked the weedy-looking man in a shirt and tie.

"Some of those," Guy said, pointing at budded branches.

"Cherry blossoms?"

"Yeah," said Guy, looking around the shop.

"Anything else?"

"Roses," said Guy.

The young man rolled his eyes, put his pen down on the cash register. "Why don't we try this?" he began in a condescending voice to an oblivious Guy. "Why don't we take your address and MasterCard—fifty dollars sound about right?—and you write out the gift card. Leave the rest to me."

"Fine. Thanks," Guy said gratefully. He wrote, I love you too much for words. "So long," he said, floating out of the shop.

"Give me one 'kitchen sink' to go," yelled the young man into the dark interior of the store.

"I love you too," Hanna wept, hugging him, wiping her wet face on his shirt, carrying dripping blossoms and twigs everywhere, sticking them in pitchers, an ice bucket, a rain boot, the umbrella stand. She thought, a boyfriend, I have a real boyfriend.

"Don't flush the toilet, Hanna," Guy said, heaving himself back into their still very early Sunday morning bed.

"Why not?" Hanna called in from the bathroom moments later as she pulled the handle. And then, anxiously, "Guy?"

"You didn't do it, did you?"

"Guy. What's wrong with it? Help."

Guy sighed heavily and swung his legs over the bed. "Why don't you listen to me?" he asked rhetorically from the edge of the widening lake on the bathroom floor. She never listened to him because inside this woman lived a ten-year-old kid. To Hanna, the word "no," was a challenge. It meant "maybe," or "why not?" or "we'll see about that."

"Get me a mop," he said to her. And when she brought it, "Get me a bucket. And the plunger." Hanna padded back and forth, carrying tools and rags to Guy, who plunged, mopped, and when the overflow was cleaned up, put the toilet seat lid down and looked his brown-eyed girl square on. "The answer to what was wrong with it is that someone in this apartment flushed a salad down it last night."

"But, you see, I didn't want to put all that oil down the sink . . ."

". . . and she should know better. I'm going back to bed."

"Mmmmmf. I'm sorry, Guy. Thank you, Guy."

"You're welcome, you nut." He slapped her on her backside and when they were back in bed, surrounded her curled-up body with his.

Oh, my God, thought Hanna, wide-eyed in bed, viewing images of Guy standing naked in the bathroom swabbing the floor with her ratty mop at yow! 6:30 in the morning. She had no experiences to compare with this one. Oh, my God, she thought again, captions inscribing themselves under the pictures. Guy is a husband! She stared at an electric socket in the wall until, much later, the sounds of Guy's breathing lulled her to sleep.

In Guy and Hanna's fourth month together, Guy said, "I love you. Let's live together."

"Guy," Hanna said, "the two of us are such slobs, we need all the room we can get. Look," she said indicating the oak library table by her living-room window about to crash under the weight of the electric typewriter, the sewing machine, cartons of books, reams of paper, bolts of cloth. "Look," she said sweeping her hand toward the closets bulging with wardrobe. "There isn't enough room here for another pair of socks." She thought, not yet. I don't know if I can give up my own separate life yet.

Guy said, "It will work out great if we live together. We can use my apartment for storage. We can live down here."

"I don't think I'm ready yet, Guy," Hanna admitted. "I love you, but living together . . . I need a little more time to get used to the idea. Will that be okay with you?"

"Okay," he said with a smile and a warm kiss.

At six months Guy said, "Please. Live with me. It's stupid," he said. He loved her, she loved him. They were sleeping together almost every night. "I'm not ready yet, Guy," she said again. She thought, is this it? Is this the man I'm going to marry? She loved him, but did she love him enough? He brought so much of his old life into hers. Depression, anxiety, alimony, Joanne's still dependent needs. Sometimes being with him made her see the way her life would end—with a period, not with an exclamation mark. She'd never thought about that before. What good could come of telling him this? "It's too soon, Guy," is what she said. "I need more time." Something in Guy's face flattened out. He got cool.

That summer Guy and Hanna shared a beach house with Frank and Mahelly. Guy didn't mention love for the entire month of June. Turning a bend in the footpath, on a hot July day, Hanna caught him with his hand in a bikini top filled with a ravishing pair of breasts belonging to a woman with a mass of brunette hair. Hanna raged. Guy was abashed, but not sorry.

In August they were still living apart. Guy snaked the phone cord down through a drilled hole in Hanna's linen closet, and his telephone with a football player sculpture grafted onto the receiver now sat on the shelf with the towels. The phone frequently rang when they were making love or watching Dynasty. ("Sure, Charlie, I can meet you for breakfast tomorrow. Why? What do you think is going to go wrong in the creative review?") The conversation which followed would go on for so long, Hanna would in exasperation move into another room. The phone also rang if Guy was in the shower. ("Please get that honey.") When Hanna answered it would inevitably be Joanne. "Hi, Hanna," she'd say. "Is my husb—I mean, is Guy around?" On the way out of the bathroom, she'd see Guy standing in front of the linen closet wrapped in telephone cord. "No, the warranty for the roof is in the tin box in the pantry, Jo. I'm quite sure."

"Guy, honey, do you have to have the phone down here?"

"Yes," he said, simply and firmly.

78

"Mel, I don't know what's wrong with me," Hanna said, rubbing her nose with the palm of her hand. "I love him, I'm sure of it. But I'm getting anxious." Hanna was lying on the floor of Mahelly's living room with her feet on the radiator. The two were sharing a pack of red licorice. Frank and Guy were at Hanna's watching the Steelers and the Raiders do battle on the hundred yards of striped turf.

"I don't know what's wrong with you either. He's darling to look at. He loves you. You have terrific sex. You're complaining because he wears too much orange? And because he watches football on Sunday? Every man in this country watches football on Sunday."

"I know," Hanna wailed. "I'm crazy, but I'm scared. I hate myself for being so critical of him. He's so wonderful to me. Nobody has ever treated me the way he does. He protects me. He cooks for me. He stands up to me. I love him. But Mel, is he the man I envisioned all those years ago when I was fantasizing about my husband-to-be; an account man with a pot belly, alimony and a rubber stamp collection?"

"Hanna, I don't want to call you stupid or anything, but these can't be the real reasons. What's going on?"

"Mahelly, I don't know!" Hanna said balling up the cellophane candy wrapper and throwing it ineffectually against the window for emphasis. "That's why I'm talking to you. I'm thinking in circles."

"Sorry. Go on."

Hanna slapped the floor softly, repeatedly with her hand. "I'm wondering what's going to happen when the romantic sheen wears off as everyone says it does. Do you know what I mean?"

"Sort of. Yeah." Mahelly's thoughts sped off tangentially, homing in on her own marriage before she forcibly pulled them back to her friend.

Hanna sighed deeply. "I'm worried about how normal he is and how normal I'm not. I suppose I mean traditional. When he says 'let's live together,' it makes me think we're moments away from 'let's get married.' Am I supposed to marry him? Is he the one? He's cute, but he's not the most handsome man in the world. He's never going to be famous or anything. He's a regular guy. Is that what I wanted? Right now, I've still got options. Once we move in together, I've made a nearly irrevocable commitment to marry him.

"And what about this marriage business, anyway. Guy already

knows how to be a husband. I don't think he can wait to be a husband again. But am I a wife? What will I be expected to be like? What's my job supposed to be? Remember that time you said if I had your job I'd kill myself."

Mahelly nodded. "Yeah, but Frank and Guy are two different people. Guy isn't going to expect you to Wisk his ring-around-the-collar."

"How do you know? What went on all those years he was married to Joanne? I would have hung myself if I'd been in that marriage, I would have been so bored." Hanna sighed heavily. "Doesn't it make sense that after thirty-two years of being single I'm scared about marrying a man I've known for nine months?"

"Mmmmm," Mahelly said plumping the pillows on her sofa, tossing the cellophane into the trash basket. "I'll tell you what you've got. You've got," she made monster hands and put a spooky warble in her voice, "*fear of commitment.*"

"How do you know? You never had it."

"I read a lot of magazines." The two laughed with relief. "Look, this seems obvious, but why don't you talk all this out with Guy?"

"I have sort of. I've told him I'm not ready yet. If I tell him any of these dumb, mean little excuses, if I tell him I'm not sure I'm meant to be a wife, he's going to leave me."

"Yeah. Don't tell him you can't marry a man who wears orange, Han."

"Arrrgh."

On Hanna's thirty-third birthday in November, they were still living on 12 and 13 and Guy had stopped pressuring Hanna. He was hooked. He knew it. She knew it. He could try being patient. What did it really mean to live together, anyway? They were together more than they were apart, and when they were apart it was only by six inches of plasterboard and oak flooring. Hey, in the hallway they could hear one another's toilet flush.

In December, Frank and Mahelly and Hanna and Guy went to Key West for the holidays. They biked and fished and played tennis. Hanna thought it should have been the most wonderful time in her life. But where was Guy when she wanted to bike? Sleeping. And when she wanted to play tennis? Reading. And when she wanted to go to Hemingway's house, Guy and Frank wanted to play tennis. And before they could make love, Hanna would lie in the creaky iron bed and stare at the ceiling fan while Guy called the office.

"I don't know how I'm going to pay for this," Guy said toting up the American Express receipts on the plane home.

In January, Guy and Hanna celebrated their first year anniversary. One year! "Let's get married." Guy said.

"Guy," she said walking over to where he was sitting in her oak desk chair, wrapping her arms around his head and pulling his face to her bosom. "I can't yet."

"Hanna," Guy said flatly, putting bionic hands on her waist and putting her away from him. "You will be old and toothless and your tits will be hanging down to your knees before I ever ask you again. If you ever want to marry me," he said before walking out the front door, "you'll have to ask me."

Hanna stared at the closed door. In a while she wiped her cheeks, took Guy's keys off an antler on the hatrack, went upstairs and climbed into his bed. "I just need a little more time," she said. "I do love you, Guy. I swear."

On the night or two a week they slept apart, Guy missed Hanna. He resented his solitary TV dinners, but had no ambition to cook for himself. If he went out with a friend or client, he wished Hanna were there to observe, comment, delight them with her wit. In bed he packed himself in with pillows so he could pretend the heat they stored was Hanna's warm flesh pressed against his.

On the night or two a week they slept apart, Hanna reveled. She could be on the phone all night without Guy asking her to lower her voice or move into the next room. She could stretch out in bed. She could wax her bikini line without being imprisoned in the bathroom. She could eat garlicked cheese on celery and stay up half the night yakking with Mahelly. She could have fantasies about movie stars and trips to Cannes and chauffeur-driven limousines.

Hanna's Valentine gift to Guy was a big taupe sweater, handmade in Scotland. Guy gave her a pair of sapphire earrings. Hanna's gift to

Mahelly was a monthly column at *Urban Life*. It had been submitted and then prayed for. Stein had wanted to run a trial column on physical fitness and after reading Mahelly's almost literary prose, he agreed that Hanna was right. Mahelly was the right writer.

The column, "Fitness First," ran as a test in the March issue. It ran again in April and three sporting goods manufacturers signed up to advertise in *U.L.*

In May, two things happened.

Mahelly opened up her own gym. It was small but very beautiful. The room was very light with big arched windows, white carpets and a clientele who wanted to be taught by Mahelly Colucci who wrote the fitness column for *Urban Life*.

Frank, looking for an aspirin or an exit, took the Harkness Life Priority Seminar. After seven twelve-hour sessions of list making, life experience exercises, and life story sharing, Frank concluded the two most important things in his life were being a radio broadcaster and his wife. In that order. He bought a copy of *Broadcast News*, read the classified ads and applied for a dozen open disc jockey jobs. One of his letters was answered with a telegram and a plane ticket in the next mail. He found that in order to "let the natural forces of living propel him," Frank propelled himself to Sioux City, Iowa.

When Frank returned home from Sioux City with the good news, that he had an early evening slot on WMAP and that he had taken a very nice apartment they could afford near the studio, Mahelly was shocked. He had taken a job in Iowa without asking her? And he wanted her to move there too? Was he kidding? How could she leave? Leave her home? Leave her new business?

Frank packed. He flew.

7

FOR THE FIRST TIME IN HER THIRTY-THREE YEARS, MAHELLY WAS ALONE.
True, Hanna and Guy were in the building, but when she came home
at night from the gym, the apartment was dark and quiet. Every little
thing was the way she had left it in the morning, and every little thing
would stay that way until she moved it. There were no cigarette butts
anywhere, no brown socks, no jockey shorts, no meatball sandwiches
moldering in the refrigerator. Dinner could be a small green salad and
a slice of cheese on a cracker. The sheets stayed clean and crisp. They
didn't need shaking and straightening and smoothing. Mahelly bought
a pair of ice-blue glass candlestick holders, screwed long white tapers
into them, and placed them on the night tables flanking the bed. At
night, after her bath, Mahelly would light the candles, put something
soft and fluty on the stereo, get into her white silk pajamas and fresh
clean bed, and watch the candlelight flickering on the ceiling, reflecting
in the mirrors. In an hour or so, her thoughts would soften and when
sleep gently tugged at her eyelids, she'd turn off the music and snuff
out the flames. Mahelly felt wonderfully, gloriously free. So why was
her sleep thick, seamless and dark as a hole?

Mahelly went home to Massachusetts a few Sundays right after Frank
moved to Iowa. How nice it was to be asked, "What would you like
for dinner, dear? Chicken? Tell us every word about your new business," but she was horrified at her family's reaction to her situation
with Frank. What did they mean when they said Frank had left her?

Why were they pampering her? He hadn't left. He was just getting a job that he wanted after all these years of sacrifice for her. He wasn't going to live in Sioux City forever? Was he?

And what was Hanna saying when she said Frank wasn't right for her anyway? Mahelly had known Frank for fourteen years and now she was supposed to accept that he wasn't right for her?

"Which is it, Hanna?" she'd wanted to know. "I've been married to this man all these years and you've never told me how you feel? Or you're trying to make me feel better now that he's gone?"

"Both," Hanna had said miserably.

"Do you think he's left me?" Mahelly's voice cracked.

"I don't think so," Hanna opined, evaluating every syllable. "I just don't see how you can put your relationship back together without one of you giving up everything."

Mahelly took a valium for her headache, and went to bed at 7:30.

Mahelly was unprepared for Donna's explosion at her over lunch. What had come over good old Donna, supportive friend of many years? "A good wife would follow her husband anywhere," she said. "You're castrating your husband, that's what you're doing," she spat, spraying egg salad with each word. Mahelly, shocked, just stared. "Poor Frank," Donna said.

Poor Frank? Poor Frank was happy. He called every night, usually while on the air. He was breathless with excitement. He sounded younger, stronger than Mahelly remembered him. He practically sang into the phone, laying it down by the turntable when he cued up another record and then turning it low while he talked to her. Now all of her conversations with Frank had background music. When was she coming out to Sioux City? he wanted to know. "I don't know," she said. She couldn't close the gym for a whole weekend right now she said, but when the Memorial Day weekend showed up and with its four-day presence called her bluff, Mahelly booked a flight to small town, U.S.A.

Frank looked wonderful. He seemed taller. He was tanned. He had bloomed. He showed his wife around Sioux City and then around the station as if he had created these places himself. In the control room, his hands lingered on the knobs of the board, gently frisking this, his multinippled concubine. Mahelly remembered the hundreds of college nights spent sitting on a swivel stool like the one on which she now sat, listening to rock, staring at the back of Frank's head and at the muscles moving under his T-shirt, singing, as the nights turned into mornings. How young she'd been!

Frank's apartment was furnished with the heaviest furniture Mahelly could imagine. The couch was the color of ink and the size of a battleship. The armchair looked like a tank. The bed stretched from wall to wall in the bedroom, and was covered with a white fake-fur spread. "I got that for you," Frank said with pride.

Frank's lovemaking was more tender than it had ever been. He missed her so much, he said filling her mouth with kisses. She missed him too and was even sad when she said good-bye and waved to him from the airplane window. Funny thing, though. There was no talk of what to do next. Frank had a two-year contract at WMAP and Mahelly was not going to move there. Period.

For the first few months Mahelly overworked. She worked all day at the gym six days a week, and on the seventh day she did paperwork. When she wasn't working, she ran—five miles every morning. She had been lean before. Now she was hard. She hired another instructor; then two for a total of three. Mahelly started giving private classes. She stopped knitting, shopping and going to concerts. When she broke a plate or a lamp separated from its cord, she would put the pieces aside as she'd always done. Days later, she would realize the pieces wouldn't get fixed by themselves and she'd throw them away. Her sleep was still dark and it was shorter. When she woke up, she would find herself in midthought.

Mahelly took another weekend trip out west. Frank was still the Sioux City sensation. He had applied for his first-class engineer's license; if he got it, he'd get a raise bringing him up to $32,000 a year, which was quite enough for a single man who worked nights. He showed her a survey of a little piece of wooded land a few miles out of town. The down payment was really small, he said. Mahelly didn't ask what he intended to do with the land. Hanna's words, and her mother's and Donna's were tapping on her skull. He has walked out on me, she thought. He has no intention of leaving here and he isn't considering me at all. If she stayed in Sioux City another hour, something red and hot would consume her and everything in her path.

When Mahelly got back to New York, she started taking the phone off the hook at night. When Frank did get through, she was short with him. "I've got to write my column," she'd say. Or, "I'm getting ready to go out with Guy and Hanna." She had a pole installed in the hall closet. Soon all of Frank's clothes were hanging in WPOM. She never opened the door after that.

When Frank came home to New York (both times) he put his feet up on the white couch, presumably as he did at home in S.C. He forgot where the can opener was kept and the garbage bags. He watched the ball game while Mahelly cooked. Mahelly found herself doing what she used to think of as being the wife, only now she saw it as being the chambermaid, the social director, the cook and room service. It was at the end of his second visit, when he had left the plates on the table, his shoes and socks in the living room, and had disparaged the new watercolor she had hung in the hallway, that Mahelly focused her anger on its cause.

"OK, Frank," Mahelly said, turning from the saucepot she had futilely scoured and had now left soaking in Lemon Fresh Joy. It had been months since she had cooked anything with tomato sauce and garlic and she was faintly nauseated. (It was the garlic that was making her sick, wasn't it?) She dried her hands on an apron. They were shaking. "I think it's time we talked."

"Shoot, Bird. What do you want to talk about?"

Mahelly took her apron off, moved the chair closer to the sofa and sat on its edge. "Us, Frank. I want to talk about us. What are we doing?"

"Uh, oh. I'm in trouble." He pulled a Dagwood Bumstead face. "You're doing the dishes and I'm doing nothing again, right?" Frank put the newspaper he was reading on the floor and started to get up.

"Don't be cute, Frank. I'm serious. I want to talk about what we're planning to do about this, this marriage," she sputtered in exasperation. "What is it you think we're doing?"

"We're um," (Frank fumbled through his mental file cabinet looking for the appropriate Priority Seminar catchphrase) " 'forming two strong pillars supporting a mutually beneficial structure.' "

Mahelly stared at him. This was the macho man she'd married? He was spouting pop-psychology bullshit. "Bullshit, Frank. You got that answer wrong, so it's my turn. We're not supporting a 'mutually beneficial' anything. You live in one city and I live two thousand miles away." Mahelly realized her voice was moving up and down in her throat, out of control. "One day, without saying one word to me, you take a job in Iowa, you call in when you feel like it, and when you come home you act as if this is a hotel! *You* are thrilled with yourself and I'm furious all the time. I'll tell you what we're doing. We're letting our marriage go down the drain and we haven't even discussed it. Do you realize that?"

"Calm down, Bird," Frank said, feeling suddenly chilled in the summer night. She looked serious. And ugly. He sat up and reaching over, took her hand. It was cold. "We'll fix it, whatever it is."

"We will? How Frank? Are you coming back to New York?" Say no, she thought almost audibly. I don't want you in my apartment any more.

"Mary Helen, you know I can't do that," Frank said quickly. Mahelly waited for Frank to say something else, but he didn't. All he seemed capable of was squeezing her fingers rhythmically, and looking unhappy.

"What then, Frank? I'm not dropping everything to move out there."

"You haven't really given it a chance . . ." Frank looked at his wife's face. There were lines in the corners of her eyes, and without her makeup she looked pale and old. Where was the little girl who'd followed him around all those years ago, the little girl who sat in the control room with him all night, rubbing his back, stirring sugar into his coffee? She had to be there somewhere. Frank squinted and still could find no softness in her face. Where was his wife? Was he losing her?

"I don't want to give it a chance, Frank." A pot slipped against another in the soapy water, making a cymbal sound. Mahelly winced and continued. "There's nothing for me in Sioux City."

"*I'm* in Sioux City."

"I know, Frank. But it's not enough." She'd done it. She'd backed him against the wall. She took her hand away from Frank and put it in her lap with her other hand. She was frightened. This was the man she had sworn allegiance to and had trusted since she was in college. One part of her desperately wanted everything back the way it used to be—safe, secure, predictable. The other part of her, the strident, pressing, angry part, knew she didn't love him anymore and wanted to be free. What would happen to her if he stood up, kissed her on the forehead and said "good-bye." Could she be alone? Could she find someone else to love? Yes. She could try. Say it, Frank, she found herself hoping. Leave me.

"You *want* to break up, don't you?" he said.

"Frank, you've *already* left me." He didn't understand. He'd never understood. "You have, Frank." He was looking at her openmouthed. "That's what they call it when a man walks out on his wife. You left me."

He felt dizzy. How had this happened? He was being maneuvered and he had no idea how it had happened. Maybe he had been too cavalier with this move after all. He hadn't thought she would go this far. Be smart, he cautioned himself. Save what you can. Live to fight another day.

"Mary Helen. You're upset. If I didn't have to catch a plane, we could talk about this some more, but anyway, we'll talk again. I'll call you from S.C."

Mahelly nodded. She felt weak, exhausted. She had done as much as she could do. She returned to the kitchen, took the sponge from the sink edge, dusted cleanser on an enamel surface and with brisk movements, scrubbed at the encrusted tomato spills on the stove. She hoped by the time she looked up, Frank would have vanished.

Frank called, suggesting he visit again the next weekend. Mahelly said, "No. Let's face it, Frank, this is a separation. I don't want you to come home. I want my own life, and I want to figure out what to do with it."

Frank set the phone on the floor, punched the sofa pillows and leaned back against them. He considered what Mahelly had said. She wanted to call this a separation? Fine. Let her try that out for a while. He couldn't blame her for being mad. He *should* have consulted her before he moved here, but he hadn't, and that was that. Everyone makes mistakes. She'd forgive him sooner or later, and they'd work out something. They were having a marital crisis, but there was nothing that could really destroy the love they'd had all those years. Maybe they would both have to have this separation in order to appreciate each other again.

Meanwhile, he was doing great here. The station manager took him to dinner every week, and bragged about discovering him. He couldn't go back to New York now, but maybe later. It was possible, given a little more time he could get a really decent spot in New York. He was a much better DJ than he had been in the old days, and if he couldn't get a New York City gig, maybe Mahelly would change her mind and come out west. They hadn't even discussed other cities. There were other places in the world besides New York and Sioux City. Hell, anything could happen. He clasped his hands behind his head. A new thought was forming. If this was a separation, he could do what he wanted, right? He was a star and the women in this town were mad for him. He stretched out on the big blue velveteen couch and thought about the tall redhead at the diner who always tucked a free donut into the paper bag with the coffee he took back to the station before he went on the air. Her name was Josie. Jo-wo-sie. He said her name a few times. It sounded like a mouthful of water. Frank smiled. He wondered if Josie would like to come sit in the control room with him sometime.

Mahelly stretched out in the steam room. The gym was empty. She sluiced the water from her body with the edges of her hands. Her right hand absently found its way though damp blond curls to the little pink tip of tissue between her thighs. But her hand didn't move, it just rested. Sexual excitement was far away from her body but it was in her mind. We're separated, she said to herself. I wonder what it would be like actually to sleep with another man. I wonder if I know how to do it. I wonder if anyone would find me sexy. I wonder how I'm going to find out.

They were lying on the floor of Hanna's apartment gazing at the stucco swirls in the ceiling, cheek to cheek, one set of feet pointing north, the other set pointing south.

"I want to get laid," Mahelly said to a contemplative Hanna. "I feel like a virgin. Frank is the only man I've ever slept with in my life. Think about it."

"I know," said Hanna.

"I want to know what it *feels* like. I almost don't care who I do it with."

"You don't have the flu, you know, Mahelly. Sex isn't like getting an injection. It helps if you feel something for the guy."

"Hanna, you've slept with a lot of guys. You don't know what it feels like to be me. I don't even think Frank is good in bed. I bet I don't even know how to do it."

"Yeah," said Hanna with a sigh. "I had gobs of fun sleeping with those guys. Remember?"

"Yes, I remember. You liked it fine while it was happening and you love it with Guy. I'm not even asking for a wonderful lover like Guy. I just want to get laid."

"You will. Don't worry."

"When?" Mahelly asked.

Hanna laughed. They both did.

Mahelly's libido became a heat-seeking missile. Paul was the first object. Mahelly invited him to her gym to show him around. Then she invited him back to her apartment.

"Where's your husband?" he wanted to know.

"Away on business," she said. "He works in Iowa, more or less permanently," she added. "Would you like a glass of wine?"

"No, thanks," croaked Paul. "I'll be late for my class. Thanks for showing me around your gym and everything," he said backing out of the door. He fled.

She got Arly's number from Hanna and called him.

"Who?" he asked into the phone. "I'll be there in a second," he said over his shoulder to a party unknown.

"Oh, yeah," he said when Mahelly described herself from the Valentine's Day party.

"Yeah, sure I'll take your picture sometime. Give me your number and I'll be in touch."

When he hung up, Mahelly knew he hadn't bothered to write the number down, but regardless, she and hope formed an unnatural attachment to the telephone. "I'm expecting a call," she said to her mother, to Hanna, to Frank when the phone rang and it wasn't Arly.

Guy and Hanna took Mahelly to dinner in Sam's deli. Guy ordered a corned beef on rye with coleslaw and potato salad. Hanna gnawed on a turkey wing between forkfuls of mashed potatoes and gravy. Mahelly sipped at her glass of iced tea. Iced tea could be a full meal for Mahelly these days. She was flat and hard enough to be used as a backboard for a small handball court. The only sags on her entire five-foot one-inch frame were the two dark square inches, one under each eye.

"I don't know what I did wrong," Mahelly was saying. "He was flirting with me, you said so yourself, Guy," she added with a sniff and a wipe with her napkin.

"I'm sure he was," said Guy putting down his sandwich. "People don't always mean something when they flirt."

"That fuck shouldn't have teased me," Mahelly said with a pout.

"You're right, baby," said Hanna wanting to give her a hug.

"Fuck, fuck, fuck," said Mahelly head in her hands.

"For a girl who doesn't do it, you sure can talk it," Guy said with a laugh.

Mahelly met Aaron when she was jogging in the park. He was the most beautiful man she'd ever seen. He had blond curly hair on his head, legs, arms, and peeking out of the top of his T-shirt. In the early morning sun, he glowed, a halo limning his muscular physique. He slowed his run on the cinder path so Mahelly could keep pace with him and then he had to stretch to match her incredible stamina. They met again that week and soon started waiting for one another at quarter to seven on the 97th Street entrance to the park. Running with this sunlit morning god put a smile on Mahelly's face that lasted all day long and into her dreams. She went off her iced tea diet and actually started putting cheese and peanut butter into her body.

Aaron was young, she told Hanna, about twenty-eight, but he was single and he used to be in the physical fitness business so they had a lot in common. He was back in school now, full time, getting a degree in law. They met for dinner and a movie. Aaron walked her home and said good-night. After their second date, he kissed her good-night. To Mahelly, that kiss was a feast. She thought for days about the texture of his skin on her cheek, the feel of his mouth and taste of his tongue. On their third evening together, Aaron told her he was wild about her. He never hoped to find a woman so perfect for him. She invited him upstairs. Time and objects blurred. Her skin burned. Her breath came in shallow pants, as he kissed her and undressed her with practiced hands. Aaron's strong arms carried Mahelly to the bed where moist and trembling she locked her legs around his thigh, buried her face in his neck and moaned his name. She felt hands stroking her body, then stopping, then stroking her again.

"Please," she begged. The stroking stopped again. She was afraid to look. What was he doing? Touching himself? Yes. "Let me," she said, taking his alien, recalcitrant penis into her small hand.

"It's no use," he said.

Embarrassed, they called it nerves. Mahelly was so glad to be kissed and held, she shushed the tiny voice that wanted to claim, see, you're not sexy enough to turn on anyone but Frank.

"I'm so glad we waited," said Aaron on their next date. He undid little heart-shaped buttons with trembling fingers. He unsnapped a blue lace brassiere. He slid his wide hand slowly into blue nylon panties and cupped folds of flesh that nearly quivered at his touch. Mahelly covered her eyes with her arm and heard the clank of a buckle, the swish sound of jeans falling to the floor, and then he was naked, beside her. She put her arms around his seventeen-inch neck, snuggled flat against the front of his body and waited. God. Shouldn't he be hard? Her breath was loud in her ears as she reached for him. "I can't," he said, holding her hand still. "I just can't." He touched her then, gently but firmly in a detached way, and after her shudders and sobs subsided, he put on his clothes and went home.

There was no next time because Mahelly never saw Aaron again. He wasn't waiting for her in the park although she waited for him nearly every day for two weeks. He didn't answer his phone.

"Aaron," said Hanna thoughtfully. "Aaron Lefkowitz. I know that name from somewhere . . . Oh, my God! It's Lefty."

Mahelly was stricken. Hanna was stunned. "I've heard about this," said Hanna. "I think it's called a madonna/whore complex. It's when a man can only have sex with women he doesn't respect. When he has real feelings, he can't get it up." The two friends blinked at one another. "I don't know which one of us should feel worse," Hanna said at last.

"Maybe I should get my breasts enlarged," said Mahelly.

"Guy," said Hanna in bed that night. "I hated to leave her alone. She thinks she's a misfit."

"I know," said Guy yawning. "She's having a rough time."

"Is she doing something wrong?" Hanna asked rubbing slow circles in the fur on Guy's belly.

"Not really. I don't think so. She's a bit overeager, I guess, but mostly her judgment is off and she's picking the wrong guys. I certainly would have nailed her." Guy unbuttoned the top buttons of Hanna's nightgown.

Hanna stopped rubbing. She thought for a moment. "So you think she's attractive?"

"Are you kidding," Guy asked, liberating a breast, lifting it with his hand. "She's a doll." He reached over and turned off the light.

MAHELLY'S EXPERIENCES AND HER OWN OVER ALL THOSE YEARS, HAD given Hanna the idea that was resting now in her briefcase as she waited for the editorial meeting to begin. Guy's suggestion had sparked it. Thousands, no millions of women, no men. What could women do? There was really only one thing to do. They would have to get together and *share* the available men.

How do you think you'll like that, David Stein? Hanna thought as she surveyed the conference table. How many copies do you think we'll sell with this headline on the December issue?

"MANSHARE. By Hanna Coleman."

She had rehearsed her presentation, sanded off the rough edges, verified every fact. She was ready. Where was Stein?

Others in the room seemed to be wondering too. The buzzing continued but it was only light, tense chatter, conversational stones skipping across a deep body of water. Atkins had taken an empty seat to the left of the chair Stein customarily graced (the chair Hanna had fantasized taking) and seemed to be nonchalantly perusing the *Wall Street Journal*. She noticed though, even *his* fingers were tat-tat-tatting on the table's glossy surface.

From her seat next to Mahelly, she calculated how long the rotation would take. The first round would take between an hour and two. Then, depending on how many people had story propositions, how much Stein had to say, her moment would come. Her stomach felt empty and cold at the thought.

Would Stein's thumb point up or down? Would she win or lose? Proposing such an ephemeral concept as mansharing as a feature story idea was taking a chance, she knew. David Stein was the only editor in the city, probably on the planet, who insisted that the proposal of story ideas be exposed to the entire editorial staff. Other editors asked for these proposals in one-on-one meetings, but Stein loved the tension, the competition these open sessions provoked. He theorized the competition and the resulting fear of failure produced better ideas. Maybe he was right, Hanna thought, but could it really be good to feel as if she had a very frightened rabbit in her stomach? When she proposed her idea, she was not only risking Stein's rejection, she was risking humiliation before her peers. She was terrified but there was no other way. It would take a bold stroke to get that man's attention, approval and, she hoped, her reward. If she couldn't create the job she wanted for herself at *Urban Life*, she'd probably been fooling herself about her talent all along. Hanna knew it was time to find out how good she was. The time was now.

There was a stir in the room, like the flapping of wings, as people collected their belongings and found their seats. Then there was silence.

David Stein had entered the room.

"All right boys and girls," he intoned. "Let's settle down." The room *had* settled down since he had opened his private door entering the conference room at the far windowed end, but the few remaining midsentences, the isolated twitter, stopped, executed.

Stein stood another moment, sipping his coffee from a blue stoneware mug, glancing over papers in his hand, and then he sat.

"You've read my memo," he began, "but its message is worth repeating. The September issue has had to date the highest newsstand sales we've seen in over two years. Atkins' landlord story should get most of the credit, but frankly, I don't want to see events like last month's sales results be so noteworthy . . ." Stein stopped to look at his thumbnail, which Hanna could see from her seat was blackened. Was that the thumb she was pinning her hopes on? It seemed a bad omen. Before she could scare herself further, Stein continued. "I want to keep features in-house," he said, hefting a sheaf of manuscripts and setting them down on the table with a slap, "but I've been getting some interesting queries from free-lance writers . . ." He paused to let his words drench the editors in the room. "Now," he continued with a smile. "Let's see how we are doing for November and hear your thoughts, if any, for December."

Around the table, one at a time, they reported. Some coughed, some swallowed, some twitched. Some were as comfortable as if they had been sitting at the kitchen table of their own home. Resentment was visible in the faces of some of those who had been with *Urban Life* longer than Stein. Those faces reflected what they said in noisy corners of the newsroom. They were reporters, writers, journalists. Nothing in their training had prepared them for this deadly inquisition. Yet if they wanted to keep their jobs, and most did, they had to become adept at coping with Stein's brand of aggression. The younger editors rarely spoke with the older generation. They looked at Stein with awe. And with envy.

Roger Wilson was one who was comfortable. He had been a theater critic at the *Post* for twenty years before joining *U.L.* He considered his monthly section recreation. He stood up in his baggy glen-plaid suit and quickly commented on the Times Square theater renovation story he was concluding for November and his plans for a children's theater story for December.

"Do you like children, Wilson?" asked Stein.

"Not much," admitted Wilson without flinching.

"Nor do I," said Stein.

"But they are rather necessary," continued Wilson as if Stein hadn't spoken.

"True. Very true, Wilson," said Stein, unruffled. "Necessary, but not interesting. Shall we try for an idea just a touch less boring? By Friday?"

Wilson smiled, genuinely amused, and sat.

Art Haskins, named the art mouse by his colleagues, brought photos of the new exhibit at the Museum of Modern Art and tacked them to the back wall of the room, described them, lingered lovingly over some, and then with a nod from Stein, smiled appreciation at the approving staffers and scurried back to his seat.

Atkins' column, UrbanBeat, was unpredictable. The December column would be written in November, days before deadline, events of the day dictating his column's contents. Today, his pale hair lank, his face moist with sweat and success, Brian Atkins described his interview with Ron and Nancy for the November issue.

"Bravo," said Stein dryly. "Broome," he called out.

Kathy stood, slightly pale under her brown satin skin. Pages rattled in her hand, but her voice was smooth as she proposed "Breaking the Christmas Tree Tradition," for December.

"Gutsy," Stein remarked with something like sincerity. Kathy beamed. And then Rosenthal, the financial columnist, described his proposed attack on Christmas clubs.

"Coleman," Stein announced. Hanna took a deep breath. With a clear voice she presented her next UrbanWear column called "Knitwear for November," and her idea for a "White Christmas–White Fashion" story for December.

Mahelly spoke out, her voice quivering for a moment, and made her proposal for a home-gymnasium gift catalog. Stein approved it by nodding once and shifting his gaze.

"Johnson," he called out in a bored tone, licking the edge of his thumbnail. Johnson reported on Dance, and Walker was next with the Nation's News. Fergusen followed with Movies and so the imaginary baton was passed until the circuit was completed and Stein once again held the floor.

"All right," he growled, "who has a feature idea for December?" He raked the table with his eyes, searchlights in a prison yard. The editors shifted as if their seats were not padded antelope skin but slats of wood. Hanna felt her stomach drop. Two black spots pressed in on her brown eyes. I'm not going to faint, she said to herself. Not.

"I have something," she announced to the quiet room.

"Go ahead, Coleman," said Stein, looking up, tapping a pencil audibly on the table.

Hanna stood for several long moments, while she put herself together inside. She said nothing. Her external awareness seemed heightened. She sensed Stein's watch measuring off the seconds. She heard Mahelly's soft breathing next to her. She felt a lump the size of a grapefruit in her throat, but the rest of her body felt numb. She knew she had to speak but somehow she had misplaced the opening line she had rehearsed over and over to herself, the line that would launch her past this first terrible moment. And then it was there in her mouth.

"Just as you suspected, there are eight million more single women then single men in this country," Hanna said, one conscious part of her relieved that her voice hadn't squeaked. "This isn't such good news for women who want a mate of their own but the eight *million* too few men is good news compared to how much worse the disparity gets for *Urban Life's* female readership." Hanna cleared her throat and glanced at her notes. "In suburban communities and small towns the numbers are very close to equal, one-to-one single men, single women. In some rural areas the men outnumber the women. It's in the urban areas where the single, upwardly mobile, professional women

96

congregate and where the largest disparity between the numbers of men and women shows up. In a city like New York, not only are there more single women than single men, but a full fifteen percent of the single men are homosexual against a much smaller and less documented female homosexual population."

Hanna turned a file card over and making sure not to break her rhythm, continued. "Here's where the bad numbers become really sinister. Speaking psychographics now, not demographics, women have historically aspired upwards when seeking mates, and despite raised consciousness and shifting roles, they still do. Men have never had difficulty socializing below their business and/or social level. In fact," she added as an aside, "they have problems socializing above it. Common examples to illustrate my point: male doctors and female nurses, male executives and secretaries, working men and women who choose to manage their homes, etcetera. Women, however, still show a marked preference for men who are older, taller, more experienced, more successful, richer. As women have elevated themselves, moved into historically male-dominated occupations, they have found a small and shrinking stratum of more successful males above. Obviously many women are finding acceptable mates and some women are comfortable with men who are not older, richer, more successful and so on—or are compromising in this regard. But, and I have no hard data here, it seems a very conservative estimate to say that our single female reader, our sophisticated, chic, successful urban woman, who is psychologically traditional when it comes to mating—this woman outnumbers her male counterpart an easy two to one."

Hanna paused to take a breath. Gee, this was going great. She hadn't stumbled once. She looked up with a smile expecting to see it returned by whom? Atkins? Stein? Mmmmm. No. They were both tapping pencils. Atkins, that sycophant! But at least she hadn't been stopped. She turned two index cards over and moved another into focus. "To those of you who are married, the numbers I cited are just statistics." Hanna swept her eyes around the conference room. "To those who aren't, and I think that's three quarters of us in this room, and to our readers who aren't, many of whom will be thinking of killing themselves as the holiday season and the December issue hits the stands, it would be very nice to give them some kind of solution to this depressing state of affairs." Hanna stopped. It was so quiet. What was going on? She was doing great, wasn't she? Why then did everyone look so solemn, so bored! She was going to die here. Her throat was closing up. She took a sip of Mahelly's coffee and looked over the rim at Stein. He was frowning (*oh, God*) tapping a pencil more quickly now.

"Let's get to this brilliant solution *today*, all right, Coleman?"

Hanna nodded and plunged back in, afraid to deviate from her prepared presentation. "We can't even out the odds," she ventured, "but maybe it's archaic to think in terms of one on one when the actual numbers are dramatically different. What I'm suggesting is an end to what exists now; something I would characterize as mortal combat, despair, and sexual musical chairs. I'm suggesting women get together, face the facts, and under certain circumstances, agree to share the available men. I'm proposing a story on mansharing."

Hanna exhaled and sat. There, she was through. It was her turn to listen now. Oohs and ughs rose in a low verbal cloud.

"Ick, Hanna," said Linda Johnson. "Has it really come to this?"

"Hmmm," hummed music critic, Teddy Ross. "Not so original; the Beachboys predicted it first. 'Two girls for eve-ry boy-y,' " he sang. He laughed at his own cleverness, and the volume increased. A boo was heard and more than one hiss. There was some laughter, and then a sharp pencil rap from Stein.

"How would you go about it, Coleman," he asked into the newborn silence.

Hanna cleared her throat. Oh, God. Was he buying it? Was he going to say OK? "Statistical analysis first," she heard herself say, "and then a series of interviews with existing triangles of men and women who are involved in mansharing situations now. Then, I'll sum up and project the trend." Hanna held her breath and stared straight at Stein.

"Johnson," he said. "I get the feeling you don't like this idea. What's on your mind?"

"Sorry, Hanna," said Linda, sitting to Hanna's right, tipping her pixie head in Hanna's direction before continuing in a strong voice. "It's just disgusting, that's all. Nobody would ever do such a thing willingly. No woman anyway. It's a downer idea."

"I don't know about that," said Kathy Broome. "Hanna, you don't mean all women would share their men, do you?"

"No," said Hanna, glad she'd talked this over with Kathy during the month. "I said some circumstances, some women, not a wholesale abandonment of monogamy."

"It's like this, Linda," Kathy added. "There might be some circumstances where it would benefit all parties. Like if a friend was in desperate need somehow."

Thank you, thank you, Hanna thought in waves at Kathy. What a friend.

"Mmmm," said Wilson. "That reminds me of when I was in the war. I was seeing this pretty Italian girl. Her sister's husband had been shot. She was inconsolable. So naturally, when my girl asked me to spend time with her sister, I couldn't refuse . . ."

"Spare us, please, Wilson," Stein interjected dryly. "Some of us don't care to visualize you in bed with inconsolable Italian waifs." Laughter erupted in the room, breaking tension.

"No, no, that's not what I mean." Hanna spoke loudly over the noise. "This is not a piece about war victims. It's a story about contemporary supply and demand. Women in supply. Men in demand. I don't know where this story would lead. Some unpleasantness may exist. A woman might have to accept sharing her man at the man's request, possibly even suggesting it to him as a way to keep a fixed relationship intact. With men in demand this may turn out to be a new fact of life. But what I want to explore is mansharing as a workable option for all kinds of women; especially high-achieving single and divorced women. Mansharing would take the place of a permanent, perhaps demanding relationship, either replacing the need for marriage or filling in for marriage until a permanent mate is found. This would include Kathy's point and even the implied intent of Roger's remarks; altruistic mansharing—helping out a friend by loaning out your mate. How about bi-coastal relationships or any relationships where one lover is frequently out of town? I see possibilities in relationships where the sexual aspect is not complete or is unsatisfactory but the love aspect binds the two. Wouldn't a woman in that situation consider sharing her man and perhaps sharing another herself? What would make this different from simply dating, or cheating, or commiting adultery, would be the knowledge and *agreement* of the parties concerned. I don't necessarily see mansharing as limited to two women sharing one man. I find it very feasible that one woman might share *more* than one man. It might be the woman who travels and shares a lover in New York and another in L.A. I'm not married, so perhaps, if Jackie were willing, I might share you, Roger," Hanna put her hand on his shoulder, "and I might share you too, Ben," she said to Rosenthal.

"Anytime, Hanna," Ben winked at her.

"Hey, I'm married," said Roger Wilson. "You think Jackie would want to share me?"

"She'd jump at the chance of getting some peace from you," Ben cracked, getting laughter around the table.

"Did you check with any men about this?" Fergusen asked. "I mean, do you think men are going to like being shared?"

"Don't worry about the men, old boy," Wilson hurrumphed. "It's a well-known fact, most men will bleep anything."

"Wrong-o," said Johnson. "Not the men I know. And no healthy, self-respecting woman would consider demeaning herself by sharing a man for any reason. You, for instance, Hanna. Would you really do it?"

Will you kindly shut up, Linda, Hanna thought. Are you trying to torpedo me or what? "Absolutely," said Hanna into the rumble of voices.

"What do *you* think, Atkins?" Stein asked, swiveling his chair slightly to the right. Hanna gripped Mahelly's knee under the table. Her worst fear was going to come true. Brian Atkins would influence Stein and that would be the end of the mansharing story and in falling domino fashion, UrbanWoman would follow and Features Editor, and her rosy projection of a future work life of fun, thrills, glory and a carpeted, not linoleum floor. Brian pushed his yellow pad in front of him and centered it exactly with both hands before he spoke. "I guess it's OK," he said, looking across at Hanna. "It just doesn't seem very big somehow. I picture a bunch of desperate women scraping along on crumbs and pretending it's dinner. Not a terribly attractive thought." He swiveled his chair and looked at Stein.

Adrenaline flooded through Hanna's body. She could actually feel the blood in her face. Beside her, Mahelly said very quietly, "ow," and touched the top of Hanna's hand. Hanna winced and muttered, "sorry." Then, heart still pounding, she watched Stein.

He was thinking. He held his pencil in the middle and seesawed it lightly, rapidly on the table. "There seems to be some controversy here. That's good. But as you say, Atkins, Johnson, there is something very distasteful about the concept." His pencil was still. Something seemed to come together in Stein's mind. He paused and spoke almost to himself. "Of course, if Coleman is right, if attractive, desirable people, *our* people, *elect* to manshare . . ." Silence hung over the table. Twenty-five pairs of eyes focused on Stein's face. He saw none of them. And then his eyes swung to Hanna.

"Coleman, I think you told Johnson a moment ago that you, the very embodiment of the *U.L.* woman reader you so passionately describe, you wouldn't object to mansharing yourself. Is that so?"

Hanna sat erect in her chair, put both arms flat on the table, and swiveled slightly with her feet. Don't get thrown by the put-down, Hanna, she cautioned herself. "Right," she said, tilting her chin up and looking defiantly, straight into Stein's face.

"Fine," he said. "I'm starting to like this idea. Your proposal is accepted conditionally. Do the statistics as outlined, but consider all of that material as backdrop. This seems to me a perfect opportunity for a first person story, Coleman. Straight reportage would be very dull. I've been looking for an opportunity like this; a story that doesn't hang on hard fact and can be used to reach out and pull the reader in. What do you say?"

"I'm sorry. I don't understand the question," Hanna said, breathing shallow breaths, groping to make sense of Stein's verbal thinking.

"I'm asking you," Stein ennunciated clearly, "if you can write this story in the first person."

Hanna looked at him blankly. Did he mean do the interviews and use first-person narrative to link up the stories?

Stein was speaking again. "I want you to do this thing, manshare, and write it from the participant's point of view." Stein paused, looked at Hanna and asked in a strangely gentle way, "Do you think you can handle it, Coleman?" He smiled as he tapped his pencil.

Hanna's thoughts were foaming. There was too much happening. "Don't do it, Hanna," Linda warned in a low voice. What? There was so much noise in the room. Stein was waiting for her to answer. Didn't he say he approved the story? First person? She could write in the first person. Narrative style was her forte.

Hanna looked across the table. Brian Atkins was smiling at her, daring her, tapping his pencil just as Stein was doing.

"Of course, I can write it," Hanna said, her nostrils flaring. God, she thought, I've got the assignment. She felt elated. "Of course, I can."

For a moment the only sound in the room was the sharp whoosh sound of Mahelly sucking air immediately followed by a rush of group noise, penetrated by Stein's voice.

"Good," he said with finality. "But you'd better get started. I want to see a very good first draft by the end of the month if we're going to consider headlining this in December. Who else has something to propose?"

Hanna never heard another word of the meeting. Her body didn't return to normal, though. It stayed numb, and as the meeting broke up, Mahelly and Hanna stood virtually nailed to the floor by the door.

The disbanding group of editors parted around the two, some stopping to give Hanna a little tap of support, some a small smirk. Stein was in the throng and as he passed with Atkins following, he put his hand on Hanna's arm for a second, smiled and said, "Brave girl." Then, brushing her breast with his arm as he moved past her, he walked out of the room and down the hall.

Mahelly and Hanna stood in the empty conference room surrounded by crumpled coffee cups and thundering silence.

"What did you just do, Hanna?" asked Mahelly, her face pinched and white. What had she done? Hanna thought wildly. Stein had noticed her, that was for sure. Her arm still tingled where he had gripped it. She had a go-ahead from Stein to do the story and he had said "headline," hadn't he? He had loved it. But what had she said she would do? Realization, like cold water creeping up her spine, chilled and sobered her.

"Did I say I was going to manshare, Mel?"

Mahelly nodded, her blue eyes huge and unblinking.

"Oh, God," Hanna said in a dead voice. "I think this is what they possibly mean by more balls than brains."

Mahelly squeaked nervously, "Han. What are you going to do?"

"I don't know," she said, her voice floating out of her mouth, disembodied, a ghost of her former voice. Her insides sloshed around. Her blood pounded in polka time. To Mahelly she said, "Let's have lunch."

It was only 11:15. Charlie Brown's hadn't really opened for lunch but Bert, the maître d', said OK to Hanna's plea for a booth in the back. "We'll just drink until you open, I swear."

"What're you going to do, what're you going to do?" Mahelly chanted mindlessly.

"Could we get a drink first?" Hanna asked rhetorically. "Come on, Mel. I'm the one in the jam. Don't crack up on me."

"Sorry," Mahelly said. She waited.

"Two glasses of the house wine, please. One red, one white," Hanna ordered from the waitress who stood with pencil poised at their brown formica table.

"OK now, Hanna? OK if I speak?"

Hanna nodded.

"What were you thinking about? What did you think you were doing? Were you out of your mind?"

"Please, Mel. Please don't scold me. I can't take any more today."

"I'm sorry, Hanna, but I can't help it. I just saw a traffic accident in there. In slow motion. Please talk to me. I'm your friend. Whatever you do, it's OK with me. But please explain to me what you just did."

Hanna let out a long sigh and buried her head in her hands. When she spoke, her words addressed the table. "I didn't realize what I was committing myself to. I was completely adrenalized. Do you know what I mean? It was as if my hearing were impaired or something. I couldn't absorb everything . . . Wilson . . . Johnson. Johnson! Whatever was she doing! And Atkins, that creep. And the Prince of Darkness himself, grilling me on whether I could handle my own story!" Hanna looked up at her friend in disbelief. "After a month of preparing every word of this presentation, he threw me completely off with this first-person stuff. I didn't even understand what he was talking about! I told you what I was going to propose. Did it ever sound to you as if I was planning on mansharing?"

Mahelly shook her head slowly, no. She kept shaking it until Hanna touched her hand to bring her out of her trance.

Hanna continued speaking. "It felt like a traffic accident to you? To me it felt as if my apartment were on fire and people were yelling all different things at me. Get the hose. Call the police. Hide in the bathtub. Jump out the window. Let it burn and collect the insurance. Come stand under my cloak little girl. I'll protect you." Hanna paused and shook her head sadly. "Mahelly. What am I going to do?"

Mahelly shook her head again and stared.

"OK," Hanna sighed. "What are my options here? I told him I would manshare so I can either do it, or tell him I changed my mind."

"Good idea, Han. Tell him you changed your mind. I don't think it's too late."

"It's not too late, Mel. I can tell him I changed my mind. Then I can take a cab to the George Washington Bridge and jump over. I'll leave you the purple fox. It's not your color, but maybe you can dye it, and make sure my Mom knows where I put the diamond studs—in the box in my sewing drawer. The sweater-dress copy for the next issue is in my file marked 'This Month,' and my autographed picture of me and Debby Harry is in the bottom drawer of my desk at home, and my black angora sweater is in the refrigerator—you can have that too, it will look great on you, and I want Guy to have my C.D., and any souvenirs he wants."

"Stop, Hanna. You're nattering."

Hanna folded her hands on the table, took a deep breath and looked at Mahelly. Mahelly said, "I take it you don't think you can change your mind."

"I won't ever be taken seriously at *Urban Life* again. Forget my career. I'll be doing fashion work when the century turns."

"Uhhh," grunted Mahelly. A long silence followed. "What does this mean? You're going to have to find a man to share?"

"Right. Or share Guy," Hanna said, the blood in her face draining out.

"Share Guy?" Mahelly whispered, a strange chill coming over her. She had a premonition. "Share him with who? Whom?"

Hanna didn't say anything. She looked out of stark eyes and pale skin. Except for her nose, Mahelly noticed. Her nose was red. "You don't mean share him with me?" she asked incredulously.

Hanna nodded. "I could only do it with you. You would be the only one in the whole world I could share him with, but I think with you it would be OK."

"Guy? And me?"

"Don't you get it? You're a friend in need. Like Kathy said. You can borrow Guy. I don't have to do the borrowing. I just have to be part of the triangle."

"Hanna, no. You're crazy. It's a terrible idea."

"Melly, listen," Hanna was glimpsing salvation. She leaned across the table. "It's perfect. You like Guy. He likes you. I love you both. It's perfect."

"Hanna, I can't do it."

"Mel, look. All you've been talking about for the last six months is how you want to get laid. Am I right?"

"*I didn't say I wanted to get laid by your fucking boyfriend and have you write it up in fucking* Urban Life," Mahelly yelled.

"Thanks, she gets the white," Hanna said to the waitress.

"Will there be anything else?" the waitress asked, oblivious or seeming so.

"No thanks, not right now, but will you let us know when they open the kitchen?"

"Did you hear me?" Mahelly screeched very quietly.

"Melly, calm down," Hanna said reaching for calm herself. "I wouldn't use names." Hanna paused and then asked leaning back in her seat, "How do you feel about Guy?"

Mahelly didn't say anything. She had taken all the pretzel nuggets out of the plastic bowl on the table and was lining them up head to toe on the table. She shrugged before answering. "I like him," she said. She looked at Hanna out of the corners of her eyes. What did Hanna want her to say?

"Could you sleep with him?" Hanna pressed.

"I guess so, but . . ."

"But what?"

"But what makes you think Guy would have any part of this? He loves you."

Hanna sighed. "I don't know if he'll do it. He's going to be mad, that's for sure. It's not a favor on the order of asking him to pick up my dry cleaning." Hanna sighed mournfully. "I'll just have to tell him the truth. If he doesn't do this my life is over."

"How can you be funny at a time like this?"

"That wasn't meant to be funny."

"Oh." Long pause. "What do you think he'd say about sleeping with me?"

"He's always going on about how cute and sexy you are," said Hanna reflectively. "And if we all agree it's all right, well, he wouldn't be cheating on me . . ."

"He really thinks I'm sexy?" Mahelly asked incredulously.

"Really."

Silence.

"Mahelly, would you do it? Sleep with Guy?"

"I don't know," she said, hiding her burgeoning excitement. "Are you sure you know what you're doing? What if I fall in love?"

"Why would you do that, Mel? You just want to get laid, remember?"

Mahelly nodded. She allowed herself a smile. "How would it work?"

"I don't know yet," Hanna admitted. "Can we decide one thing at a time? Are you in?"

"Yeah, sure," Mahelly said, smiling broadly at Hanna. "What wouldn't I do for a friend?"

They clicked glasses with identical cat-with-cream smiles covering identical fear for their lives.

When Hanna opened the door to her office, the blue envelope was the only thing she saw. Stein used blue stationery. She put her thumb under the flap and ripped a ragged tear. The note said, "Well, Hanna, shall we have a drink to discuss? Wednesday?" And it was signed,

"David." Hanna. David. He'd never called her Hanna before. What was this? Monday? Yes, Monday. She dialed his extension. "Is Mr. Stein there?" she asked Jillian Cruse, his administrative assistant.

"Sorry, no, Hanna. He'll be back at 3:00."

"Will you tell him I called, and that Wednesday is fine?"

When Hanna hung up the phone, she had big wet patches under the arms of her creamy silk blouse. And a headache the size of an oven-stuffer roaster.

9

GUY HAD A HEADACHE. HANNA WOULD BE HOME ANY MINUTE NOW and maybe she'd feel like going out for dinner. He didn't feel like cooking or watching her do it, but he was hungry. The headache was work-induced, he knew. He never got them on the weekends. Today's headache was the product of four terrible storyboards, hastily presented to him at the last minute by the creative group, and each one of the storyboards was worse than the one before. He'd objected that there was not one execution along the lines the client had asked for and the creative director had shouted (in front of everyone, of course), "Listen, just go out there and sell the campaign. That's your job. Leave the creating to us," and he'd stamped out of the room. Tomorrow Guy was going to have to try to get this campaign approved by the group brand manager in Chicago and he knew by the end of the day tomorrow he was going to be carved very gently into slices, so gently he wouldn't even feel it until he brought home the no sale to the creative group.

Guy wished Hanna were home. She would listen and stroke his hair, and then after they ate, he could fold her into the curve of his body and sleep. If he could sleep like that for a week, it would be all right with him.

Hanna was walking home a good three miles. She needed time to think. She'd been too stunned after the meeting to think about Guy but after her talk with Mel, Guy's big, loving image confronted her. God, what an insulting thing to do to him. She had offered him up to Mahelly like a piece of cheese. He was going to kill her. Could she forget the whole thing? She imagined again the scene in the conference room. Dummy, she thought to herself. She had a big, fat mouth. What did she have to be so macho with Linda for? Sure, I'd manshare, she'd said stupidly. Let's face it, if she hadn't said that, Stein would have dumped her idea and if that had happened she would have been devastated, so devastated she wouldn't have known what to do.

Maybe she shouldn't be so hard on herself. She had come up with a good idea. She'd worked really hard on her presentation. She couldn't have known that Linda was going to be so provocative, or that Stein was going to turn her idea back on her. Face it, Coleman, she thought to herself, he manipulated you and he was, in fact, right. This story would be a hundred times more interesting in the first person. She sighed. What in God's name was she going to say to Guy?

A horn honked at her as she walked through a red light. She looked up, shot the driver an obscene gesture she'd picked up in a Greek restaurant, and kept walking. The blocks blurred. Could she appeal to his sympathetic side? Could she say, Guy, you know how horny Mahelly is? Nah. Could she be casual, urbane, say, Guy, remember that great idea you gave me last month? Well, Stein wants me to do it . . . She cancelled the thought. Don't be ridiculous, Hanna, she said to herself. She was going to have to be straight from the start, but she wished she could pay someone else to have this horrible conversation. "Can you spare some change, Lady?" asked a tall, ragged man in a cowboy hat on the corner of 74th Street. "Buzz off, Slim," she growled. "Thank you and have a nice day," he replied with a genuine, toothless smile. Shit, she swore to herself, going back and giving him a pocket full of change. "God bless you, Lady," his sibilant voice followed her. Maybe God was watching, you never knew. God, if you're watching, she thought looking skyward, please shit on David Stein.

Hanna loped through the 80s. If only she could predict what Guy was going to say. She honestly had no idea. He was going to be extremely pissed off, that was for sure. Would he actually refuse to go along with this? Maybe. It was a fifty/fifty chance. God, what if he refused? What could she do? Although if he said no, it would certainly take the burden off her. David, she might say, I'd love to write this article but my boyfriend won't let me. Yecchh. No, Guy just couldn't refuse to do this. He just couldn't. On the other hand, if he did go along with it, would he ever talk to her again? Would it break the good feeling and trust between them? Her career wasn't worth that, was it? Maybe it was wishful thinking, but was there any chance he just might think this was a cool idea and he wouldn't be mad? Not much chance, she admitted to herself. She entered the cool marble lobby of her apartment building, said "hi" to Pat, the doorman, looked at her mail and unable to postpone the inevitable, took the elevator to the thirteenth floor and knocked on Guy's door.

Guy opened the door with a bleat, "Where have you been? I've been waiting for hours. I'm starved. My head is killing me." Hanna pushed past him and threw herself onto his brown and white striped sofa. "What's the matter, honey?" he asked looking at her, immediately concerned. "You look awful."

"I feel awful. No, I feel worse than awful. I wish I only felt awful. I hope I get lucky enough to feel awful pretty soon."

Guy laughed at his miserable darling. She looked at him. Gee, he was cute. What a cute face all crinkled up like that. He loved her. Would he still love her tomorrow?

"What, baby?" he said sitting on the edge of the couch, kissing her downcast mouth.

"I've done something so dreadful I don't know how to tell you."

"Honey, it's me. You can tell me anything."

Hanna stared at him. He looked at her entirely. Gosh, she was cute. Even sad, with big blue circles under her eyes, all creased up and shining with sweat, she was the most huggable woman he ever met. "Hanna, what is it?"

Hanna didn't say anything.

"Do you want to change? Do you want to tell me over dinner?"

She shook her head, no. "I can't eat."

"Want me to guess?"

She smiled. "Yeah."

"You lost your wallet with your cashed paycheck in it?"

"I wish."

"Ahhh, you left all the layouts for the next issue on the subway?"

Hanna shook her head, no.

"Wait. You had an editorial meeting today. You got shot down?"

"You're getting warm," Hanna said the ends of her mouth turning down. Her nose prickled and some tears collected in her lower lids. "I think I have to go to the bathroom."

"Hanna, what? What happened?"

Hanna picked up one of the cotton throw pillows and put it over her face. "Guy," she said, her voice muffled.

Guy plucked the pillow off her face. "Yes?"

"Guy you know that mansharing idea I've been working on night and day?"

He nodded.

"Stein said I can write it if I do it."

"No." he said, feeling the slightest prick of alarm. She was going to have an affair. Joanne's shadow fell across him. No. How could she be? He wouldn't permit it! What did she mean to do? "Are you talking about seeing someone else?"

"No. 'Course not. Guy." She swallowed in the silence. "I was thinking you might."

"Hanna," Guy said, not playfully. "Make sense."

"Guy, you know what this story's about—the lack of men, Guy."

"Yeah, I remember." What was Hanna up to? What flaky thing was she about to do? Sometimes he had the feeling that Hanna was the 1980s version of Lucy Ricardo. "Go on," he said.

"It's about what's happening to Mahelly, and what I went through with dating before I met you."

"Yeah, but what's this got to do with you now? You have me."

"I know Guy, but everyone isn't so lucky. Mahelly for instance."

Big silence. Something was occurring to Guy, but he was sure he'd got it wrong. "What about Mahelly?"

"Honey, will you lie down? I can't say this with you looking at me."

"Okay, Hanna, but get to it, will you? If you take any longer to tell this I'm going to die from arteriosclerosis." He pushed Hanna in towards the back of the couch with his hip and extended his body horizontally. It was a tight fit. Hanna turned on her side, put her head under his arm, and her arm over his belly.

She felt false comfort, like finding a mountain ledge to sleep on in the middle of a snowstorm. She hung on nevertheless. "Guy. Would you sleep with Mel if it was all right with me?"

"Wh-a-a-a-t?" He pulled back to look at her.

"Would you? You've told me you think she's attractive, you know."

"HAN-NA. SPEAK!"

Hanna took a deep breath, perhaps she thought, her last. "Guy, would you please think about sleeping with Mel because, because, I presented this story idea about mansharing today at the editorial meeting and Stein didn't like it and Atkins pissed on it and Linda Johnson said no one would ever do such a disgusting thing so I told her off and then Stein said he'd put the story on the cover only if I do the mansharing myself and then I write about it in a first person account and he asked me if I could handle that and I was so scared and so mad I agreed to it in front of everyone at *Urban Life* before I could think about what I was saying or even what he meant and I can't back out of it or my career at *Urban Life* is over, and the only thing I can think of is for you to sleep with Mahelly, and I'm really sick to my stomach Guy but that's what I did.'' She took in some air and then pulled back a couple of inches to look at Guy's face.

He was frozen in the same expression Mahelly had had today in the meeting. He was aghast.

"You want me to sleep with Mahelly and you want to write about it?"

"Something like that, Guy. I'm not going to mention names."

"You love me and you want me to sleep with your best friend?"

"Guy. I didn't plan this. I'm sorry. Truly sorry. I jumped out without a parachute on. I was out of my mind. You know me. Please forget I ever said anything." Hanna sighed. She looked into Guy's face. It was crazy but she was feeling relief. Almost. "Do you have any sharp blades around here? You know I shave with those built-in plastic things and you can't cut anything with them."

"Hanna, don't screw around. What seriously will happen if you back out, tell Stein you made a mistake."

"Nothing. That's the problem. He'll say 'Fine, Coleman,' and I'll be writing fashion articles for the rest of my life. He'll never give me a shot like this again, ever, that's for sure."

"I see. If I don't help you out with this, your career is over and it's my fault."

Hanna started to protest, "Of course not, it's all my . . .''

Guy interrupted. "What did Mahelly say to all this, I'd like to know?"

"She said 'fine.' ''

"Oh, really?"

Hanna nodded. What was that on his face. Interest? Was he thinking of doing it?

"Will you do it?" Hanna asked, exhausted. Her mouth was dry and tasted of dead tongue.

"I'll have to think about it, Hanna," Guy said, disengaging himself. "I don't like the idea of being used by anyone, not even you, and especially not by that manipulative asshole, Stein." Guy stood, and angrily tucked his shirt into his pants. "I have to go to Chicago tomorrow and I have to think about my presentation right now. I'll call you when I get in tomorrow night."

Hanna stood too. He was asking her to leave. She smoothed out her clothes, pushed back her hair, and tried to accept the rejected feeling she was having. "OK," she said quietly. "G'night, Guy." She thought of twenty other things to say, some of them were please, some of them were please don't. Her sensible self, fighting for life, knew she had said enough for one day. She kissed Guy and let herself out. Guy had never been this mad at her ever, not even close. She was scared. And she felt sorry for herself.

Once in her apartment Hanna disrobed quickly. She scrubbed her face hard with a washcloth as hot as she could bear, slathered night cream on her face, covered her body with a long nightgown and got into bed. Her stomach growled, but it was the most inconsequential sound she could imagine. Eat? Probably never again.

The phone rang. Mahelly. "Well?" she asked.

"He wants to think about it," Hanna said, her voice flat.

"Oh." Pause. "If he doesn't want to fuck me, I'm going to kill myself."

"It's not about you, Mahelly, OK? He's mad at me."

"Shit. I'm sorry, Hanna. I'm a clod. A one-track-minded clod. I'm really sorry."

"It's OK. Can we talk tomorrow?"

"Sure."

They hung up. Hanna didn't have enough strength to wind her clock or shut off her bathroom light. She woke up very early in the morning with the bathroom light in her face and the remains of a dream in her mind. She'd been in a slatted cage, and from outside the cage the devil poked at her with a long carrot-shaped stick. The devil had one blue eye, one green.

10

MAHELLY AWOKE WITH A SENSE OF EXCITEMENT. WHAT WAS THAT thought? What was that smile off to the side of center? Wait a minute. It was coming. Guy. It was Guy. If everything worked out OK, pretty soon she was going to be sleeping with Guy.

Water bounced from her skin in the shower. Her running clothes barely touched her body as she slid them on. She did her warm-up exercises on the sidewalk outside the park, and began an effortless morning jog. She was a racehorse off-track, taking a leisurely romp in the meadow. She smiled at every jogger and dog walker she passed. Mahelly was a girl with a secret. The secret was that pretty soon she'd be in the arms of a man. And they'd be making love.

Mahelly was so happy she wished she could gather up the feeling and rub it all over her body with both hands. Imagine being in bed with Guy. He was handsome, he was her friend, he wouldn't reject her, and she wouldn't have to guess about anything. He was very tender and sweet in bed, Hanna had said, and a great kisser and he could get it up! Wow. And Hanna really didn't mind. What a wonderful thing this was that Hanna was doing for her. Incredible.

Mahelly had thought about Guy before but had never really allowed her imagination to range all through the inside of her head like this. She thought about him now though. She thought about how sexy he looked in corduroy pants and those nice, soft cashmere sweaters he wore. She remembered how nice and broad he looked in a bathing suit and how she had looked up the leg opening once when he had his leg cocked up on a chair at the beach. His penis had looked so nice and thick lying quietly in the nylon sling of his trunks. He hadn't been aware of her gaze and she looked at it for a long time. Soon, she hoped, she was going to touch it all she wanted. Then he would put it in her really hard and deep. She flushed as she ran.

I hope nothing goes wrong, she thought to herself for the hundredth time. I hope Guy says yes. I hope Hanna doesn't change her mind. She had one brief dark consideration. What if Frank finds out? Naahhh. Never. She abandoned the thought. A low log barricade enclosed a lawn of grass. Mahelly took the hurdle, ran through the deepest pile of leaves she could see and sprinted home. In her head were endless chains of pictures of her body entwined with Guy's.

Guy was mad. Flakiness he could tolerate, but this mansharing thing was damned insensitive to him and dangerous to all of them. The more he thought about it, the madder he got. Did Hanna think he was like the army reserves, that he was on tap for sexual emergencies? Women. They had this idea that all a man had to do was get it up, and stick it in. Didn't she know him at all? How was he going to treat Mahelly like a pickup? She was going to need a lot of hand-holding, that girl. She had been talking like a hooker lately, but that was just artificial virgin-itis. Anyone with brains could see she was going to be goo inside. Shit, that's why she couldn't get laid.

Guy raised his hand and a cab came to a halt. He gave directions to the driver and sat back in the seat. Good. He had gotten a driver who was not a maniac for a change and was driving a nice neat course to LaGuardia. He could leave the driving to the driver and really stew. Tonight when he got back into town he was going drinking with Bo. After that he'd decide.

Hanna knew she wouldn't be able to work. She was so anxious she was getting hives. She called the office, said she'd be in the garment center all day, and then went to the Museum of Modern Art. She sat in front of the Rothkos for three hours, seeing nothing. She wandered upstairs. She sat out in the garden. She went inside to the restaurant and drank tea. Now I get it, she thought. Tea is what you drink when you can't keep down a hot dog.

114

She was worried about Guy. What was he feeling? What was he thinking about? Would he say yes or no? Guy, if you love me, she thought, say yes. Or say no, but whatever you do, tell me before Wednesday.

Tomorrow night's drink date with Stein was scaring her to death. What if Guy said no and she had to tell Stein she was withdrawing her proposal? She tried to imagine the conversation and got chills. She sucked in the lemon wedge and it was so horrible a sensation, it gave her relief. She took a bitter sip of tea. Why was Stein having a drink with her anyway? That was an interesting question. Lunch was business. What was a drink? Was he interested in her? Don't be stupid, she thought. She ought to know when a man was interested in her by the age of thirty-four. She thought about her contact with Stein. Most of the time, she was so nervous in his presence, so on-trial, she never considered how he was regarding her. She considered it now. Wasn't there a sort of softness when he smiled at her? Hadn't she caught him staring at her breasts more than once?

Yow. Stein. David, she corrected herself. She was going to think of him as David. Was David about to make a pass at her? God. What would happen if they ever slept together? Was that a possible scenario? She tried to imagine. She thought of his intense face focused on hers; the bicolored eyes, those nostrils flared in passion. She imagined him taking off his white shirt and . . . stop, she commanded herself. This was crazy. He was taking her out for a drink, probably a short one, to discuss her story. They would probably go to noisy, unromantic Charlie Brown's. All business. Probably. And thank God. Her life was complicated enough. She shook her head to clear it and found she was still thinking of Stein. So, anyway it wouldn't hurt to wear something nice. Like what? She should wear her black dress. The black wool dress with the leather cummerbund. It was sexy but businesslike. She'd worn it to the office before so that was good. She wouldn't want it to look as if she'd gotten all dressed up for their drink date. She loved the way she looked in that dress, demure and vampy at the same time. She imagined herself standing next to David in that dress, him in one of his incredible Armani suits, staring down at her and smiling into her face. Yow. Didn't she need new eye shadow and patterned stockings? And what about her hair? It needed a trim badly. By six o'clock, Hanna had a charge card record of her entire day.

"What is it about me?" Guy asked Bo. "Do I have a sign around my neck—'Crazy Women Wanted, Apply Here'?"

Bo laughed. "I don't think so, but it's a funny idea."

"Do you believe it? She wants me to sleep with her best friend so she can get ahead in her career." Guy shook his head in disbelief. "Have you ever heard of such a thing? I'm trying to imagine my mother asking my father to sleep with her friend Vivian, so she could become chairman of the Westport Free Library."

Bo laughed uproariously. He wiped his eyes. "I'm sorry," he said. "I shouldn't laugh. But it's so funny." He laughed again.

Guy pushed the bar stool back onto its hind legs, then let it drop forward with a heavy thunk. "You *should* be sorry. This isn't amusing."

"Hmm-hmm-mmmph," Bo muffled his laugh behind his hand. "I'm sorry. Mmmph." He let out the tail end of his laugh and put his empty glass on the bar. "Whose turn is it?" he asked.

"Mine," said Guy sliding the three beer bottle caps over to him. He put a half peanut kernel under one, and moved them quickly in circles.

"Wait, I wasn't ready," Bo protested.

"Don't do that to me, Bo," Guy said with a glare. He lifted up one cap, showed the peanut to Bo, replaced the cap, moved the three around, stopped and looked at his friend.

"That one."

Guy lifted the bottle cap disgustedly, flicked the peanut at his friend, and slapped some bills on the counter. "Another round, Jake," he said.

"OK, Guy," Bo said. "I'll be serious. What part's bothering you?"

"It *all* bothers me. I'm insulted for one thing. *I love her.* What does she think I've got, some sort of automatic prick-on-a-stick? Sleep with her, jump on Mahelly a few times—who knows what's next. 'Guy, I'm about to get this great job at *National Geographic*. There's just one little thing. Would you mind fucking a turtle for me so I can write about sex in the Galápagos Islands?' "

Bo put his arms on the bar and his head on his arms and laughed. When he stopped, he said, "Uh, Mahelly's not exactly hard and green, you know. If I recall correctly, she's a tight little blonde with great legs, a high ass, and eyes the color of a desert sky. Could be Hanna didn't think she was asking you to do something too awful, you know what I mean?"

"You mean, you think she thinks Mahelly turns me on." Guy

paused. "Hell, she isn't entirely wrong. I've thought about putting it to Mahelly once or twice. A week."

"Well, you *have* mentioned it a few times to me. It's natural Guy. It's hard to have a woman friend and not think about what it would be like to do it with her."

"Mmmm."

"You get my point? Hanna didn't suggest you fuck a stranger or someone you don't like. You like this Mahelly. You think she's hot, and presumably, this could solve a problem for her."

"Yeah, that's me. Man on a white horse. Lance in his hand."

"Well?"

"You're right. I feel sorry for her. She says fuck so many times in a sentence the other two words get whisker burn."

Bo laughed. "And she's not getting laid at all, right?"

"Not since old Frank left town. And he doesn't strike me as a Warren Beatty kind of a lay to begin with."

"Poor girl," Bo said sweeping the bottle caps with the side of his hand. "Ready?" he asked.

"Yeah. Go."

Bo moved the bottle caps in tight circles and stopped. Guy concentrated, picked up one of the lids. Under it was a bare bar. "Shit," he said. "Jake, do it again. So," he continued, "even if drilling Mahelly makes me a good fucking Samaritan, I'm still pissed at Hanna," Guy said licking foam from his top lip.

Bo belched noisily and thought for a long time about what Guy said. "But you love her, right?"

"Yup. Diff'ren' girl ev'ry night."

"She loves *you*?"

"So she says."

"So, how's she gonna feel with you upstairs banging her girl-friend?"

Guy turned to his friend. "She's gonna hate it."

"Right," said Bo with a smirk.

"She's gonna be jealous."

"Right."

"She's gonna get crazy."

"Right. You're gonna bang the little blond. She's gonna get crazy and then . . ." Bo clapped his hands together.

"Clap? I'm gonna get VD?"

Bo shook his head no. "You're gonna get Hanna."

"Ahhh," Guy said, understanding. "If I handle this right, I'm getting married."

Bo put thumb to forefinger, then drained his glass. He pushed the bottle caps over to Guy. "Again?"

"Uh, uh. Gotta go home. Sober up. Talk to Hanna."

"Goooood man," said Bo. "Have a goooood time. Call me if you need any help." He laughed and the two walked out of Jake's together.

By nine o'clock, Hanna had been home for hours. Packages had been unwrapped and put away. She had spooned some yogurt into her body by way of dinner and now she sat alone in the dark. She found a little roach of marijuana left over from a party, which she had stowed in her night table. She smoked it. She poured herself a large water glass of $3.00 wine, put on a roomy rust-colored caftan, plunked herself down on the couch, stared out the window into murky night air, and waited.

The bell rang, two beats. Mahelly. Hanna floated to the door and let her in. Mahelly seemed to be shimmering. They hugged.

"Want some wine?" Hanna asked.

"No. Thanks. I don't need anything." Mahelly also seemed to be on springs.

"Please," said Hanna. "Have something. I can't bear you jumping around."

"OK," said Mahelly, accepting a large tumbler of Hungarian bordeaux. "Heard from Guy?" She hid her anxiety in a sip.

"No. But he'll be here soon."

"Are you really sure about this, Hanna? Have you really thought about how you are going to feel about the two of us in bed together?"

"Mel," Hanna thought lazily. "I'm past thinking about any of this. I really am. I seem to remember the last time I thought about it, I thought you'd really like sleeping with (pause) Guy, and I want you to."

"OK," said Mahelly, dubiously. The fantasy was great, but this was getting real.

"Don't forget, Mel. This is just a loan. I want him back."

Mahelly nodded. Hanna almost recognized a feeling. Nervousness? Was Mel liking this idea too much? Hell, why wouldn't she? Hanna tried to remember why she was doing this again. She couldn't. What was the question? She inhaled herbal air.

The bell rang again. Guy. He seemed very big in the doorway. Gigantic. Pyramidal. "OK, Hanna," he said without coming inside. "I'll do it. Mel?" he called out to Mahelly. "Want to talk?"

Mahelly nodded. She scrabbled off the couch and went to the door. She said, "Hanna, I'll call you later."

Hanna walked them out of the door. The ground was spongy for some reason. "How was the trip?" she shouted down the hall to Guy. The words came out of her mouth one at a time and hung in the air.

"Fine. Great," Guy answered over his shoulder. Mahelly, trailing behind Guy, turned and shot Hanna an anxious look. Then the elevator came and Guy and Mahelly got in. Hanna closed her apartment door and after several attempts, chained it. Her whole body was numb. She hadn't felt so abandoned ever.

11

IT WAS LATE WEDNESDAY AFTERNOON. HANNA SAT AT HER DESK. HER
light box was on, and the slides from the knitwear shoot were lined
up on it, making bright luminescent patches. She moved the slides
around, arranging the order, seeing them on the imaginary page. Yes,
the red mohair sweater with the strips of mink woven in would work.
And the electric blue dress with gold thread was good. Very good.
She would describe it in the copy as thunder and lightning, yeah.
Yowee, that pink knit suit was bad. It looked on film like poached
salmon. She had told the art director it was wrong but he'd felt nothing
could be lost by shooting it. She tossed the slide in the garbage. But,
oh, look at that. The beaded black sweater dress was the best. It was
simple, straight to below the knee and it had a bib of shiny, jet-black
bugle beads glittering upon and defining the model's bust. Ooh, she
should get that dress. She opened another box of slides and spilled
them out onto the light box.

As she poked the slides into place she thought about Guy; about
how he had pounded on her door late last night (early this morning?)
after he had talked with Melly, and after she had fallen into a woozy
sleep.

"These are my conditions," he had said standing in her hallway as
she squinted and blinked into the sudden light. "Fine," she had agreed
before he had uttered another word. Any conditions would have been
fine with Hanna. Any hour, any day, any position. She would have
agreed to anything. She couldn't bear the tension any more.

Guy's terms were simple and actually agreeable; two predetermined days off every week. ("How do Tuesday and Wednesday sound?" "Fine.") They could both do what they wanted, no questions asked. When would it be over? she had asked. He had shrugged. There was a little burr in the agreement, she couldn't help noticing. He didn't say he would be with Mahelly on those two days. He just said that he and she wouldn't spend Tuesdays and Wednesdays together. What did that mean? And what did he mean they could both do what they wanted? There had never been any contractual agreement about what they could or couldn't do; but there had been an understanding. Was Guy changing the understanding? Sounded like it. Hanna sighed. He was going to put her through something, she was sure. His whole demeanor toward her had changed.

Hanna tenderly touched the bruise on her wrist left by Guy. It hadn't been anger exactly. After she had agreed to his terms, he had grabbed her with force, kissed her hard before bending her over the living-room chair and plunging into her body. She couldn't have resisted him had she wanted to. She felt so weak from the wine and the grass and besides, she knew what he was doing. He was branding her, claiming her, telling her he was her man. She almost wanted him to hurt her more. And in a way, he had. Afterwards, he had gone upstairs to his own bed and again she was left alone.

She touched the bruise with a finger and watched it whiten, then color again. By making love to her like that, Guy had, she thought, told her in the most primitive way that she belonged to him. He might have to be a caveman for a while but she deserved it, and it wouldn't be worse than that. She knew Guy pretty well and he just wasn't mean or vindictive. He wouldn't fall in love with Mel and Hanna knew Mel would be loyal. It was all going to work out.

A snapshot of the four of them, Frank and Mahelly and Guy and herself, taken on the deck of their summer house, was pinned to the wall above her typewriter. Mahelly was in the middle between the two men and it was easy for Hanna with her great visual sense to eliminate Frank and herself from the photo. Hanna looked at Guy with his arm around Mahelly, protective, her friend. Tonight, she supposed, would be their first night together. She watched the two figures in the picture come to life, turn to face one another. She imagined Guy kissing Mahelly chastely then rather clinically re-deflowering her. That was OK. She exhaled and smiled. That was good. That was really sweet.

Hanna took some pressure-sensitive labels out of her drawer and started tagging the slides. And what would she be doing tonight, she wondered? It was five. Stein, she meant David, should be calling her now. She had avoided him all day so he would see her for the first time in her dress. Her lipstick was fresh, her hair looked great; after turning off the harsh overhead light, she had styled her office and posed herself at the desk. She thought she would look irresistible when he poked his head in and saw her bending over the colored slides, bosom moving under the v-neck, her face lit only by the soft glow of the light box.

It was vanity, she knew, but it would be fun to flirt with David. She wondered what that man was like in jeans and a sweater. Was he a warmer man when he wasn't pushing the magazine around? Was he actually human? Was he ever out of control? She tried to imagine him with a baby in his arms and failed. She tried to imagine herself in his arms and thought she saw something. He was so hard, muscular, and she was so soft. Yow. He would probably find the contrast pretty appealing. She saw him bend over her, and press his mouth to hers. Oooh. She shook her head and rubbed both her arms.

Where was David anyway? It was 5:30 and Hanna started to feel impatient. She opened her center desk drawer and looked at the note he had left on her desk two days before. It read the same. Wednesday. Had Jillian forgotten to give him the message? No. She was meticulous. Anyway, 5:30 wasn't late. She'd keep working.

At 5:45 and not one second sooner, Hanna called David's extension. No answer. She tried it again with the same result. What was going on? Was he in the men's room? Had he forgotten their appointment? She walked down the hall with a firm tread and stood before David's office door. The glass transom was dark. She pulled on the handle. Locked. He wasn't there. The disappointment was sudden and total. Her limbs felt heavy; the strings to something above had been sheared away. Numb, Hanna returned to her office and turned off the light box. She covered her sexy black dress with her lavender cloak and the purple fox boa. She gently closed her door. She walked out to the elevators, took one when it came, clung to the rail and instead of taking the subway, went out to the street and caught a taxi.

Inside the comforting black interior, Hanna pressed herself against the door, put her head against the cold window and allowed disappointment to take over. She remained immobile until she had to pay the driver and go upstairs to her apartment.

Her apartment was dark in the early fall evening. Through her numbness, Hanna knew Guy wouldn't be coming over. She knew she couldn't go upstairs and climb onto his friendly sofa. She couldn't even call Mahelly.

She took off her clothes one piece at a time, treating her body and her garments with the deference one would show to fragile art objects. She hung the black dress on a padded hanger. She rolled the leather belt neatly and put it in a drawer. She lined up her shoes carefully on the floor of her closet and unhooked her new black lace bra. She fingered the lace before dropping it and her matching panties and her lace-patterned pantyhose in a laundry bag. She slid on her caftan. She opened the freezer compartment of the refrigerator, took out a pint of chocolate-chocolate-chip ice cream and dumped it whole into a big crockery bowl her mother had given her last Christmas. She took the ice cream and a big silver serving spoon with her into bed.

It was then that Hanna noticed the red light of her answering machine was blinking. She set the bowl down carefully on a paperback book on the nightstand and then, with trembling fingers, flipped the dial to rewind. Ten seconds, twenty, thirty. More than one message. The first, "Hanna," Mahelly chirped. "I just wanted you to wish me luck. Talk to you tomorrow." Please don't, thought Hanna. I won't be up to this by tomorrow. Beep. The next message began. "Hanna. This is David." David? Her body was instantly electrified. "I'm calling from Kennedy Airport. I'm sorry about our drink date. Frankly, I got caught up and just remembered now. I'll catch up with you when I get back on Friday." Then the receiver had clicked and there were long seconds before the beep tone. Forgot? How could he forget something that had been on her mind for three solid days? She played the message again. She liked the sound of his voice. Be sensible, she said to her stress-fatigued body. People stand people up for drinks all the time. It wasn't like a real date. And he called. That was good. What did he mean he would catch up with her on Friday? See her in the office or make another date?

Hanna got out of bed and turned on the TV. She found a program that she hoped would prevent her from thinking her own thoughts. She lifted the bowl from the table and started spooning in the soul-nourishing food. Wonder where they are, she thought. Out to dinner, or did they make this an early night? Would they be in Mahelly's baby-blue bedroom enveloped in Bach and candlelight? Or would they be tangled up in Guy's masculine plaid sheets? Would they be making wild love, or tender love, or educational love? Educational, she decided with finality. Where were they? If she got up and went to the hall closet she might be able to hear footsteps.

No. Stop it, she told herself sternly. She finished what she could of the ice cream and put the bowl in the sink. "Time to start thinking about writing the damned story," she said out loud. Tomorrow would be Thursday, which would mean it wouldn't be Tuesday or Wednesday or even Friday. Thank God. It was time for Wednesday to be over. Hanna went to the medicine chest and took out a package of over-the-counter sleeping pills. She took one and without pausing to listen in the hallway, dived into her bed. By 8:30 P.M., Hanna Coleman was deep in troubled sleep.

The tape, Vivaldi's "Four Seasons," had ended. Mahelly turned it over and looked at Guy sitting across the room on the sofa, sipping his white wine in the dim light. He looked too big for the dainty white sofa as had Frank, and that reminded her of Frank and that made her sad. That small white sofa was just one piece of evidence that showed her how self-absorbed she'd been during their marriage. Had she been a good wife to Frank? She wasn't sure. Certainly not as good as she had thought at the time. She fiddled with the stereo as she thought. What she was about to do with Guy was so calculated! She had to *think* about what she was doing. She couldn't just call sleeping with Guy getting laid. Sleeping with Guy would be something real and would separate her truly from her husband.

"What are you thinking about, Mel? You look as if you just had a sad thought."

"A lot of things, Guy. I think I'm afraid to do this."

"I know," said Guy, "Me too."

Mahelly sighed. She stared into her wineglass and twirled it by its stem.

"Do you want to call if off?" Guy asked in an even tone of voice.

"I don't think so. It's just that this whole thing is starting to feel a little cold-blooded all of a sudden." Mahelly paused. "I know you, Guy. I don't know how to pretend that this is a sex education class of some kind, or that I never met you before. You are real to me; my friend."

"I know," said Guy. "I care about you too, Mel."

Mahelly laughed a small ironic laugh. "You know, I'm embarrassed to take my clothes off in front of you. You're Hanna's boyfriend."

Guy smiled.

"And you know what else? I'm afraid I'm going to embarrass myself in bed with you. What do I know about sex anyway? I want to feel more like I know what I'm doing, or that since I don't know what I'm doing I won't ever have to see you again. Isn't that dumb?"

"Yeah," said Guy. "Or maybe it would be better still if you were in love so the mechanics didn't matter."

Mahelly nodded and two silent tears traveled down her cheeks.

Guy said, "How would you feel about just hugging for a little while and then going out for a pizza?"

Mahelly wiped her eyes with her sleeve, nodded with a tight smile and said, "I'd like that a lot." She walked over to the couch and perched on the edge. Guy put one arm around her, drawing her close to his body, and then the other arm went around her too. He held firmly but gently. He touched her hair, moved it off her face, and kissed her on the forehead. She waited a minute before she looked up at him. "Do you think we could hug in the bedroom?" she asked in a soft voice.

Guy nodded yes, picked up the bottle of wine and the glasses from the coffee table. Mahelly turned off the stereo in the living room and the two entered the hallway at the same time, both slamming into the hallway wall, rebounding, laughing finally. They sat, then lay together on the bed, fully clothed except for their shoes.

It was strange, Guy thought, almost exotic to have this small frail woman in his arms. Hanna was so voluptuous, so substantial, and Mahelly was—tiny. He was afraid to hold her too tight, afraid if he rolled over wrong, he'd break her bones. There was a talcum powdery smell about her and maybe a hint of something sweet, like jasmine in her cloudy hair. Holding Mahelly was like holding . . . a girl, a young, prepubescent girl.

The light was off and Guy couldn't see her tiny face which was buried in his chest, but he could see her little feet in their white socks, just touching the tops of his. She moved closer into his body, pushing one of her legs between his. Her pelvis pressed his hip and he became aroused, but his desire was not to push into her, to rend her flesh, it was a desire to kiss her throat, to suckle her childlike breasts, to hold her up on his shoulder like a baby and rub her back.

"I'm terrified," she said into his soft wool chest.

"Talk to me," he said into her hair.

"It's crazy. But once we do this, I won't feel married to Frank anymore."

Guy kissed the top of her head. He stroked her sweatshirted back with a fleshy palm; up and down, up and down, and then Mahelly started to cry. The cries were just whimpers at first and then they were sobs. "Go ahead and cry," Guy said, and he kept rubbing her back. She pushed her face deeper into his chest and let months of pain roll out of her lungs and belly. She cried for herself. She cried for the loss of Frank. She cried for the wounds she'd received at the hands of men who weren't Guy, and mostly she cried because she was so afraid; afraid, she knew, to open herself up, to expose all of the soft wet parts she had hidden behind rough talk and overwork and muscles of steel. She cried as she abandoned her bravery and let herself trust this man who knew her. She blew her nose, and then she cried some more, and Guy just rubbed her and rocked her and murmured her name. When the tears were gone, Mahelly found a dry spot on Guy's soft sweater and then she fell asleep.

Mahelly didn't feel Guy lift her leg and slide her under the blanket. She was only aware that the night had passed when she awoke at dawn still clothed and still in Guy's embrace. She thought, I haven't been this happy in years. When Guy awoke, he looked at Mahelly who was looking at him. He gave her hair a little tousle, kissed her lips, and swinging his feet to the floor said, "I've got to go. Next Tuesday night?" he asked. She nodded, yes. He put on his loafers and padded out to the front door. "Don't forget to chain the door," he shouted in a loud whisper, and then he was gone.

Mahelly chained the door, and then stripping off her yesterday's things, showered cool then warm, put on her jogging clothes and fairly skipped to the park. What a beautiful day, she thought.

It was fifty-five degrees and overcast.

12

HANNA WOKE UP WITH A BAD FEELING—A FEELING THAT SHE KNEW something she didn't want to know but was going to know soon. When the specifics moved from the back of her brain to the front, she realized it was not just one thing, it was two. One: her lover had slept with another woman. Two: the other woman was her best friend—and now she didn't know how to talk with her about her troubled heart.

The sleeping pill had made Hanna's head heavy. Maybe she could wait awhile before getting out of bed. Maybe she could stay in bed the whole day. It was gray outside, dreary. If she just covered up her face with the goose-down comforter, maybe she would be invisible. She tried it. It was sort of nice but hard to maintain. The air got stale quickly. I should get up, she thought. I should get going on the story.

Dread joined her in the hot soapy shower. Anxiety accompanied her over coffee and Danish. If I put on my red sweater, I'll have to live up to it, she thought, slipping it on over her head. It was a big sweater with bat wings. It ended just above her knees. She tugged on black tights, then pulled on her soft black kid ankle boots. Sharp, she thought glancing at herself in the bathroom mirror. Try to be depressed in this. Not exactly whistling, she entered the subway and exited in Grand Central station.

She breezed past the receptionist on the 33rd floor, who buzzed her through the security locked door. She poured a cup of coffee from the communal pot on the file cabinet, dropped a quarter into the coffee can kitty, stirred milk and sugar into her cup, ducked inside her cubicle with a window, and shut the door. She punched her two telephone line buttons and the "hold" button in succession. Putting each line on hold meant no calls could get through.

Her bunker secured, Hanna opened her file on mansharing and took out a sheet of legal paper on which she had written some notes. She had written the notes awhile ago in a more innocent age. When was that? Two weeks ago? The sheet looked organized, sane. Hanna was impressed. She had wanted to do a roundup, a woman on the street sort of thing. Ask a few hundred women what they thought of mansharing. She had phrased the question:

ROUNDUP

The odds are two and a half single women to every single man. Given this and that there may not be an acceptable available mate for you, would you:

A: choose to share someone else's man (men)?

B: accept sharing a man of your own, if not sharing him might mean losing him.

C: reject mansharing and hold out for one man of your own or no one?

Required to qualify as mansharing:

The parties involved must agree to the arrangement.

Hanna put her head down on her arms. She qualified all right. She knew she had put the telephone lines on hold because any minute now, Mahelly was going to call and tell her about her wonderful night, and Hanna, as much as she wanted Mahelly to be happy, didn't think she would be sincerely happy for her yet. Maybe in a couple of hours. After lunch.

Hanna looked at her work sheet. It was obsolete. She had no materials to work with. No market research was required. First person, Stein had said. Hanna stared at the walls. Where to start? Start with Mahelly. Stop being so squeamish, she said to herself, trying to fight the desire to book a flight to Egypt to avoid ever talking with Mahelly again.

Come on, Ms. Urban Woman, she commanded. What's the big deal? What's the worst thing Mahelly could say? Guy is a phenomenal lover and she had a million orgasms, she answered herself. Hanna thought about that. So what? Orgasms. That wasn't it. She could live with orgasms. She *hoped* Mahelly had a million orgasms. Orgasm, she thought. What a stupid word. Anyway, it was the wrong word. Labeling her nameless fear "orgasm" didn't make it go away. Was she worried about what a softy Guy was? That was closer. Guy needed about a half inch of soil before he started putting down roots. Ninety-seven percent of the men she'd ever met had been terrified of marriage—that is to say, all of them except Guy. Guy had married Joanne without even deciding he loved her. He'd dated that account woman, what was her name—Constance, Confidence, no, it was Courtney—for a year and a half a couple of months out of his marriage, and what's her name, Barbra, the punk rocker, was almost fucking living with him. And let's not forget, Guy had proposed to her, Hanna, after about three months of dating. She had never known a man so willing to make a commitment.

Hanna wrote Mahelly's name on the styrofoam cup. Ball-point pen ink sure loved to be written on styrofoam. It went on so nice and easy. And blue! Hanna drew a lacy balloon around Mahelly's name and continued her thoughts. Mahelly. Her pal, her roomie. Mahelly, who married the first man she had ever slept with, now thirty-fucking-four years old and he's *still* the only man she'd ever slept with. Frank, the paperback Lancelot, and now what? Here comes Guy, a gift-wrapped, no threat, no sweat, romance novel hero right down to his big brown eyes and curly brown hair. "Unnnh," Hanna groaned. That was it. That was what was scaring her. Were those two, her two closest dearest people in the whole world, going to fall in love and do what Hanna had told Guy she wasn't ready to do yet? Were they going to fall in love and get married?

Hanna stared at the beach house picture. They say you can tell a lot from photographs, she thought to herself, photoanalysis or something. She unpinned the picture from the wall and held it under the light. The four of them were sitting on the railing. The sun going down behind the camera cast a rosy light on their faces. There was Frank on Mahelly's right. He was beaming at the camera, his arm around Mahelly's waist and her hand caressing his leg. Guy was sitting next to Mahelly on her left and had his arm over her shoulder. His other arm, the arm around Hanna, was pulling her in to his body. His hand was millimeters from her breast and Hanna remembered, he had squeezed her breast playfully, a fraction of a second after the photo was taken. She had shoved him away in mock anger and then the two of them had raced down the footpath and onto the beach. The last time she had looked at this picture, she had imagined Frank and herself removed from the ends. Looking at the picture as a whole, the couple-ness of the two pairs was evident. Guy loved her. She was sure of it. If sleeping with Mahelly was going to undo all their time together, all their love and closeness, well, it would probably be good to know now what Guy meant by love. That didn't mean she had to give in. She didn't have to give Guy away. She would let him know how much his love meant to her and she would spend time with both Guy and Mel; as a threesome, as they had often done.

Oh, could that be done? Because right now she felt so left out. How would she survive the loneliness and that terrible abandoned feeling she had had last night? She had wanted to be with Guy. And he had been with Mahelly. She had lost something. What was it? Suddenly she knew. What she had lost was the special feeling of "we two" she shared with Guy. Even if nothing permanent happened between Guy and Mahelly, sharing the intimacy was her real gift to her best friend. Could she bear this? She would have to. She would not let the sadness grip her. Quickly she punched out Mahelly's number on the phone. She had to get her girlfriend back. Get plugged in.

"Hanna, I've been trying to reach you all day." Mahelly's voice was effervescent. "Your line was busy."

"I've had a frantic morning, Mel," Hanna said. Why are you so damned happy, Mel, she wanted to ask. "I've got this story to write. Maybe I've told you about it. It's about mansharing."

"Oh, really?" Mahelly laughed appreciatively. "What a droll idea."

"What do you think? Do you think anyone would ever do it?"

"Yeah. Me. I'd do it."

Hanna felt a bolt to her heart. Mahelly, you jerk. Could you please stifle the glee, she thought in angry waves over the phone. So much for the pep talk. "May I assume from that, you are having a wonderful time?"

"Wow! Yes, Hanna," Mahelly chortled. "But it's not because we had, you know, sex."

Hanna couldn't help it. She felt her blood vessels relaxing, the nice red fluid extending out to her fingertips. "What then?" she asked.

"We didn't do it, Han. We just, you know, slept. It was enough, believe me."

"Well, what happened?" To Hanna, Mahelly's voice was the only sound in the world. She clutched the receiver with both sweaty hands.

"I was scared, Hanna. I just choked."

Oh. Poor Mel, Hanna thought to her surprise. "Of course you were scared. It's a big thing to do, get intimate like that with someone."

Mahelly sighed. "I cried a lot, Han. I cried all night. And Guy was so sweet. Hanna, I think he's the nicest man I've ever known. I'm sure glad you guys are letting me . . . you know."

Hanna swallowed.

"Really, thanks," said Mahelly gratefully, her voice cracking. "I'm going to try to do better next time."

Goody, Hanna thought facetiously, but didn't say.

"How are you?" Mahelly asked.

"Fine." Hanna said. "Fine and busy."

"Oh," said Mahelly. "Well, we'll talk later. OK?"

"OK, 'bye."

" 'Bye."

Fine and busy and nervous and jealous and ready to jump out of my skin, Hanna thought, completing the sentence she hadn't uttered to Mahelly. Who wouldn't be crazed from this, Hanna thought. Was Guy going to call? Was he going to come over tonight? Should she call him? Think about your article, you dope, she admonished herself. Stein said he wanted a draft from her in three weeks and all she had was one sheet of obsolete notes. She tacked the beach picture back to the wall, pushing the pin in hard. Little flecks of plaster fell on her desk. She blew them off. Stein, she thought, her mind leaping deliberately to another track. David. Tomorrow is Friday and he's going to be back in town. Get to work.

Hanna dug in her drawer and found a leather-bound notebook a friend had given her for Christmas one year, which she had never used. She opened it to the first page and wrote her name in with marker pen. She put the date on the second page and dated the following pages consecutively. This would be her journal, "The Chronicle of Lois Lane and the Mansharing Story."

She found an empty typewriter paper box and scraped every paper on her desk into the box and put the box on the floor. She stared at the journal. The thing to do was start jotting down her feelings. She blinked at the clean page with the date on the top. She took a pen out of the jai-alai cup on her desk, scratched it on the back of a file folder, and thought about her feelings. She drew a box on the first page and then quartered it. She had once seen a research grid like this in *Popular Psychology*. In the upper left-hand quarter, she wrote "Anxious." In the upper right-hand quarter, she wrote "Happy for Mahelly." In the lower left quarter, she wrote "Fame, Fortune, Approval." In the lower right quarter, she wrote "Guy." Her grid didn't look exactly right, but it looked close enough. She drew an arrow from Guy's name to "Anxious," and another arrow from "Fame, Fortune, Approval" to "Anxious." She considered her drawing. She was anxious, let's face it. She wrote:

"Beginning an adventure. Excited. Mahelly is going to be very happy." She tried to write, "I feel generous," but the pen ran out in the middle of the last word. "I feel gener," the sentence said. Hanna ran the pen tip back and forth on a folder trying to elicit more ink. None came. She threw the pen in the garbage can. She had nothing more to add anyway. She took the folder for the December column out of the toast rack on her desk. She opened it, rolled a piece of paper into the typewriter. She began to write copy. If I work, she thought, maybe the day will somehow end. Somehow, it did.

Hanna was in bed, almost asleep, when Guy called.

"Hi."

"Hi." Hi who? Hi what? What happened to "Hi, Nan?" OK, Hanna thought. Bound to be a little stiffness. She could let it go. She wanted to make love.

"Want me to come down?" he asked.

"Uh-huh, sure do," she replied.

He opened the door with his key. She heard him hang his coat on the antlers of her demented-looking Victorian hall-seat-coat-rack-umbrella-stand and throw his keys into its tray. A few clumping footsteps later, Guy was standing in her bedroom.

"Hi," he said again.

Hanna sat up, went to her knees and held her arms out to him. He came to her and gave her a good kiss. It felt wonderful to have his mouth on hers.

"Tired?" she asked.

"Yeah. You know Mulholland, that jackass. Had to tell him how smart he was for about twelve hours." Guy took off his clothes and threw them loosely over Hanna's gray armchair.

Hanna loved seeing him naked. He was picking up a roll of fat around his middle and his shoulders were slumping, but it was her familiar almost middle-aged lover draping his clothes over her chair just like always, scratching his balls, roughing up his hair. Just like always. He walked around to his side of the bed and got in. He lay on his back with a groan.

"How's it going?" he asked.

"Good," she said. "I worked most of the day on the December issue, and after that I made some notes about, you know, the man-sharing story. I think I'm getting somewhere, sort of, and tomorrow I've got to start writing a little bit for the draft I've got to show David . . ."

"David?"

"Stein, he wants to see a draft in a couple of weeks."

"Honey," Guy interrupted, "will you turn off the light?"

"You don't want to hear?"

"Sure, I do. I just want you to turn off the light. Keep talking."

Was she chattering? Sure. She only wanted to know one thing. What had Guy thought about his night with Mahelly. "Guy?"

"Mmm-hmm." Guy yawned.

"Guy, how did things go last night?"

"Didn't you talk to Mel?"

"Yes."

"So you know."

"Yeah, but I want to know what you think."

"Come here, Nan," he said. He turned her on her side facing away from him and surrounded her with his big body, knees tucked into the backs of hers.

"Guy?"

"I don't know what you want me to say, Hanna." Guy said into her back. "She's a little messed up, and since I've been elected to take care of her, I guess I'm going to do it."

Hanna felt a shock wave. Her worst fear.

"What do you mean?"

"Hanna, I don't know what I mean. We're all people here. I'm going to treat her as one. I'll try to do what you asked me to do, but I'm not sure I'll be able to talk about it very much. I've made a little commitment to Mel and that's important, more important than your story."

"More important than me?" Fear engulfed her. She thought she might faint.

"Don't be silly, Nan."

"Guy, I'm scared."

"Of what?"

"That this is going to break us up. All of us. Could we please call it off? Cancel it?"

"Hanna, it's too late for that."

"But she said you didn't do anything . . ."

"Hanna, a commitment was made, a connection. Do you really want to call Mel, your friend, and tell her the answer is no? That you've changed your mind? I know I couldn't do it."

Hanna thought of Mahelly, the skin stretched tight across her pinched little face, her voice cracking on the phone, of this wonderful man, Guy, helping her over a very rough spot. She thought of how long Mahelly could be alone and wanting before she ever found a man as good as Guy. She thought of Lefty and Oscar and Robin and Frank. Mahelly would survive the obstacle course, but at what cost? And to have Guy offered up and then withdrawn? It was too cruel. They had always come through for each other. Backing out after all Mahelly's expectations had been raised would do irreparable damage to their relationship. How could Mahelly ever trust her again?

"No, I can't do that," Hanna said at last. Guy squeezed her and kissed her nape. He filled his hands with her breasts and settled farther into the bedding.

"Do you still love me, Guy? Is this going to turn out all right?"

"Yes, I do. Of course it will."

"Tell me."

"I love you, Hanna. Everything is going to turn out all right. Now, go to sleep." She felt Guy's warm body against hers but it was not comforting. It was hot and sticky. She pushed away from him and turned over onto her stomach. He shifted and turned facing the other direction, not aware of her, really, just getting comfortable. His breathing deepened and then Guy was asleep. Hanna didn't have any choice. She followed.

Hanna arrived late to the office. She'd had a closet crisis, a battle with her wardrobe. She'd lost. Knowing she looked terrible seemed appropriate to her mood. By the time the morning sun had moved from one side of Hanna's office window to the other, Hanna had booked lunch dates, drinks dates, breakfast dates, crammed her week with people so she wouldn't find herself waiting to find out if her relationship with Guy and her relationship with Mahelly would be alive by the end of the week.

Along with purely social phone calls, she called the showroom managers at Perry Ellis, Norma Kamali, Ralph Lauren, and Calvin Klein to see the white wools she would select and have shot for the December issue.

Hanna had chewed off the skin on her lips and fingertips and was digging in a box under her chair for some hand cream when David Stein's voice cut into her world.

"Free for a drink tonight?" he asked. She looked up. He was lounging against her doorway, one hand in the pocket of his, Hanna couldn't help noticing, Adolfo suit. She tried to focus, pat down her hair. She knew she looked grubby. What had he asked? Drink?

"Oh, I can't tonight, David," she said. "I've got to get to the Lauren showroom right after work. They're staying open until seven just for me."

"Oh," said David. He stepped into her office and sat in the chair next to her desk.

"When are you free next week?" What was that pull in his face? Hanna wondered. Was he disappointed?

Hanna looked at her appointment book, hands trembling. What month was it? What year? Had her deodorant let her down? She flipped through pages, tried to absorb what she saw. She knew she was booked solid next week. She had done it quite deliberately. She was having lunch next Friday with Robin, of all people. She'd wanted to see Robin, see what his life was like, wanted to talk to someone who loved her and wasn't sleeping with someone she loved. But she could cancel that date. "How's next Friday for lunch?" she asked.

"That's fine," he said. "unless you hear otherwise from Jillian." He looked at her in silence. "You look as if you've been working hard, Hanna. How's your mansharing piece coming along?"

"Good, I think," said Hanna setting her jaw. "I'm not ready to talk about it yet, David."

"How are you feeling?" David asked with a smile.

"Perfectly fine," Hanna said looking into his handsome face with all the bravado she could muster.

David smiled at her, winked, and was gone.

13

GUY SAT AT THE KITCHEN TABLE WATCHING. AS USUAL THIS HAD BEEN one of Hanna's flaky ideas and as usual, having left no way for anyone to bail her out, she was going to have to work it out herself.

She had picked Tuesday night, the night he and Mahelly were supposed to consummate Hanna's nut-job scheme of the decade, for her to invite them both for a Chinese takeout dinner in her apartment. How could either say no?

Guy thought both women looked as if they were on drugs even though they were not. Mahelly in her pale yellow sweater and white pants was careening around the kitchen like a canary on amphetamines. She was caroming from the counter to the cabinets, to the sink and back again, squeezing little packets of duck and soy sauce into saucers, neatly smoothing out the white cardboard cartons before she threw them away, for Christ's sake.

Hanna just looked as if she were stoned. She moved in slo mo as the creative people at the agency would say, and m.o.s., mit out sound.

Guy was having trouble figuring out how to be himself. Mahelly had flattened herself against the refrigerator when he had gone past her to the sink, made herself almost part of the door in an attempt to prevent him touching her anywhere. No doubt she was protecting Hanna from the image of their touching and carrying it out to an absurd length. Relax, Melly, he thought, pinching her little-boy bottom, an action causing her to squeal and spring away knocking a quart of wonton into the sink which she had miraculously retrieved with her adrenaline-charged reflexes before it hit porcelain.

Next, he put his arms around Hanna and kissed her lips, lips he had kissed perhaps five million times in front of Mahelly, and found Hanna's lips dry and his back being patted as she extricated herself from his embrace.

OK, Guy thought, so affection isn't going to loosen things up. Perhaps he should try being the buddy. "So," he said. "How was your day?" Hanna said two words that sounded mysteriously like "erp, erp." Mahelly rattled, "bleep-de-bleep, new exercise machine, ya da ya da, new member fainting," never quite noticing that Hanna had been in the bathroom for almost the whole monologue.

His last attempt to inject reality into the evening was as group therapist. "Let's get honest here," he said. "Do we all want to talk about this again? Hanna?" he asked.

No, she shook her head.

"Mel?"

"No."

Fuck 'em. He sat at the table and watched.

Hanna put the spareribs and fried rice on the table and with Mahelly speed talking and with someone's occasional comment about the food, the meal was eaten and over at last.

Help with the dishes? "No, no," Hanna said. She could do them herself. "You two go ahead."

Guy looked at Hanna and was reminded of the legendary draft candidate who shoots off his toe so he doesn't have to go into the army. He felt sorry for her and he didn't want to feel sorry for her. "Talk to you," he said.

Hanna leaned against the closed door. She felt anaesthetized. Better make note of these feelings, you asshole she thought, before you forget them. She looked at the counter and the table and the sink. She hadn't let Guy and Mahelly help her with the dishes because she knew she was going to need something to do. She thought about Guy saying, "Talk to you," as if he were going upstairs to watch TV. Mahelly had pushed her cheek up to hers and held it for a long time. It was the only quiet moment in the whole crummy evening. "Thanks, Hanna, love," she'd said. "I'll call you tomorrow."

Poor Mahelly, Hanna thought. Why should she feel guilty because of all this? None of this was her doing and she should have the freedom to have fun with Guy without worrying about her. "Unnhh," Hanna groaned out loud.

If this had been a stage play, Hanna thought, the curtain would come down and the audience would go out to the lobby for coffee and a smoke. She couldn't think of any way to turn this into a stage play. Hanna looked again at the counter brimming with dirty dishes. Some people would have seen sparerib bones, cold fried rice and shrimp tails in congealed lobster sauce.

Hanna saw scrambled eggs—scrambled eggs she had made all by herself.

Frank hung up the phone. It had rung about twenty times. He had gazed off into space, cued up another record, and just let the phone ring in the bedroom he used to share with Mary Helen two thousand miles away. While it was ringing, he felt connected to her.

"Call ya' on the telephone," he sang with the record, "but you're never home . . ." He listened to the song, lit a Marlboro, and wondered what she was doing. He hadn't seen her in months. When they spoke, it was, "Hi, how are you? I'm fine. How are you? That's good." Neither spoke about making the separation permanent, neither spoke about getting back together.

Frank missed her, but he didn't know what to do about it. He didn't want to go back to New York. He liked it here. He felt so comfortable in this station, in this town. It was hard to believe he'd only been here six months. Six months, and he still got a little ache under his arm where Mahelly used to put her fluffy blonde head, and that ache would not go away. He remembered her sitting on the floor in those shiny exercise clothes she wore, stretching and sweating. He missed scrubbing her back in the tub. He missed fooling around with her in bed; playing acrobats. Mahelly would stand on his knees, balance on his hands, then she'd fall over and he'd hug her until they'd find they were making love. It made him smile thinking about it. All those years, and he still wanted to make love to his wife. And the truth was, they never fought. Could they reconcile?

Frank picked up the phone and tapped out the numbers again. Maybe Mary Helen missed him too. Maybe she wouldn't say no to another visit. The phone rang and rang. A shadow appeared on his board. He turned in his chair.

Josie swept in on him from behind, grabbing him around the neck and almost tipping over his chair. "Hey, watch out," he exclaimed.

"You watch out," she said, plunking her big body onto his lap, pushing her tongue into his mouth. Frank raked his fingers into the thick hair at her nape and put the phone down. By the time he'd cued up the next record, Josie was the only woman on his mind.

Mahelly got into the elevator with Guy. She wished her mouth didn't taste like lobster sauce. Maybe she could rub some toothpaste on her teeth real quick. She thought about how her nylon string bikini was pinching her hips and how the care label in the new bra with peekaboo nipples was scratching her back. She wondered if Guy noticed how much makeup she had put on. She wished the light in the elevator wasn't so harsh.

"Your place?" Guy asked as the elevator doors closed. Mahelly nodded. By now the incense she had lit earlier would have permeated the living room. She had put the stereo on a good music station, so the sound and the scent would greet them when they opened the door. She'd been afraid to light the candles, though. She hadn't been able to judge how long they would be at Hanna's and she was afraid she might burn down the building.

They walked toward Mahelly's apartment and from halfway down the hall, they could hear the phone ringing. Six rings, seven, Mahelly put the key in the lock. Eight rings. She paused. No one lets the phone ring that long but Frank. Nine. She looked helplessly at Guy. Ten. "That's Frank," she said. Eleven.

"How about we go to my apartment?" Guy asked.

"Yes," said Mahelly, the only short sentence she had uttered all evening. The combination of desire and anticipation were making her teeth chatter.

Guy pressed the button marked "13" and in a moment the elevator stopped with a lurch. The doors rumbled open, Guy fumbled for his key, and then they were standing in the entrance to his studio.

It was dark. Guy flipped on the hallway light switch, and then the Oriental-carpeted living room showed itself. Bookcases lined one long wall, the striped sofa faced them along the opposite wall, at the far end were the windows and the sleeping alcove. The bed was barely visible because the wall turned sharply to the left, but Mahelly knew it was there.

"I have this book," Mahelly said, taking one out of the bookcase and putting it back.

"No kidding," Guy said.

"Frank," she said shaking her head. "He hasn't gotten it yet."

"No," said Guy. "Listen, is it warm in here?" He walked to the window, opened it a crack. He walked back to the bookcase and turned on the stereo. He slipped a tape into the slot. He ran his finger across the top of the metal case then wiped it on his pants. Christ, there was dust on everything. He never dusted. Hanna never dusted. Mel. She dusted. Hanna. What was she doing right now? Crying. Was he really going through with this? "Like something to drink?" Guy asked.

"OK, thanks," she answered.

Guy turned on the light in the kitchen, found a corkscrew, uncorked a bottle, and poured out two glasses. "You're gonna be banging the little blond . . ." he heard Bo say. Right, Bo, he thought. Clap. He handed a glass to Mahelly who smiled at him and took it. They clicked glasses, but no toast was made. They stood in the living room and swallowed some wine.

"Guy," said Mahelly in a small voice. "Will you take me to bed?"

"Are you sure?" he asked.

Mahelly put her glass down on the table, stepped close to Guy, tilted her head up for a kiss, and as Guy kissed her, she put her hand between his legs and held him there. His immediate arousal sent waves of liquid heat through her. She felt her muscles contract. She knew her breathing was loud, too loud, but she could no more quiet her breathing than stop it completely. She put both her hands on Guy's buttocks, raised herself to her toes and pressed her pelvis to his. "I want you," she croaked, blushing.

Guy put his hands on her waist and set her away from him. He looked into her face. OK, Mel, he thought. OK. He stared at her for long moments before he put his arm around her and walked with her to the alcove.

Mahelly got into the center of the bed and took a pillow into her arms hugging it tightly. Guy, lit from behind, was faceless, a huge black silhouette. He sat on the edge of his bed, took off his shoes and socks. He pulled off his sweater and then his trousers and opening the sliding closet door near the bed, tossed his things on the closet floor. His erection was pushing at the elastic band of his jockey shorts and he wanted to take them off. Not yet. He quietly burped a little breath of fried rice. He ignored it.

Guy turned to Mahelly. She was holding a pillow in her arms and watching him with big eyes. Her features were softened by the distance the hallway light had to travel. Her childlikeness was almost overwhelming. Guy lay down on the bed next to her and turning onto his side, propping his head on his arm, he leaned over and kissed her mouth. Her mouth was so small. He kissed her again and this time, she opened her lips and her small tongue flicked out, shyly, then boldly. He took the pillow out of her arms. She resisted at first, and then let it go. He tossed it to the floor. Guy put his hand on Mahelly's collarbone and then one at a time he slipped the pearly buttons from their buttonholes until the black nippleless bra Mahelly wore under her cardigan was exposed. Do not laugh, he cautioned himself, bending and touching her nipples with his tongue. "Very nice, Melly," he said. He opened the snap of the waistband of her pants, and then in a slow movement, pulled the zipper down.

Carefully, thoughtfully, Guy unsnapped the bra and caressed each breast. Mahelly gasped and putting her arms around his neck, pulled his face to hers and kissed him hard, taking his tongue into her mouth and sucking on it with such force, he had to disengage. He took off her sweater then, and her pants and panties as if they were one, and removed his shorts and pushed all of the clothes to the floor. Guy stood, undoing the blankets and sheets, sliding Mahelly in between them and sliding in after her.

And then she was in his arms. The feeling of his naked flesh on hers warmed her. His erection pressed hard against her belly and made her squirm. Guy could feel her moist breath on his chest. When he touched between her legs, she was wet. When he slipped his finger inside her, she clamped her muscles like a baby enclosing a finger with its fist.

I can't get in there, Guy thought, no way in the world. "Mel," he said and kissed. "Mel, try to relax. Try to let go." He kissed her again, lingering, letting his tongue know her mouth, her taste, her teeth. He felt her body warm and mold itself to his. He heard her inhale deeply and exhale and as she did so, her muscles lost their tension; as she kissed him, savored him, she lost herself in the feel of their mouths.

With their breathing loud in their ears, Guy eased himself slowly inside. One slow inch at a time was fast enough. Mahelly struggled to take him inside her completely and as she did so, the bed, Guy, everything around her blurred and blended. She felt she was falling. She clutched at Guy and called his name. He moved into her then, harder and faster, enjoying the tightness of her body, and again a cry escaped Mahelly's lips. One part of his mind making sure not to fall on this sexy, fragile woman friend he now knew in a new way, Guy released himself into her. And then they lay together in a close embrace.

"Are you all right, Mel?" Guy asked when his breathing slowed.

"Oh, yes, Guy," she said her voice languid. "Thank you so much."

He squeezed her. She kissed his neck and he separated from her body. She burrowed her head into his chest, and thinking how completely undone she felt, melted to the bone, Mahelly fell asleep.

Guy was awake. What now? he wondered. This had been very nice. Nice and take that, Hanna, but now what. He had an urge to go down to Hanna's bed and crawl in with her. Not a good idea. Would Mel expect him to sleep with her tomorrow too? Yes, but should he, or should he not?

Guy thought about what he should do in the future. He decided. He would let Hanna think he was with Mahelly. But what he would actually do was be by himself.

In the morning when they woke up, he said, "Mel, I have plans tonight. See you next week?"

"Sure," she said. "I have muffins in the freezer. They'll take just a second."

"No, no thanks, Mel. I've got to go."

"Was I terrible?" she asked, fear in her eyes.

"No. Of course not. It was wonderful. You are wonderful."

"Really?"

"Really. Sexy. Beautiful. Heaven, if you really want to know. But we both know I love Hanna. I don't want us to get into a spot we can't get out of. A lifetime habit, you know what I mean?"

"Yes, I do," she said. He was so right. He was only hers for a little while, and so, especially so, she wasn't going to let anything cloud the elation she felt. "You are a very nice man, Guy." They smiled at one another and kissed. "And," she kissed him again, "the best lay I ever had in my life." He laughed. They kissed again and there was heat between them. Mahelly reached for him and he groaned. He took her small buttocks in his hands and pulled her on top of him. She took him full into her body, greedy for more and more. This time when they galloped toward fulfillment, morning light was shining through the windows and for Mahelly the fear had gone. It had been replaced by joy.

14

IT WAS AN OUTSTANDING IDEA TO GO TO THE BEACH. GUY WAS IN
Westport celebrating his parents' anniversary. Hanna had called and
had said, "Let's go to Fire Island and pretend it's still summer," and
Mahelly had enthusiastically agreed.

"How?" Mahelly had asked.

"We'll take Guy's car. He won't mind."

"When will you be ready?"

"I'm dressed now. You get dressed. If we leave in a half hour we
can catch the 11:15 ferry and get about five hours on the beach before
we have to come back."

"Brilliant," said Mahelly. "I think I have some fruit in the fridge.
I'll bring it. And the cheese."

"Great," said Hanna. "I'll meet you out front."

Hanna wore jeans and a red sweatshirt. Mahelly wore all blue. The
beach blanket Hanna had brought was green and the size of Oklahoma,
but the two women lay together almost touching. A small plane flew
silently overhead. Hanna pointed to it, followed it with her finger. "I
bet we look like a flag from up there," she said.

"Of what country?"

"Not a country flag. I meant semaphore."

"Oh. What letters?"

SOS, Hanna thought. Mayday. "Oh, I don't know. I was just being
creative."

"Albania," said Mahelly.

"Seriously?"

"No."

"Oh."

"Hanna," Mahelly began tentatively. Someone had to bring it all up. The ride in the car had started out fun, but the longer they were together, the harder it was to ignore the gigantic undiscussable "IT." They were lying so closely together, Mahelly could almost hear Hanna blinking, but they weren't talking about anything real. She was afraid if they discussed "IT," it was going to be over, but this was lousy. "Hanna, I don't care how great a sport you are, you aren't happy about this thing." She saw herself step around it; call it a thing. "I know you. You haven't been this quiet in fifteen years."

"I'm all right. I'm fine."

"Sure. Sure, you are."

"You're right, I'm not happy. I'd like to be happy though. I'm trying to be happy. I *want* to be happy."

"I want to be happy too, but I'm feeling guilty now."

"Don't. It's my problem, not yours. I'm feeling left out and possessive and you're so terrific, and so is he, I'm afraid you and Guy are going to fall in love, and besides that I couldn't be happier."

Mahelly laughed. "Hanna, no!" she said. "No way. We're not going to fall in love. He loves *you*."

Hanna turned her head sideways and looked at her friend.

They listened to the waves.

"So how was it?" Hanna asked at last, afraid of asking, more afraid of not.

"It was great," Mahelly said with relief. Thank God they could finally talk. Her eyes were closed against the sun. She smiled. "I feel like a woman again, I really do. I was right. I *knew* Frank was lousy. Or maybe Frank is average and Guy is superb. It's hard to know with my vast experience. Anyway, it was sensational. I came like a slot machine hitting sevens or cherries, or whatever." She turned to look at Hanna, expecting her to laugh with her and saw instead Hanna's face wrinkled up in anguish.

"You *bitch*," Hanna said. "*Are you out of your mind?*"

Mahelly gasped. "But, you asked . . ."

"*God.*" Hanna sat up and covered her face. "*God.* Did you have to draw pictures?"

"Hanna, I'm sor . . ."

"STOP. Leave me alone. Don't talk to me, OK?" Hanna clasped her knees and with closed eyes pressed her face into her arms. Tears flowed. She rocked. This couldn't be happening. Mahelly. Her friend. Her friend had killed her. She was dead. She rocked. She heard Mahelly saying her name, but she shook her head on her arms. No. Leave me alone. Oh, God, oh, God. What had she done? Mahelly hadn't killed her. She had killed herself. She *had* asked. Why? She asked because she had to know. Had to. God. Why couldn't Mahelly have just said it was good. Or OK. Or best yet, she was disappointed. That had been a possibility, hadn't it? Sevens! Sevens, she'd said. Jackpot. She saw golden coins pouring out of a chute between Mahelly's legs. The coins turned into little golden rings, spinning, twisting. She saw Guy scooping them up, laughing. She gritted her teeth and rocked. If Mahelly thought Guy was superb, how did he feel about Mahelly? Jackpot for him? How was she going to make love to him ever again? How was she going to still love Mahelly? This hurt too much. Much too much. She became aware again of Mahelly's voice.

". . . but he loves *you*, Hanna. He loves you a lot and he wanted me to know it. He was very clear he doesn't want me to get any ideas. I swear to God. Hanna, he's not doing this for *me*. He's doing it for *you*. Hanna, please talk to me."

Mahelly was crying and shaking her arm. Hanna was afraid to look at her. What would she see? She turned to her weeping friend. She pulled a napkin out of the basket and blew her nose. She asked, "Mel, if I asked you to stop now, would you?"

"Absolutely. This minute. Say the word."

Hanna felt relief. This pain could all go away. She blew her nose again. There was sand on her eyelids and she brushed it off gingerly. Mel said she would stop. OK. They were still friends. Her eyes hurt from pressing them. She closed them and saw images. Cherry popsicles. Bruce, the ecologist, her first lover. Clumsy. Terrible. Guy. Guy and Mahelly. Superb. "Yeah," Hanna said. "Would you?"

"Yes," Mahelly said, touching Hanna's face.

"Oh, God, Melly, I'm sorry," Hanna said, crying again. "I did ask you. I didn't realize how raw I am. You were right. You are both doing this for *me*. I shouldn't have yelled at you."

"You should too have. I was a supreme jerk once again. I'm so used to telling you everything . . . I should have had a shade more tact. A *ton* more tact. So, let's stop, OK? I wanted to get laid. I got laid. Nothing too serious has happened. Let's stop."

Hanna found a dry spot on the napkin and blew her nose. She handed a fresh napkin to Mahelly who did the same. She looked out at the ocean. "We can't," she said finally.

"Hanna. We can."

"We can't stop, Mel. It's an excellent idea, a 'superb' idea, except for one thing. Here's the new title for my brilliant cover story. 'I Manshared for One Day,' by Hanna Coleman."

Mahelly touched Hanna's arm. "Stein might accept that, you know, Han. He didn't say you had to do it for the rest of your life."

Hanna blew hair out of her face. She rubbed her teeth with the back of her hand. "Right. Sure, he would. I don't even want to imagine what he would say to me. Probably nothing. Probably he'd hold the story in two fingers like a bag of dog poop and drop it in the trash. I might not be that lucky. Knowing him, he'd photocopy it and pass it out for comments at the next editorial meeting."

"Hanna, that isn't a good enough reason. If we're going to break up over this, it isn't a good enough reason."

Hanna lifted a handful of sand. "I'm OK now Mel. We're not going to break up over this. I wanted you to have fun. Just, you know, spare me the graphic details."

Mahelly was quiet. She was glad she'd still have Guy to look forward to, but she could make it without him. "Hanna. Honestly. I'd like to do this for a while, but I don't have to. Aren't we being stupid if we keep doing this?"

"I think the stupid part is over. The thing is, the thing is, the worst is over and as long as we've gone this far, I might as well give the bastard what he wants." Hanna thought and sifted sand. A little pyramid formed between her feet. When it wouldn't get any higher without collapsing onto itself, Hanna gave up and swept it away with her hand. She brushed her hands together. She sniffed. "I wonder what the bastard does want."

"Huh," said Mahelly, shading her eyes.

"He's different since I decided to do this story."

"Different how?"

"Poking around. Telling me to call him David. Asked me out for drinks a couple of times."

"No!" Mahelly propped herself up on one elbow. A flirty breeze blew their fight right down the beach. "You didn't tell me! You *went out* with him?"

"No. Not yet," Hanna said with a conspiratorial smile. "Once he cancelled. Once I couldn't make it. But. I'm having lunch with him on Friday." She grinned a shy, brave smile at Mahelly. Roommates again. Big date on Friday.

"Wow, Hanna, I don't know what to say. And here I thought he was going steady with Brian Atkins."

Hanna laughed.

"David Stein could be the most handsome man in America, perhaps the world," said Mahelly. She poked the sand with a piece of shell. "I wonder what he's like in bed."

"Mel, you *pig*!" Hanna shouted in mock horror. "You want David Stein too. My boyfriend isn't enough for you?"

"My new life ambition," said Mahelly, eyes downcast, "is to become a slut."

They both laughed until helpless. When the laughter subsided, they looked into each others' eyes. They kissed the other's sunburned cheek. Then Hanna found a good station on the radio and they sang together. They ate avocado and tomato slices stuffed in pita bread, pears buttered with Brie, and drank warm red wine in thick blocky glasses. They ran on the beach and napped in the warm air. The sun baked their bodies, and the wind came up from the ocean and cleansed them. Their hair mingled together on the blanket. It was all good.

15

THE ELECTRIC PING OF THE CLOCK ALARM SOUNDED. DAVID STEIN
stabbed the shut-off button and allowed himself to the count of sixty
to open his eyes. And then he did. He always loved this moment. His
bed faced the East River. The windows were arches eleven feet high,
five feet wide, divided into beveled rays at the top, and there were three
of them. David's black-lacquered bed frame was centered with and
facing the middle window. The window on the right was a door opening
out to the terrace. At this moment, 6:15 A.M., the sun was slashing
in, flinging rainbow fragments through the beveled glass, scattering
colored lights on the indigo-blue spread, the pale-blue sheets, and
David's furred arms which were now stretching overhead. He lowered
his arms, one hand finding his morning hard-on, holding it for a
moment before the pressure from his bladder exerted pressure on his
brain. He walked to the black marble bathroom and relieved himself.

David showered quickly. Then, wearing the black terry-cloth robe
Miranda had given him, he returned to the bed, found the remote
control switch and summoned a television picture from the cool black
instrument on the slick black-lacquer storage unit.

"Thank you, Bill," Miranda Wu said into the camera. "At the
Beirut Airport this morning, the U.S. Marines began pulling out . . ."
David felt a tightening in his groin. Looking at Miranda on television
was enough to excite him. Her hair was rolled back at the sides and
back in a nineteen-forties hair style that only Miranda could make

stylish today. She was wearing a pale lilac suit with a white blouse and scalloped collar. She looked so demure. So pure.

Tonight Miranda would do the Seven O'Clock Report, have a light meal, take the limo to the airport, catch the nine o'clock flight from Washington to New York the way she did every Friday night. She'd arrive at his door at 10:00 P.M. She'd walk into the dark marble foyer dropping everything as she walked—coat, bag, keys—and click, click with her pointy heels, she'd walk to the bar and pour a Scotch.

David liked to lie on the black leather chaise by the fireplace, the night-lights of the city the only lights illuminating the room, and watch her. Drink in hand, Miranda would pace, clickety click and she'd talk, staccato. "Damned camera went out three times this week," and "lost my damned place in the middle of the Israel story," and "who does he think he is?" Click, click. And then the outer garments would come off. Jacket first, fling, into a chair, step, click, step, click, the skirt left in a heap. Then the blouse, impatiently untied, unbottoned, discarded on top of the skirt, and then, standing in her satin slip and heels, Miranda would say, "Good-night, David, I'm going to bed." And then the game would begin. The Empress of No, he called her. The Empress of No.

David had been aware of Miranda Wu long before he met her. Hers was a familiar face every morning, every night; hers and Jane Pauley's and Michele Marsh's and Sue Simmons's and all the other pretty professional TV reporters. He had had no feeling of expectation when Gloria called him from her magazine and asked him to attend the fund-raiser luncheon for Southeast Asian refugee children at $75.00 a plate and for him please to take a table of ten representing *Urban Life*. He owed Gloria a favor or two, he was new to New York, and it just made good political sense for him to attend.

The luncheon was to be at the Grand Hyatt Hotel on 42nd Street over Grand Central and a scant block from the office. He took the table, gave nine tickets to senior staff.

David arrived late to the reception before the luncheon. He ordered a glass of wine from the bar, affixed his name sticker to his jacket and as he did so, the lights flickered and a voice announced it was time to move into the meeting room.

"David!" he heard someone call. "David, over here. We have just a minute to say hello." He kissed Gloria, shook hands with the three women standing with her, the third being the beautiful Miranda Wu.

"Miranda, David Stein," Gloria said.

"Oh, David Stein," Miranda spoke with a smile. "You've just taken over as Editor-in-Chief of *Urban Life*."

"Why, yes," he said, surprised and flattered. "I'm surprised you know who I am."

"Not at all. You are a very visible man. Besides, it says on your jacket, 'David Stein, Editor-in-Chief, *Urban Life*.' "

David looked down. "Yes, it does, doesn't it. But you don't have a name tag."

"I will have a big sign in front of my place on the dais," she said with a broad smile.

"You're speaking," David said dumbly. Such a clever remark, he thought to himself. What was coming over him? Starstruck? Him? No, he didn't think so. It was her beauty. Miranda Wu was simply dazzling. Her flowered silk dress clung to her body. Her teeth were small and white and even, her face flawless, her long black hair hanging straight and smooth down her back. She was extraordinary.

"My parents were refugees from China," she explained. "I know about this subject firsthand." The lights flashed again.

"I'd like to hear more," David said. "Are you flying back to Washington tonight?"

"No, I'm taking a holiday tomorrow," she said. "I'm staying here at the hotel tonight."

"Will you have dinner with me?"

"Yes," she said and turning with a smile, walked into the other room and up the steps to the dais.

David hardly worked the rest of the day. He left a message at the front desk. He'd pick her up at 8:00.

Dinner had been easy. The hotel restaurant had been decent, the service almost excellent. Conversing with Miranda had been easy. She knew a great deal about many things. Walking her to her room had been easy. It would have been hard for her to refuse him the privilege of walking her to her room. Taking her to bed had been easy. She invited him in. The bed had been turned back by the chambermaid. Her silk dress fell into a soft heap on the floor. Her lovemaking had been the mirror of his, cool, practiced, successful.

"I'll call you when I come to Washington," David had said sliding on his watch, slipping on his shoes.

"No, don't, but thank you, David."

"No? Why not? Are you living with someone?"

"No."

"Then why not?" he found himself asking, one shoe still in his hand. A second ago, he hadn't seriously planned on calling her. It was done. A complete relationship with a woman he would never see again. He supposed he might have called her if the thought struck him when they were in the same city, maybe, but here she was turning down his polite small talk, his civilized amenity, an imitation invitation to a rematch.

"Once is enough, don't you think, David?"

No, he didn't think so. Not any longer. "Whatever you say, Miranda," he said with ice in his voice. He found his tie and put on his jacket.

"Yes," she said with a smile.

David Stein spent the next two weeks not thinking about Miranda Wu. He didn't think about her every night when he turned on the news. He never had had a favorite news show before, and that hadn't changed. Now he had an unfavorite news show. If her face came on the screen accidentally, he flipped past it quickly. He didn't think about Miranda Wu when he saw an Oriental woman in a movie theater. He didn't think about her when Brian Atkins covered the fund-raising luncheon in "UrbanBeat," not even when the photograph used was a picture of Miranda on that day, her silk dress clinging, her small glasses on her nose, her mouth parted in an appeal to the audience. David remembered kissing that mouth, and then he angrily pushed the thought away.

When David couldn't stand it anymore, he called her office in Washington. When she didn't return his call, he called again the next day. This time she picked up the phone.

"I've been thinking about you," he said.

"Oh," she responded, no inflection in her voice.

"I want to see you again," he said.

"Oh," she said. "Well, I'll call you sometime."

"You'll call me?" he asked incredulously.

"Yes," she said. "I've got to go."

She'd call him! He was infuriated. What was she doing? Brushing him off? Did she mean it? Well if she did mean it, she could ring until the world ended before he would see her. What was he supposed to be? A one-night stud?

When she called the next week, she was in New York. He had a date that evening. He told Jillian to cancel it. Where was Miranda? At the Palace. He'd meet her. They had dinner at the Palm. His steak was medium rare. Hers was cold and purple in the center. She finished hers. After dinner, he walked her out to the curb. Her driver was waiting.

"Good night, David," she said. "Thanks for the lovely dinner."

"I'll call you," he said as her driver opened her door.

"No," she said. "I'll call you." She leaned through the window, kissed him, and left him standing on the curb. He didn't know how he could wait to see her again.

David had her biography pulled from the morgue. He asked friends casually what they knew about her. He asked Gloria, who answered him with, "I guess you'll have to find out for yourself." He found out very little. She lived at the top of the Bismarck, Washington's most exclusive cooperative residence. She had no husband, no steady lover, although she had many men in her life. He knew where she had gone to school, where she lived, and where she was every morning at 6:30 A.M. and 7:00 P.M. every Monday through Friday. He knew she was serious about her career. That was all. No. He knew she wanted things her way. And he knew he wanted her.

He knew he wanted her enough to let her choose the pattern of their affair. For one year now, it had been the same. Every Friday night at 10:00, Miranda came to his apartment in New York and every Sunday afternoon at 4:00 she caught the Washington shuttle. That was the way she wanted it. That was the way it was.

Tonight when Miranda came home, she would drop her bags and keys on the floor. She would drop her clothes. She would say no. And right after she had said no, David would have her, and he would have her any way he wanted her. In bed, there was no Empress of No. In bed, Miranda Wu said yes. To everything.

At the foot of his bed this morning, David watched Miranda smile engagingly at her TV audience. He rejected the notion his new erection was forcing on him. Not now. Soon enough he would have the real thing. He switched off the television. "See you, later, Miranda," he said.

David got dressed. He had an 8:00 breakfast with a reporter from the *Wall Street Journal* and he was meeting with the ad manager from Mercedes-Benz at 10:30. Then he was having lunch with Hanna Coleman. Where to take her? Some place very rich and intimate. He'd mention it to Jillian when he got in.

16

HANNA AWOKE TO THE SCRATCHY FEEL OF WHISKERS ON HER NECK.
Guy had been ignoring her tentative morning advances lately, so even
though she wasn't feeling sexy, Hanna wanted Guy to want her. She
felt almost grateful that he did. She turned to receive his kisses, and
opened herself to his embrace.

Their lovemaking was different now, Hanna thought as she enfolded
Guy in her arms. It was still Hanna-and-Guy-sex, their own special
touch-talk ways, but openness had gone and had been replaced with
something cool and private. Once upon a time, two weeks ago, they
had laughed, teased, watched one another open-eyed as love, passion,
delight, brushed their features. Now the air around them was heavy
with unspoken thoughts, and they weren't laughing in bed anymore.
Hanna tried to find her old, safe feelings. She wanted to abandon
herself to physical sensation and love, but as she wrapped her arms
and legs around her lover, what she thought about was Guy making
love with Mahelly.

Was it better with Mel? Hanna asked herself again. Mahelly was
so girlish and domestic. Was Guy having nice, homey sex with Mel?
Or was there something much more exotic going on? Mel had gotten
so hot since Frank left. Was she a seductress in bed? Was she taking
those wonderful new muscles of hers and doing tricks Hanna couldn't
even imagine? Was Guy loving it, loving her? Was Guy adoring Mahelly's flat stomach and flawless thighs and wishing that she, Hanna,

would drop a couple or ten pounds? Was it possible he wasn't happy sleeping with Mahelly and not willing to tell Hanna about it? Was he hoping all this would be over soon? Or was it already over and she had lost?

Hanna tried to stop thinking, tried just to be with her lover making love. She moved her hands over his buttocks and back and hugged him to her. Still the voice in her head queried on. What was it like for Guy and Mahelly? Hanna was aching to know although she thought the knowledge could kill her. She also knew Guy was fully capable of telling her anything and he was choosing silence. It was awful having silent, secretive sex with the man she loved. She wanted to tell him to stop pounding into her body. She wanted to tell him to stop and hold her and look into her eyes and tell her that he loved her and only her. But she couldn't. She couldn't even allow herself to cry.

Hanna sighed as Guy's plunging ceased and he relaxed his full weight onto her body. What a mess, she thought winding Guy's curly hair around her fingers, kissing his neck. And it's your fault, David Stein, you creep, she thought viciously. She stroked Guy until his breathing slowed and then she pushed him gently off her and got out of bed.

"What's up, honey?" Guy asked, eyelids barely parted. "Something wrong?"

"Big lunch today with Stein," she said telling half the truth.

"Oh?"

"I'm really nervous." She opened the closet door and peered mournfully inside.

"How come?"

"I don't know what that bastard's going to say or do. He just plain scares me, that's all." Hanna disappeared into the closet and moved some hangers around. "What do you think I should wear?"

"Your gray suit."

"At the cleaners. Do you like this?" she asked pulling a bright blue wool dress out of the closet.

"Love it," said Guy.

"Or this?" She showed him the black dress, "with a red belt?"

"Do you want him looking down your front?"

"No."

"Blue dress."

"OK."

Friday was closing day. At 7:45, Hanna was not the first person in. The office was swarming with frantic people. Hanna gulped her coffee, then walked down the hall to Matty's office to look at layouts. Matthew Gerbin was the magazine's executive art director. He was in charge of the magazine's design from front cover to back. He showed her the layouts for her section for November. Hanna located the tiny fraction of her mind still interested in her actual job and that part was pleased with the layouts. She told Matty so, strode back to her office and closed the door.

She opened her top drawer, plopped her journal on her desk, turned to the proper page, and wrote: "Cathartic fight with Mahelly. We'll be even closer as the result of sharing Guy. Relationship with Guy," Hanna put the pen down. She hated to commit to writing that they were feeling distant. What could she say that would be true? "Relationship with Guy temporarily cool," she decided and wrote. Temporarily. The ice age had been temporary. It only lasted twenty billion years and when it was over all the mastodons were dead. Hanna drew a picture of a mastodon in her journal. She stroked in shading, indicated a gleam of light on the end of a tusk, added a mop of hair on the top of its head. It didn't look right, but it had some charm. Poor mastodons. Poor her. How was she going to write about mansharing in *Urban Life* if she couldn't stand to write about it in her own journal? Was Brian Atkins going to turn out to be right? Was mansharing going to turn out to be a sick story?

As a reporter she was obliged to report, not slant. If the idea stank, she would have to abandon it. If she didn't have a story, Stein would simply drop her proposal and that would be it. He would know she had tried. Everything would be OK. OK except for one little thing— for the sake of this story, she had transformed her wonderful, happy, love affair and best friendship into a gigantic pot of goop. Well, dammit, the goop had happened, and she couldn't let it be goop in vain. She wasn't a quitter. Hanna looked at her watch. Oh, boy, 9 o'clock already. Three hours until lunch. She found a sheet of canary yellow typing paper, and hoping the color yellow would improve the tone of her story, Hanna typed "MANSHARE" in the center of the page. She continued typing.

Le Jardin Blanc was a glass arboretum extending behind an ordinary-looking brownstone building on East 65th. Trees banked the glass walls outside. The inside was scented with gardenias trained as trees and growing proudly out of square clay pots. Twelve tables planted their iron feet on the brick floor. The table linen was green. The silver was real.

Across from Hanna at last, sat David Stein. Hanna felt giddy and girly and incredibly young. She had never seen David in daylight before, never had a chance to study his features. How could he be this good-looking and be real? Had he made a pact with the devil? Did mortal women actually take their clothes off for this man? How did they have the courage? She could do nothing but stare and try not to. David's tweed jacket was open. His blue cashmere sweater-vest, dark tie and white shirt provided the perfect foil for his tanned face and blue-black hair. His nose and his mouth were perfect. And those incredible, fascinating eyes. One matched the tablecloth. The other matched the sky. He was smiling.

"I'm very glad you proposed this feature, Hanna," he said offering her the basket of warm bread and rolls. "Your writing is excellent, but you've been so important to us in fashion, I selfishly hoped you'd stay happy there."

Hanna took a pumpernickel-raisin roll, put it down on her bread dish and looked at him. Had he said she was an excellent writer? She thought so. She swallowed some wine and felt her own self return. Thank you, God. She spoke. "I can't write fashion forever, David. It's not enough for me. I've been writing fashion in some form for twelve years. Can you imagine what that must be like?"

"Tell me," he said.

"It's like eating chocolate sauce every day. Chocolate sauce on bananas and cereal, chocolate hollandaise on asparagus, chocolate béchamel on steak." David laughed. Hanna continued. "I love chocolate sauce, but really, every day? Sometimes I have a fantasy that fashion is outlawed and everyone has to wear one-size-fits-all T-shirt-sweater things down to their ankles. These things would come in two colors, black and white, and they'd have big pockets and hoods, and you could sit cross-legged in them and wear them out in the rain, and for a big night on the town, you could put on a diamond necklace and be ready to go."

David threw his head back and laughed. "Do you really fantasize about that or did you just make that up?"

"Made it up," Hanna said looking into his impossibly handsome face. God, she'd never heard him laugh before and she had done it. She clasped herself with her arms and put her elbows on the table.

"But it's a good idea, don't you think? If there were no fashion, I'd either be out of work, or you'd be giving me real writing to do."

"I see," said David. "Well, I'd be giving you real writing to do."

"You would?"

David nodded his head. "I would. You've got a special style, Hanna."

Hanna unfolded her arms and pinched the stem of her water glass. She moved the glass an inch forward, an inch back. The water sloshed and the ice clinked against the sides. She stared across at David and waited anxiously for him to continue.

"Your writing is very, mmm, human, and your pacing is remarkable." David buttered a piece of bread for himself. "Granted, the fashion section is brief, but the two features you wrote earlier in the year, the birth control story, and what was the other one . . . ?"

"Public schools."

"Public schools, were very well done. Honestly, Hanna, it was bad of me not to think of something bigger for you to try."

Hanna couldn't believe what she was hearing. Praise. Honest to God real praise from David Stein. She wouldn't interrupt him for anything in the world. She drained her wineglass and set it down.

"So," he said, "I'm glad you took the initiative and proposed this feature. After it's in, maybe we'll have to think of a way to take you off chocolate sauce." He paused. "So tell me. How is it going?"

God. This was why she was writing the story, Hanna remembered with a wine-softened jolt. She'd almost forgotten. She wasn't writing the story out of some masochistic urge to destroy her personal life. She was writing this story so David Stein would give her recognition and a fulfilling career. And now he was practically taking the thoughts out of her head and making them his own idea. She wanted to hug him. She wanted to say, "whheeee!" She wanted to go back to the office and pound out the first Pulitzer Prize winning article in the history of *Urban Life*. Instead of doing any of those things, she beamed.

David filled her glass. "Hanna?"

"Huh?"

"I asked how it's going. The mansharing story." David watched Hanna move around in her seat. She was very appealing, this Hanna Coleman, when she got a little wine into her. Not so intense as she'd been, or was that fear he had seen when he'd spoken with her in the past? Not that he'd spoken with her much. He had told her the truth. He hadn't been interested in anything about her beyond her fashion section until she proposed that mansharing idea. What an idea! The two most important words in America were "career" and "sex," and not necessarily in that order. They would sell a few magazines if this story of hers could be written correctly and promoted well.

Now that he had a little wine in *him*, he couldn't ignore Hanna's almost too tight blue dress and the flushed pretty face. And she liked to swing that auburn hair around. Was she flirting with him? He wondered. Maybe not. If she was flirting, she would be direct. Hanna was incapable of disguising her feelings, and it seemed to him she was unaware that this was evident. There was something wonderfully naïve about this girl and he liked it. Guilelessness and naïveté were qualities completely lacking in Miranda.

David noticed that Hanna looked agitated. What had he asked her? Oh, about the story. Was she having a problem?

Hanna struggled with what to say. He had asked her about the damned story. She had wanted to be honest with him. Tell him how badly she was feeling, get his help or maybe his permission to cancel the whole idea. She couldn't do that now. He'd told her he was watching this story and thinking about promoting her. If she said she was feeling insecure, that her relationship with Guy had cooled off, what would he say? Forget it, that's what he'd say.

The wine was making her buzzy. Where the heck was the food? Oh, a reprieve. She watched as the waiter set steaming plates in front of them. She looked up and saw David still waiting for her reply. God, he was different outside of the office. He was so real. So nice. He had laughed at her jokes and told her how good she was as a writer. She couldn't let him drop the story. She wouldn't be able to bear losing this David Stein and getting back the David Stein who called her Coleman. She composed her thoughts.

"Um. The story is coming along just fine," she lied, twirling her fork in her hand. "I'm learning a lot about myself and the other two people I'm, um, involved with. With whom I'm involved," she corrected herself. "It's a real growth experience."

"What do you mean?" David asked spearing a snow pea pod and folding it neatly into his mouth.

She looked up and smiled at David. She hoped she looked positive, confident. "I'm still at the exploration stage," she added. "I'm not ready to sum it up for you yet."

Oh-oh, David thought. That crooked smile means trouble. "Tell me more," he said. "I'm not getting a very clear picture."

Hanna broke off a small portion of tilefish and chewed it very, very slowly. It tasted good. Somewhere she read that tilefish ate lobsters. How? What kind of fish munched on whole live lobsters? What did a tilefish look like? Tough probably. With a big mouth. Like hers. She said, "I don't want to talk about it yet. I've probably said too much already. It's still a new arrangement, and . . ."

"And you're still at the exploration stage."

"Yes."

"Oh, come on, Hanna," David said impatiently. "You are going to tell the whole world about it in a few weeks. Surely you can give me a preview. I'd like at least to look at your notes."

Hanna sighed. He was pressing hard and she didn't want to say another word. Here she was in this beautiful restaurant with this attentive, appreciative man who was her boss, and now she was going to have to tell him that half the time she thought the whole idea was a terrible mistake and the other half of the time she knew it was. On the other hand, she could lie. Things could pick up next week.

"I'm not ready to show you anything in writing yet, but I'll tell you this much. It's nice, David. It's really nice. I decided to share my lover with a friend who shall remain nameless. She was in great need of some loving and my man is providing it. He likes her. He loves me. I think I've done something nice for both of them." She lifted her chin in his direction.

"And you don't feel jealous."

"Maybe once, but that's where the growth comes in. Anyway it's important that I push through that. Obviously that's the area where women are going to have to, to, mature!"

"Uh-huh." Stein acknowledged, registering her obvious discomfort. "And what about you? Are you sharing anyone's man?"

"No."

"Any plans to?"

"Not really." Not at all, she thought, but what was that from David? A hint? A suggestion? She looked up out of her lashes. David intercepted her look and gave her a steady smile. Hanna blushed, backed down, and returned to her tilefish.

"How does your arrangement work?" David asked forking some asparagus into his mouth.

"Guy, that's his name, spends Tuesday and Wednesday nights with my friend." Oh, it sounded weird to say Guy's name out loud to David. Almost sacrilegious. "Every other night we spend together just like before."

"What do *you* do Tuesday and Wednesday nights?" David asked, balancing his asparagus-laden fork in his hand.

"Anything I want," Hanna answered, hesitatingly. She was feeling unsettled again. It was one thing to have idle fantasies about a devastating man. It was something else to be at dead center in his sights. She couldn't be mistaken. David was prepping her for a pass. She glanced up at David just before she knocked over her wine. It was just as well. The wine wasn't working any more. She was straight, sober, and nervous as bees.

17

MAHELLY SURVEYED HER SMALL OFFICE. EVERY SPACE-SAVING DEVICE developed by modern Italian designer technology had been employed. The desks were file cabinets supporting white Formica slabs. Locker keys dangled from pegs in the walls and the walls themselves were hung with rubber-coated wire baskets holding metallic jumbles—combination locks, hair dryers and found items. She loved this place, but it was no longer possible to deny the obvious: The gym was too small. The phones were ringing off their little hooks. She had two people working in the ten-foot by ten-foot office. She had hired three instructors and a floater to teach classes, and now complaints were coming in that there were never enough clean towels, not enough floor space during the classes, not enough hot water. I have to get more space, she thought.

Mahelly had seen 3,500 feet of warehouse loft in Soho that she imagined could be turned into a gym. The space wasn't lovable but it was big and in a trendy part of town. The money she would need to buy the loft was staggering and in addition to the purchase price she'd have to do major renovation. Even so, buying this loft and renovating it might be cheap when compared to renting a similar-size space over a period of years. Maybe, if her father would co-sign the loan . . .

Mahelly closed out the sounds and sights of her present office and thought about the big loft. Every surface including the floor had been sloppily painted many times with thick coats of battleship gray. The steel columns rising to the sixteen-foot ceilings at twenty-foot intervals interfered with the overall size of the room, and the ordinary windows with their splintered sashes and broken panes hadn't been opened or closed in twenty years. Then there were the siren sounds of the fire station directly across the street.

Mahelly tapped pearly nails on Formica and mused. What if the whole interior were sandblasted back to brick, steel and wood? Those floors wouldn't be anything special, but if they were sanded down and waxed, not poly-ed, they might look rich. Then she could paint the whole interior in some very warm pastel, a color that would promote a feeling of youth and well-being. Peach. Pale peach would be perfect. She'd even paint the brick wall pale peach, but the columns should be white. And then she could use the back portion of the loft for the locker room and showers. The L-shaped alcove where the front of the loft curved out to the right would be perfect for her office if an entrance could be opened through the outer wall. The windows could be re-framed, the sashes painted white . . . Oh, it was starting to feel dreamy. Could she do it? Could she buy the loft, move her business, set up the new one? She had never done anything this enormous in her whole entire life. If it hadn't been for Guy she would never even have thought about it.

"Mel, there's nothing to it," he'd said. "You've already started one business. This is the same thing again, only bigger."

"But, Guy, buying and renovating. The money. Supervising the construction. Finding new clients. If I blow it, I'm dead."

"Mel, you won't die. And you're not going to blow it. It would be utterly impossible."

Was he right? Knowing he believed in her made her almost believe in herself.

Last night Guy had come downtown with her to see the loft. They had ridden in the taxi holding hands as Guy told her about his day. Then they had taken the creaky old service elevator and Mahelly had coaxed open the stubborn door. She had held her breath as Guy strolled through the loft, which was illuminated only by purple twilight.

"You can breathe now, Mahelly," Guy had said touching her shoulder with his hand. But she only exhaled when she heard him say, "I like it. I can see what you will do to it. To anyone else this would be an ugly, old loft in a printing building, but in your hands Mel, it's going to be special. You are going to make it something else." Then they had walked down empty streets in the cool air until they found a small Cuban restaurant. Dinner had been pepper steak, dark coffee and creamy flan and now, as if a blessing looking for something to do had elected to give itself to Mahelly, there was this.

Mahelly sat in a mound of snow-white bedthings and watched Guy. He was adding, subtracting and giving her the benefit of his MBA. He had opened his briefcase, removed paper and calculator and "worked up the numbers." He had divided the dollars into the square footage, estimated the cost of the renovation, evaluated the worth of the location and told her he thought it looked good to him. Then he looked in the pocket of his briefcase and pulled out a tissue-wrapped packet. "This must be for you," he said, placing the parcel on her lap.

Mahelly looked at the colored paper for a long time and then she looked at Guy.

"Go on. Open it."

She didn't want to. Nothing inside could be as perfect as the evening had been, and now she was staring at one more gift from Guy, this one wrapped in lavender tissue and bound with a white ribbon.

Mahelly untied the bow, and carefully lifted the tape holding the package together. Then she parted paper leaves which at last revealed a perfect pair of ballet slippers, the toes of which were encrusted with baby pearls and frail banners of pink ribbon.

"They look like you, don't they?" Guy said, watching Mahelly who was holding the slippers in both hands and looking down at them. She didn't speak. "If you don't like them, I can take them back."

"Never," she replied through the frog in her throat. "I love them." And then she put her arms around his neck and smeared teary eyes on his undershirt.

"Melly, don't cry."

"I'm not crying," she said. She crawled over his body to reach the tissues on the bedstand and blew her nose. Then she set the briefcase on the floor, put the shoes reverently on the night table, and then Mahelly made love to Guy with all her heart.

Guy. Mindless of the phones and the noises around her, Mahelly put her head on her hands and her elbows on the inky surface of the real estate section. She was spending nearly all of her night and day dreaming, thinking of Guy. She waited the whole week for the night they would spend together. The hours they spent were so simple; supper, some conversation, bed. It was all she wanted to do. She was jealous of the time Guy spent away from her and grateful for the time they had. And she was terrified of the inevitable. Sometime, without her saying it was OK, this would all stop. The article would be written and Guy would go back to Hanna. Wouldn't he? It would be very stupid to think otherwise. He would have to. And then what would she do?

"Mrs. Colucci," a voice called. Pam, her youngest instructor, a girl with a dancer's body and a squeaky voice, broke into her thoughts. "Mrs. Colucci, the hot water's out again." Damn. She'd have to get serious about moving. And soon. What would she have to do about financing? She'd ask Guy. He would know.

Guy balanced his coffee container, the *Times*, his briefcase and overcoat. "Getting out," he said from the back of the elevator. He politely sidled out of the elevator and headed for his office. He was still dizzy from last night. Something very strong was happening between him and that "little blond" he was supposed to be "banging." She had cried last night over the ballet slippers and then she had melted against his body. No one had ever melted against him like that. Ever. My God, he felt appreciated in every way, and yet she asked for so little. A couple of numbers on the little tape, a thirty-five dollar gift, a little conversation and she did flip-flops when she saw him. Melted. This morning when he left her, she looked so bereft, it hurt him. And yet, he knew if he stayed with her tonight too, it would be trouble. He would go home tonight, unplug the phone, get a little distance and cool off. It was the only thing to do.

The phone on his desk was ringing as he got the key out of the door. He set his briefcase on the floor, let his coat fall, let the paper fall, eased the coffee container onto his desk and picked up the phone.

"Spencer," he said. "Be right there, Charlie." He hung up the phone.

Guy thought, you aren't supposed to be surprised by being fired or by being promoted. At least that's what they had taught him in business school, and here he was, surprised out of his socks.

Charlie Jackson, Guy's management supervisor, was moving up to Management Director and Guy was being promoted right along with him.

"Congratulations, fella, on a new stripe," Charlie had said pounding him on the back. "Your new business cards will say 'Senior V.P.' "

Senior Vice President. Holy Cow. Would his Dad be proud! "You'll need to get briefed on your three new brands," Charlie said, "and your new staff. Courtney Rand is your account supervisor on the cocoa brands and the brown sugar. You remember Courtney." Charlie looked at Guy with a conspiratorial smile that Guy did not return. "You'll want to meet with her before you do anything."

Guy remembered Courtney all right. One of the things he remembered about her was how pissed she had been when they broke up a few years ago. Hell, he'd done the only thing he could do. She wanted to get married and he didn't. He'd felt cornered and he'd snarled and she'd snarled back. Today he would have been gentler, more responsive to her feelings, but then? He'd been too green. For the last couple of years, they'd said hello to each other in the halls and borne civil silence in the elevators, but that was about it. Won't she be pleased to learn that I'm her new boss, he thought facetiously as he dialed her extension. Hey, knowing Courtney, she already knew.

"Courtney, can you come up?" he asked without needing to identify himself.

"OK," she said without enthusiasm.

Damn, he thought. I should have gone to her office. Shown a little contrition.

"Congratulations, Guy," Courtney said with scantily clad insincerity. She shook his hand, and arranged her skirt and herself in the chair in front of his desk. A torrent of hair tumbled forward over one eye. She pushed it out of the way with a casual hand. "I brought the files on Mom's Cocoa Mix, Diet Cocoa and Swanee Old Fashioned Brown Sugar." She slapped the files down on the desk as she named them. "Do you want to go over them now, or should I leave them for you to review?" She swung her amber, wavy mane behind her shoulders and folded her hands in her lap. She gave him an even, expressionless stare.

"Courtney . . ."

She waited.

Guy exhaled through his mouth and folded his hands on his desk. "Court, I know you're still mad at me, but I don't want you to be." He paused, knowing no matter what he said, Courtney was going to make him sweat. He hadn't dated her for eighteen months without learning something about her. "I didn't mean to, uh, hurt you . . ."

She rolled her eyes slightly, sighed impatiently, and gave Guy a baleful look.

Guy continued, "I didn't. I missed you like anything. I was crazy about you. You caught me by surprise and I reacted poorly. You probably couldn't tell, but I was trying to be fair to both of us. I wish you'd try to understand that."

Courtney shifted in her chair. She recrossed her legs and spoke with a thrum in her voice. It was a dangerous sound, like that of a fallen electrical line. "Don't insult me by making it sound worse than it was. I'm not having a problem, Guy."

"Bullshit," he said meeting her gaze.

She swallowed and swung her leg nervously in the silence. "All right, it's bullshit. I loved you and you didn't love me as much and it hurt like hell."

"I didn't know that then, Court, and when I figured it out I didn't handle it well. I'm not a mean person. You know that. I should add my feelings were kind of hurt too."

Courtney shrugged.

"It wasn't exactly pleasant, you know. Not only were you gone but I had to think about you and Jackson."

"Tough," she said blinking and swinging her foot into his desk.

Guy thought, I don't think I deserve all this, but even if I do, how in the world am I going to get out from under it? He had forgotten how seriously Courtney took her anger. He dimly remembered her telling him that she hadn't talked to her brother for five years because he'd taken her car for the weekend without asking her permission. And wasn't there some story he'd heard about Court having her secretary fired for flirting with a man Courtney had been dating? Wait, the secretary story was a rumor, and her brother had smashed up the car, totaled it. And it was an Aston Martin. Anyone would have been mad about that. Come on, Court, he silently pleaded. Let me off the hook. "You're right to be mad at me, Courtney, but I did care, really, and I'm a better person now, I swear. Will you please forgive me?"

"Yes," she said.

Was that a yes? Had she smiled?

"I forgive you. We had a pretty good time while it lasted." She smiled the smile of a woman with inside knowledge.

Was that a truce? Could they be friends? Could he take a chance? He looked up shyly. "Better than pretty good, I'd say. That stuff we did in the office without locking the door? I'll never forget it as long as I live."

She grinned. He smiled. There was a moment of peace.

"Thanks, Court," he said. "And now, will you please, please, tell me about the damned stuff I'm supposed to be responsible for. Mulholland is getting off the noon flight and we're supposed to spend the day with him."

"I know, I know," she said grinning. "I'll take you through the brands one at a time. Just you pay attention." She opened a file and scanned the top sheet. "Briefly, Mom's and the Diet Cocoa are holding their share of market and Mulholland is happy with the advertising. It's good old Swanee Old Fashioned Brown that's the problem." She looked up at Guy and moved the opened file in front of him. "See? Here. The curve for the whole category is down and where we had the bulk of the consumer loyalty out West, the instant food generation is ignoring our brand right off the charts."

"So where are we?"

"We have to make a recommendation pretty soon. Come up with a marketing plan and a campaign that can move the product, or recommend abandoning the brand and hope they don't give it to one of our competitors who might do what we can't."

"What's our current position?"

"Fight. We're talking about a budget of five million. That's paying for a few salaries around here. Mine," she said. "And yours." Courtney grinned at him. "Oh, and we've got to get the old ducks in a row pretty soon. You know, we've got the annual account review coming up right there. And you're 'it.' " She reached over Guy's desk, flipped through pages until she found the right date and circled it with a pen. An earthy floral fragrance moved with Courtney as she bent over him. Guy remembered that scent. His brain sent memories of a flowered bedroom, and Courtney bent over pillows as he . . . No. He shook his head. No time for reminiscing. Keep your stupid eyes on the business, you asshole, he chastised himself. "Could be a great opportunity, Court. Show them what we can do."

"I agree, Guy. I don't want Swanee Brown to be a swan song."

Guy smiled. "Then let's do it."

"You have my support all the way, Guy. You can count on me. It's going to be great working with you."

"Shake?" he asked when she finished.

"Shake," she said taking his hand, giving it a pull, then kissing him on the mouth. "I've booked lunch at Lutèce," she said from the doorway, "but Carter's going to be here for the night, so think about where you want to take him for dinner." Then Courtney Rand turned on the shapeliest legs on Madison Avenue, tossed her hair once more, and walked out of Guy's office.

Courtney closed the door to her office, put her legs up on her desk, leaned back in her chair and stretched. Against the wall opposite her desk was a small rose-colored sofa and a pale wooden coffee table. On the table was a heavy crystal vase in which was clustered a fat bunch of old-fashioned roses. The painting above the sofa was a seascape; roiling waves of dark green crashed against steel-gray rocks, sending up a frothy spume that seemed to rest in the air and then fall back into the sea. No matter how often she looked at the objects before her, Courtney found them pleasing. The colors of the fabric and the roses. The never-ending motion of the painted sea. It was like a little play of her own devising. The pieces were familiar characters, almost friends. They looked today as they had looked when Guy used to come here way back when. Back when they made love on the little rose-colored sofa. When they were in love. When she *thought* they were in love.

Well, they weren't in love now. Now they were colleagues. Teammates. And it was wonderful really, how it had all turned out. She could be very useful to Guy. She knew her brands down to each and every granule. If she weren't so young, she'd have gotten the brand group supervisory position herself, but Guy was in line before her, and she was in no hurry. This was truly a sensational opportunity. The clients out in Chicago adored her and if she backed Guy, so would they. Mulholland, *the* man in Sugarland, said she was a real talent in marketing. Said she was one of Hastings and Goode's most important assets. She'd heard him telling Jack Bitner, the president, she was gifted. Gifted!

Courtney wiggled her toes in her fine Italian shoes and regarded the shape of her shoe, her ankle, her calf with the same loving satisfaction. She flexed her fingers above her head and yawned deeply. Carter Mulholland wasn't wrong. She *was* gifted. And she believed in sharing her gifts. She was going to share her marketing gift with Guy. For a while anyway—until he really depended upon her. Then she would pull a string. Do a thing. Do unto others, Courtney thought with a smile. She hadn't forgotten what Guy had done unto her. She couldn't wait to do unto him. And she hoped she could cover him with as much public humiliation as she had endured. Fair was fair.

18

WHAT WAS THIS, JILLIAN CRUSE WONDERED AS SHE GLANCED AT MR. Stein's appointment calendar. Right there on the upcoming Wednesday page, opposite 6:00 P.M., a name and a notation. "Hanna C. Dinner." Hanna Coleman? Was he having dinner with Hanna? First a drink, cancelled. Lunch at Le Jardin. Now dinner? What was he up to?

Jillian threw a coffee container in the garbage can, blew some ashes off the desk, wet her finger and rubbed a spot off the shiny black surface. Whoo, she whistled to herself. Coleman and Stein. Goldfish in a shark tank. She smoothed the wrinkles in the lap of her beige suit skirt, ran a manicured hand through short, nappy hair, stood in the doorway and surveyed the office. She should remind office services to get the windows washed. Otherwise the office was tidy. When he got back from lunch, the office would look as though he hadn't even been in it this morning. He liked things clean, this man.

Mr. Stein liked things clean, he liked things clear, he liked to have things his way. When everything was as he liked, Mr. Stein was a doll. "Hello, gorgeous," he'd say every morning. "These are for you, beautiful," he'd say every now and then, setting down a cone of paper-wrapped flowers on her desk. "Turn around and let me see that dress," he'd command her when she wore something new. That's how he was when things were going fine. When things weren't going fine, you better look out. Hide under the desk and pull the rug up over your face.

Jillian shook her head. From the minute she was introduced to Mr. Stein, she thought she was sure glad he didn't turn her on. This man was trou-ble. She liked Hanna. She hoped she didn't get chewed up like what was her name? The woman who used to be Features Editor. Doreen. She hoped Hanna was smart enough to take care of herself. Somehow she didn't think she would be. Too soft. Not like the dragon lady. Now, those two were made for each other.

Jillian placed the appointment calendar flush against the marble-based penholder and squared the phone with the edge of the desk. She put two memos and a file near the phone in order of his need for them that afternoon, took a short stack of paper out of his out-box, and added an appointment to his calendar. She looked again at the notation for Wednesday. Hanna. Whoo. Good luck, baby, she thought.

She took one last look around the office and then closed the door behind her.

19

IT WAS ON THE CORNER OF RUSKIN AND WALSH IN A SECONDHAND car lot in a thirdhand neighborhood. A misty rain was falling and bouncing off the car in the hazy light. A halo seemed to outline the ancient metal, but it was no angel. It was a 1957 Mercury Turnpike Cruiser, streamlined, three shades of green and bedecked with enough chrome to plate a submarine.

Frank pulled his own sporty red Datsun up to the curb and got out. He walked into the lot and over to the car. Was it an illusion? No. There they were. Distinctive. Unique. The TC signature vent pods punctuating the windshield peak on both sides, pierced at dead center with fake aerial-spears. They made Frank think of Martian eyebrows. It was the '57 Merc TC all right.

Frank couldn't breathe. This was entirely too unbelievable. He opened the door and sat in the driver's seat. He closed the door with a thunk. That sound. Cast iron. His hands fit naturally on the steering wheel. It was high and flat across the top; the capital letter "D" lying on its belly. He peered out the windshield. The wraparound glass was distorted at the corners but the width and height of that transparent expanse created a sensation of indescribable roominess. Sitting in the TC, Frank felt he was sitting in a chapel. His eyes stung as he recognized the familiar perforated vinyl ceiling, the rubber bezeled instrument panel, the power seat memory dial. He leaned forward and looked at the dial. The last driver had set the dial at 3-A. Frank twisted the knurled knob and reset the hands to 4-E. His setting. He hadn't forgotten. He sighed with satisfaction. This car had been made for him.

Frank turned the steering wheel experimentally. He tenderly touched the gear buttons on the panel box to the left of the steering wheel. "Merc-o-matic," he said out loud, pressing the buttons in sequence; N/S, L, D, R, N/S again. He opened the glove compartment, half expecting to see his registration and maybe some top 40 charts from 1968 to 1972 when he was driving his own TC. Of course the glove compartment was clean. Of course it couldn't have been his car. His upholstery had been gray. This car was upholstered in black.

As Frank sat in the car the raindrops flattened up and fell in heavy splats against the windshield. He was glad the power windows were in the up position. He moved aside a double-jointed sunvisor and adjusted the vents which were the inside face of the outside pods. Look, there was the leak. Here came the rain. Even with the baffles and the louvers to shut off the air passage, the guys who engineered this car hadn't been able to figure out how to keep out the rain. Frank smiled as the rain outside the car became a downpour.

This couldn't be more perfect, he thought, sitting in the old car with a privacy curtain of rain all around. How he had loved his Merc TC. He loved parking it every morning in his special parking space at WKIX, his name painted on the concrete wall in bright blue with a star before Frank and another after Colucci. He loved driving around Cobleskill, acknowledging the waves and KIX-tattoo horn beeps from other drivers who recognized him at traffic lights. He remembered sitting in the car at night with Mahelly, his little princess nestled under his arm, the aroma of pizza filling the vaulted interior of the car. Damn. He'd felt invincible then. Loved, powerful, completely in the right place. He'd forgotten he'd had all those feelings.

Geez, he wondered what Mahelly was up to. He missed her. He missed her little birdlike ways. He missed talcum powder all over the bathroom floor. He missed the freshly ground coffee beans and the crisp sheets. He missed standing above her and looking down into her small face surrounded by cloudy yellow fuzz. He missed being able to pick her up as easy as pie and carry her into the bedroom . . . All that history didn't disappear because someone said separation. All those feelings. They could find a way to get back together. They would.

There was a rap on the window of the passenger's side of the car. Reality. The broad face of a young salesman, who looked to Frank as if he'd been a junior college fullback not too long ago, was visible through the condensation on the glass. The salesman opened the door, and peered into the interior.

"Hello, sir, I'm Ed Beaton, Jr., and you are . . . ?" The huge young man shook water off his closely shaven head and climbed into the car.

"Hi. I'm Frank Colucci."

"Frank Colucci, the disc jockey?"

Frank smiled modestly and nodded.

"Nice to meet you, Mr. Colucci. I listen to your show sometimes," he said, and shook Frank's hand. "You're real good," he said earnestly. "Real good."

"Thank you. I have a good time."

The salesman nodded thoughtfully, absorbing Frank's remark. "Real good," he said again. He looked at Frank. "You like this car, Mr. Colucci?"

Frank shrugged slightly and smiled.

"I don't blame you," said the young man. "I love this car myself. It's flamboyant, wouldn't you say that was the word? Flamboyant. A happy car. Where do you see a car like this any more?" He gave the padded dashboard a hearty thwap for emphasis.

"Nowhere. Which is where you find the parts for this 'happy car.' Nowhere," Frank added, to make his point.

"Parts? It's an American car, sir." Ed Beaton looked insulted as if Frank had uttered an anti-American slur. "The parts don't wear out and you can always get engine parts all right, anyhow. Besides, this car is as good as new."

"You notice this?" Frank asked using his handkerchief to dab at the trickle of water dribbling down his side of the windshield.

"All the TC's did that, Mr. Colucci. That's the way they made 'em. A little eccentricity, that's all."

Frank nodded. He hadn't expected this kid to know that. The kid hadn't even been born in 1957. "Got the keys with you?"

"You bet," said Ed.

Frank pushed the neutral/start button and turned the key in the ignition. The car seat moved down and back. No kidding! It still worked. The seat memory was usually the first part to go. Wonderful. Frank gave the horn a little push. Instead of a deep hoot, the car emitted a creaky beep. Good. Frank turned to the young man.

"This car wasn't as good as new when it was new, but let's give it a little spin, if you don't mind." The young man smiled knowingly. He knew this game. He leaned back in the seat and folded his arms.

The car lumbered out of the parking lot. She wasn't facile, but she sure was comfy, Frank thought, rounding the corner, taking the car from low into drive. Compared to his Datsun, the Mercury felt like a truck. No, like a truck on balloon tires. It was the feeling Frank remembered. It was a safe feeling. Sitting high on the broad bench seat, tires skimming the asphalt of Walsh Street, the rear springs floating on those amazing air-cushioned shackle eyes. There was that feeling again. Nothing could touch him in this car. It was magic. He was glad the boy had the sense to be quiet in the car Frank already felt he owned.

"I'm a sentimental guy," he said to the young salesman when the Mercury was once again berthed in its space. "And you're right. I like this old beast. What do you want for her?"

"Well, sir, I'm going to have to ask my dad what he wants for this automobile. This is an American classic. My dad's not in today, so maybe you'd like to see something else or come back toward the end of the week . . ." The young man took the keys out of the ignition, fumbled for the door handle.

"No," said Frank. Stop, he thought. "This is the car I want." He wiped the condensation from the window on his side with the edge of his hand. "See the Datsun at the curb?"

"Yeah. So?"

"How about an even trade?"

The young man thought. The old Merc was worth five to seven thousand, somewhere in there, if he could get it. That car, classic or not, had left impressions in the asphalt, it had been on the lot so long. People liked to look at old cars. Old cars brought 'em into the lot as a matter of fact, but they didn't buy 'em too fast. Heck, his mother had suggested planting petunias in the trunk. Seemed to him the Datsun's book value was maybe a couple a thou more than the Merc's and he could get rid of it quick. Maybe he'd keep the Datsun himself. No matter how he looked at it, this was a good deal. Too bad his dad hadn't lived long enough to see how good he was at the used car business. He would have been real happy.

The young man pulled a melancholy face and rubbed his chin a few times as he pretended to consider a poor offer. "OK, sir, if your car is in satisfactory condition, you got a deal," he said, offering his hand to Frank for the formal shake. "I'll go make out the papers while you sit right here and stay dry. What a honey," he said looking around the car as if it were a condominium apartment. "Mr. Colucci, you got the best of me on a bad day." Frank took the steering wheel into his hands and silently exulted. It was his. He had his car back.

Frank toweled his hair, made himself some hot chocolate and removed the band from his packet of road maps. Hell, if you're going to have a Turnpike Cruiser, better get on a turnpike, right? He stretched out on his big blue couch, mug in one hand, map in the other, and planned. It wasn't such a bad drive. It would be a stick straight cruise across the country and would take about three days. He'd pick up I-80 about seventy miles south of S.C. and take it to South Bend, Indiana, where he'd spend the night. It would take him the whole next day to get to Youngstown, Ohio. That would be a drag, but the next day would be worse. Pennsylvania would take forever. On the other hand, he would barely feel New Jersey at all. A couple of minutes in Jersey, then over the GW bridge onto New York City's West Side Highway, get off at 96th Street and home. He looked at the mileage chart and totaled up the numbers. Wow, 1,300 miles, but so what? He hadn't seen his wife in months. She couldn't say so, out of pride, but she had to miss him as much as he missed her. Fifteen years of marriage didn't just disappear overnight.

Now that he knew he was going, he was impatient to leave. The sooner he could go, the happier he'd be. He'd take the car into the shop for a checkup and if everything went well, and he could get someone to take his shift at the station, maybe he could leave this weekend. Monday at the latest.

He traced the route with his finger. It would be great to get out on the road and just drive. He'd take a portable tape player for the stretches where the radio in the old Merc wouldn't be able to grab the airwaves. A field trip. What a terrific idea this was.

In his mind, he could see parking the car on Central Park West where Mahelly would be able to see it by looking out the window. Maybe she'd feel like taking a trip up to Cobleskill to see the school and the radio station. Frank smiled to himself as he folded up the map. What a great surprise this would be! Mary Helen would just flip when she saw the old car.

20

HANNA SCRUNCHED AROUND IN HER CHAIR. THE CROTCH OF HER BLACK wool pants was too short and made her feel as if she were straddling a rope. She was wearing these killer pants because she knew she looked taller and skinnier in black, especially when the tapered pants were topped with her silk and angora sweater with the big pads in the shoulders. She wore the six twists of jet beads because she was having dinner with David Stein tonight and they'd probably leave from the office. No telling where they'd be eating, and black would go anywhere. She could always take off the beads to play the outfit down if he took her to McDonald's.

She looked at her black shoes. The heels had run down on the outside edges to the white plastic under the rubber. Why was it she forgot about her shoes the second she took them off? Other people seemed to think about their shoes more than she did. Men didn't really notice things like heels, did they? Anyway, what if David did? This wasn't a date. This was a dinner. A business dinner. And the one thing she was going to have for David by the end of the day, run-down heels, strangled crotch, and all, was a nice neat outline of her story to keep him happy while she found a way to write the damned article.

But first, she wanted to talk with Guy. He'd been with Mel all night and she wanted to talk with him. She was allowed. He was her lover. He loved her. Hanna pressed the receiver of the phone into her ear. She poked the numbers with the rubber end of her pencil and with her other hand turned to the day's page in her journal. The phone rang at Hastings and Goode. Hanna asked for Guy and as she waited for the connection, she wrote his name on the page.

"All the lines are busy," the agency operator said. "Do you wish to hold."

"Sure," said Hanna. She added a three-dimensional outline to the letters of Guy's name and then ringed it with a fluffy cloud.

"The lines are still busy," the operator said.

"I'll hold," said Hanna. She took a yellow marker pen from the Dania Jai-Alai "World's Fastest Sport" mug and began doodling lightning bolts lancing the cloud.

"Still busy."

"Forget it," Hanna said, dropping the receiver onto the cradle from a height of eight inches. Hanna watched it crash, rock, and settle. Then looked at the page now embellished with electricity and Guy's name ominously framed in thunderclouds. It looked ugly. Hanna ripped out the page, tore it in half, then quarters, then eighths. She dropped it in the ashtray, rummaged around in her desk drawer until she found a book of matches, and then set a small blaze in the glass hemisphere. When the flame was out, Hanna rolled paper into her typewriter and looked at it. "Outline, outline, outline," she said to the typewriter, as if it could proceed without her. OK. Three sections. One, 'He.' Two, 'She.' Three, 'Me.' Hey, that was good. Four, 'We Three.' She typed, leaving large white spaces a quarter of the page deep between headings. She stopped. She considered.

This relationship between the three of them was actually working, right? It wasn't fun, but still it was working. Hanna mentally listed the evidence. She and Mahelly had renewed their friendship that weekend at the beach. Mahelly was happy with Guy. Guy was . . . what? Between Guy's weekend in Westport, his trips to Chicago, and his nights with Mahelly she was seeing him practically never. Once for dinner in the last week to be exact. After dinner on that one unexceptional night, he was so tired they had uttered a dozen half sentences each, then Guy had fallen asleep without kissing her good-night. And they hadn't made love.

Hanna hugged herself. God. She and Guy used to make love almost every single night. And, not to be denied, she used to talk with Mahelly every single day. Now neither of these things happened. No wonder she was feeling alone and frightened. Was Mel avoiding her? Was she avoiding Mel? Probably. Guy was too tired to talk, too tired to have sex. Whose fault was that? Her. Own. Hanna banged a row of exes across the white page, hit the return key, and banged the x key again. Holding down the x key was more efficient. She held the key down, watched the printing ball clack across the page, and hit the return key. She repeated those movements until the whole page was full of exes. Then she took the uniformly printed page out of the typewriter and stood it neatly in the trash can.

She slid a crisp new sheet of paper carefully behind the platen, making sure it would roll into the typewriter perfectly. She turned the platen knob back and forth, back and forth, making sure the top edge of the paper came exactly in line with the ruled bar that held the paper with its rubber rollers. Then Hanna flipped the paper release lever, open, closed, and when she was absolutely sure there was no other mechanical procrastinating trick she could exercise, she wrote a lead paragraph and retyped the outline. Below each heading she typed the motivation of each individual, questions to be asked, possible conclusions. None of the conclusions sounded as good as never having embarked upon mansharing to begin with. That wouldn't do. She slashed out the conclusions with a satisfying barrage of hyphens and rethought how she should end the story. She was still thinking when the sound of her name startled her. She looked up from her typewriter. How had it gotten so late? David Stein was standing in her doorway. Her heart paused in midbeat.

"Is that my outline?" asked Adonis, the man.

"Yes. I mean no," Hanna sputtered. She rolled the paper deep into the typewriter and covered the top of the machine with her arms and bosom. "I mean, yes it is, but I'm not ready to give it to you yet."

"I thought, Hanna, we were having dinner to discuss that outline." David pointed to the now invisible page.

"I want to give it to you David, I really do, but things are just about crystallizing, only they haven't yet." He didn't say anything. She went on. "David, this isn't like covering a fire, or an auto show or something. This is a process, not an event. I can't draw a conclusion to it yet."

"All right, Hanna," he said, jingling coins in both pockets. "But you don't have much time. If you don't give it to me by next week, midweek at the latest, I'm going to scratch the story."

"OK." Hanna said weakly. That was incentive. The bright side was, if she did the damned piece, she could go back to a normal life.

"Are you hungry?"

Hanna shrugged.

"You can go comb your hair if you like, and meet me in the lobby in ten minutes. I'll take you someplace where they serve red meat. You look as if you could use some protein."

Hanna nodded. She felt tears gathering in the corners of her eyes. They stayed there. David left.

"You're not eating," David said.

"I can't," she said. They were seated opposite one another in a booth. The leather banquettes were slippery and seemed unfriendly. The hanging light suspended between them moved slightly in the breeze created by the restaurant's frequently opening front door. The shifting shadows seemed sinister to Hanna. She sighed. She actually knew her dark mood wasn't caused by the swinging light or the slippery banquette. The cause of her mood was sitting across from her happily enjoying buttered new potatoes. Hanna pulled at her pants surreptitiously. The pants were tight, but she could wear them. Last month she couldn't pull up the zipper. She was losing weight. One of the many benefits of mansharing. Make a note, she thought to herself. She arranged her fork and knife neatly on the far edge of her plate.

"You don't like the prime rib?"

"The food's great. I can't eat and worry about the story at the same time."

"Oh." He gave her a lopsided grin. "What's the real reason?"

"Pants are tight."

"That's better," he said laughing. "Have some of the spinach. It's light."

Hanna pulled the plate over and wound some of the vegetable onto her fork.

"Did you see the story in today's *Journal*?" he asked.

"Uh-huh," Hanna said, chewing.

"That reporter ought to go back to Boise or wherever he's from. L.A. probably. Did you see how he described us? 'On the way up.' Didn't he look at the financial statement?" David's face closed up. "We're doing a full twenty-seven percent better in newsstand sales than we were doing only two years ago. I don't know of another publication past or present that can say that."

"It was a sloppy story, David, but it was still a good report. He said very good things about you."

"'At the helm, young David Stein.' Young? Made me sound like a kid."

"I think it was a compliment. You are young." Hanna was surprised. David was opening up to her. Wow! Was it possible, when you spent time with him, that David Stein would turn out to be human? And sensitive! He was hurt by that article. What do you know? He was a person. There was a chink in that gorgeous armor. Hanna looked at David's wrinkled brow and imagined smoothing it with her hand. What would it feel like to soothe him? She imagined pressing her cheek to his and holding it there so she could feel the temperature of his skin and smell his hair. She held his gaze for a moment and he held hers.

"Did you know I can read minds, Hanna?"

"No." He could not.

"Well, I can."

"Then you know I was thinking about cleaning out my closets," she said, saying the first full sentence that came into her pushed-off-balance mind.

"Exactly."

They laughed and Hanna blushed. The moment lengthened. Hanna felt her smile stiffen, then fade. She fingered her wineglass. Took a sip.

David said, "I can't help but wonder how your relationship with Guy is faring."

Hanna's stomach dropped. No fair. Just when she was relaxing, getting to like him. She blinked. "I thought you said you can read minds."

"I can. Would it be a wild guess if I said the friend you are sharing Guy with is Mahelly Colucci?"

"Not too wild."

"Would I be wrong if I guessed you are having problems?"

Hanna shook her head "no" and looked at the mess of stewed spinach. Had she really been eating that disgusting stuff?

"Do you want to tell me about it?"

Tell him about it? Tell him Guy was never home anymore and they were making love about once a week. Down a full four-hundred and twenty-seven percent. No. "Not now, David."

He looked at her sad expression, reached over and touched her cheek. Then he changed the subject. Soon Hanna felt at ease again. They talked about politics, gossiped about competitive magazines. It was good time spent with him. For the first time Hanna felt that she and David were colleagues and equals.

Driving to her apartment changed everything. Just being in David's car moved her off center. Where was she? What was she doing? It was only 10:30. It would have been rude not to invite him to her apartment for a drink, so she had and he had accepted. Hanna greeted the doorman and entered the elevator, thinking as many thoughts as she could have at one time. (Did she still have that bottle of Rémy someone had given her for Christmas? Did she have peanuts? No, not peanuts with Rémy. Is there any soap in the bathroom? Did I close the hamper? If he turns the light on in the kitchen, will the roaches do a cha-cha on the counter? What does he think we're going to do?)

The Rémy still had a red bow on it but the glasses had water spots. She rinsed the glasses, handed one to David and finally, at his request, stopped moving around.

David was sitting on Hanna's maroon velvet settee swishing Rémy Martin around in his wineglass. Hanna sat in her Art Deco armchair and saw her apartment through new eyes. Her new eyes hated it. Each piece of furniture had been a found object, selected for its individual character, bargained for or landed at auction. The eccentricity of the pieces dictated the eclectic nature of the whole. Before David Stein walked in the door her living room had seemed, to her, warm and friendly, as if it were peopled by a collection of slightly wacky grandparents having a few cups of rum punch with their fruit and nut cake. Now the eclectic effect seemed cheap, confused, and the Victorian versus Art Deco conflict, downright antagonistic.

It had occurred to her this morning that she might want to invite David up to her apartment after dinner, but cleaning things down to the shine seemed a commitment to having him there. The idea of his powerful physical presence in a place with a bed brought up too many fantasies—wanting him, letting him know, not letting him know, fighting him off, not fighting him off . . . What would happen if she said no to David Stein? What if she said yes? Would she have to tell Guy? No, it was too much. Too much to consider. So as protection, almost insurance against a contrary inclination, she'd barely made the bed, had run a damp sponge over the counters and sinks, and let cleaning the apartment go at that. Now David was sitting in her living room and Hanna was mentally running a hand over all the dust-collecting surfaces and checking the trash containers for empty tampon tubes.

Alone together in her apartment, her feelings of equality had fled.

David was real. He was her boss. He was attracted to her. Her nervousness was making her jumpy.

Finally David had said, "Do sit down, Hanna. I don't need anything else to eat or drink," and she had made an easy decision. Not the couch. The chair. So she sat on her familiar gray chair that didn't seem familiar any more, and thought: Did I shave my legs? Should I make coffee? Should I turn on another light? Should I talk about Guy? What should I do if he makes a move? Say, "David, it wouldn't be good for our working relationship." Say, "not tonight, I'm having my period." Say nothing. Kiss that face. God. To run fingers through that hair. Would he have hair on his chest or would it be smooth? Is he bored? Does he still like me? What can I talk with him about? None of her thoughts led anywhere.

Hanna watched David as he smoked a cigarette, tapping ashes into a clamshell she had picked up at the beach and declared an ashtray. He had loosened his tie, spread both his arms over the back of the velvet couch that was losing its nap, and crossed his leg at the calf. (He wore sock garters, she noticed. How interesting.) The couch was his now. The time was 10:45, David had taken possession of her couch, and everything she thought to say sounded so stupid inside her head, she knew if she said anything, she would get hives all week remembering. In a minute, she was going to have to show him her baby pictures. She didn't know what else to do. She had a sense she was holding a balloon all soaped up on the outside and filled with nitroglycerine on the inside. If she dropped it, it would explode.

The problem was, it was entirely too quiet, Hanna decided at last. Music would help. Her shoe box full of tapes was truly the bird's-nest mess Guy had told her it was, but looking for exactly the right music was beyond her present capabilities anyway. What would be the right music? She popped a peppy selection of 1950s classics into her stereo and offered David some more Rémy. She prayed with all her might that he would decline the offer and take his problematic self out of her apartment. Her prayers worked.

Setting his glass down on the mosaic coffee table made from shards of antique ceramic dinner plates, David said, "Well, I've got to be going." Hanna sprang to her feet. "Yes, it's a work night, isn't it?" She hustled his coat out of her closet and handed it to him. She walked him to the door, opened it, and pressed herself to the wall.

"Good-night, Hanna," David said, and Hanna, without looking him in the face, replied, "Good-night, David. I had a lovely . . ."

but before she could finish, she felt David's finger under her chin, lifting it and her eyes to his gaze. When he had her attention, he bent his head and kissed her softly on the mouth. It was a very soft kiss and brief, not what Hanna had imagined at all. When David looked at her after the kiss, he saw something that made him kiss her again. And this kiss was a longer kiss, a hungrier kiss; when they broke apart, Hanna knew the skin on her chin would be raw from David's beard. She put her hand to her chin and covered her mouth. She didn't say a word.

"I'll see you tomorrow," he said.

"Good-night," she said faintly. And she closed the door. She stood, her back up against the door for a long time tenderly touching her face, running and rerunning the kisses through her head. Weak, she went to her bedroom, and taking off her shoes, got under the covers. I think I'm in shock, she thought to herself.

Dizzily, Hanna rolled over and reached for the phone. She dialed four of the seven numbers before she remembered. I can't call Mahelly tonight. It's Wednesday. She took off the rest of her clothes, and without washing her face or brushing her teeth, Hanna went to sleep.

What she didn't know and wouldn't know until the next day was she could have called Mahelly because Mahelly was home. Alone.

Mahelly was wearing her plain old gray sweats. She was sitting in a chair pushed right up to the front window so she could look out and she had tucked her knees under her chin so she could look at her ballet slippers. She had been waiting for Hanna to come home so she could talk with her. She'd waited and waited and then she'd seen the navy blue Bentley pull up to the curb, make a U-turn, and park across the street. Then she'd seen David and Hanna walk across the street into the building.

Good for Hanna, Mahelly thought, and then she'd gotten a soft mohair blanket, pulled it over her legs, curled back into her chair and just watched the city lights and the stars over the treetops.

Guy had left at around 7:30 that morning. Holding him and being held by him all night had made her feel so secure and so at peace that his leaving in the morning, leaving and telling her he'd see her next week, caused a ripping in her that seemed almost audible. He was going to be out late, he said. Client coming in from out of town, he said. He didn't want her to wait up for him, he said. She would have been happy to stay up all night, all week, for a hug, a kiss, another night of sleeping in his arms. But she couldn't say so. Couldn't beg.

Mahelly tried to remember last month when there was no Guy as a lover. She remembered she had felt so lonely and cold. Maybe she could have borne the loneliness. At least last month she hadn't been aching so. Hell, this wasn't Guy's fault. He was doing her a favor. He was giving her so much, she should just be grateful for the bits that she had. Still, she ached from missing him. If she couldn't be with Guy, she wanted to be with Hanna. She wanted to wrap herself in the blanket and run downstairs to Hanna's apartment, crawl into bed with her and just feel the presence of her old friend. But her old friend probably had all the company in bed she wanted tonight.

This wasn't meant to be my night, Mahelly thought, hugging her knees and rocking. Last night had been her night. She allowed herself a moment of pleasure. She traced baby pearls with a fingertip. She remembered tracing Guy's backbone with the same fingertip as he slept in her arms. She put her cheek on her knees and closed her eyes.

She wondered what Hanna and David were doing right now. She could almost see them kissing, deeply, passionately. It was easy to imagine David and Hanna making love. Having imagined that, she felt a sharp visceral jolt. Oooh. What beautiful, sexy love they'd make. A new thought. It would just be wonderful if Hanna and David got involved. Wonderful for Hanna and wonderful for her. She wouldn't have to feel guilty about Guy, and maybe she could have him for a little longer. Maybe forever? No. Stop. She bit her lower lip hard. You are asking for it, Mary Helen. You are asking for punishment. You are being avaricious and gluttonous and covetous. Not to mention adulterous. Four sins at once. She hadn't thought about God in a long time, but maybe one little prayer would be heard. She wouldn't pray for herself. She'd pray for a happy ending for the three of them.

Guy and Courtney stood outside the restaurant on a desolate street in Tribeca. Guy closed the top button of his raincoat, wishing he'd put the liner in this morning. Fall was such an unpredictable season. Warm last weekend. Supposed to be in the low forties tonight he'd heard, but it felt colder than that. They'd given Carter the first cab instead of sharing it with him. Of course, neither of them had realized it would be so cold or that they'd be standing and waiting for so long.

It was late now. Well after midnight. The smallest taxi Guy had ever seen buzzed up to the curb where he and Courtney stood. It was a cartoon taxi, more a yellow-jacket wasp than a vehicle. It was a gypsy cab, in Manhattan illegally, but what was their choice? Waiting for another taxi would be trusting luck too far. He looked at Court. She shrugged. And before the decision had been made, the driver had dismounted from his seat and opened the passenger door for Courtney with a flourish.

The heater in the minicab was out of order and Guy pulled the collar of his raincoat closer around his neck. Court leaned her head against her side of the taxi and in seconds was sleeping. Guy closed his eyes too. He leaned his head against the back of the seat and let his thoughts find their own path.

They took him to the crumpled bed in Mahelly's bedroom this morning. He could see it vividly. The morning light on the blue sheets, the pale blond hair against the pillow, Mahelly's breasts clothed in a sheer white camisole, her blue eyes fixed on his, and her hand grasping his thigh. He grimaced in the dark. The need she'd felt before was now focused on him. Those slippers. He'd seen the slippers in the window of a lingerie shop and thirty-five dollars seemed very little for such a charming gift. He knew she would like them, but he'd forgotten how much meaning women attached to gifts. He realized what they meant to Mahelly when he saw the slippers leaning up against the table lamp this morning like religious relics. Damn. He was making things worse for her by caring. That look on her face, that silent pleading for him to stay, was trouble. Trouble for her and trouble for him too. It hurt him to leave her this morning. He couldn't tell her. It would mean too much.

Guy sighed. Melly. She was sweet and tender, and she pampered him. The patting and fluffing and housewifey things she did were both new and familiar to him. New, because he hadn't been patted and fluffed in a very long time. Familiar, because Joanne, way back at the beginning, had made his toast and hung up his clothes, and felt his forehead for fever if he complained of a headache. There was a certain kind of man-of-the-house feeling that came over him when he was with Mel. She calmed him, soothed him, made him feel somehow broader across the chest. It was a good feeling and so different from the feeling he had with Hanna.

What he got from Hanna was a new way of looking at the world. Hanna was upside-down cake. Her thought processes were so different from his, so different from anyone's, being with her was a constant adventure. She was nutty and unpredictable and utterly lovable. How could you not love a girl who ate popcorn with milk for breakfast, named her clothes (her fox boa was Fred and she had a summer dress named Sally), and glued your picture to the bottom of her underwear drawer? Guy grinned in the dark. He thought about Mahelly. The grin faded. Hanna. How could he excuse her for lending him to Mahelly as she might lend a dress or something? That wasn't fair. She hadn't planned it. Still, she'd done a dumb thing, a bad thing, and a penalty was going to be exacted from all of them. Hanna was already suffering. He could tell. Mahelly was going to get hurt when he went back to Hanna . . . he was going back to her, wasn't he? Well, wasn't he? He didn't know any more. He loved Hanna but. But what about all these new, tender feelings for Mahelly? What did they all mean? If he could feel something suspiciously like love for Mahelly, could he really love Hanna? He didn't used to be confused about his feelings for Hanna. The confusion was *his* penalty. The confusion and the responsibility. Jesus. Bo. How would Bo handle all this?

Guy clenched his jaw and shifted slightly in his seat. He opened his eyes. They were still downtown. Still only in Soho. A streetlight briefly illuminated his wristwatch. He could barely make out the time. It was later than he thought. Almost one. Damn. What a long day. He'd been up at seven, in Jackson's office by nine, with Mulholland and two brand managers by half-past twelve. He'd spent the whole day since lunch reviewing the Cocoa Division sales reports. In the afternoon, he'd watched the reel of competitive commercials, and spent the evening with Courtney and Carter discussing what he'd learned.

He sighed. Tired as he was, he appreciated how well the day had gone. First day in his new job, and Mulholland had flown in to see him. Ironic. He'd told Mel he was going to be out late with a client, but he hadn't known why Mulholland was coming in. It was a good sign. And Courtney. What a treasure. She had grown so much since they had worked together two years ago. They sure thought a lot of her out there in Chicago and he could see why. She was incredibly bright, incredibly motivated, and determined to succeed with her brands. He couldn't have been luckier than to have her working for him.

Courtney braced her knees against the rear of the cab's front seat so she wouldn't roll as the tiny vehicle took corners far too fast. She had posed herself, hand upturned in her lap, jacket slightly open, lips parted in pretend slumber. She sensed Guy was gazing at her with affection, and she wanted to look vulnerable in a very sexy way.

She knew Guy felt close to her earlier today. The meetings had been politically complicated and intense. She had darted from point to point, guiding him, backing off when he was on firm ground, unobtrusively laying down planks across gaps in his knowledge. It had been a full dress rehearsal for her new role: the able aide, the supportive Courtney, a role she knew would win Guy's complete faith and trust. What a convincing job she'd done of being the woman-behind-the-man! Her acting had been a triumphant success, but she had a little more work to do before the night was over. Could she manage it? She bet herself a million dollars she could. Had he just sighed? She didn't dare open her eyes yet. He might see something she didn't want him to see.

Guy watched Courtney sleeping. Her hair had slid unevenly out of its clip, her jacket was askew, and she was breathing peacefully. Even in an exhausted sleep, Courtney was a beauty. He had never felt so close to her as he had felt working with her today. She had been incredible. She'd been there in the most invisible way. She'd made him look smart and solidly immersed in the accounts he'd been given only a few hours before. Now here beside him was a different Courtney; a young woman, asleep. He gazed at her affectionately and sighed. He'd seen her only as a hot lay when they had dated so long ago. He guessed that was all he had wanted to see in her. No wonder she had been so angry. She was an amazing woman. Why hadn't he loved her? He couldn't remember. Anyway, she was taking care of him in his job right now, being a good friend, and he felt indebted to her. She would never be sorry. He would take care of her too.

Guy rubbed his hands to warm them. Jeez, why did it feel colder in the cab than it felt in the open air? He thought he could see Court's breath. He exhaled experimentally. Sure, you could see your breath in here. Courtney's coat was folded neatly on the seat beside her. Guy lifted it and tucked it gently around her shoulders. She stirred.

"Are we home yet?"

"Not yet. Go back to sleep."

"I'm cold, Guy," she said, snuggling under his arm. He wrapped the other arm around her and reflexively pulled her close.

"I think my lips are numb," she said, tilting up her face to him.

Her movements released fragrance from within the folds of her clothing and her scent engulfed him. Instinctively, he bent his face to hers, touched her lips with his. Her mouth opened easily, naturally. He put his hand in her hair and cradled her head. His tongue, remembering its way, led him into a warm, living place. He closed his eyes. Courtney tasted of sleep and something sweet and familiar; those violet candies she liked. He held her tighter, explored the whole of her mouth, and as he kissed her, he heard himself groan. Startled by his unexpected surge of desire, Guy pulled back slightly. He was hard! He looked in amazement at the woman he held in his arms. Courtney touched her hand gently to his cheek.

"My God," he said, staring at her. "I'd forgotten."

Courtney took Guy's hand, closed her fingers around his thumb and squeezed it. She brought his hand to her breast and pressed it to her. "I haven't forgotten," she said quietly. "You were the best, Guy. It has never been as good for me with anyone else."

Nothing he could say would mean as much as kissing her again, and so he did. He was uncomfortably aware that there were too many constraints around him; his coat, the size of the back seat. If only everything around him would melt away. Did someone speak? "What?" Guy asked, looking up.

"Sorry, man," said the cabdriver. "This is your first stop. Gramercy Park."

"Just a minute," Guy said. The driver turned away and put the cab into neutral. It settled on its springs. Guy turned back to Courtney. He absently lifted a length of her hair and let it fall back onto her shoulder a little at a time. Street lamp light glistened on the strands. He remembered grasping that hair in his fist, twisting it at her nape, hearing her cry out that she wanted him.

"Come upstairs with me," Courtney said softly, running a finger across the back of his hand. She cocked her head and smiled at him.

"I want to, Court, very much," he said, touching her hair wistfully. "But it would be risky for us both. I'm committed, you know."

"I know." Courtney straightened up. She seemed to be thinking. She unfastened her hair clip and, holding it in her teeth, raked her hair, bunched it, clipped it again. She turned to Guy, touched his knee. "It would be all right just this once, don't you think? To celebrate your promotion?"

Would it be all right? Guy wondered. Yes, he was committed to Hanna, but Hanna had altered that commitment. If it was OK to sleep with Mahelly, it was damned well OK to sleep with Courtney. Two nights off, no questions asked. Right? What about his meeting in Chicago tomorrow? He could sleep on the plane. But what about Court? She had been so angry with him. Could they really sleep together once more, then resume their working relationship? The promise of undressing her, touching her everywhere, was an unasked for gift, undreamed of moments ago, and now it was what he wanted to do more than anything in this world. "Just this time? You're sure?" he asked.

"I'm not in love with you anymore, Guy, if that's worrying you," she said with a laugh. "Honestly." She leaned toward him and kissed him lightly. "Say yes. Please?"

"Do it, man, or we've got to move," the driver's voice said matter-of-factly over the sound of the car horn behind them. "This is a 'no parking anytime' zone." He nudged the cab into gear for emphasis. It lurched. Guy reached into his coat pocket, took out a clump of bills, stuffed some into the tray. Then he was standing in the cool air in front of the building where Courtney lived. They walked up the front steps and two more flights, and then Courtney put her key in the lock and opened the door.

"You know the way," Courtney said, giving him a gentle shove toward the bedroom. "Light this, OK?" she whispered. She handed him a glass sphere half-filled with water, in which floated candle wax in a little tub. Guy heard the bathroom door close. He set the globe on the vanity in front of the hinged triple-paned mirror. He struck a match and the wick caught. He walked to the bed and sat on its edge. He took off his shoes and socks. He looked around the room abloom with floral-printed fabrics. The air was fragrant with potpourri. Candlelight bobbed and flickered in the vanity mirrors; one fiery, beckoning finger, three reflections. Guy gazed at the flame and allowed himself to be mesmerized by its dance. He looked up as Court came toward him. She was wearing a short silk kimono that just covered the tops of her thighs. Her hair was loose. She put her hands on his shoulders and looked down at him. "You're still dressed," she said. Guy wrapped his arms around her and pulled her toward him. He pressed his face to her breasts. He found the sash and tugged it. With an easy, silky swish, the cloth parted. Courtney shrugged her shoulders and the robe dropped to the floor. Guy held her hips easily with his hands. He stared at her breasts, as firm as those of a twenty-year-old. He dropped his gaze down the length of her body, over her flat stomach to the tangle of blond curls. He pressed his palm there and raised his eyes to her face. Courtney bent to kiss him. Her hair tumbled past her shoulders and caressed his cheeks. Her scent overwhelmed his senses. He stood, and with trembling fingers, Guy undid his clothes.

"Be still," Courtney said. "This is my gift to you." Guy reached for her. She knew he wouldn't be able to take this much longer, but she wanted to stretch him to his limit. "Stop," she said. "You can't move, Guy. Pretend that I've tied you down." Courtney parted her lips again, tasting him, teasing him with darting flicks of her tongue. This was fun. It hardly seemed like work at all. She remembered all of it now. Where he was the most sensitive, how long he could tolerate her lips there, her tongue there. Her finger—there. She heard him groan again. She slowed her rhythm, stopped completely until, sensing the peak of his anticipation, she took him deeply into her mouth again. "You're killing me," she heard him say. She lifted her face and smiled. Almost, she thought. "Don't move," she said, straddling him. What she couldn't remember was why she had ever loved him. She held him to the entrance to her body for long moments before slowly lowering herself.

"You outrageous bitch," Guy said, grabbing her haunches and rolling her over. Courtney gasped as he wrapped her hair in his fist.

"Tell me when it hurts," he said.

"Now."

"Good," he said, tightening his grip, thrusting himself into her.

She ran her nails over his buttocks, up his back. "Harder," she said, listening to his grunts with satisfaction. This was almost too easy. "Now, Guy," she said, kneading, probing, biting into his shoulder, "Now." She was rewarded as Guy screamed his orgasm into the pillow.

Courtney listened as Guy's breathing lengthened and deepened. Crouching beside him, she cupped his buttocks in her hands and traced a path up the cleft with her tongue. Guy stirred and turned. I'm not through with you yet, Courtney thought, taking him into her hands. She permitted herself a smile as he became erect.

Courtney blinked her eyes in the dark. She lifted her watch from the night table and turned it until the dial was illuminated by a weak shaft of moonlight. Five-twenty. They'd made love three times in four hours. Not too bad for a man Guy's age, but as good as he was, even Guy couldn't make love and sleep at the same time. Time to wake him up again, but this time it was to pack him up and get him to leave. He had to meet Carter at the airport, and from there, Chicago and an all-day round of introductions to Carter's brand management team. She got out of bed and unceremoniously wrapped her kimono around her. "Wake up, Guy," she said, shaking his arm, gathering up his clothes, piling them on the bed. "You've got to catch a plane."

"That was great, Court," Guy whispered at the door. "You're sure you're all right?"

"Of course. I'm fine," she said stiffly. "Get going. If you want to go home and change, you have to hurry." She kissed him coolly and shut the door a little too hard, a little too fast. She went back to her bedroom. She slid back into the warm sheets. She had almost blown it for a second by letting her anger surface, but he probably hadn't noticed. He was worried about her? He ought to save his concern for himself. She'd kept him all night and until she sucked him dry. Good luck in Chicago, Guy, she thought sarcastically. Try to stay awake. She, however, could get in about three hours of sleep if she started right now. She closed her eyes.

21

HANNA LOOKED AT THE PAGES OF TEENY, TINY TYPE. WHEN SHE HAD asked the librarian for the latest U.S. Census data, it had come in an interoffice envelope with a handwritten note, "If you need any more help, just call. Irene." Now Irene was on vacation in Bermuda, where Hanna would like to be, and Hanna needed help all right.

"Kathy," she called over the partition.

"Yeah?" Kathy Broome replied from her cubicle on the other side.

Hanna grabbed the sheaf of statistics and knocked on the door.

"C'mon in."

"Check me on this, will ya' Kath? I think I've got it, but these numbers are starting to look like crazy little ants to me."

Kathy laughed. "Let's see."

Hanna sat in the chair next to Kathy. Kathy always wore tea rose, a scent that smelled wrong on everyone but Kathy, and big loose dresses in warm prints and colors. She probably baked her own bread, Hanna thought as she considered crawling into Kathy's lap and hiding in her bosom for a few years. The image faded as Kathy spoke.

"What is this? The 1980 Census?"

"Yeah. And a few other depressing little pieces of data. Now check me on this." Hanna picked a ruler off Kathy's desk and lined it up across a page. "This is New York City, total males, total females, over the age of fifteen."

Kathy nodded.

"OK," Hanna said. "Total females in round numbers, three million one. Total males in round numbers, two million five. So, right away, in New York, we've got six hundred thousand more women than men. Right?"

"I'm following you. That's what it says."

"Now here's a chart breaking down marriage availability by age category. New York City. For every 100 women aged 25 to 29, there are 90 men. For every 100 women aged 30 to 34, there are 75 men. How's that sound, Kath?"

"Grim."

"Not grim yet. Here's grim," said Hanna. "To continue ever downward: For every 100 women aged 35 to 39, there are 57 available men. For every 100 women 40 to 44, 42 prince charmings, and if you want to hear the capper, if a person, male or female has not married by the age of 45, the chances of marriage after that are almost zippo. One in a hundred. *That's* grim."

"Whew," said Kathy. "I'm glad Mike and I are in the married column. So your story has real basis in fact. Right?"

"Yeah." Hanna rolled the sheets into a cone and tapped it against her knee. She looked up at her friend. "You smell nice, Kath."

"Thanks. Where are you going?" she asked as Hanna stood up.

"Bergdorf's."

"Getting what?"

"I don't care. Something expensive."

The smell of garlic filled the kitchen. Guy was sautéing two fish fillets in a pan. "It happened a couple of days ago. Why?" he asked, tipping the pan so the butter coated it evenly.

"You got promoted and didn't tell me?!" Hanna exploded.

"Hey. We don't see each other on Tuesdays and Wednesdays, sweet one. Remember? Besides I was in Chicago yesterday."

"Gee," said Hanna. "No phones in Chicago. I thought Chicago was a real city with elevators and toasters and phones and everything." Hanna banged plates onto the table.

Why hadn't he told her? Damn, he was angry with her, that's why he hadn't wanted to tell her the good news. That moment had belonged to him and Courtney. "I'm sorry, Hanna. I meant to."

"Hmmmph."

"Come on, Hanna. Don't pout. I said I'm sorry."

"Well, congratulations," she said without looking up.

"Thanks. Give me a kiss."

She complied but didn't put any tongue into it. Guy took her into his arms and held her. Then he kissed her again. She relented. "Congratulations," she said and extricated herself from his embrace. "I mean it." She patted him on the bottom.

"Are you happy with your new accounts?" Hanna folded the napkins.

"Love them. Especially Swanee Old Fashioned Brown Sugar. It's got zero market potential, but we see a real opportunity to turn the business around and score some points out in Chicago."

"Yow. Can you really do it?"

"We think so. It'll be rough, but if we can keep the five million dollars in the agency, your lover is going to be a hero."

"You're my hero and you don't need to give me five million dollars," Hanna said, giving him a smile. "How many people do you have reporting to you now?"

"A bunch. A dozen." Guy nudged the fish. The oil crackled. The sizzle made Hanna's mouth wet.

"Who's this 'we' you keep mentioning?" she asked.

"I'm ready for the platter now, Nan," Guy said lifting the fish out with a spatula. Christ. Never underestimate Hanna. How in the world had she picked up that innocuous "we"? Was she going to remember Courtney's name and make something out of it? Both the question and the smell of fried flounder hung in the air. Hanna looked at Guy and then carried the fish to the table. Guy went to the refrigerator. He started to open a beer, put his hand on his gut, and changed his mind. He opened a club soda.

"Courtney Rand. She's my account supe on the Cocoa brands, and the Brown Sugar."

"Courtney?" Hanna turned. "She's the one you went out with for a couple of years. Right?"

"Right," said Guy, pouring out two glasses of soda.

"Well, is it going to be a problem working with her?"

"Nah," said Guy, busying himself with the silverware. "No problem at all." He was sure of it. Courtney had sworn their night was a one-time thing. What a night it had been! And what a relief to screw someone Hanna hadn't asked him to screw. Christ, he'd felt like a seventeen-year-old! Had he really slept with three women this week? Incredible. Court was almost three women all by herself. He couldn't remember how many times he'd made love to her. But what had happened? When he kissed her good-bye at the door and told her it was great, he saw something change in her eyes. Her irises had contracted. He remembered now. The cold, in-control Courtney; the business Courtney. This had been her seduction and she had chosen her time and way to say good-bye. How was she able to go from so hot to so cool? He could be captivated by the challenge she presented, and he respected her self-control, but this sexual power game of hers wasn't a lovable trait. Anyway, they were comrades again, not lovers. He needed another lover like he needed another foot. He had enough problems on 94th Street.

Guy checked the knobs on the stove. All were off. He tested them anyway. Goddamn it, last month life had been so simple; job, home, woman he loved. Agreeing to sleep with Mahelly was supposed to be his scheme to get Hanna to marry him. He hadn't wanted to be torn between the two women and he *was* torn. Did he still love Hanna? His underlying anger at her, combined with his new soft feelings for Mel, made it hard to be sure. He was a one-woman man. Always had been. He looked over at Hanna filling the salt shaker, straightening the table settings—Hanna, whom he had recently believed he would love forever. Unbelievable how things had changed. Change the subject, he decided. "What have *you* been up to?" he asked, hoping she wouldn't hear the flat tone of his voice.

Hanna brought the covered dish of broccoli to the table and sighed. They sat facing each other. "It's the worst, Guy. The worst. I'm disgusted. I miss you. You won't talk with me about Mahelly. I never see her. I never see you. I feel stranded all the time. High and dry. But I've got to write about all this somehow. Write a big, happy, brave new world of the future story." She put food on her plate and stared at it. "Somehow I convinced Stein we're going to sell at least a million magazines with this crappy idea. Now he won't give it up and I can't write two sentences without getting the heaves."

Guy's fingers tensed around the silverware he was holding. "I can't tell you how much I hate hearing you talk about this story, Hanna," he said in a low, breathless voice. "It's scaring me, how angry I am and how confused. I wasn't confused before this. I used to be very sure of my feelings for you."

"What are you saying?" Hanna asked. Nothing he could say after that would be reassuring. Hanna braced herself against the table.

"I'm angry, Hanna. Angry at you." Guy dropped his fork into his plate with a clatter. "I know that doesn't seem fair. I know I didn't have to go along with this stupid idea, but I did it. And now I don't know what I want any more. I don't know how I feel any more."

Frozen, Hanna stared at Guy. He stared back. It was then that the phone rang.

"Han, it's me," said Mahelly. Her voice was hoarse, as though she'd been crying. "I've got to talk to you. Can you come now?"

"I'm coming upstairs." Hanna hung up the phone. Guy had said he didn't know if he loved her any more. She couldn't face the thought of her life without Guy loving her. She wouldn't face it. She wouldn't have it. Guy would love her again. Go, she said to herself. Go before he says anything worse. Move. Run away.

"I have to go upstairs," she said. "Mel needs me."

"I just made dinner."

"I'll be back." Hanna put her plate in the oven, pushed the "warm" button, dropped her napkin on the table and fled.

Mahelly's front door was open. She was sitting at the kitchen table. There were plates on the counter, a tea bag lying on the table itself, and laundry in an ice-blue heap on the stove. Hanna had never seen this much disarray in Mahelly's apartment before. Mahelly was smoking. Mahelly didn't smoke.

"Hey," said Hanna walking on soft feet, sliding into a chair. Worry about Guy later, she thought. Talk to Guy later.

"Hey," Mahelly said, looking up, waving smoke away. "Are you crying, Han?"

"Borderline. I will any minute. I missed you Mel. You look bad. Are you all right?"

"Not really."

"What's the matter, kiddo?" Hanna asked.

"Can I get you something? Tea?"

"OK."

Mahelly piled the sheets on top of the refrigerator. She shook the kettle, opened the refrigerator, poured distilled water into the kettle, and put it on the stove. "Red Zinger? English Breakfast? Earl Grey? Stop me if you hear something you like. Peppermint Perk, Morning Thunder, Rosehip?"

"Have anything in Deadly Nightshade?"

"Oh, great. What a pair. The suicide sisters."

"You're smoking? Marlboros?"

Mahelly shrugged. "Frank's. Found them in the junk drawer." She adjusted the flame.

"Mel, that makes them about six months old."

Mahelly didn't answer.

"What's this?" Hanna asked dangling the cold tea bag by its string.

"A & P, I think."

"That'll be fine."

Mahelly sighed. "I feel the same way. Why waste the good stuff on this mood? I don't even know where I got this tea." She dropped a new bag into a cup, dropped the used bag into the cup she'd been drinking from and waited for the kettle to boil. She filled the sugar bowl, put a clean spoon on the table, ran water on the dirty plates. She sat down and looked at Hanna. "I don't know which of us looks worse. Do you want to go first?"

"No, you go. You called," Hanna said.

The kettle's whistle blew. Mahelly took the pot off the flame, turned off the stove, poured hot water into the two cups. "I know you're the wrong person to talk with about this," she said looking at Hanna and looking away, "but I don't know who the right person is."

Hanna felt an extra measure of dread spilling onto a mountain of the same substance. She looked at the cheerful red and white cigarette box. Marlboro country. Those old TV commercials. Dum-dump-ty-dump. Dah-dahdy-dahdy-dum-dump. She'd like to be on a horse right now. In Marlboro country. She looked at Mahelly. "Please don't tell me this is about Guy."

Mahelly sighed. "OK."

"It's not? It's not about Guy?"

Mahelly looked at Hanna with red-veined eyes.

Hanna sighed deeply. "I thought so. I hoped not, but I thought so. Go ahead." She put her elbows on the table, her hands into her hair, the palms half covering her ears. She was afraid she wouldn't hear what Mahelly had to say. She didn't want to.

Mahelly said, "I think I'm getting hooked on your boyfriend."

"You're falling for Guy?" Hanna asked with a dead voice.

Mahelly nodded her head miserably. "But don't worry, the feeling isn't mutual. And I haven't told him how I feel and I won't. I just don't know what to do with my feelings." She didn't move. She was looking at Hanna.

Had Mahelly said "don't worry"? Was that a joke? OK, don't worry. Don't worry that Guy said he was confused about his feelings and that Mahelly was confused about her feelings and that she, the perpetrator and the victim was supposed also to be Ann Landers. "Mel, I'm sorry but I don't know what to say to you. I really, really don't."

"Please, Hanna. This is all so awful. Could you just be my best friend like always and tell me what to do?"

Hanna shrugged openmouthed. She turned her palms up and waited. Mahelly took this as a sign of encouragement and spoke. "It's feeling abandoned that I hate the most. With Frank, it was boring, but he was always here. With Guy, I wait all week for the two nights with him. Then he usually comes over for one night. I don't know where he's going to be the rest of the week. We never talk during the week at all. Then I have this one precious night to talk," she rubbed her nose on her sleeve, "and get close, and then in the morning, he's gone. I sometimes feel as if my stomach's been ripped out when he leaves."

Hanna opened her mouth to speak, closed it, opened it again. "Mel. This is too weird. I have about a thousand conflicting thoughts about this. I love you. I don't want you to be in pain. I don't want you to be in love with Guy either. I love *him*. Damn it!" She slapped the table with both hands. "This was supposed to be about sex, remember?"

Mahelly nodded and pressed tissues to her eyes.

"What do you want me to say? That you can have him? He's all yours. Is that what you want?"

Mahelly shook her head from side to side. Her face was covered with her hands. She was crying.

"OK," Hanna said. Her temples were throbbing. This was the stuff the damned story was supposed to be made of. She pushed the teacup out of the way of her shaking hands. "I'll try to be some objective third party. If your feelings for Guy aren't returned, why don't you just stop seeing him?"

Mahelly blew her nose and took a deep breath. She looked at Hanna. "Hanna, I have to be honest with you. I'm not ready to let go yet. I suffer so much when he leaves, I don't think I can bear to be completely alone yet."

Hanna sighed. She flipped open the cigarette box, closed it. It was absurd. She shouldn't be here listening to this. She didn't even understand what was going on. If Guy was so confused about his feelings, how come Mahelly thought he didn't care about her? Hanna looked up at Mahelly. How was this going to turn out? Were the two of them going to be friends when this was over? Was she going to be the maid of honor at Guy's and Mahelly's wedding? She'd move to Rio if that happened. Mahelly had little blobs of gook in the corners of her pink-rimmed eyes. She looked like a rabbit when she cried.

"You know, I think I could stand this if I saw a little more of him,"

Mahelly said, blotting her eyes. "He makes me feel good when he's here but the fact that he could be with me twice as much as he is, hurts as much as his absence." Mahelly's face looked puffy and the wrong color. Hanna couldn't reach out to her. She just took something in. Mahelly had said something like this before, but it hadn't registered the first time.

"What do you mean, he doesn't come over both nights? Where is he?"

"I don't know. He's vague. He's going to be out late. He has other plans. I don't think I should grill him, do you?"

"He's probably home. You know, taking a rest from the two of us."

Mahelly shrugged. "But why on one of *my* nights with him? Selfish of me, I know, but I can't help but think if he's not with me, he's with someone else."

"Mel. That's crazy. That's not Guy. Believe me, he's home in bed giving his cock a break."

"When I saw you coming in with David the other night, I called him at home. I called him a few times. He wasn't in."

A big bright light went off in Hanna. It was jealousy. And it was fear. Where was that prick if he wasn't home and he wasn't with Mahelly? Where? With Courtney? NO. Absolutely not. He was probably out getting drunk. This was too much and she wasn't going to let Mahelly's paranoia push her over the edge. "Mel. I don't think I can handle this," she said, holding her feelings behind tight lips. "I realize this isn't your fault, but I can't take this any more. You're going to have to work out your problem with Guy by yourself. I would like to suggest we all go back to normal life, but I don't have much faith this thing could be called off now anyway. Guy seems to be working from his own script." Hanna stood. "I think, Mel, I don't want to know any more."

"Han, what are you saying?"

"I'm saying that I can't help you and the things you are saying are hurting me too much. Maybe you and I have to take a break in our relationship until this is all over."

"No, Hanna. I don't want to."

"Look, Mel. You're going to have to live with it. I don't want to hear about your falling in love with Guy. I don't want to hear Guy is hurting you. I don't want to wonder where he is. I want to be in the dark. OK?"

"But you have David."

"David? *What the hell are you talking about?*" Hanna heard her voice vibrating in the quiet room. Too much, Hanna thought. Too much. She might scream in a minute. "David's got *nothing* to do with this. I *work* for him. That's *all.*"

"Oh, I thought . . ."

"Wished, you mean," Hanna said, seeing an image through Mahelly's eyes. "Wished I was going out with David, so you could have Guy? What a pal."

"Hanna, I didn't. I'm sorry. Please don't be angry with me." Mahelly was holding her own throat loosely with one hand. "How can you be angry with me for this? This wasn't even my idea," she said pitifully.

"Don't remind me."

The two women stood and faced one another. Their faces were white.

"I can't talk any more, Mel. I'm bloody from this."

"I'm sorry. That sounds so feeble, but I mean it. I've been selfish and you've been . . ." Mahelly shook her head, ". . . my best friend. Only, believe me, Han. I thought it would be what we agreed. Sex."

Hanna let out more air then she knew she had in her lungs. This was going to be over soon. She was going to leave this room and go back to her apartment. "I'm sorry too," she said.

"This will be all over soon, won't it?" Mahelly asked looking away from Hanna. Looking out the window.

"Somehow. I have to leave." Hanna kissed her friend's cheek and ran down eight flights of stairs.

Guy had left a note pinned to the refrigerator door with a yellow Day-Glo banana magnet. "Went home to do chores. Come up when you can."

Hanna threw the note in the trash. She clutched the banana Guy had brought home from a business trip. "A relative of yours," he'd said. He had been right. She leaned against the refrigerator. She was relieved to be alone. She needed time to think. She didn't know what to say to Guy. She thought about what he'd said to her just before Mahelly had called; how angry he was at her, how confused he was about his feelings. Well, damn it, where was his damned loyalty? Damned right, he hadn't had to go along with mansharing, but he had done it. What was he so confused about, anyway? Mel said he didn't love her. What the hell was going on? Well, she was pretty angry herself. If he'd ever simply said "no," none of this would have happened.

That thought made her cry. She unfurled a three-sheet length of paper toweling illustrated on both margins with a parade of aquamarine-colored vegetables. Holding the towel to her nose, she sobbed over the kitchen sink. She blew her nose hard and dropped the wadded paper into the trash bucket under the sink. Why wasn't he supporting her, that bastard? Was this supposed to be easy for her? Fuck Guy anyway. If he was going to back away from her, she was going to enjoy whatever happened with David Stein. Maybe it was fate that the mansharing story had thrown them together as man and woman. Mahelly had said, "You have David." She had been trying not to look at that, but maybe she *did* have David. That kiss at the door. He liked her. A lot. And he was single. Maybe they were meant to be. She arranged the syllables in her head. Hanna Coleman Stein. That sounded pretty damned good. Hanna went into the bathroom and washed her face furiously.

22

WAIT A MINUTE. JUST WAIT A MINUTE. NUTS. THE DREAM HAD GONE. Guy tried to remember, but all he could recollect was a sense of pulling things out of both pockets, and not knowing what he was looking for.

Last month, he would have told Hanna the dream and she would have interpreted it, embellished it with her wacky little insights. This dream didn't need much interpretation. Both pockets. Both women. What was he looking for?

He turned his head and looked at Hanna lying still asleep beside him. Hanna was the most complex human being he knew. Being with her was like being home, only home was a recreational vehicle. You could go to sleep one night parked by a lake, and wake up the next morning in a fast-food parking lot. Being in bed with her, wrapping her up in his arms and feeling her soft warm flesh conform to his, was the most comforting feeling he knew. At least it had been before all this stiffness had come between them. The old Hanna he used to have would be enough for him forever if he could count on it. But how could he? She'd gone and upset the whole contented fabric of his life by doing this damned mansharing thing, and he didn't know how they were ever going to get out from under what they all had done.

Guy stared at the ceiling. A few floors away, he knew, Mahelly was thinking about him. This had been going on for what, a month? Not even, but it seemed like a lifetime. Mahelly had fallen in love with him, and as much as he cared for her, he couldn't make a commitment to her. Hiding from her hadn't worked. That had simply intensified her feelings. He was not going to be a passive participant in this mansharing crap any more. He had a date with Mel tonight and he was just going to have to tell her it was time to stop. Dealing with his situation with Hanna was a different matter. He did love her. He would have to work through his anger at her somehow, or stop seeing her, but he had to separate his relationship with Hanna from his relationship with Mahelly. Tying the two together was what made it so confusing.

It was too bad Hanna and Mahelly had broken up. He was going to hate to leave Mel alone. But maybe with his relationship with her back to friendship, she and Hanna could resume theirs. And then maybe, he could love Hanna again.

Hanna threw her coffee container in the garbage and thought about Guy. Funny how great their sex was this weekend. They were furious at each other, could hardly talk, but the sex was great. Primitive, but great. She'd wanted to ask him about Mahelly, but she couldn't. She knew he'd tell her the truth and she didn't really want to know. She wanted to ask him please, please, to stop seeing Mel so they could have their life back, but she could tell from the distance between them, he would say no. If she asked and he said no, the rejection would kill her. What in the world should she do? She needed to think.

There was no ignoring it any longer. The story stunk. First, she'd tell David. Then, when she'd resigned the assignment with honor, she'd tell Guy. What would he do? Whatever he wanted, that's what. Despite what Mahelly had said, it was possible Guy did love her, and was hiding his feelings until he was sure.

Shit. The thing she had to do was get rid of the story. The rest she'd just have to feel out. Telling Guy who he should or shouldn't sleep with was never going to work again, never in a hundred million years. She was going to have to fight for Guy and take whatever lumps he dished out. Right now, she was going to see David. She clutched her journal in her hand for moral support and closed her office door behind her.

She waved unseeingly at Jillian as she strode past her and stood in David's doorway. "David. I've got to talk to you."

"Come in, Coleman."

Coleman, she thought. Wonderful. Last night, she fantasized marrying him. Now it was back to Coleman. She could see he was buried in something he had been concentrating on, but it was too late to turn back. "I think the mansharing story is lousy," she said from halfway across the large room. David was backlit by the windows behind his desk. His face was a featureless eclipse. Was he scowling? She couldn't tell. "I think the story is lousy," she said again. "I don't know why I ever thought it would be good, but I have given it a very good try, and I can tell you, it stinks."

"Hold on, Coleman," David said with a tone he reserved for the most scathing public criticism. "It *is* a good idea. If you can't write it, possibly it's because we overestimated your ability to write about a subject in which you are emotionally involved. Perhaps I should turn your notes over to someone else."

Hanna felt her blood pressure drop. Maybe she was going to have a heart attack. "Maybe you should," she said, she hoped strongly.

"Let me see what you've got."

Hanna walked into his office. She imagined throwing open her journal, giving him a good look at the mastodon. That would impress him. Let him turn that into something. His face came into view. He was mad all right. "I don't have them with me."

"I'll see them tonight," he said with finality. "Tell Jillian to cancel my plans." He turned back to a stack of layouts on his desk. Hanna just stood. She was transfixed.

"I'll talk with you about this later. I'll come by your office at six." He went back to the layouts. She had been dismissed. Hanna left the office.

"Jillian," she said in a monotone, the voice of a zombie. "David wants you to cancel his plans for tonight." She walked away, seeing nothing. Could he be right? Maybe she was too close to the story. Was it possible David might see some way to write this that she couldn't see? She had certainly bombed in every possible way. Her relationship with Guy was cracking up. She'd lost her best friend, who was getting hurt. David had just told her she was an asshole, and she was in fear for her life. What else could possibly happen? War? Pestilence? Famine?

Hanna went to the ladies' lounge and glanced at her reflection in the mirror of the fluorescent-lit room. Her face looked green. Her hair looked limp. She had visible panty line. And she didn't care.

23

DAVID AND HANNA BARELY SPOKE OVER DINNER. THE RESTAURANT was small and specialized in Italian peasant cooking. The food looked good, not that Hanna had eaten much, but the restaurant was ugly, overlit, and the waiters tended to drop the plates onto the table from several inches above its surface.

David was wearing glasses. He went through Hanna's first draft line by line, sometimes marking the margin with his blue pencil, sometimes crossing out whole paragraphs. Hanna tasted some salad, pushed bread crumbs around on the tablecloth and drank wine. The wine was red and tasted very rich. It seemed wholesome to Hanna, so she drank as much as she wanted. Twice, David asked her questions, then, scribbling notes on the back of her clean white draft, he wrote busily for minutes without looking at her. His meal was eaten in silence and he drank very little.

"You've done an amazing job," he said finally, taking off his glasses to look at her. "An amazing job, considering this is a superficial, dishonest piece of crap that doesn't deserve to be called journalism."

Hanna shrugged. "Can't write it, David. I told you. It shtinks. It's a shtinkeroo." This seemed funny, so she laughed. David looked at her. He didn't want to be amused. He wanted to sell a few hundred thousand copies of the December issue, and he was pinning some hopes on the story this delicious, drunken, fruitcake was writing.

Despite his intentions to the contrary, he smiled. She's a little shtink-eroo'd herself, he thought. He pushed the breadbasket toward her, hoping she would eat something, and went back to the draft.

"I don't know how yet, but you're going to have to put some teeth into this pollyanna piece of shit," David said, clicking his tongue with disgust. "What happened, by the way, to your 'mature woman' angle?" he asked after a while.

"Growing up an' liking it?" Hanna asked dreamily. Wait. Wasn't that the title of a pamphlet on menstruation she'd read as a teen-ager? "Hold it. That's been used." She tapped her lower lip with her forefinger. "I tried to be mature," Hanna said, and with no warning that her mood was going to change, it did. A rivulet of tears broke over her lower lids and streamed straight for her chin.

"Hanna. Are you all right?"

Hanna's elbows were on the table. She wriggled her fingers in the air. As quickly as the tears had come, they were forgotten. Of course she was OK. Why had he asked? She nodded yes. There was a loose smile on her face. Gee, David looked cute with glasses. Like a boyfriend. Or a husband. Not like the boss who was going to kill her. He was nice.

"I'd drop this damned story this minute if I could, but I can't. I've left a huge hole in the December book and I hired Crandall-Edwards to do a painting for the cover." Was Hanna listening to him? He didn't think so. He leaned across the table. "Are you interested in the cover, Hanna? The cover I've commissioned for your story?"

Hanna nodded, mesmerized by those unmatched eyes enlarged by the lenses of his glasses.

"People entering an ark in groups of threes. Played straight. Burberry's held overhead to keep off the rain."

Hanna nodded. David sighed in exasperation, took off his glasses and tossed them lightly onto the table. "I'm not letting you off the hook. I'm going to think about what to do about this garbage and then you're going to write it and write it right."

Hanna screwed up her face and looked at him quizzically. "What?"

David laughed. "Never mind. I'll tell you tomorrow. It's time to go." He paid the check, helped Hanna on with her coat and out the door.

Hanna closed her eyes in the car. When she awoke, she was on 94th street in front of her apartment building. The engine had stopped, and the sound that woke her was David's door slamming as he left his side of the car to open her door. Her door opened and a rush of cold air assaulted her. She swung her legs out of the car and tried to stand. She steadied herself against him. He closed the car door behind her and taking her into his arms, pressed her up against the Bentley's cold metal side. She looked up at David and for a long moment their eyes engaged. Then he placed his mouth on hers and Hanna felt herself dissolve. His kiss filled her mouth, her body heated, trembled. She met his hardness with a softness and a yearning of her own, and she pressed her body even tighter against him. Oh, he did like her. He wanted her. She wanted him. She reached her arms up around David's neck and brushed her cheek against his. She blinked against his whiskers. The wind burned her eyes and as she blinked them, they cleared and focused. Was she doing this on 94th street? In front of her own building. With David Stein?

She dropped down from her toes and, embarrassed now, looked at David through half-closed eyes. His large hands slipped inside her opened coat, under her arms, and slid very slowly downward along her ribcage. His thumbs blazed a hot trail down the upper slope of her breasts, across her nipples where they halted as her flesh peaked to meet his touch. His thumbs lingered there, flicked side to side, twice, three times, before his hands traveled to her waist.

Hanna was aware that her cheeks were stinging from his beard and the cold air. Her underwear was wet and she was panting. This had to stop. She was sober now. Her eyes darted wildly over David's shoulders, up to the windows of the building she faced. Anyone could see her out here. The doorman. Mahelly. Guy. *Guy*.

Hanna unsteadily sidestepped David's embrace. She opened the car door behind her and finding her handbag on the seat, clutched it in front of her. "Thanks for bringing me home," she began.

"Invite me in," he said.

"I'm sorry," she said. "I can't."

"It's Wednesday, isn't it?"

"That's not why not." Images appeared. Her passion with Guy this past weekend. Her lover. "I love him," she said.

David stepped toward her. He put a hand through her hair and held her head at its base. He put the other hand around her waist. She felt his erection against her thigh as he pulled her toward him. He bent to kiss her again, but she pushed her hands against his chest. "No, David. Really."

Something flashed in his eyes. Something that amused him. "I'll walk you inside."

"OK."

When the elevator door closed, Hanna remembered David's eyes flickering, surveying her face as she said "no." He hadn't been hurt. He hadn't looked rejected. He looked as if he liked it. Huh. Thank God, he hadn't been hurt, but huh, anyway.

Hanna didn't turn on her bedroom light. She peeled off all her clothes in one many-layered piece, left them in a heap on her chair and climbed naked into bed. *This* is maturity, she thought, tucking a pillow between her legs. She rocked a little as the bed warmed to her temperature. God. She could be fucking him right now. She squeezed her thighs together. She bit the corner of the pillow case. She had said "no," without needing to think about it. "No, David," she'd said. Fantasies of being Mrs. David Stein had been only that. It was true. She loved Guy. Tears came to her eyes. She rubbed her face into the pillow. She thought about making love to David, but she could not hold the image. She hugged the pillow and saw Guy's face, a loving face, behind her closed eyes, then that face blended and ran and was replaced by pictures of pastures along a highway as seen from a speeding car. Green. Serene. Silent. And then Hanna was asleep.

Mahelly liked her apartment so much. It was so creamy and white, the perfect backdrop for her trees, her paintings, the clothes she wore. She was wearing white satin flannel-lined pajamas and a long pink satin flannel-lined robe. Her socks had lace around the cuffs and she wore a strand of baby pearls. She went into the bathroom and brushed her teeth again. She looked at herself. She was pearly. A pearly girl. She brushed her eyebrows with a damp toothbrush, put some Vaseline on them and rubbed some more onto her lips. She sprayed Diorissimo on her wrists, her throat. She went back into the living room and reclined on the white sofa. She pulled the lap throw over her and closed her eyes. If she fell asleep it would be OK. It was late, and Mahelly was waiting for Guy.

She remembered his call at seven, could still feel her disappointment when he said he'd be working late. "Don't worry about the time," she'd said.

"It could be ten, eleven, later. I'll probably go out with people at the office so we can work at dinner."

"It's OK. I don't mind how late you get here. Use your key." Then she took a two-milligram Valium, nothing really but a placebo she thought, but she needed it anyway. She knew she was bordering on being out of control. Some of it was her infatuation with Guy, but even in her coldest, loneliest times, she knew that the desperation she felt was based on her recent discovery, her realization of how enormously deprived she had been of a full adult life. It was wrong to confuse the emotional void of fifteen years of marriage to Frank with a longing for Guy. She knew what she was longing for was real love and a real relationship. She saw just enough of the possibility of that with Guy to arouse longing beyond anything she had ever imagined.

Mahelly sighed deeply and straightened a fold in the mohair afghan. This affair with Guy couldn't go on forever and she had better start planning ahead. She'd already wasted fifteen years being a housewife to Frank. How much time did she want to waste pining away for a man who didn't belong to her? Dear God, all those years of being Frank's diminutive little "Bird." She'd only been a semiperson. It was time to fly on her own. Really be a bird. If only she could. She'd talk to Guy about it tonight, hear what he had to say. Above all, he was really her friend. When should she talk to him—when he walked in? No. She'd talk with Guy after they made love. She didn't want to take any chance that talking about separation would somehow interfere with their making love tonight. Was she serious? Was she going to be able to give up making love to Guy and be completely alone? She heard her door open.

"Guy," she called out, her desire to see him, erasing her earlier thoughts. "Is that you, Guy?"

"No," a deeper voice said. "It's Frank. Come over here and give your husband a kiss."

The room shifted. Where was she? What was happening? Was she crazy? Had she summoned Frank into existence just by thinking about him? Damn. The locks. She'd never changed the damned locks.

"Frank! What are you doing here!?" She swept the blanket to the floor and stood.

Frank laughed. "I wanted to surprise my little wife." He strode towards her, grabbed her in his strong arms and lifted her off the ground to his kiss. She kissed him back, more out of shock and reflex than affection. He put her down and crossed to the window. "And look out here, Mary Helen," he said. "Look at what I've got. Can you see it?" He'd parked the car just where he'd planned. Across the street with the park wall and all the trees behind it, right under the streetlight. You could photograph it right there. It looked so great.

Mahelly walked to the window. What was he doing here? Had he truly used his key and walked in? Fucking Frank didn't call, didn't even have her rung on the intercom. Was he completely out of his mind? She pushed the curtains to one side. "What am I looking for?" she asked in a tight voice.

"Right there. Under that light in the middle." He put one arm on her back and tapped the window with his finger.

Standing this close to him, she could smell his odor—meat sandwiches, milk, cigarettes. God knew what else. She'd forgotten his smell. She'd wanted to forget it. She stepped away from him. "There?" Her heart was beating furiously. She put her hand on her chest. He would have to leave now. "You got a *car*?"

"Not just a car, Bird. A 1957 Mercury Turnpike Cruiser!"

"Uh-huh," Mahelly said. She thought, a car. He wants to talk about a car. He hadn't grown an inch. Records and cars. He still lived in 1971.

" 'Uh-huh'?" he said, repeating her remark in disbelief. "Mary Helen it's the TC! Like the one we used to drive back in Cobleskill!" What was the matter with her? Didn't she get it? Damn. Women. He'd forgotten all cars were the same to them except for the colors. The disappointment would have to be measured later. He felt suddenly tired. "Got anything to drink?"

"Scotch?" she asked. He nodded. He kicked at the bathroom door. She could hear him urinating through the open door. The toilet sounded its rumbled flush, the water in the sink ran, and then Frank flung himself heavily onto the sofa. Mahelly brought his drink to him with a cocktail napkin. She put a cushion in her lap and sat on a chair. She looked at him. He'd cut himself this morning. There was blood on the collar of his shirt and a crust of blood on his neck. And that awful jacket. He'd had that jacket for twenty years. What was he doing here? She bit her lip. How dare he break in on her as if he still lived here without even a phone call! How *could* she have left that lock in place? With a little foresight, Frank would be outside ringing the doorbell and she'd never let him in. Shit, she wasn't crazy. How could she have known he was going to drive here in a car? Guy was going to be here any moment. Frank was going to screw up the best night in her week and maybe her last with Guy. She sniffed at the cigarette smoke that was tainting the air. Frank had to go. "Seriously, Frank. Why are you here?"

Frank frowned. He'd driven three days for a weak Scotch and a weaker reception. What was going on here? Why was she being so cold to him? "I wanted to surprise you, Mary Helen. But why do I have to explain myself? I'm still your husband, remember? 'Til death do us part, I seem to remember."

"Death!? 'Til Sioux City do us part, you mean. How dare you break in on me like this? We haven't spoken more than two dozen words in the last six months. Didn't you think to call at least? Did it occur to you I might have plans this evening?"

Frank was so tired. His eyes felt gritty. His undershirt had shrunk in the wash and was chafing him under the arms. This wasn't anything like he'd planned. He wanted to take off his shoes and his clothes and go to sleep with his arms around his wife. "OK, maybe I should have called," he conceded. "I wanted to surprise you," he said again, almost to himself this time. "Please let's not fight. I've been driving for three days. I just wanted to see you, Bird." Frank got up and walked across the room to Mahelly. He wanted to take her in his arms. If he could do just that, everything would be all right.

Mahelly watched him come toward her with outstretched arms. Hadn't he heard her? "Frank, no." She ducked away from him, sat at the window seat on other side of the room, and pulled her knees up under her chin. "I hate that you did this, but I'm not surprised. Isn't this just the way you are, though? The way you always do things? You decide what *you* want to do, then you decide that's what I want and without *asking me*, you *do* it."

"Always? That's what I *always* do?" Frank returned to the sofa. It was lower than he remembered. He fell off balance as he sat and the Scotch splashed onto his wrist. He licked it off with his tongue. He stared across the room at Mahelly. "Made my own decision? Is that what I did when I moved to New York to begin with? Did I make a decision without asking you then?"

"No, Frank. You asked me then and that was the last time you asked me anything."

"Stop it, Mary Helen. You're getting me mad. I drove fifteen hundred miles to see you."

"So what, Frank? That's my point. I don't want to see *you*. I told you the last time we spoke that I didn't want to see you, but you drove here anyway. I don't even think you really wanted to see me. I think you bought that stupid car and wanted to go somewhere with it."

"Don't talk to me that way. You're being disrespectful."

Mahelly hugged her knees. How was she going to get him out of here? She hated the way he looked in this apartment. Army clothes!

That jacket, the rough brown slacks, the combat boots. He was a gross insult to her eyes. His smell revolted her. "Are you being respectful to me, barging in on me like this?"

She paused, waiting for an answer. Frank ignored the question.

Mahelly felt like walking over to him and kicking him in the shins, but she didn't dare go that far. "This is my place, you know, Frank." she said. "You can't tell me how to talk any more. Or what to talk about. And I want to talk about how our marriage is shit, and how you thought I'd be overjoyed to see you and your fucking car. Doesn't that strike you as pretty funny, Frank?" Mahelly laughed.

"No, I don't think that's funny. I don't think you're funny. Don't laugh at me, Mary Helen."

"Well, then, why don't you leave, all right? Why don't you say 'good-bye,' and give me the fucking key to the fucking apartment, and get in your fucking car and go back to Sioux City?"

"I've had enough of your filthy talk, Mary Helen," Frank said glaring at her from his seat on the sofa.

"Fuck, fuck, fuck," she said spitting the words at him, holding on tight to her knees. She watched as Frank put the glass of Scotch on the table and unfolded his body from the tight crouch the low seat had forced upon him. As he stood, she had to lift her gaze. Shit. He was big. What was he going to do? A finger of fear touched the back of her neck.

Frank walked to the window seat and with a deliberate motion, took her jaw in his hand and squeezed her cheeks. "*Stop that*," he growled, bending over her, pulling her face up to his. "You sound like a whore. A cheap little whore."

His breath stank of Scotch. "Don't you DARE touch me," she hissed at him. Mahelly pushed his arm away, sprang up from the seat and walked to the bar. She clasped a glass in her hand, set it down hard on the bar surface, rummaged in the ice bucket with the tongs, breaking up the ice. She dropped three ice cubes in the glass, one at a time, wincing at the brittle sound. Now what? Now he was mad and he wasn't any closer to leaving than he had been before. She was getting frightened. Her hands were shaking. Where was Guy? She didn't want him to walk in on this. She splashed Campari into the glass. Club soda fizzed over the ice, lay in a bubbly layer on top of the vermilion liquid. She stirred the drink with a swizzle stick. She gulped it down as if it were cherry soda. Ask him to leave again. Try to be nice.

"Frank, I'm sorry I spoiled your surprise, but don't you understand? You don't live here anymore, and you caught me off-guard. We can talk, *should* talk some other time, but I'd like you to leave now. I'm expecting a guest."

"Oh, you have plans." He felt defeated. She had a date. He never thought of that. He never thought she would go out with anyone. But wait a minute. She didn't have a date. She'd called out Guy's name when he walked in the door. "But it's only Guy and Hanna, right? I'll come with you. They'd be glad to see me. It's been a long time."

"It's not exactly Guy and Hanna." Ow, she thought. The words "Guy and Hanna" reminded her of a couple who used to be her friends. They had been a happy couple made up of her best friend Hanna and a man she had waited years to meet—a man she loved. Now she thought of two people, two faces. When she thought of Guy's face, she saw it contorted in passion above her. She saw Hanna's face contorted in pain. Frank was speaking.

"Who exactly is it then, Mary Helen?"

"Guy. I'm expecting Guy to walk in any minute." Mahelly got up and went to the bar. She nervously poured herself another glass of Campari and soda. The ice crackled ominously in the glass. Maybe the glass would break. Don't push me Frank, she thought. Just get the hint and leave. That he was here was bad enough, but being here on her night with Guy, especially a night when she wanted everything to be calm and beautiful, was too much. On some other day or night, she might be more patient with Frank. But she hated him right now. She knew if Frank pushed her, she would tell him everything. She wanted to hurt him for breaking in on her now and for all the rest of it. Marrying her. Leaving her. Everything. She had so much pain and he didn't have any. He had a big-deal DJ job and his stupid green car, but he didn't have her. He didn't have his "little Bird."

"Guy?" Frank asked, standing up, walking over to the bar behind Mahelly. He couldn't resist touching her. He encircled her waist with his hands, bent down and kissed her neck. "I don't get it," he said.

His smell was so strong, his lips unwelcome and damp on her neck. Leeches, she thought. Her skin prickled. She shrugged out of his embrace. She could feel the dam breaking. She couldn't stop. She spun around to face him "I'm seeing Guy," she said. "*Dating* him."

Frank looked at her. He didn't understand what she was saying. "*What?*"

"I'm *dating* him. You know. Man. Woman. It's called 'dating.' "

Frank flicked the air with his hand, pushing aside the words, ignoring the sarcasm. "How far has this gone?" he asked. "Are you telling me you're sleeping with him?"

"That's right, Frank. He's my lover." She stared at him, defiantly.

Frank rocked on his heels, took a step back. He had never imagined Mahelly in bed with anyone. Anyone at all. And now she had gone to bed with another man, and it was Guy? "What's Hanna got to say about this?" he wondered out loud.

"It's a long story, but it's OK with her."

Jesus Christ, she was flippant with him about having a lover. Just like that. Cheating on him, and as far as she was concerned it was a long story she couldn't bother to tell. First she'd ridiculed him for his what? Romantic intentions. She'd called him a fool for trying as best he could to show her how much he still loved her and now . . . now she was telling him she was sleeping with another man! A man he knew as a friend. How casual. How hip! She'd turned into a regular New York City bimbo, hadn't she? His wife. His sweet little wife. Hanna had said it was OK? Hanna would. Typical bimbo thing to do. *"Well, I don't care that your bimbo friend said it was OK. You forgot to get my approval,"* Frank roared, grabbing Mahelly by the arm. If only he could take her in his arms and kiss her. If only he could hold her as he used to do, she'd stop saying all this stuff she was saying, and pay attention to him. She'd see that he was here and loving her. She'd stop this craziness with Guy.

Mahelly jerked her arm away and turned her back to him.

"Stop that," he shouted, grabbing her arm again, shaking it. The glass of bright fluid flew from her grasp and sprayed red all over the creamy white carpet, the creamy white sofa. It looked like blood.

"You stop!" Mahelly shouted back, pulling herself free. He was wrecking everything. He was wrecking her life. She hated him. He was coming at her with those arms again. He was trying to kiss her. Couldn't he see how much she hated him? *"Leave me alone! Just leave me alone!"* She struck out at his chest with her free hand. She hit him again.

"I'll leave you alone," he said grabbing her by the front of her robe and dragging her into him. Her body went rigid. He shook her hard back and forth, her head rocking violently in a beat with his words. *"I'll leave you alone when I'm good,"* he shoved her away still holding onto her robe, dragged her body toward his, *"and ready!"* With his last word, Frank seized Mahelly's shoulders with both hands and shoved her with all his strength into the wall.

Her head cracked against Sheetrock and she slid to the floor. Her pain alarm went on but did not register at the point of impact. The pain felt like rage.

"You bastard," she said quietly. *"You bastard,"* she said again. She viewed Frank's reactions in slow motion. She watched his hands return to his sides and his face change from anger, to fear, to concern.

"Bird," he said kneeling, stretching his hands to her face.

If he touched her, she thought, she would shrivel. She would die. She shrank from his touch. *"Don't.* Don't come near me."

"Bird, please. You're hurt." Blood was running out of her nose. Her robe had opened and he could see his fingerprints on her collarbone. He had to fix her back the way she had been. He had to touch her. He reached for her.

"I'll scream!"

"I'm not going to hurt you. I just want to help."

"Don't you dare touch me!" Frank looked stricken. What was wrong? She felt her nose running. She touched her hand to her nostrils. Blood. She looked down. Blood was dripping on her robe. It was everywhere. Frank was coming toward her again. She opened her mouth and screamed wordlessly. When she ran out of breath, she stopped. Then she screamed again.

Frank put his hands to his head and looked wildly around. He didn't know what to do. She was bleeding. She wouldn't let him touch her and the blood was all over her face. The screaming—it had to stop. He was getting frightened. She was hysterical. "Stop, Mahelly. Please stop fighting me. It's only me. I promise I'm not going to hurt you again."

"Bastard!" she cried. Oh, her head hurt. She wanted to put her head down on the floor and sob, but she couldn't. He was still here. "Go away! Just leave me *alone*."

She was screaming again. If only she would stop. He had never heard anything like the sound of her screams. He put his hands to her mouth. Her fists beat against him futilely.

Guy heard noises when he got out of the elevator. Someone was fighting. The sounds of screaming got louder as he got to the end of the hall. It couldn't be Mahelly. It was. She was being murdered!

The doorknob turned in his hand. It wasn't locked. What the hell was going on? He rounded the foyer wall and saw a man crouched over a pink heap. Mahelly!

"Hey!" he shouted. "Get away from her!"

The man turned, looked at his bloodied hands, cupped them over his eyes, and began to cry. The man was Frank. Guy stared and knelt beside Mahelly who was sobbing. "What's going on here?" he asked looking from Mahelly to Frank. "What's happened?"

"Guy," Mahelly said. "Guy."

"How badly do you hurt?" There was blood running down her chin.

"I'm OK, Guy. Nothing's broken." She struggled to sit, touched the back of her head and winced. She reached for him and he held her. She was shivering. He stroked her back and Mahelly began to weep. "It's OK, Mel. I'm here now. I'm taking care of you."

Mahelly buried her face in Guy's chest and let her tears flow. She took in big gasps of air through her mouth. Guy's here, she thought, consoled. Guy's taking care of me.

Guy rocked Mahelly as she cried in his arms. What had that ape done to her? There was a dent in the wall about five feet from the floor. Her head had made that dent. He'd thrown her into the wall. What else had he done? If he'd broken anything, if he'd, God forbid, seriously hurt her . . . "I'm calling an ambulance," Guy said into the room, "and then I'm going to kill you, Frank."

"I shoved her," Frank said blubbering. "I didn't mean it." There was blood on his face now, where he'd touched it with his hands. He looked as if he'd been in an accident.

"Guy. I'm OK," Mahelly said, holding Guy's arm as he started to get up. "It's just my nose."

"Are you sure?"

She nodded, an abbreviated movement. "I don't need a hospital, Guy. I just need you." She started to cry again.

"Shhhh," Guy said surrounding her with his arms. "I'm here. Lie back. Be quiet." He lowered her head and straightened her limbs. He rolled up his jacket and placed it under her neck. "Keep your head back and hold your finger under your nose."

Mahelly gulped air. She couldn't be still. She wanted to explain. She didn't want them to fight. "It's all over with me and Frank." She inhaled another shallow breath. Her teeth were chattering. "It shouldn't have taken all this, but it did. And I shouldn't have, but I told him about us," Mahelly said finally, pressing her finger again below her nose.

"Oh, brother," Guy muttered under his breath. He put a hand on Mahelly's forehead. He smoothed the hair away from her eyes. Guy looked at Frank. He looked pathetic. Whatever fury had come over him wasn't with him any longer. "Do you suppose you can find me a damp towel?" he asked Frank.

Frank went into the bathroom and returned with the towel. He held it as if it were an alien object, as if he'd never seen a towel before. Guy took it from him and sponged Mahelly's face. He took a tip of the towel and wiped each eyelid. He lifted her forefinger from her face; seeing the flow of blood had stopped, he took the fingers of both hands and cleaned them one at a time. He closed her robe gently and retied the sash.

Watching them, Frank was again overcome with remorse and sadness. They loved each other. He was nothing to her any longer. He sat down beside her and wept helplessly. His romantic fantasy was just as she had said it was. Completely his idea. It had nothing to do with her. No wonder she was so angry. It *was* over between them. Jesus. He hadn't cried in twenty years. Mary Helen. He wanted to touch her. He wanted to be forgiven.

Mahelly had never seen Frank cry before. He was speaking to her through his tears. "Bird, Bird, I didn't mean to do it," he said.

Mahelly touched her head. It hurt, but it hurt on the outside, not as if her skull were crushed. She looked at Frank, rocking, water dripping from his cheeks. Good, she thought, you deserve this. She found to her surprise she didn't mean that.

"I'm sorry, so sorry," he said thickly.

He was. She could tell. Something moved inside her. Something shifted. She felt sorry for him. He could be so thick, but he loved her. He loved her. And she had provoked him.

"Frank," she said. She slowly reached her hand into her pocket and pulled out a tissue. She touched it to his cheek.

"Frank," she said again. "I'm sorry too. I'm sorry I was so mean."

Guy looked at them. They should be alone for this. He draped the mohair blanket over Mahelly and looked into her eyes. "I'll be back," he said. He got up and went in to the bedroom. He needed to use the phone.

"I don't understand," Frank said sadly. "What happened to us?"

Her head hurt. She didn't want to talk, but if she didn't, she'd have to see him again. "Frank. Help me sit up."

"On the couch?"

"No. Here against the wall."

Frank lifted her back as she struggled to sit. She was dizzy, but this was better. She was OK. She pulled the blanket over her knees.

"Are you OK?"

"Uh-huh."

Frank put his back up against the wall too. They were sitting side-by-side. Mahelly took in a deep breath. "What happened to us was, you left me. That's what you did, no matter what you call it. We never talked about it. You took a job and you moved out." Mahelly dabbed at her nose with the towel. She wasn't bleeding any more.

"I wanted you to come with me. I *asked* you to come with me," Frank said with a crack in his voice.

"I couldn't go. I had my work and I would have hated Sioux City."

"You don't know for sure. You never gave it a chance."

"Frank, I have a business," she said tiredly. "I was finally feeling like a whole person."

"I wasn't. Feeling like a whole person."

"I know."

"Do you? I was working my butt off being a cruddy salesman and going nowhere, which I could have stood, but you . . ." Frank's voice cracked again and he stopped speaking. He swallowed. He put his hands through his hair. "But you weren't here any more. You didn't need me any more."

"I needed you, Frank. I just needed myself more. I needed to know what I could do on my own, not as just Mrs. Colucci."

"Just Mrs. Colucci?"

"Frank, you know what I mean. Not just a housewife with no kids, waiting to get old and dull." Her breath was running out. Please understand, Frank, she prayed. Please. I want to go to sleep with Guy next to me. "Listen," she said. "It didn't turn out so bad. Your leaving and me staying was the right thing for each of us. It just made being together impossible."

"You know, Mel, you say I left you, but I think you left me a long time before I went to Sioux City."

They were both quiet as they thought about what Frank had said. Mahelly finally nodded. Frank looked so miserable, so mournful sitting on the floor. She *had* left him. She had become a different person· from the one he had married. Frank hadn't changed though. He was the same man she had met when she was in college. "I guess I did leave you in a way."

Silence bathed them. They could hear Guy on the phone in the other room. Frank spoke.

"So is this it, Mary Helen? The end of the Mr. and Mrs. Colucci Show?"

"Yes. But don't think I won't miss your brown socks draped over everything, and hairballs in the drain."

Frank laughed.

"And pesto sauce on everything. And it's been quieter around here since WPOM went off the air."

"Do you still line up your toenail clippings on a square of tissue and wrap them up all neat before you throw them away?"

"Oh, Frank. You know that?"

"Sure." Frank grinned. He gave her a sidelong glance. "You get to know a girl pretty well when you live with her for more than a decade."

They basked gently in the silence. Mahelly touched her head and pain gripped her. It was getting stronger as the alcohol wore off. She couldn't hold the pain silently longer. She released a whimper.

"What can I do?"

"Nothing. Thanks. I'll just sit here for a while. Guy will be right back."

"Do you love him?" Frank pointed his thumb in the direction of the bedroom.

"Maybe. But it doesn't have anything to do with us."

Frank sighed. He wiped at his nose with the shredded tissue. A little piece of paper stuck to his nose. Mahelly touched it off.

"That separation talk. It wasn't because of Guy?"

"No. Please believe me, it was only because of us. We need to get divorced, Frank. Hanging on like this, we can't have free lives."

Frank grunted and ran his sleeve across his face. He took a deep breath and let it out. He looked at his wife. "I'll do whatever you want, Bird. If you'll forgive me for doing what I did."

"If you'll forgive me for doing what I did."

"If only I could hold you," Frank said sadly, tears filling his eyes.

Mahelly held out her arms.

Hanna blinked in the dark and tried to get oriented. It wasn't a dream. Guy had called and told her to come upstairs to Mahelly's apartment. He sounded urgent. Why? Had Mahelly done something? Said something? The wine she had drunk at dinner had left her dizzy. Dinner. David. Oh. She lifted the blanket. She felt cold air on her skin. She was naked. Where was her robe? She switched on the small lamp on her night table and looked around her bedroom. Clothes were heaped on every surface. The robe could be anywhere. Her nightgown was hanging on the footboard. Could she go up in that? Yeah. She put it on gingerly, pushing out the inside-out sleeves. They'd both seen her in her nightgown a million times. It was the elevator she had to worry about. If she got in the elevator in her nightgown, she'd run smack into Mick Jagger. No, George Bush. It was a guarantee. She put her door key in the nightgown pocket, pulled on her sweatsocks. She'd take the stairs. She went to the front door and had trouble with the knob. Stairs? Was she kidding? Eight flights up? She turned, went into the bathroom, used the toilet, and spotted her robe on the back of the bathroom door. Wrapping herself in it, she headed for the elevator.

The door to Mahelly's apartment was open a crack. Hanna pushed it open. Who was that? Frank. God. Guy had said Frank was there, but she hadn't gotten it. She saw Guy and Mahelly on the floor. She eyed them sideways.

"Hi, Frank."

"Hi, Hanna."

"Guy, Mel. What happened?" Mahelly was sitting up against the wall under a big dent. Guy had a bloody towel in his hand. There was blood all over Mahelly. Hanna went to her and got on her knees. How bad was this? She regretted the fight they'd had. Mahelly was as pale as a geisha girl. "What happened?" she asked again.

"Ask him," Guy said indicating Frank.

"Frank?"

"Hanna, no," Mahelly said softly. "Let him alone, Guy."

Frank looked miserable and embarrassed. Hanna had never seen him look so lost, so old. "I think I'll go, Bird, OK? You've got your friends here."

"I'll call you next week," she said.

"You'll call?"

"We have some things to discuss."

"Oh. OK. You'll be all right?"

"Yes. Don't worry."

Frank put his hands on his knees. " 'Bye, Bird," he said. She nodded carefully and smiled. He bent to kiss her cheek and she moved her mouth to his. It was a brief kiss, but it was a love kiss. They held one another for another moment before they broke their embrace. "I should go, right?" Frank asked again. She nodded. Frank got to his feet; looking once behind him, he slipped out the door. He closed it quietly, precisely, as if doing this exactly right would protect him from doing violence again as long as he lived.

220

"Hanna, give me a hand," Guy said, easing his hands under Mahelly's arms. Hanna couldn't figure out what to do, so she watched.

"Should we put her to bed?"

"That would be best. Can you manage, Mel?"

"Yes, slowly." Was he going to stay? No.

"We're getting divorced," Mahelly said to Hanna.

"I know," Hanna replied. "I know." She touched Mahelly's hair and opened the bedcovers so Mahelly could slide in.

"Wait. I need to soak my robe," Mahelly said holding it out in front of her for examination.

"Mel. Screw the robe," Guy said. "It's time for bed."

"It'll be ruined," she said pushing him away, untying her sash.

"Give it to me," Hanna said. "I'll do it."

"Hanna, it's nothing. It'll take me a second."

"Forget it," Hanna said, stripping it gently from Mahelly's arms.

"Will you be all right for a while without me?" Guy asked Mahelly.

"Are you coming back?"

"Of course. I want to talk with Hanna, but I'll be back in a little while."

Mahelly nodded.

"No, I *don't* understand, Guy," Hanna was saying. She poured Woolite into the sink, ran the cold water. She dunked the fabric a few times. The icy water felt good. The sensation of frigid fingers gave her something to think about other than what Guy had just said. The pink water swirled around her wrists. She ran clean water into the sink, rinsed her hands, dried them and walked stiffly out of the bathroom. She sat on the sofa and Guy followed her. "I *don't* see how bad this is. She's all *right*. She had a *nosebleed*."

"Hanna, I don't expect you to like this, but try to understand. It's more than a nosebleed. Frank used her head as a wrecking ball. She's getting divorced. She's been having a ridiculous relationship with me. I'm here one minute, gone the next. You two have fought. She has no one. I can't just leave her messed up like this. She's a *mess*. It's all a mess. And I have to get myself straightened out too."

"What? You're a mess too?"

"Yes, in a way I am. I love you, Hanna. I love you, but I have feelings for that person, too," he said pointing to the bedroom. "I want to resolve the confusion I'm having. I want to suspend the Tuesday night-Wednesday night deal we have and take Mahelly to the lake for the weekend.''

"You're asking me?" There was so much fear in her body, there was no room for air. She could hardly breathe. Guy was feeling sad and tender, and it wasn't for *her* pain. It was for Mahelly.

"I'm asking you to understand that Mahelly needs me badly."

"Don't you know *I* need you badly?" Her face crumpled. She didn't want to cry. She put her hand to her mouth.

Guy nodded. "I do. But I can't be with you both at the same time. Please understand. I have to do this."

Hanna stood and retied her robe. She felt nauseated. The wine was bitter acid in the back of her throat. She couldn't talk to him any longer. Too much again. She hurt too much and she had too much anger. "Do what you want, Guy," she said. She strode toward the door.

"Han, I'll call you tomorrow," Guy said behind her. She didn't acknowledge his statement. She walked out and slammed the door behind her.

24

HANNA'S HEAD HURT. SHE TURNED ON HER TYPEWRITER SO SHE
could pretend imminent productivity, but she couldn't work yet. With
the sound of her typewriter providing a comforting background hum,
she scrutinized the cover of the November issue.

"Winter Holidays" was the cover story, and the photograph on the
cover was of a predictably blazing fireplace, the backs of two huge
armchairs presented to the viewer with only the elbows and tops of
the heads of the chairs' occupants visible. The heads and elbows
belonged, presumably, to *U.L.*'s prototypical readers, "Urban Couple." Jennifer and Joshua were their shorthand names at *U.L.*, and
they were referred to frequently when story content was debated. "Jen
would never wear purple spangles, Matty, I swear," Hanna might say.
Or, "Do you think Jen and Josh would like a current listing of Sotheby's
antique valuations?" someone would ask. "Do you think Jen and Josh
will cough up three bucks for the December issue if 'Mansharing' is
in big purple letters across the cover?" David Stein had undoubtedly
wondered in his own way and decided capital Y, capital E, capital S.

Gee, Hanna thought wistfully. Here's an idea. How would Jen like
to share Josh with Mahelly? That would be a nice break. Come to
think of it, this fireplace scene could be Guy and Mahelly. At the lake.
Cut. Hanna cautioned herself. Cut it out. Do not think about that now.
Think about your job, Coleman, or you are going to have problems
that make this one look like a Sunday picnic in the park.

The November cover was so uninviting that Hanna hadn't opened the magazine when it flopped into her in-box an hour ago, but now, putting off the moment when she would actually have to work, she opened the book. She found her section in the table of contents and turned to it. It looked just as she thought it would. There was her by-line under the bold "UrbanWear" heading. There were the colorful playing-card-size photos along the left margin of the left-hand page and along the right margin of the opposite page. There was her copy, tra-la-la, unfurling in skinny pastel-colored ribbons across both pages of the double-page spread.

She sighed. She had been so bored a month ago. Fashion. Yechh. Boring, boring, boring. How she'd love to be bored now instead of sick to her stomach and scared all the time. Well, an opportunity to be bored was coming right up. She was shooting the December photos on Saturday and the shoot wasn't entirely organized. If she wanted to be bored, she would have to concentrate for another few hours and make sure the details were double checked. If she didn't go over everything herself, something would get fouled up and then she could get scared again. OK. Number one on the agenda today, make sure the shoot is buttoned down. And of course for the famous number two, she should spend a little time trying to write about the ever-present thousand-pound boulder on top of her head—the mansharing story. But how? She couldn't write it, and David wouldn't drop it. In fact, he had told her if she didn't have the story in in time for the editorial meeting on Monday morning, he was going to write it himself. What kind of threat was that? Would he really write her story? No. He'd trash it and pull out something he'd saved as a backup. Brian Atkins was probably writing a story right now on something really juicy. Pit bull fights in Manhattan. Earn stud fees in your own home. How to build seventeen major appliances in your spare time.

Hanna flipped pages carelessly, not reading, not absorbing anything. She found her fingers at the back of the book running down the column of personal ads.

"Sushi eater seeks slender sylph who eats same . . ." Pass, Hanna thought. B + for alliteration, D − for literacy.

"Toad, 32, never married, seeks princess any religion for kissing . . ." Pass.

A long, expensive ad was next. "Moral character is important to me. You should be a woman who has a strong self-image that you are proud of coupled with the courage necessary to act in a manner that confirms and reflects the values you believe in. I am a handsome entrepreneur who tries not to take himself too seriously. I run 65 miles weekly, teach at NYU, est graduate, psychoanalyzed, amateur cellist, co-author of well-known condo investment guide, involved father of three, looking for an intelligent, pure, robust, athletic woman, strikingly attractive in a wholesome way . . ." Hanna rolled her eyes and skipped to the next ad.

"Successful MD, 33, incurable romantic. Seeks urbane, multifaceted, professional female with a vivid imagination for strolling through porticos and gondola rides." Fine until the stroll through the gondola rides. Pass. The ad from the toad was starting to seem attractive. Don't worry about me, Guy. I've found a virgin toad to call my very own. God. It wouldn't come to that, would it?

Maybe she should run her own ad. How should it read? A poem. "Messed-up female, 34, former life was such a bore, lent her man to her best friend, seeks—da da, da da, da da, mend." No. Bend. Send. Oh. "Seeks way to get together again." The meter was crooked, but it would do.

Hanna slapped the magazine shut and stared at the snapshots she'd pinned to the wall in front of her desk last year. Four ignorant, happy faces smiled at her. There she was with Guy and Mahelly and Frank, all four draped over the deck railing of the beach house they'd shared, slick with suntan oil, healthy, innocent, bathed in that incredibly rosy, found-only-at-the-beach, summer sunset color. She wished she could go back in time and tell the Hanna of last summer to smarten up. Hang on to that good man, she'd say. She felt the inside of her nose prickling and if she didn't get control of herself, she was going to cry all over her desk.

Her phone rang.

"How are you?" David asked.

Hanna didn't say anything. She wasn't sure who was on the phone.

"It's David," he said.

"Oh. Hi. (David!) Fine, I guess. My head hurts."

"You drank a little wine last night. About a bottle."

Hanna let a little animal sound escape. Something between a grunt and a whimper. A whole bottle. Ow.

"Oh," she said.

"Hanna, I'd like to see you."

"Now?" Oh, God. She'd been fooled by his new friendly voice. She was in trouble. What had she said last night? Not that she would have something to show him? No. She told him the story stunk. Well, it did.

"No, not now. I thought we could have dinner tonight."

"Oh. David, I haven't anything else to show you yet." She wasn't going to write about that nightmare in Mahelly's apartment no matter what he threatened. God. If only it had been a nightmare.

"I'm asking you to dinner, Hanna. I'm not saying we won't kick around a few ideas about your story. We need a few."

Hanna laughed nervously.

David continued. "But this is dinner, not work. I want to see you."

He wanted to see her again! She wasn't just Coleman-the-delin-quent-writer to him. He was asking her out. A date. Even though she'd been dumb and drunk. That kiss. Damn. He liked her. He did. So there, Guy. Somebody wants me and he's not a toad. He's David, drum roll, Stein. Yeah. "I'd like to see you too," she said softly into the phone.

"I know tonight isn't one of your nights off but . . ."

"Don't worry about that," she interrupted quickly. It *wasn't* one of her so-called nights off, but the Tuesday-Wednesday deal was "suspended," Guy had said.

"Good. I'm expected at a gallery opening in Soho. Why don't I pick you up at your place at around eight? We'll go to the opening, and then we'll eat downtown."

"OK. Sure," she said. "See you later." Red Vittadini dress, she thought. Black patent leather Maud Frizons.

"Nan, I want to talk to you," Guy's voice said into the earpiece. Hanna held the receiver away, and then brought it back to her face.

"Go ahead."

"Not on the phone. In person. Tonight. I'm not happy about leaving while you're so mad at me."

"So, don't go. You don't have to go." She twiddled a pencil. She knew what he would say and he said it.

"Hanna. I do. Can we have dinner tonight? We'll go out."

"I can't tonight. I've made other plans."

"But Hanna, I'm leaving tomorrow night and when I get back from the lake, I have to fly out to Chicago. Can't you change what you're doing?"

"No. I'm having dinner with David."

"Again? David? Is this David Stein the monster we're talking about here?"

"He's not a monster."

"Oh." Jeez, she was cold. OK, she was furious. He couldn't really blame her. Taking Mel away to the lake, good reason aside, was inflammatory. Why *was* he taking Mahelly away? He wondered suddenly. Was Hanna right? Mel *could* survive without spending the weekend with him. Hey, he felt a little responsible for that pounding she'd taken at Frank's hands. It was crazy for Mel to have told Frank about him, it really was, and surely that pushed Frank over the edge. Was he just assuaging his conscience because of that? Was he deliberately trying to hurt Hanna? Come on, Guy, he counseled himself. You don't have to look for motives here. Fuck it, his instincts were right to take Mel away. She needed him. He still didn't like leaving Hanna feeling as angry as she was. After he got back from his weekend with Mel, he wanted to address his relationship with Hanna minus the entanglement with Mahelly. Also, he didn't like the sound of this "dinner with David" crap. That man wasn't trustworthy. Not a bit. And Hanna was no match for him. David Stein and his lovely, soft Hanna. Made him shiver to think about it. But what could he do?

"Hey, Nan. I don't trust that guy. Don't do anything rash, OK?"

"Have a great weekend, Guy," Hanna said sweetly and, without waiting for a reply, hung up the phone.

Hanna contemplated the now quiet phone. She was glad she hung up on Guy. What nerve, telling her not to trust David! She needed Guy and where was he? How generous of him to sandwich her in tonight between his date with Mahelly last night and his weekend with her starting tomorrow. Did she really deserve this treatment for making one cruddy, innocent(!) mistake after two years of bliss? No, she didn't! Fuck you, Guy. Fuck you, fuck you, fuck you! Hanna cocked her leg and kicked at the garbage can under her desk, and it dented with a satisfying crunch.

"Are you all right in there Hanna?" Kathy called over the partition.

"Fine, Kathy. Thanks."

Hanna drummed her fingers and hurled angry thoughts against the walls, wishing they were paperweights. Well, if she couldn't have her old life back the way it had been, maybe she could have a better life. A life starring a tall handsome editor of a national magazine who could have dinner with any woman in the universe and wanted to have dinner with her. Fate, that's what this was. A date with Fate. No blue pencil tonight. No sandwich between Mahelly and Mahelly. She was going out into public with David Stein. There would be someone there from *WWD*. Probably a photographer from the *Post*. She could be on Page Six tomorrow. She was up for it. She would be.

The sun was going down over the trees in Central Park. The air was cool, not cold, and Mahelly was wearing heavy-duty sweats and sitting against a rock. The sky was turning colors not unlike the colors of the bruises on her arms and shoulders, although there was a touch more pink in the sky. A soft breeze riffled through her fuzzy curls. It was a friendly breeze and Mahelly felt more peaceful than she had felt in years.

She closed her eyes. It was so dear of Guy to take her away for the weekend. He was the nicest man in the world. But no matter how nice he had been to her, she knew affection was the most he felt for her. Her heart hurt as she held this thought, but hold it she must. She had to face it and put hope away. Guy didn't love her, would never love her. She had gotten exactly what she had bargained for and the trouble that had resulted, her breakup with Hanna, the ugly fight with Frank, were the fruits of a relationship that was just plain wrong.

That knock on the head had been good for her, she knew. It broke something. Changed something. Not that Frank should be excused, but she found she really wasn't angry at him any more. She'd been angry at him for too long; and for what reason? For just being the person he was. Now she could let go. She didn't need the anger any longer. She wanted to be clean.

Letting Guy go had to be accepted too. She was going to learn to be a woman without a man and she was going to do a better job of it this time around. It would be nice to be with Guy over the weekend though. They could spend the time relaxing with one another and saying good-bye. She wanted to catch up on the parts of his life he hadn't had time to share with her. She wanted to tell him how important he'd been to her, and then she would like to be a real friend to him again. She hadn't been that in a long time. Then on Monday she'd call Hanna and try to see her. She missed Hanna terribly.

Where the sun had been was now just an inky pinky-blue stain in the sky. Mahelly got slowly and painfully to her feet. She'd go home and get a good night's sleep. When she got up tomorrow, she'd pack. There would be plenty of time. They would be leaving after lunch sometime and would be at the lake this time tomorrow night. Then they'd have Friday night and Saturday night and part of Sunday together. She would try to heal very fast.

Guy riffled through the stack of bound papers on his desk. The damned Market Planning Meeting was on Monday, and his morale, energy and ambition were in the cellar. Hanna and Mahelly. Mahelly and Hanna. Thank God for Courtney. She'd clipped the important material for him and since he wasn't having dinner with Hanna tonight, he might as well go home early and give this stack of crap a good read.

He squared the edges of the papers, put a new battery in his pocket calculator and threw all of it into his briefcase. Without asking his permission, his fingers went to the phone and dialed a familiar number.

"Bo. Hey, buddy. Want to go out for a couple of brews?" There was no point in trying to cram a dead brain, Guy reasoned, locking his office door. If he and Bo had a nice loose evening, he'd probably be able to puzzle this whole mess out.

Courtney patted dark green mud on her face. She ran the tea bags under cold water, squeezed them out, eased herself into the steaming bath water and when the bags were in place, molded them against her eyelids. She patted the surface of the water with her fingertips and teased herself with her favorite notion. She was going to get this man where she wanted him and then she was going to do him in. And there was nothing he would be able to do about it.

Wasn't it amazing? She'd asked him to marry her, and he had said no. No, after nineteen months of passion and being vulnerable, and having everyone in the office know what she was feeling. No, after he had met all of her friends and her parents. What could be more rejecting than that? Then that dope actually believed she would forgive him as though nothing had happened. Amazing. It had been a special kind of thrill to tug him into bed. She had crooked her finger and said pretty please, and he had dropped his trousers. Weren't men simple?

Courtney lifted the tea bags from her eyes and dropped them in the trash. She stood in the tub and scrubbed her skin in long upward strokes with a loofah mit. When her skin was pink and tingling, she released the bath water and turned the shower on hard and hot. Guy was different now, she thought. Softer than he'd been. This was good. She was going to do something really big to him in the one place she owned him—H & G. She wasn't sure how or what she was going to do exactly, but she loved considering the possibilities. It would be something very graceful, very subtle, but it would be something everyone would know about. Whatever she did, she would be protected from him should he try to retaliate. They loved her out in Chicago. They loved her at the agency. She was a star. In fact, if he didn't watch his ass, she would get his job.

Courtney stepped from the tub, toweled herself, wrapped her hair, took her kimono from the hook behind the door and slipped it on. She took small pots, jars, a bottle of oil into the bedroom, and spread a towel over the flowered comforter. She combed back her hair. She shook baby oil on her feet and massaged her toes, then she put the bottle on the night table.

From where she was sitting on the bed, Courtney could see herself reflected in the cathedral-shaped vanity table mirrors. Her short silk kimono was open, revealing long, straight limbs. She stopped massaging her toes to stare at her image. She was beautiful. Her wavy blonde hair, combed back, wet, fell below her shoulders. The bones in her face were sharp, her lips, large and soft, her pale greeny-gold eyes, complemented by the watery green silk robe, looked huge. She dusted bronze powder on her cheekbones with a soft brush, then dipped the brush to the valley between her breasts and dusted there too. She knew some women had good days and bad ones. Courtney didn't want bad days, or even bad moments. She liked to be prepared for anything. She was having dinner with good old Charlie Jackson this evening. They'd discuss the upcoming Plans Meeting and she'd pick up a few ideas. Afterwards, maybe she'd sleep with Charlie for old time's sake. One hand washing the other.

I'm scared, Hanna thought to herself with surprise. Today, still angry with Guy, she had made a date with a handsome, confident man whose perfectly timed phone call rescued her from the bleak prospect of her life without Guy. Now, standing before the bathroom mirror wiping mascara from her eyes, preparing for the evening ahead, Hanna wondered what she thought she was doing going out on a date with her boss. The lunches and dinners she'd had with David recently had blurred the usual sharp line between superior and subordinate and overrode what should have been her instinctive response to his invitation as well. When he asked her out, she should have said no. She hadn't put "don't go out with your boss" on her old, tattered don't list, but then it had never come up before. David was the first man she'd ever worked for. "Don't go out with your boss" belonged on that list, she was sure, even if your boss is the most eligible bachelor in the northeastern United States. But. On the other hand. What about fate? What about how her body had responded to his kisses? What about that?

All right, she thought in the shower. A date is just a date, she decided, shaving her legs. I'll be a woman on a date with a man. I'm not going to bed with him. She rinsed the razor, soaped her underarms. I'm going to enjoy myself tonight. There's no reason to be nervous. She stepped out of the shower and dried herself. I'm going to an art exhibit and out to dinner with a man who likes me. She creamed her skin and when her face was a satin canvas, she stroked colors on her cheeks and eyes. She stretched black-dotted hosiery with elastic tops over her calves and thighs and slipped into sublimely silky underpants and matching bra. She sprayed Ralph Lauren's scent in the air and walked through the damp cloud so that the fragrance clung to every part of her.

How long had it been since she had last dressed her best? Months, surely. She was going to be seen tonight and she wanted to be gorgeous. This evening with David would be fun. She wouldn't let it go too far. If things fell apart with Guy, well then maybe she could consider having a relationship with David, but not now. Too risky twelve ways. So why am I so nervous? she asked herself, stepping into the black patent leather high-heeled shoes. What's the worst thing that could happen? She saw herself clasped in his fist. Fay Wray and King Kong. Stupid girl, she chided herself, he's not going to ravage you. Love me, David, sang a silent soprano voice. Please. Hanna threw her glorious auburn hair forward, brushed it hard, and flung it back so that it was fuller with more mass. Then she slid the red knit dress over her body, feeling it settle into place with a satisfying whoosh. She hooked a black snakeskin belt around her waist. Its smooth silver buckle clicked and caught. She adjusted the dress's voluminous cowl neck until it presented the perfect frame for her face, she pushed the sleeves up to her elbows, and last, clipped black metal disks onto her earlobes. She stood back from the full-length mirror. She looked like a flame. She looked on fire. And she looked worried. "Relax, Hanna," she said to her reflection. Then the buzzer buzzed.

25

THE LIGHT INSIDE THE HORNE GALLERY WAS DAZZLING. IT BOUNCED off the white walls and formed lucent lakes on the gleaming wooden floors. The moving colors and shapes inside the huge open space were kaleidoscopic. It was impossible to absorb and decipher everything she saw from the entrance, but Hanna tried.

As she looked around the room, even Hanna Coleman, *U.L.*'s Fashion Editor, thought the quality and variety of clothing styles worn by the guests remarkable. There were plaids mixed with prints, electric-colored tunics over painted hosiery, neon-colored shoes, somber three-piece suits and penny loafers, prom dresses, short-short skirts, huge overshirts and jackets, some buttoned to the adam's apple, some swinging away from the body, casually exposing breasts as they did so.

Don't look as if you've never seen this before, she said to herself. You've been to a million openings just like this. But never with David Stein, some other self answered back. It made a difference. It did. Walking through the gallery, her arm linked through David's, Hanna felt proud and perfectly escorted. David was wearing black tie. She was wearing body-hugging flame-red mohair and three-hundred dollar shoes. Individually, they looked sensational. Together they looked regal. They couldn't have been better matched. He smiled at her and winked. She smiled back shyly. Could he tell the side of her body that touched his felt to her as if it had hot little bugs traveling under the skin? Was he feeling it too? She had never felt this particular feeling with Guy. Never. Was that good or bad? She squeezed his arm against her body and looked around the room.

There were people here she knew from other places, other times. Hanna left David's side and flirted with Woolsey from Lauder, Weber from the *Voice*, but she quickly returned to David. Being in public with him made her see something new. This was a life she could have. She could be walking always arm-in-arm with this handsome, important man in an environment filled with exciting people. This had been her college fantasy! Exactly.

Hanna watched how David handled himself, how easily he moved in the crowd, how many people wanted to speak with him, even simply to shake his hand. The part of him she had seen at the office, the despot, had vanished. Here, his power was transmuted into charm; his tyrannical nature into easy confidence. Who could resist David Stein's alchemical transformation to a social self? David touched the arm of a woman and Hanna watched the woman turn toward him, preen under his gaze. Hanna remembered David's fingers moving slowly over her breasts and involuntarily, she gasped.

Stop, Hanna, she commanded herself. Grow up. Tonight is simply an evening out—an art exhibit and dinner, remember? She would not go all girlish and stupid. She couldn't let him know how much she desired him, how weak she felt. She had to keep herself under control. David was exciting but dangerous, and as long as she was in love with Guy, sex with David was crazy and wrong. Hanna sipped at her plastic glass of white wine, being very careful not to drink too much. It took so little to get her drunk. She had to, no matter what, stop being so flaky around him. She must try to be a little sophisticated for a change.

Hanna shifted her focus, stepped forward, and squinted at one of the enormous oils. Officially called "Intergalactian Sexual Responses," quickly dubbed "Space Sex," by *Interview*, the huge ten-foot by twelve-foot canvases were tangles of not quite human beings engaged in sexual play. To show that the beings were alien was what had made the possibilities so rich for the artist. In this, one of the largest paintings, two male figures embraced, their skins iridescent, the slightest suggestion of scales on their thighs and hands, translucent fins sprouting from their spines. It was their state of sexual arousal that was making Hanna squint. She was standing too close to the open-mouthed baby yellow kisses. She could almost smell the streams of pearly sweat running from downy yellow underarms, touch the half-closed golden eyes. The whole damned exhibit made her uncomfortable.

"What do you think?" David asked when he found Hanna standing before a fourteen- by twenty-foot depiction of a tentacled *ménage à quatre*.

"I'm not sure, but I think I know this guy from somewhere," she said pointing to one of the beings in the foreground. She looked up at David's surprised face and laughed. "No, seriously, it's interesting," she said. "I sort of like them," she lied.

"Really, I would have thought this work a little too, ah, vivid for you."

"Not at all, David," said cool Hanna. "It's just sex with a few extra parts, that's all. What do *you* think of the work?"

"It's hard for me to be, ah, objective. I know some of the models. Which painting do you like the best?" he asked, turning into the room.

"I guess that one," Hanna said pointing to a rather small painting of a womanish creature.

The painting was hanging on a wall by itself. The subject of the painting had her back to the viewer, but she had been caught looking behind her as if she had been called and had turned her head. The face was in three-quarter view. A patch of lavender fur started at her eyelid and continued upward, merging with her hairline. Her hair was a braided rope of purple and blue and gold and it hung to the small of her perfectly formed back. Her skin was faintly gilded where light struck, and in places where there was shadow—the indentation of her spine, under the ledge of her jaw—lavender fur gleamed. Her expression was anticipatory, mischievous. Her eyes flirted with the viewer. "Look at me," they said, and Hanna looked. In the background another creature, male and shadowy came toward her. There was something so engaging about this painting, so familiar, Hanna almost felt she knew the subject; felt she had seen her before.

"That's my favorite too," David said. "In fact, it's mine."

"Really?" Hanna exclaimed. Yow, how about that? Good guess, she congratulated herself. "Do you know the model?"

"Mmm," David acknowledged.

"Yes," said a brassy female voice behind Hanna. "It really captures 'Randa, don't you think?" The woman, fiftyish, wearing a man's white shirt and blue velvet painter's overalls, smiled at David and moved on without waiting for an introduction.

"Who was that?" Hanna asked, disturbed, feeling a jab she didn't understand.

234

"The artist," David said, irritation in his voice.

"Well," said Hanna, watching the woman until she was out of sight. "Who's 'Randa?"

"It's Miranda. Friend of mine."

Oh. She'd almost seen it. Now it was obvious. Miranda Wu. The newscaster. What kind of friends were she and David? She started to ask, but stopped herself. They would be lovers, of course. She saw the scowl in David's expression. Were they still? Don't get possessive for God's sake, Hanna, she cautioned herself. Anyway, how close could they be? She was here with David and Miranda Wu was not. David had put his arm around her and squeezed her. She turned to him.

"How about dinner?" he asked. "Are you hungry?"

"Not very," she said. She couldn't realistically consider the concept of food consumption. She still felt the lingering effects of the wine last night, and the fight with Guy, and anxiety about what would happen next with David. She was a walking "before" for an antacid demonstration, she thought. She asked. "Are you starving?"

"I can wait. Why don't I fix us something light at my place. We'll have a drink and go out for dinner later on." It wasn't a question, Hanna noticed.

The car was two blocks away. As they walked, David surrounded her shoulders with his arm. He asked, "Your story aside, how's your mansharing arrangement coming along? Any improvement?"

Why did he want to know? "Why do you ask?"

"I care about you, Hanna. I want to know how you are."

"It's perfect," Hanna said in a self-mocking tone. She snuggled in closer to David's body, protecting herself against the chill air. She didn't know what to do with her hands so she used them to tick off items off on her fingers. "One, Guy is mad at me for getting him to do it so he's taking it out on me by being hostile. Two, there's less of him to go around these days. Three, Mahelly has fallen in love with him so four, I can't be close to her anymore because hearing about how she loves him hurts so much I want to kill her. It's just perfect," she concluded, smiling brightly into David's face. "That's the story you are looking for, isn't it David?" she asked facetiously.

"Go on, Hanna. I sense you've left out a few more fingers."

Hanna sighed. Might as well give it all. "You'd like more? Five." She made a fist and stuck her thumb in the air. "Guy and I aren't as close as we used to be. There are new areas now that are private." She looked at David, and put her arm around his waist. "He considers his relationship with Mel too intimate to discuss, which I have to admit is pretty honorable of him." She dropped her gaze and watched where she was putting her feet. "This weekend he's going away with her and the truth is, at this moment she needs him more than I do."

"Why is that?"

"Oh," Hanna said sadly. "I didn't tell you. Mahelly's husband dropped by her apartment last night unannounced and before he left he bounced her off the wall."

David winced. "Because of Guy?"

"Not really, but it was probably a factor."

"Is she all right?"

Hanna nodded and sighed deeply. David walked her around to the passenger side of the car and unlocked the door for her. She got in.

The darkness in the Bentley was comforting. The motor was purring and the car was vibrating a little bit. The car was resting on the incline to an underground garage. David had gotten out to discuss something with the attendant and Hanna hoped he wouldn't hurry back. She pulled her sleeves down to her wrists to warm herself and crossed her arms over her chest. She was glad for the few minutes alone so she could think. Talking about Guy had cooled her passion for David briefly, but it had also revived her feelings of loneliness and fear of losing Guy. Now, poised on the brink of David's apartment, she could feel herself weakening. Could she keep the evening free of sex? She wanted to be held badly. She wanted to feel loved and desired. Hey, Guy, she thought, I *want* to do something rash. What about it, Hanna Louise? she challenged herself. Can you have a simple one-night fling with David and then work for him as if nothing had happened? Could he? If only she didn't have to make a decision. If only David . . . A fantasy intruded into her thoughts; David holding her, kissing away her protests, telling her everything would be all right, that he cared for her . . . She put a hand to her mouth. Oh. God. Could he care? And what about *her* feelings? His looks, his worldliness, his undeniable masculine power, made him exciting to her. But was there a tender side to him that she could love? Wait, she cautioned herself. Wait until you know.

A sound broke through her reverie. Hanna became alert. She heard David's voice amplified by the hollow concrete cavern of the garage. The attendant followed David to the car. Hanna and David got out and walked two blocks to his apartment building. They walked through the tiled lobby into the wood-paneled elevator cage. At the twenty-second floor, the operator opened the gate. David opened his front door and Hanna stepped into a marble foyer.

The living room was stupendous. Huge arched windows bordered one side of the room that opened out onto a terrace, and beyond that, darkly, silently, flowed the East River. Hanna noticed the parquet floor was stained green—just stained, so the wood grain showed through. There was a fireplace in the center of a black marble wall which rose to a ceiling that looked to Hanna to be fourteen feet high. In front of the fireplace was a plum-colored Chinese rug splashed with woven sprays of flowering branches. On it was a black leather chaise. The lighting was dim and indirect, glowing from behind cut-glass sconces. Large abstract paintings hung on the walls. No wonder he liked my apartment so much, Hanna thought wryly. It looks like his.

David left Hanna in the living room. She could hear him in the kitchen, could hear the sound of plates clashing together. She followed the sound until she found herself surrounded by blue tile and bright light.

"Look at this," he said, unwrapping a blue-veined cheese and placing it on a platter. "Stilton. And taste this," he said, slicing a thin circle of savory sausage and putting it in her mouth.

"Mmm."

"Good?"

"Uh-huh."

"Champagne?" he asked, arranging powdery crackers next to the cheeses and sausages.

"Great."

David opened a bottle, put it on the tray with the small feast, said, "I think you'll like this. Grab those glasses, will you?" He walked past Hanna to the living room. The chaise stretched elegantly across the space before the fireplace. It was wide enough for two, and David indicated she should go there and she did. He put some spacy electronic music on the stereo, poured two glasses of Champagne, handed them both to Hanna and moved a glass table over to the chaise.

"A fire. We need a fire," David said without looking at Hanna.

"That would be nice," she said, gripping her glass. A fire and a little hug were what she needed. Nothing would be wrong with a little hugging, she thought. She ached everywhere.

David lit a match to the neat pyramid of logs and paper stacked in the hearth. When he was sure the fire had caught, he sat near Hanna, removed his shoes and hers, and reclined.

237

"Taste the wine," he said. "It's a good vintage."

The Champagne *was* good. She sipped, then she drank, letting the effervescent liquid fill her mouth. David refilled her glass. He hadn't touched her. Would he? She lay next to him, feeling his warmth along the length of her, wanting to snuggle close to him, not daring to. Her stockinged foot nudged David's. Oh. She hadn't meant that. She hadn't meant to touch him. He took the glass from her and put it on the table with his. He turned to her and, surrounding her with his arms, brought her to him. Hanna was afraid to look in his eyes. The whole lower half of her body was in flames. He would know. She raised her eyes. His kiss was gentle at first, then less so. Hanna struggled as his tongue probed, pried, called her bluff. Hanna felt her resolve to be in control this evening melt away as her body fought her mind's desire to be chaste. She thought her breath must be steaming. A whimper escaped her throat. She couldn't call it back. If she was going to stop this, it would have to be now.

"Are you warm?" David asked, his face inches from hers. He lifted damp hair from her face.

"No."

"That's what I thought. Much too warm." He put his hand on Hanna's leg and pushed her dress to her waist.

"Lovely," he said, placing his hand under the elastic top of her stocking and stretching it.

"No, David," she said. "Stop."

"How? How can I stop?" he asked, running his hand the whole inner length of her thigh, from knee to the very soft skin above her stocking. "Do you know how often I've thought of touching you this way?"

Hanna's fantasy of being taken, of not having to make a decision, came back to her. This was what she had imagined. But this was becoming real. If David were only a handsome stranger—but in fact, he was not. She worked for him and she had to be responsible; responsible for how their relationship might change; responsible for her commitment to Guy. "Please. I can't." She pulled down her skirt, swung her feet to the floor. She covered her face with her hands. "I'm sorry," she said.

David shifted his position, sat next to her. He touched her back, rubbed her, soothed her. He said, "Hanna. Look at me."

She shook her head and looked at the floor.

"Look at me," he said again.

She turned to him. She knew he would see her conflict; see how weak she felt. She wanted to look away, but he held her gaze.

"I like to think I can read people pretty well." He paused. "You want me to make love to you. Don't you?"

Hanna shook her head once, almost imperceptibly, no. There were tears in her eyes. "No," she began. "I mean, I want to, David, but this would be a mistake."

"I don't understand."

"I'm angry at Guy. That's a bad reason to, to, get involved with you."

"That felt like real passion a minute ago."

"I know. It was." She looked at him for a brief instant and then looked away. "I want to wait."

"Do you think I don't care about you? Is that it? I do."

Too much. Hanna felt hot tears running down her face. She covered her eyes. She gulped and breathed hard. She did not want to cry here. Not with David. "Sorry," she squeaked. "I'm sorry."

"It's all right," he said.

David gave his handkerchief to Hanna. He watched her blow her nose, dab at her eyes. She held the crumpled handkerchief in her lap and looked at him. Her chest was heaving. He had never seen Miranda cry. Not once. God, Hanna was appealing. She made him think about fruit somehow. Plums. Soft, satiny, very sweet. Hanna. Even her name was soft. She would be soft and sweet to her center. He would have to turn her a little bit, warm her up again, reassure her. Soft women like Hanna never knew how beautiful they were. Had the boyfriend told her lately? Probably not. Guy had left an opening for him, and if he just moved slowly and carefully, he would be deep in plum nectar tonight. She already knew how much she was going to love it with him, but she was fighting it. He would have to get her to relax.

"You don't have to apologize for anything," David said. He smiled at her, ruffled her hair. He went to the fireplace and poked at the logs. He opened a box on the mantel. Hanna watched him light a thin cigarette. He came back to the chaise and lay down again. "Lie back," he said. "We'll be quiet together for a little while. Then I'm taking you out to dinner."

Hanna looked at him. His arms were open to her. Was it safe? She swung her legs back onto the chaise. She turned toward him, and as he slipped his arm under her neck and around her shoulder, she tentatively rested her face on his hard chest.

"You understood me, David. Didn't you?"

"Shhh. Don't worry anymore. The grass will give us an appetite and then we'll go. Have some of this."

Hanna inhaled the marijuana, exhaled, and touched her face to David's stiff shirt. She put her hand on his chest. The cloth was so starched, her fingers made whispery sounds as she moved them tentatively across a small expanse of his chest. Damp paper touched her lips. She inhaled. As she exhaled, her breath followed an electronic note that sailed above her, reverberated against the windowpanes. She inhaled again. And again.

David kissed her forehead. It was a warm kiss and he held his lips to the tender spot for a long time. She liked the feeling of that kiss. It was an affectionate kiss. She tilted her head to him and smiled. He smiled back. His look crossed her face, taking in her mouth, each eye, her hair. He put a hand to her face, touched her earlobe with his thumb. He slipped an earring off. The other followed. She heard them clatter on the glass table. Hanna's smile disappeared. A thrill shot through her. She looked at his face so near her own. She knew his face and yet she didn't know it at all. She raised her hand and hesitantly touched his hair. It was so thick and dark. She closed her eyes. This movement took a very long time. David brought his mouth to hers and kissed her.

When David kissed her, Hanna felt her mouth expand. It was a forever kind of kiss. It was a kiss made up of many parts and she could almost name them. It was a kiss that had nothing to do with any part of her body below her head. She felt whiskers sanding her chin. She moved her tongue into the warm mouth connected to hers and felt it grow fatter and fuller as it slicked across the edges of his teeth. She felt David's hands moving over her body. So loving, so warm. She was in a soft red cocoon. She didn't want to stop this kiss of many parts, but she had to so David could pull her dress over her head. The neckline caught the bottom of her nose and hurt, and then it was off. She was briefly aware that her bra had melted away, and then she felt her breasts being warmed in Guy's, no, David's hands. Her nipples tightened and then her mouth and his were one again. She was free. Her body was floating, flowering, aching. She opened her mouth wider and swallowed him, drank deeply.

"You are magnificent," David said, lying beside her, propping himself up with one arm. "Absolutely magnificent." He shook his

240

head slowly. He reached out a hand to touch the soft skin of her throat, her breasts. He touched her lightly with the palm of one hand. Moving his hand slowly downward, David skimmed the surface of her body, touching just the pale hairs on her body, brushing the darker, tighter curls, lingering a moment. She was so wet. He teased her gently, gently. He heard her gasp. Good. Make her commit. Ask her.

"Do you want me, Hanna?"

"Please," she said. "Please."

He stood with his back to the flames, his shadow falling across her. He would have preferred to take her to the bedroom, but he didn't trust her mood. She was vulnerable, almost too much so. If he waited too long, she might change that yes to no. He wished the air were a little warmer, that the tape hadn't run out. Too bad but he couldn't count on her. Stay with me, Hanna, he thought. Stay warm. Damn. The phone was ringing. Talk to her, he thought, as he removed his tie, his shirt.

Hanna felt suddenly chilled. David was standing between her and the fire so that it no longer warmed her. She hugged herself. She became aware that there was no music in the room. The tape had ended. A phone rang in another room; a quiet ring, asking a question, not demanding attention. David ignored it. It stopped. Should she stop too? She lost the thought.

"You are absolutely beautiful, Hanna," she heard him say. "Truly remarkable." His words washed over her and she shivered. Being the sole object of David's attention was almost more than she could bear. He would be touching her again. "Please," she said. She watched as David pulled his tie from his collar. She watched him as he unbuttoned his shirt, unfastened the hook in his pants. He wore nothing under his pants. He was standing before her, the flames seeming to lick his back, throwing red and gold lights on her body. He was to Hanna as handsome naked as he was clothed. The hair on his chest covered his body in one smooth pelt past his navel, and she thought, although she couldn't look, that the fur covered his body down to his toes.

"My God, I want you so badly," she heard him say as he stretched next to her. She kissed him. She drank him. She sucked gently on his tongue. So much better than food. She put her head on his chest. Could she sleep here? "Touch me, Hanna." His voice was deep and it echoed. She reached for him. He was so hard! She couldn't open her eyes. She felt the velvet of his chest hair on her breasts, the feelings of warmth and abandon as he stroked her thighs and between them. She was in the sky being made love to by butterflies.

"Open up, Beauty," he murmured. "Let me in."

She opened herself to him entirely. He entered her so slowly, she couldn't wait for him. Grasping his buttocks she pulled him into her. How good he felt. How strong. She pulled at him hungrily. She couldn't have enough of him. More, she thought. More. And then, weightless, she came.

Without realizing she had slept, Hanna found herself awake. She wasn't home. The darkness here was not really darkness at all. Skylight came in through the huge vaulted windows and lit the room with a pale glow. Oh, God. David was lying half on her body, his head on her breasts. He was sleeping.

Hanna nestled her face in his hair and tried to find comfort. His hair was not Guy's hair, not soft like Guy's. Guy was a bigger man, really, rounder, more solid. Guy. Hanna stared at the ceiling lit by a violet sky. Who was this man she had slept with? She still didn't know. She wanted to be with Guy. And Guy wanted to be with Mahelly! She had to go home. She patted David's back, and when he rolled off her body, she sat, bent, felt for her clothing. She touched the red dress and put it on her lap. She needed her underthings. She needed herself.

"Are you going?"

"Yes."

"Are you upset with me?"

She shook her head no. David sat up and put an arm around her. "Tell me what's wrong."

She didn't answer. She was afraid to speak, afraid she would sob uncontrollably if she did.

David rubbed her shoulder and touched her hair. "My, my, Hanna," he said at last. "You certainly aren't the happy girl you used to be. You haven't had much fun lately, have you?"

Hanna squeezed her eyes shut. No, she hadn't had much fun lately. When had she last heard the sound of her own laughter? She had to leave. If she stayed any longer, she would break. "I'm so tired, David," she said, disengaging herself from his embrace. She stood, put on her clothes, her shoes. "I have to go home now."

"No dinner?"

"Not tonight."

"Well, all right. I'll drive you home."

"No, thanks." She just wanted to be alone. "It's easy to catch a cab."

"If you're sure." He pulled on his trousers and walked her to the front door. Don't brood, Hanna, he thought. Don't hold this against me. He opened the door, folded her hand into his and held it. "Hanna. I want you to come over on Saturday after your shoot. Will you do that? I'll think of something to make you happy. I want to see you smile."

"OK," she said. Saturday was forever away. She could think about it later. Right now, she just wanted to leave. She felt awful and knew she looked worse. "We should wrap at about six," she said.

"See you then."

They kissed. Then a bewildered Hanna Coleman went home.

26

GUY DROPPED HIS BODY INTO HIS FATHER'S BROKEN-DOWN OLD ARM-chair and stared at the cold fireplace. He'd start that fire in a minute as soon as he had a little rest. He'd had a long shitty day at the office, driven four and a half hours on a stultifying, stupor-producing highway in the rain, and spent an hour poking around in the basement with a seventy-nine cent flashlight looking for new fuses. Then he'd filled the kerosene heater, found clean towels and a box of matches. He had had a half-thought that while Mahelly made up the bed and brewed the coffee, he could take another look at the plans book, but he knew after all that highway driving, his eyes wouldn't be able to focus on a printed page in the cabin's vague forty-watt light. Instead, he'd taken an ax into the yard, chopped up some firewood, loaded it into an old plastic boat with a string tied to the front, and hauled it up to the house by moonlight. Then he'd buried the dead bird that had flown down the chimney and died in the bathtub and returned to the house and Mahelly, who had changed and looked a thousand times better after her sleep in the car and a wash than she had looked the other night in her own apartment. This was good since he looked a thousand times worse.

"You look tired, Guy," she said.

"I feel it," he said. Why *was* he so tired? Hey, his day would have killed Indiana Jones. Wasn't that a pretty good reason? Sure, but that wasn't it. Something ugly was nagging at him, something he was avoiding. Was it the plans book he hadn't read, and the impending annual meeting on Monday? Mmmmm. No. He'd get that covered this weekend. Was it leaving with Hanna being so angry with him? Yes, partly. Was it Mahelly?

Boy, that was going to be lousy. It was depressing knowing he was going to have to say good-bye to Mel. He was going to hate the hell out of that. He didn't want to think about how he was going to tell her. Maybe he'd know what to say when the right time came. Jeez. Poor little thing.

Anyway, that was close, but there was something else bothering him. Some elusive something else. Was it more than the fight with Hanna? He felt a hook snag something in his gut. There was something painful there. Hanna. Was she sleeping with Stein? Was that supercilious stud, rich, powerful and he supposed good-looking, cramming his cock into Hanna? Christ. That would be something. He clenched his jaw. Was Hanna going to fall for that manipulative creep? That would be a kick, all right. Whose just deserts would that be? he wondered angrily. Stop, boy, he soothed himself. You're blowing this out of proportion. Hanna was free to do what she wanted, and she still seemed to want him. He considered that. For how long? He could just see her swooning over that bullshit-artist. That asshole had eyes like a Siberian Husky. Yeah, he looked like a wolf. Yuck. He forced himself to unclench his teeth. He wasn't supposed to get jealous. *She* was supposed to get jealous. There was no point in worrying about this now. He had enough to deal with this weekend. What was that? Mahelly was speaking to him.

"Come to bed, Guy," she said touching her hand to his forehead. "You're falling asleep."

Guy gratefully complied. He glanced at the fireplace to make sure he hadn't lit a fire, carried the kerosene heater into the small bedroom, and after pulling off his clothes fell into the bed and sleep. He awoke sometime later. Mahelly had squirmed into the narrow bed and had found a warm spot under his arm. She barely took up any room.

"Hi," he said groggily.

"Shhh," she whispered. "Go back to sleep." He hugged her first and then he did just that, face deep in fuzzy hair.

The raft-size wooden dock extended out into the lake like a square, barn-red tongue. It was the last weekend in October and still, at noon, the planks were warm enough to bake the ache out of one's bones and the sun was hot enough to make a person pink if he didn't watch out.

Guy turned over on his stomach and let out a sigh that started at

about his knees and whooshed straight out of his lungs. The plans
book lay in a canvas satchel at his side with the backgammon game,
the Hawaiian Tropical Tanning Oil, and yesterday's *Wall Street Journal*. Only the tanning oil had been opened. It was going to be a long
weekend. He had time to get into the plans book before the Market
Planning Meeting in Chicago on Monday. Anyway, he knew the contents pretty well from what Court had told him, and besides he couldn't
read on the dock in this kind of light. Too much glare. He'd get to
his reading after dinner tonight. He had slept heavily and long last
night and now, in the middle of Saturday, sleep was seducing him
again. He hadn't worked, hadn't talked with Mahelly. Surely it could
all wait.

Ooh, what was that? "That you, Mel?" he asked the hands massaging oil into the backs of his legs.

"Uh-huh," she said. "Relax, Guy. Go back to sleep. I'll wake you
before you get cooked."

"Good," he said, surrendering willingly to the strong little hands
rubbing the knotted muscles in his limbs. Later he felt a cloud of cotton
sheet drift over his body and settle onto it like cool air. He closed his
eyes and went back into the daydream place he occupied, feeling if
any harm roamed the world, it was not looking for him today.

Mahelly hurt inside. This was too nice. This is what she'd wanted
to do with Guy since their affair began—spend unlimited time with
him alone. And yet she felt like a thief. She'd never stolen anything
before in her life, but she was stealing this time, Hanna's time, with
Guy. Didn't Guy know there was nothing wrong with her but a few
black and blue marks and an achy head? She opened the dresser drawer
and touched Hanna's blue sweater. This was the sweater she'd worn
the day she met Guy in the laundry room, and Hanna loved it now.
Mahelly bit her lip. Traces of Hanna were everywhere in this house:
a muddy inch of henna shampoo in a bottle on the shower stall ledge,
the half-empty box of Count Chocula cereal in the refrigerator, the
blue sweater with the rip in the sleeve. Mahelly felt like an intruder.
She slammed the drawer. How was it she could love Hanna so much
and still feel so tied by her love with Guy that she couldn't stop
betraying their friendship? She couldn't continue these thoughts. This
was going to be her last weekend with Guy. Period. Feeling guilty
wasn't going to ease the separation. She had to be clear with herself
that they had no future as lovers beyond Sunday night, and then try

to enjoy everything with Guy between now and then. It was a lot of time, really, to store memories. They would have today and tonight and most of tomorrow.

She folded the shorts and T-shirt she'd been wearing and tugged on a clean pair of jeans. She gingerly pulled her head through the neck opening of an old chick-yellow college sweatshirt and then drew her hair onto the top of her head with a blue ribbon. She looked at herself in the small spotty mirror over the dresser. She plucked at her topknot. Why did her hair have to frizz like this, damn it? Why couldn't it lie straight, or wave if it had to? She blew up her cheeks and then let out the air. She took a critical look at her face. She had a nice pinky-tan color, and except for the frizz, she had to admit, she looked nice.

She'd better wake Guy and find out what he wanted to eat for dinner. She tied the laces of her running shoes, stuffed some bills in her pocket and stepped carefully down the rocky path to the dock.

"Don't you trust me with the car?" she asked. "I'm a very good driver."

"It's not you, Mel. It's the damned LTD. We're lucky we got here and I'm willing to risk the drive down. Other than that the car stays put. I *know* this dirt road and last year the whole exhaust system dropped out of the bottom."

"So what are we going to do for food? Order out? I checked the pantry and the provisions in stock are two cans of leek and potato soup and one can of smoked oysters."

"We can't order out, Mel," Guy said with a laugh. "There's no takeout Chinese around here and besides, there's no phone." He shrugged into his shirt, shoved legs into his long pants. "I'll walk down to the store."

"I'll come with you."

"It's a mile, Mel, both ways, and I think you should take it easy today."

Her head *did* hurt and she was wobbly on her feet. "OK," she said. "Come back soon."

Guy loved the walk to the store. He must have run up this road a thousand times a summer when he was a kid. His parents had built this house when he was a baby. Dad had designed it himself and had done a lot of the carpentry. He'd wanted a retreat far from the city and as simple a place as he could find. This little cabin on the edge of the small four-acre lake was quiet and restorative. Guy's memory held summer pictures: himself and his friend Ricky, and that black Labrador, hiding in the woods, sloshing around in the creek, the rushing noise of the water sanding the edges off their yells and laughter and the dog's playful barking and every other sound. But there were no other sounds in the fall. It was absolutely quiet. The frogs and tree peepers were gone and so were the birds. Now the only sound was that of the constant rush of water from Bart's Pond crashing over the dam and boiling over the rocky bed of Cricket Creek, accompanying the rural dirt road down its slow twisting path to the bottom of the hill.

This crazy road. The crown always wore down about now, filling the gullies on both sides with sand. Then the rain concluded that the road was a brook and used it as a throughway to the creek. After the road washed away for a couple of seasons, the rocks stuck up out of the dirt and banged the hell out of his undercarriage.

It was Hanna who dragged the tailpipe for a half mile up the road last year, trailing sparks behind her, finally dropping the exhaust system about six yards in front of the car park. "Don't take the car," he'd said to her. "Don't worry," she'd said. He smiled at the memory of Hanna. Was that the weekend she'd bought the pumpkins? Heaped in a picturesque old farm wagon outside the store, designed to pull in the tourist trade, they were priced at twenty-five cents a *pound* before Halloween, twenty-five cents *each,* after it. "Guy, they're on *sale,*" she said, loading his trunk down to the ground. She gave pumpkins to everyone on 94th Street. Guy laughed out loud and tossed a pebble into the woods.

Protecting the stupid exhaust pipe was a wonderful excuse to walk down the country road. He needed the exercise, and he wanted to think about things. Think about Hanna. Think about Mel. Think about how different the place looked in the fall. The leaves, having mostly left, opened up a new landscape. The woods on the right side of the road were strangely empty now. He could actually see the trees. How stark they seemed. How small they looked. And he could see where the creek wound down around the hill and came out at the bottom behind the general store.

The general store. What was general about it was that it was generally out of everything you wanted, unless you wanted five-dollar Korean sneakers. Or a can of stew with dust on the lid. Or night crawlers. But it did have a phone booth attached to one side.

Guy's shoes crunched gravel as he walked to the side of the old clapboard building. He squeezed a quarter in his fist, squeaked open the phone booth door, put the coin in the slot and dialed Hanna's number. He listened to the telephone company recording and dropped more change into the phone. He listened to the ring tone, Hanna's answering machine message, and then without leaving a message of his own, he put the receiver down in the cradle. She wasn't home. What would he have said to her if she had answered? He'd already said it. "Don't," he'd said. "Don't do anything rash." And she had hung up. How could he tell her what to do when he'd changed the rules and taken Mahelly away? Guy closed the phone booth door, clumped up the steps to the porch, and walked into the store. He couldn't blame Hanna for being angry. He'd done the right thing, but still, if she loved him, she had to be angry.

Guy collected groceries in his arms, and laid them out on the counter. He paid the child behind the register. After stacking the pound of chopped meat, the eggs, butter, bread, canned beans, onions, tunafish, coffee and boxed cake in a large paper bag, Guy started up the hill toward the cabin. Would Hanna still want him after David Stein got to her? He didn't know.

Guy poked up the fire. It was a good one, if he did say so himself. The wood was yellow birch, ash, and the frame of a broken lawn chair. He added another log, and lay back on the rug to watch the fire.

"Can I get you something to drink, Guy?" Mahelly asked from the kitchen.

"I think there's some Kahlúa there somewhere," he said, almost whispering. She brought two small glasses of the chocolaty liqueur, then slipped under the blanket on top of the furry rug.

"So much for doing my paperwork," Guy said.

"You can do it tomorrow, can't you?" she asked.

"Sure." Guy settled himself into the heavenly comfort of fur underneath, fluff on top and fuzzy-topped girl sticking fuzz into his nose. His fire crackled and filled the room with a homey, woodsy smell.

"This is sort of wonderful, Mel," he said. Mahelly nodded her head, yes, but she was afraid to say anything. Why did they have to stop seeing one another? She'd forgotten. Oh, yeah. Guy didn't love her. He loved Hanna. Hanna was her best friend. She closed her eyes against the pain. Mustn't let Guy know about the pain.

"Does your head hurt, Mel?"

"Not too badly, Guy."

"Then what is it? Is something bothering you?"

She shook her head "no."

"Come on. Don't lie to me. What is it?"

Mahelly pushed her face into Guy's underarm. When she spoke, her words were muffled. Guy couldn't understand her. He moved away and lifted her chin with his free hand. "I couldn't hear you." There were tears in her eyes.

"I feel so guilty," she said in a whisper.

"But why, Mel?"

"I know this must be killing Hanna. I have no right to this. To you." She gulped and looked into his eyes.

"You didn't do anything," he said. "You didn't seduce me. You haven't demanded anything. This was all Hanna's doing."

"I could have said no." She let a sob escape. She couldn't help it.

"We're all guilty then, aren't we?" Guy wrapped his arms around her. "We could all have said no." He rocked her gently. "And I'm not sure it can be put back together." Guy thought about what he had said. He was having an incredible sensation. Tonight, when he'd been cooking the hamburger and Mel had been chopping onions, stirring the beans, padding around the kitchen in her socks and that pretty yellow sweatshirt, he'd been shocked at how normal, how right everything seemed. He couldn't remember when he'd felt so completely comfortable and safe.

It was Mahelly who was so completely comfortable and safe. What wonderful, undemanding love this woman gave! She was so giving, so incredibly sweet, and he felt so natural with her—as if they were married. He guessed this was because they had been friends for so long before they became lovers. They had no secrets. And he loved making love to her. My God. He had thought maybe tonight would turn out to be the right time to tell Mel that they had to stop their affair. Now, lying with her in his arms, he couldn't believe he would never lie with her again. Instead, he wished he could cut this hill off from the rest of the world and send it spinning high into the clear autumn sky. Cricket Creek space ship. No more job, no more worries, just he and Mahelly with the lake house wrapped around them and a big fire within.

Dreamer, he thought to himself. Escapist. He settled into the blankets and pillows even farther and hugged Mahelly. Hey. Tonight he could pretend they were alone above the world. No harm in that. "What, love?" he asked. She'd said something into his armpit again.

"I'm going to miss you so much, when you're gone," she said, tears spilling down her cheeks.

"I'm here now, Mel. Hold on to me. I'm here now."

Mahelly lifted her small face to him. His big hand spanned her cheek to the back of her head. She winced at the pressure on the bruise there.

"Oh, I'm sorry. I forgot," he said remembering.

"It's all right," she said. "Kiss me," she added.

He bent his face to hers and enveloped her mouth with his. She tasted his lips with her tongue, slipping it shyly into his mouth, withdrawing it, taking his tongue into her mouth, sucking it gently. A newborn lamb might suck this way.

"Help me with your clothes," Guy said. "I don't want to hurt you." He took off his.

Mahelly removed the ribbon from her hair. She eased the sweatshirt over her head. Guy marveled at how perfectly formed she was, how delicate and yet strong.

"You've lost weight," she said, running her hand lightly across his chest and belly, leaving gooseflesh in its wake.

Guy leaned over her. "I don't want to crush you, little girl," he said.

"Oh, do, Guy. Do crush me," she said, putting her arms around his neck. He kissed her then, and stroked the whole of her body; such short distances for his hands to travel. He laid her gently on her back and taking his weight on his knees and arms, he entered her body a fraction at a time. So tight, this girl-woman. Making love to her always felt like making love to a virgin. The floor was so hard. He would kill her, he was sure of it. Scooping his arm under her, he turned them both, and then she was lying on his chest, holding him inside her body, breathing soft chocolaty breaths and shivering. He covered her shoulders with a blanket.

"I love you, Guy," Mahelly said in a small voice. "I love you."

"Oh, Melly," he said. "Mel." She raised herself, and hands on his chest, legs straddling his hips, she made love to him. If he hadn't heard what she was saying he would have known it without being told. They came together, her soft cry drowned out by Guy's undulating wail, a wail releasing fear, and pain, and anger, and embracing the absence of these things.

After, when Mahelly cried in his arms, he said, "Baby, baby," and stroked her back, and whispered, "shhhh."

"I'm all right, really," she said, wiping her face on the blanket.

The last thought Guy had that Saturday night as he kissed Mahelly, and said good-night, and held her in his arms was—this weekend we are alone in the world. I can worry about everything else on Monday.

27

HANNA WRAPPED HER SCARF OVER HER NOSE AND MOUTH AND WALKED east. She was wearing the old down-filled Perry Ellis jacket that she'd bought at their sample sale years ago, which had long since lost its sleeve buttons. The green jacket topped a $19.95 purple sweat suit from the Gap and matched, in a weird sort of way, the jungle boots she'd gotten at the Army/Navy surplus store near Cricket Creek. Her hair stood out in salty clumps, her makeup was long gone, and her sock cuffs were drooping. If only *Womens Wear Daily* could see her now. No, *Glamour Magazine*. She could almost see her photo with a black bar over her eyes in the candid snapshot fashion-atrocity section. Was she the same girl who was the first to wear the newest of the new not too long ago? When did she work at Piquant? Four to eight years ago. Imagine, she'd gone from fashion victim to fashion victimizer. And now, plunging to new depths, she'd arrived at, ta da, "features victim." What did that make David? Features victimizer, of course. Oh, wasn't self-pity wonderful? David hadn't done anything any man wouldn't have done. Yes, no, yes, no. If she meant no, she should have left. Mmmmf. Sick girl, Hanna. You're a sick puppy.

Anyway, she'd survived the shoot. The sweaters that were the stars of the photo session, once lost, had been found. The cabin cruiser location had looked elegant even though it moved around too much to suit the photographer. The model with the drug problem had appeared straight. The shortage of film had somehow lasted the whole day. The slightly off mayonnaise on the, ugh, pastrami sandwiches had made everyone queasy, but only the makeup girl had actually thrown up on deck. The art director had taken the film to the lab, and everyone had peeled off in all directions before Hanna had thought to ask for a lift home from the pier.

So now, Hudson River to her back, Hanna was walking east, looking for a cab. For the number of cabs she'd seen in the last ten minutes, she might just as well have been looking for a camel. What was Guy doing? He hadn't called last night, but she hadn't expected him to. Hanging up on him had seemed so appropriate a few days ago. How could she have known she was going to miss him so badly now? She kicked at an old hubcap and crossed West Street. Was Mahelly walking around in jungle boots hating the world? No. She was probably curled up in that nice big chair in front of the fire wearing something kittenish, smelling like an English cottage garden. Mmmf. And Guy was probably sitting at the kitchen table gluing something. Stirring a pot of Dinty Moore. Listening to the radio. And here *she* was, walking in the middle of the street so she wouldn't be attacked by derelicts, trying to figure out how to metamorphose her mothy self into a butterfly for another relaxing evening at home with David Stein. Ugh. She would have to have a talk with him this evening before she got herself into trouble again. Tell him she wanted their relationship to back up to where it had been before Thursday night: employer-employee. Friends maybe. It would be awkward, and she would have to be diplomatic, but she couldn't let him think she would sleep with him again until she had worked out her relationship with Guy.

She looked at her watch. Five. Great. If a cab pulled up right now and flew uptown, and she figured out what to wear on the first try, and she caught a cab immediately afterward, she could be at David's at 6:30. Maybe. Here was Hudson Street. Civilization. The Dover Cab company was only a short way from here. There would be a cab any second. If not, the Sheridan Square subway stop was only a few blocks away. OK. Whichever came first. There it was—a cab! She stuck out her hand and the taxi skidded to a halt.

"Ninety-fourth and Central Park West, please," she said and threw herself back into the seat. How had she made such a mess of her life? What in the world had made her think she could passively allow an affair between her lover and her best friend? How was she going to get out of this? How was she supposed to *think* over the synthesized noise emanating from the radio speakers?

"Um," she ventured, tapping on the Plexiglass transom. "I'm feeling a little sick. Could you find another station, please? Anything but hard rock?"

The driver glared sideways at her. He twirled a dial. The crucifix hanging from the rearview mirror swung wide as the cab rounded the bend of Hudson Street turning onto Eighth Avenue. A voice came up from the speakers behind her. An evangelist. "Are you trembling?" the voice intoned. "Are you trembling, I say, between the mistakes of your past? And your appre-hen-sion . . . about the fu-ture?"

Hanna stared wide-eyed at the back of the driver's head. This couldn't be happening.

"Step boldly, brethren. Step boldly to God's Throne of Grace, and *tel-l-l* him of your travail . . ." the voice assured Hanna. "Raise your voice to God in prayer, not just in time of trouble, but ev-v-ery day. God loves to hear your voice, brothers and sisters . . ." You can endure this, Hanna thought. Close your eyes. Hanna lay down in the seat, wrapped down-filled sleeves around her head, and quickly, more quickly than she could have predicted, she was home.

The little red light on the answering machine blinked. Let it be Guy. She turned the knob to reverse and waited as the tape rewound. It rewound about an inch. A hang-up. She pushed the play button. Twelve seconds of hiss noise entered her room, punctuated at the end by a beep. She reset the machine. What was worse than a hang-up? Was it Guy? Was it the window cleaner? Was it the photo lab? Was it David? Hanna sighed and put all of her clothes in the hamper. She wished she had asked David for his number. She would call now if she could and suggest they meet somewhere, not his apartment, for dinner. Dumb of her, but this moment had seemed so far away when she had last seen him. David. She touched her face. She always felt raw after he kissed her. She could almost feel his beard right now. God, he was sexy. Hanna sighed. David said he cared about her. Did he? Guy was deserting her and David was wooing her. Give that a little thought, Hanna, she thought to herself.

She turned on the shower. How would I feel about David, if I weren't in love with Guy? she wondered. She'd had hints of how she would feel, flashes. The chemistry was there. But she'd never been able to relax with him. Something extraordinary was always going on when she saw him—an editorial meeting, a manuscript review. A little fire and the most incredible grass she'd ever smoked. Hanna soaked her hair and sudsed it up. She tried to examine her behavior. It seemed to her she was always a little off when she was with David, a little tighter than her normal self, as if she were shrink-wrapped in some smaller person's skin. She rinsed her hair and thought about last Thursday night. What had he said? He wanted to see her smile. He was offering her a pleasant Saturday evening. Light. Fun. God, she needed that. She would love to sit in the same room with David and read a book, but it wouldn't work. Not anymore. Instead, she would go there, have her talk with him, and depending on how that went, they could go out together for a relaxing dinner. Hey. That's probably what he has in mind.

Hanna dried herself with fluffy white towels, turned on the blow-dryer. She tried to imagine sitting in a room with David reading a book, reading him something amusing, having her back rubbed. I need to feel cared about, she thought to herself. And I need to feel first in line. Is that so damnable? Would it be too much to hope that if she had lost Guy, she had found David? But what did David need from her if he had that TV superstar? Maybe he saw the real Hanna, the Hanna Guy saw, and maybe, just maybe, that was something he liked. Was it so impossible David Stein cared for her? Hanna sighed again. She couldn't know yet. But she knew she couldn't have a relationship of any kind with David until she and Guy either made up or broke up.

She shut off her blow-dryer and thought about her clothes. Brown pants, turtleneck, tweed jacket, flat shoes. When da-da, you are in doubt, Ann Taylor bails you out. She dressed. Did David Stein watch television, eat in bed, get gas? She tied her shoelaces and opened the closet door. She took a critical look at herself in the mirror. She needed something. She took a man's wool cap down from the shelf and put it on her head. Good. Spunky. The clothes were right, but her color was wrong. If she were going to get mayonnaise poisoning, wouldn't she have gotten it by now? She took the red scarf from her bedpost and wrapped it around her neck. That did it. Red was her best friend.

Out on the street, Hanna took a bunched fist out of her pocket to hail a cab. "Tudor City," she said to the driver. "And please drive slowly," she said, thinking about potholes, thinking about the kind of nausea-provoking ride one got from drivers who drove with a foot on the brake. She didn't want to take any chances. She wouldn't be able to handle any of that. "I'm in no rush," she said.

"Twenty-two?" the wizened elevator operator asked her.

"Yes," she said. He knew her from Thursday. How nice. The gates clanked open on the twenty-second floor and Hanna stood in the corridor. Why hadn't they put arrows and numbers on the walls? She knew whichever way she turned, it would be wrong. She turned right, scanned the apartment numbers, turned back, found the door with "Stein," in script, under the bell. She pressed the button.

Hanna heard a click at the peephole, a chain sliding, and then the door opened and she was standing eye to eye with Miranda Wu.

It took a long time for the chill Hanna felt to reach her scalp. It started at the back of her calves and crept slowly up her spine, raising the fine hairs on her back as it traveled. Her eyes were riveted on Miranda's face. Hanna knew she couldn't move. She was as pinned as a rabbit caught in a flashlight beam on a country lane. She wanted to speak but she could think of nothing to say. She stared at Miranda and would have stared forever, except that Miranda said, "Hello."

"Hello," Hanna parroted stupidly.

"Yes?" the woman asked.

Yes? Hanna cleared her throat. "Uh. Is David here? I'm Hanna Coleman."

Miranda continued to stand at the door.

"I work for him," Hanna said. What was happening? What was this. Bolt, her inner voice urged her. Turn and bolt. She couldn't move.

Miranda turned away from Hanna and, leaving the door open behind her, walked farther into the room beyond. Hanna, mesmerized, saw the long braid of black hair hanging down to the middle of her black-robed back.

"David," Miranda said in a normal voice. "One of your little friends has come to see you." Miranda turned back to Hanna, and Hanna, not knowing what else to do, followed her into the living room. Rapid movement drew her eyes to the chaise. The rapid movement was David, standing, closing his robe. Not quickly enough. Hanna saw a dense pelt of body hair and flash of dull pink between his legs. No. She didn't want to see that. He was naked under that robe. Naked with Miranda as he had been naked with her. The chaise held the impression of David's form as he leapt to cover himself. There was a blanket on the floor. Two glasses on the table. Newspapers, scattered. What was happening? God. He'd forgotten she was coming!

"I'm sorry," she said automatically, masking conflicting feelings of hurt and confusion. "I must have come at the wrong time."

"No, no, Hanna. My mistake," David said, advancing toward her. "I lost track of the time." He ran his hand through his hair, knotted the tie-belt. "Miranda, this is Hanna."

"We've met," she said sweetly. Hanna tried to smile. She watched as Miranda walked to David's side, touched his buttocks with a careless, proprietary hand.

In succession, she felt jealousy, anger and overwhelming shame. What was she doing here? She couldn't have imagined a more wretched scenario in her worst dreams. This man, this man she had revered, had followed, was so small in this bitch's presence. He was a worm. What she couldn't figure out was his intent. Had he forgotten he had invited her? Or had he planned this little scene? Why? For whom? "*One* of your little friends, David." What did that mean? How many women did he sleep with?

She felt stupid gaping at the black-robed couple. Her cocky little cap felt ridiculous on her head. How could she take it off? She would have to endure looking stupid. It was far preferable to holding her hat in her hand. She flared her nostrils. "Come in. Sit down," David was saying. He was making no move to get dressed.

"No," she said stiffly. "I just wanted to let you know the shoot went well. I'm going. It's been a long day and I won't be very good company."

Miranda looked at Hanna with a mischievous smile, a smile Hanna had seen depicted in oil on canvas. The smile, the gilt, the lavender fur. It was all there.

Hanna backed away, turned, and walked toward the front door. David followed her, securing the flap of his robe.

"Hanna, wait. Where are you going?"

Hanna shot him a disdainful look and stepped across the threshold.

"Wait," he said in a loud whisper. "You're overreacting, Hanna."

Hanna heard a whistle. Without meaning to, she turned around. It was Miranda. "Catch," she said to David, and tossed him a set of keys. He caught them and put them in his pocket as Miranda closed the door.

They were standing together in the corridor. Hanna mashed the elevator button with her thumb. She could hear it ringing somewhere below. That old man probably hated that, but she couldn't worry about him now. She had to get out of here. Her anger was returning. What David had done just now, even if this were an oversight, simple forgetfulness, revealed what she had always known about him. David's priority was David. He knew what he had gotten her into with that damned story, and he had squeezed her. He could have released her, but he had squeezed her. He had known she was vulnerable the other night, and he could have respected her wish to wait. Instead . . . she pushed away shameful pictures of her rapture. Now he was going to squeeze her a little more. Not too obviously—subtly; that was his way. Overreacting, he had said. Overreacting to finding him with another woman, he was saying. What feeling person wouldn't react as she was reacting? He had twisted her professionally, he had played with her resulting vulnerability, and now he was messing around with her mind. Frosting on the fucking cake.

Hanna stared at the wall but her peripheral vision was excellent. She could see David wriggling his hands in his pockets, looking propitiatory. She had never seen this boyish David before, and the look didn't suit him. What a desperate weakling she'd been. She'd made him up. Created him as a human being. The lovemaking. She'd imagined what? Real feelings. Promise. Future. "I want to see you," he'd said. He'd wanted to fuck her and why the hell not? Had he ever suggested otherwise? Yes. "I care about you, Hanna," he'd said. As what? A cog in the *Urban Life* machine. "A little friend" to sleep with when Miranda was out of town. "I want to make you happy," he'd said. God.

She didn't want to think anymore. She was sweating. If that elevator didn't come . . . Hanna looked at the dial above the elevator door. Three, four. In the movies, the elevator would have come by now. It wouldn't leave her standing for painful minutes in the corridor with David in his bathrobe. She had already seen the thin, embarrassed smile on his face. She had seen his black hair curling up from his chest and swarming down over the knuckles of his toes. She'd seen and would now forget that dull pink flash. She didn't want to see any more of him. She was having faint retching feelings in her stomach. She would not throw up here. She would die first. She mashed the button again.

"Hanna, come inside," David was saying. "Let's all talk. Miranda has had a couple of thoughts about your mansharing story . . ."

Hanna's look was so scathing, it stopped David's sentence. He began again. "Hanna, you're overreacting, really . . . you're being silly."

He is the worst, Hanna thought, tapping her foot. How dare he talk down to her. Why was she being civil? Why was she trying to contain her anger, her mortification? She turned to him and, finding her voice low in her throat, she said, "Don't you dare patronize me, David. Don't you dare try that crap with me. I know you now."

"Hanna, whatever you are thinking, this was just a mistake . . ."

"Really?" Hanna curled her lips back in a semblance of a smile. "I'm curious. How was that little scene supposed to 'make me smile'? Did you think Miranda and I would have a little girl-talk? Were you, perhaps, going to entertain us on the lute?"

David looked down, abashed. "I didn't expect her this weekend. I was surprised. Then I forgot. . . . I'm sorry, Hanna."

"Don't bother apologizing for *this*," Hanna said, darting a furious look at him. "I don't want you to think I'm angry only about this. Or about the other night. This is just the, the," she looked for a phrase that wasn't a cliché, gave up, "icing on the cake. I'm finally realizing how you bullied me into this mansharing thing. You manipulated me from the beginning, and you've taken advantage of my trust in you. I looked up to you, David." *Where* was the elevator? She was seconds away from tears. If she cried, she would lose whatever small dignity she had left. The floor indicator arrow moved upward a floor. The silence.

"The story, Hanna, was your idea."

"No. Not like this it wasn't. I wanted to *write* a story. You're right about one thing, though," she added. "I *have* been silly. More than silly. I've been a fool."

Hanna could hear the elevator ascending from the floor below. She looked at David. He was leaning against the wall and sighing. His eyes looked crusty. Bread crumbs nestled in his chest hairs. "Go inside, David," she said tiredly. "You wouldn't want anyone to see you looking this way."

The elevator arrived accompanied by the sound of clashing metal gates. Hanna stepped inside and gripped the brass rail at the side of the car.

"Are you all right, miss?" the operator asked when the door closed. "You look pale."

"I'm fine," she said politely, swallowing. "Thank you very much for asking."

The elevator arrived safely at the lobby. Hanna found the door leading out to the street. Once there, she looked past the doorman and strode outside into the cold autumn air. Then she walked over to the curb, leaned into the gutter and vomited.

28

IT WAS SEVEN O'CLOCK, MORE OR LESS, AND A SUNDAY MORNING, BUT Courtney was awake. She really didn't need an alarm clock. The sun peeked in her east window first, the window sash making shadowed stripes on the reverse side of the flowered curtain. At this time of year the sun paid its first visit to the east side window at sunrise through about 7:15 and then it invaded the south window. The south window was still in shade so she could laze for a few more minutes before getting out of bed.

She was going to allow herself two hours of normal Sunday morning routine and then she was going to the office. Tom Franz in media and Abby Jacobs, a young but superbright account exec, were going to meet her there at 9:30 and they were going to go over the budget plan and advertising projections for the annual meeting one more time, or until they all felt comfortable with how the meeting would go.

The Market Planning Meeting was an annual event of major importance. It was at this meeting that events of the last year were discussed and the marketing plan and budget for the next year reviewed. The market plan and budget report were described in full in a bound report three inches thick. The book was prepared by the agency and delivered into the clients' hands two weeks before the meeting, giving everyone a chance to look over the material. Not everyone did.

The key players at the meeting were the head account person from the agency and the advertising manager from the client; in this case,

Guy Spencer, Senior V.P., Management Supervisor, from H & G, and Carter Mulholland, Senior V.P., Group Brand Manager, National Confectionary Products, Inc., were responsible for the Cocoa and Sugar Divisions.

The tables in the conference room were traditionally set up in a hollow square, the agency people and the client people facing off on opposite sides of the square. Guy and Carter would be sitting across from one another, and subordinates and superiors both would flank them on respective sides.

The rules of the game were simple. Know your stuff. Be prepared. Be sure you have guessed what issues in that entire three-inch tome were going to be on the clients' minds. Remember that whatever happened in the whole world from a national psychographic shift to a tornado in the sugarcane fields, the client was going to blame low sales on the advertising copy.

The lower-ranking people on both sides had to know the fine details: how much, how many, where, when, down to the decimal. Guy and Carter were in charge of the big picture as it affected their brands and competitive brands. The big guys, George Warren and Jack Bitner, chairman and president of Hastings and Goode, were expected to have a grander, more philosophical view of the marketplace. After the hello, how's your backhand, coffee-pouring greeting ritual, questions would be lobbed by anyone in the room to anyone in the room, and if the agency wanted to hold onto their seventy million in NCP billings, they'd better be sharp.

Guy had just become the management supervisor of the cocoa brands and the smallest sugar brand. He only had prior experience on one other NCP brand, but it was the largest brand, Premium Granulated Sugar, and it had done very well under his leadership. He had only a month's experience, however, with the other three brands, so it therefore behooved him to read the goddamned market planning book cover-to-fucking-cover. Courtney doubted he'd even cracked it. He'd been preoccupied lately and Courtney knew she hadn't tried to wake him up. In a real way it was up to her to anticipate areas Guy ought to study and point them out—no, drill him on them. But it had been so sinfully easy, if not actually to run him down the wrong course, to leave out or brush over issues she was pretty damned sure would come up at the meeting.

She had watched Guy skim the list of issues she'd prepared for him last week, a list she'd thought obviously incomplete. On Friday he'd barely stuck his head into her office when she had suggested at least a two-hour meeting with him. He had to go, he'd said. He had to drive out of town and it was getting ready to rain, he'd said.

"The copy's approved, isn't it? And the media plan's about the same as last year, right?" he had asked, waving the report in the air.

"Right," she said. "Nothing to worry about."

Guy had smiled gratefully and raced out the door.

Courtney thought she honestly hadn't planned to leave him so totally vulnerable, but he was begging for a massacre. For God's sake, he was going for the weekend to a cabin that had no phone! She hoped for his sake he did his homework. Maybe if he was nice to her, she'd give him a couple of hints on the plane. Not too many—just enough so he would live to see the sun come up the day after the meeting.

Courtney stretched and got out of bed. She wiggled her toes, bent and touched her palms to the soft, rosy carpet. She would take a half hour for exercises, a full hour to read the Sunday *Times*, which was even now lying snugly against the door of her apartment, and another half hour for showering and making up her face. Then she'd walk the twenty blocks to work.

She took deep muscle-relaxing breaths as she prepared to do leg raises. She thought about the chocolate croissant and the rich Jamaican coffee she was going to treat herself to before she left for the office.

It was going to be a very long day.

29

HANNA LOOKED INTO THE MIRROR. IT WAS HER FACE ALL RIGHT, BUT the oldest, most wrinkly version of herself she'd ever seen. She had washed her face last night without turning on the bathroom light. She had brushed the taste of vomit out of her mouth, splashed water on her cheeks and eyes, promised herself she was going to call David and quit her job in the morning, and then she'd fallen into a rock-hard slumber. The ravages of that sleep confronted her now. Mascara rimmed her veiny eyes. Her unbrushed hair, flattened on one side because she hadn't changed her position all night, untidily framed her sheet-creased face.

Hanna turned on the shower, stepped into the bathtub and let the water beat very hard on the front of her body. She toed the drain plug lever into the closed position and when the water reached the tops of her calves, she sat, still letting the shower rain on her upturned face. When the water level reached the top of the tub, she turned it off and thought.

She'd be crazy to quit. Under the influence of wretched humiliation and righteous anger, she had made the easiest decision, but it was the wrong decision. A more reasonable person this morning, she knew resigning would hurt her more than it would hurt him. The humiliation had already paled. And the anger—she'd delivered it. Her invectives might have glanced off his steely hide, but she'd established her personhood to herself; that was the most important thing. She was tired.

She felt weak in body, but she liked herself again. So she wasn't going to quit her job. At least not over last night.

Before David, apart from David, and more important than David, she had a reputation and she had a calling. She was a writer and would be one after David Stein was a faded and distant memory. She would not let H. Coleman, the writer, down. She was going to write the mansharing story but not the way David wanted her to do it. He had been right. As it was now, it *was* a superficial piece of crap, but it didn't have to be. She should write the goddamned mansharing story the way it needed to be written. She could write this story from first-person experience as David wanted, but she would tell the whole ugly truth. If David didn't want that, *that* would be something to quit over.

Hanna took the little blue bear nail brush from the soap dish and scrubbed all twenty of her nails. She rubbed her elbows and neck with a rough mitt and soaped every other place on her body. She ducked her head into the bath water and lathered it with her favorite, fragrant henna shampoo. Then she stood and rinsed in the shower.

Standing on the bath mat, she patted her body dry. She carefully and lovingly massaged lotion into her skin. A creamy chenille robe had come last week from her parents, and Hanna had left it in the box in her closet. How strange they had remembered her birthday was coming, while she had almost forgotten. Well, she'd been a little preoccupied. She put the robe on now and tucked the birthday love and kisses card in her pocket.

She went into the kitchen, poured milk and chocolate cereal into her handmade ceramic bowl, and when the cereal was consumed she went to work.

The typewriter was dusty but it was ready. Hanna swept piles of magazines and fabric swatches away, clearing a wide space on all sides of her writing area. Then she spent six hours writing and rewriting eight pages—the true story of the most painful episode of her life in only two-thousand words.

Hanna took the completed piece and settled into the lap of her friend, the velvet Victorian settee. She read her clean eight pages. As a professional, she knew the fifth and last rewrite was beautiful. It was great. It told the story, gave the facts, was written in her own chatty voice. *U.L.*'s readers would start it, consider it, feel moved, and enjoy the article down to "the end," glad that someone else had tried mansharing and spared them the trouble. It was a complete five-star guided tour of polygamy for the price of the magazine. Hanna knew the writing was sensational and if David Stein didn't like it, some other magazine would. She closed her eyes.

When Hanna woke up, it was still Sunday but it was nearly night. She wrapped her new robe tightly around her and went into the kitchen. She reached for the light switch that controlled the fluorescent bulb over the sink. She found it and pressed it hard until it flickered and caught and held. Squinting against the light, she ran the water, filled her old tea kettle and put a teaspoon of instant coffee into her favorite coffee mug, the one with a macaw perched on the handle.

Hanna watched the kettle from her minor trance and soon, adage aside, the water boiled. She removed the kettle from the flame. She sliced liverwurst into thick rounds. She considered the jar of mayonnaise and rejected it with a shudder. She slathered two pieces of rye bread with mustard, added slices of red onion, closed the sandwich and put it on a big white platter. She took her steaming cup of coffee and her sandwich with her to the bedroom where she placed it on the night table. She got into her bed and pulled her goose-down quilt under her arms and stared at the lithograph on the facing wall. It was a picture of a large orange cat against a blue sky filled with fluffy clouds. The cat was staring at Hanna. The two stared at one another while Hanna ate.

If David accepted the story or didn't she didn't care. She had done right by herself. But there was more to repairing her life than settling with David and writing the mansharing story. She wasn't finished yet. She wanted her boyfriend back. She missed Guy Richard Spencer. She loved him. She desired him. Where was he? She needed to talk with him; tell him again how sorry she was, beg him to forgive her, see if there was anything she could do to restore their love affair.

She dialed his phone number. No answer. Was he still driving back from Massachusetts? She sipped her coffee and dialed again. Still no answer. She didn't have the stomach to call at Mahelly's. She couldn't consider the possibilities of reaching him there. Anyway, she would have thought after a weekend with Mahelly he'd want to go home to his own apartment. Guess not. She turned on the television and watched a movie. The plot was incomprehensible. She was so weary. Shouldn't she sleep?

She tried to clear her mind but how could she sleep with all her scared and lost feelings about Guy clumping through her head with cleats on. Please God, she thought, if you let me have him back I promise never to be bad again. She gave God a few minutes to put Guy near his phone and then she dialed again. No answer.

Wait. He had said he was going to Chicago tomorrow. She called information. She got a number and dialed it.

"United Airlines, good evening, Miss Parker speaking."

"Oh, Miss Parker, I have a problem. My boss called from home telling me to catch the morning flight with him to Chicago, but I can't find where I wrote down the flight number and I don't know his home phone number. Can you help me?"

"Surely. What is his name?"

"Spencer. Guy Spencer."

Hanna heard clicking sounds, keys being tapped on a computer keyboard. "That would be flight 903 leaving LaGuardia at 7:00 A.M."

"Thank you. Will you please reserve a seat for me? My name is Hanna Coleman."

"Surely, will that be smoking or nonsmoking?"

"I'd like to sit with Mr. Spencer. Nonsmoking."

"I'm sorry, Miss Coleman. That seat is reserved." That would be Courtney!

"OK. Nonsmoking will be fine."

Hanna checked the time on her Felix the Cat clock. It was 11:20. Wonder what Guy is doing right now? She set the alarm for 5:30 and with her old characteristic optimism, closed her eyes. She slept.

30

GUY WAS PACING. HE THOUGHT HE OUGHT TO GET SOMETHING TO EAT but he knew he wouldn't be able to swallow. He wasn't awfully hungry lately. His suit hung on him a little, which was OK with him. Let him look a little lean and hungry. He was at the airport a half hour early. He'd woken up early, tried to make love to Mahelly, failed completely for the first time in twenty years, and so now here he was.

If Courtney got here early too, they could talk over coffee even before they got on the plane. She'd underscore everything he needed to know. He sat in one of the molded plastic chairs and clutched his briefcase in his lap. If he held onto it tight enough, maybe the contents would be absorbed by his body. Hey. He'd slept with the plans book next to the bed last night. That ought to be worth something. And being impotent. That ought to appease the meeting gods, right?

Thinking about the imminent Market Planning Meeting felt to Guy like being half certain he'd left the bathtub running when he left, and no one but him had the keys. Cool it, he thought to himself. There was no point in putting himself in a panic. Hey, everyone was nervous before the annual meeting. He'd sat on the sidelines enough times to know that and also that these people were not simply clients, but friends too. He'd known Carter for about four years now, right? Something like that and more importantly he knew the big brand, his brand, Premium Brand Granulated Sugar, down to the toenails. Courtney had said the plans for the other brands were almost identical to what they had been last year. Except of course for Swanee. They were going to justify pushing the budget to counter the decline in sales. The trouble was, he hadn't taken time to check that out with Jackson who, although he'd been moved up, knew a lot more about what was going on in Chicago than he did. Courtney was smart and efficient. If he did a little boning up with her on the plane, he'd sail through.

"United flight 903 to Chicago is boarding now," a disembodied voice announced. Christ, where was Courtney? George and Jack had probably flown out last night to have dinner with their client counterparts. Would Courtney have done the same? Without telling him? There was no way she could have reached him, so he supposed it was possible. Wait, there she was. Wasn't that Court walking down the corridor, checking her attaché case through the X-ray machine?

It was. It was Courtney. She couldn't see him yet, so he needn't wave, but he was sure glad to see her. Guy felt arms go around his middle. He turned, startled, prepared to strike. It couldn't be Hanna, but it *was.*

"Hi, darling. Surprise."

"My God, Hanna, my heart. I think you've killed me."

"I'm sorry," she said tilting back her head to look at him. "But you are alive. So am I. That's why I'm here."

"Hanna, what are you talking about?" He looked nervously around. Courtney was collecting her case and her handbag, looping the bag over her shoulder. He separated himself from Hanna's arms. "What are you doing here?"

"I want to talk with you, Guy. About us."

"Now? Right now?"

"I couldn't wait any longer. We shouldn't. I bought a round-trip ticket to Chicago. I figured we could talk on the plane and I'll take the next one back. Do you think we could sit together?"

Guy felt a tap on his shoulder. No heart attack this time. When he turned, he said, "Courtney, this is Hanna. She's joining us for breakfast in the air this morning. Hanna, meet Courtney. She works with me on three of my brands."

The two women shook hands. So this is his girlfriend, thought Courtney. A little on the pudgy side. Soft-looking too. And what was that thing she was wearing around her neck? A purple fox with rhinestone eyes? Guy had chosen *her*? It was impossible to understand what some men saw in some women.

So this is his old girlfriend, thought Hanna. God help him, she looks like a killer.

"Final boarding call for United flight 903 to Chicago," the voice rang out.

"Court, would you mind switching seats with Hanna?"

"Not at all."

"Thanks. Ladies . . ." Guy shepherded them onto the plane.

"Hanna, you couldn't have picked a worse time," said Guy. "Why don't you ever do anything normally?"

"Be flattered, Guy. How many times has a woman gotten on a plane to fly eight hundred miles to tell you she loves you?"

"I'm flattered, Nan, but I'm also terrified. I've got a major meeting in two hours and I wanted to prepare for it with Courtney."

"Fine. I'll leave." Hanna started looking under her seat. "I know there's a parachute under here somewhere."

"OK, Hanna." He took her hand. "I'm your captive audience." She smiled, kissed him. He kissed her back. It felt so good just to be sitting next to him.

"I love you," she said, laying down an eggy fork. "I always did, I suppose, but being without you has taught me a terrible lesson." Her voice wobbling, she paused. "I know I want to make amends, Guy. I want to do something very big so you know I mean what I'm saying. You told me once if I ever wanted to marry you, I would have to do the asking. I'm asking now. I want to marry you and live with you forever. Will you marry me?" She stared at him for a long minute and when she couldn't any longer, she dropped her gaze.

"What happened. Did David dump you?"

"Guy!"

"Did he?"

"No, he didn't. I walked out on him. And what a shitty thing to say!"

"I'm sorry. It was shitty. I just don't get the big commitment now, after all . . ." he trailed off. Hanna pushed her tray away, but it only moved two inches to the back of the seat in front of her.

"I know. I made a mess of everything."

"Hanna, listen to me. A lot has happened in the last month. I know you're sorry, and I love you too, but a lot has happened. I need more time to think about what I want. Right now, I want to go over this damned report and get through this meeting. Then we can talk again. OK?'' Some tears fell out of her eyes.

"Hey. Don't cry. We'll talk tomorrow.''

"It's just self-pity, Guy. I'm being disgusting.'' Hanna blew her nose on a cocktail napkin. "I'm fine. See?'' She smiled bravely. She tucked her handbag between the window and her face and closed her eyes. Guy took out the horrible, unreadable, overflowing bathtub of a plans book and tried to read.

"You'll be great today, Guy,'' Hanna said with a smile. "Lots of luck to both of you. Nice meeting you, Courtney.'' She waved good-bye and headed for the gate that would take her to the plane home. She had sounded so phony. "Nice meeting you, Courtney.'' Yucckk! Her insides felt rancid. When she got home, she'd call Mahelly. She needed to talk to her best friend. Nothing could be worse than keeping all these feelings to herself. She had to talk. Had to.

"Sorry,'' Guy said to Courtney in the cab.

"No problem,'' she'd said leaning her head against the back of the seat. Not for me, she added to herself.

The conference room was half-full of gray-suited men when Guy and Courtney walked in. Carter Mulholland was there and he shook Guy's hand warmly.

"Great to see you, Guy,'' he said. "Even nicer to see beautiful you,'' he said to Courtney, taking both of her hands in his.

"You're looking wonderful too, Carter,'' she said. "Nice tie.''

"It's yours,'' he said solemnly, starting to undo the knot.

"Guy,'' Carter said, putting his arm around him, "this is your first time in the hot seat, isn't it?'' Guy smiled.

"I'm insulated,'' he said, indicating Court. They laughed and moved on to the coffee urn. Then Carter turned to someone in his company, Court turned to the president of theirs. Tom Franz from H & G's media department stood with Guy for a moment.

"Courtney went over the media plan on Mom's, didn't she?'' he stated more than asked. Guy didn't have a chance to answer. Seats were being taken around the room.

270

The half-tab of Valium Guy had taken with his juice on the plane was working. His hands were sweating but he didn't feel nervous. He felt like a gladiator. The tables were squared off around a pit. There was nothing at the bottom of the pit except floor, but Guy thought it was good to think there were lions down there. As long as he batted the answers back across the room, he was safe from the lions.

Questions about Premium Brand had been handled easily. After four years on the account, there was little he didn't know. He'd swung his bat and connected solidly with each question that came across the plate. Mulholland was warming up again for another pitch. The subject was Mom's Cocoa, and Mulholland looked worried. Shit, the meeting was only a half-hour old out of a possible two hours. How could he be looking so worried?

"Guy," Carter was saying. "I don't feel good about how the advertising is working on Mom's. What evidence do we have that we've taken the right approach?"

Guy stared blankly. Courtney had said the copy was testing fine on Mom's. He ran a hand through the file box in his head, looking for something to say. Nothing came out of his mouth. He heard Courtney sitting on his right begin to speak. Thank God.

"The advertising has been on the air for nine months," Court said coolly. "Obviously we don't know everything we need to know yet, but all the signs seem positive. First, the national business has stabilized. After two years of decline, we are seeing flat indices in all sales districts. Two, we have a heavy-up test going in Syracuse, and shipments are indexing 115 versus control. Third, we've just gotten the preliminary tracking result and we find awareness up 25 percent and attitudes toward the brand improving. We'll know a lot more next month when we get final test results and the second wave of tracking results." As she concluded speaking, Courtney riffled the edges of the marketing plan and looked straight ahead.

"I don't know," said Carter. "I'm still not sure, but I'm willing to wait a couple of months to see if you guys are right. Frankly, I'm even more concerned about Mom's Cocoa's media plan. We have been moving over the past few years to a plan that took money out of national media and put additional weight into strong business areas with local spots. You've reversed this trend this year and put considerable weight back into national media. I'm concerned that you are thereby overspending in weaker business areas. I'd like some rationale, Guy, for why you've changed direction.''

Guy felt his stomach contract. Hadn't Courtney said the media plan was basically the same as last year? Good Lord. This is what Franz had tried to tell him about. Where was that media plan? Guy looked down at the plans book in front of him and searched for the media plan section. Please, God, give me a miracle.

Courtney spoke. "We've given this a lot of thought, Carter. And we certainly didn't make a major change in the media plan without considering every alternative. The major reason for increased network weight was our ability to be part of an extremely efficient package that would allow us to lower our CPM's by 15 percent. This makes local spot weight relatively inefficient. The net result is we're able to provide as much weight in prime areas as we did last year and get bonus weight in less developed areas. We end up with a plan that is significantly more efficient and we think more effective too. Of course," she added, "we will be watching local spot rates very carefully during the year. If relative costs change, we may be back to you with a revised plan."

"You sold me," said Carter giving Courtney a brief smile. He ran his finger down a page of itemized questions. His finger stopped and he looked across the room to Guy. "Could someone please sell me on why you folks want to keep Swanee alive?"

Whew, thought Guy. He'd discussed this often enough with Courtney. "I'm glad you asked," Guy folded his hands in front of him, put on his most confident smile, and began. "Swanee is a product with an amazing history in the brown sugar market, and although its share has eroded in the past, we feel by reaching down to the younger consumer and selling them on old-fashioned, nonadulterated, natural prod–''

"Excuse me, Guy," Jack Bitner interrupted. "I see you are not quite up on our new thoughts. Carter, we did propose taking a more aggressive stance with Swanee, but this weekend, after reviewing the projections one more time, we were forced to arrive at a different conclusion. Guy has only been on this brand for a month, so Courtney, why don't you take it from here."

Guy felt hollow inside. Bitner had covered for him, but it was simply good manners and team play that made him do it. He was in serious trouble. A half hour with Courtney and he would have been briefed. Damn Hanna and her stupid plane ride. Not fair, another voice in his head rebutted. He should have been in the office this weekend. He at least could have phoned Courtney from the pay phone at the general store. Would she have told him? His hollow feeling turned cold. She could have *insisted* she talk with him on the plane. She could have tipped him off in the cab, not just to Swanee's advertising plan but to all the other mistakes he'd made. He was sure, now that he thought about it, she had deliberately misled him. He could hear her saying emphatically that the media plan on Mom's was identical to last year's plan. He'd been had. That bitch had set him up. He turned his face to her and tuned in her voice.

". . . so even though we feel very loyal to old Swanee, and will miss the billings, if you don't mind my saying so," she smiled charmingly at Carter, who winked at her, "we can't find a way to justify the advertising budget. We recommend instead the following: Cut the budget from five million to one. Spend in print and direct mail merchandising only. Put a million into in-package coupons and promotions. Reduce the pricing and keep it low. Our target market is our current consumer. As the market tapers off, reduce the budget accordingly. We figure Swanee will be a profit maker with this plan for five years, maybe six, and then we wrap her up. Say good-bye. Maybe even have a nice party."

"I must say, Courtney, that seems right to me," said Carter, leaning over the table and making a final note. "I think we can slide the media savings into a special project we've been thinking about launching with some agency still to be decided."

It finally ended. The meeting ended with the sound of bones being gnawed by lions.

Jack Bitner walked over to Guy. "Nice tan, Spencer," he said pointedly. Guy swallowed. Jack continued. "I expect my senior people to be on top of their business. It's pretty clear you're not." He paused. This was not an invitation for Guy to speak. "This isn't the kind of client you can fake out, and you know that. I hope you won't forget it again."

Jack Bitner turned to Courtney. "You saved this meeting, Courtney. Our thanks." He shook her hand and walked away.

"What did you do to me?" Guy hissed at Courtney. She gave him a perplexed frown and smile in one as Carter stepped over.

"Court," he said turning his back on Guy. "Are you free for dinner? There are still a few issues I'm not sure about."

"Actually," said Guy, "I had planned to stay in town tonight. Maybe we three could have dinner together."

"That won't be necessary, Guy," Carter said, taking Courtney's arm as they walked from the conference room. It took Guy several moments to realize he was standing in the room by himself.

Guy went outside the room and dialed New York from a secretary's desk. He knew where he wanted to be. He wanted to be with a fuzzy-haired woman who would pat him and comfort him and hold his head. He dialed her number. Oh-oh. Carter was using a phone on the next desk and Courtney was leaning against the wall waiting.

"It's me," he said when Mahelly answered the phone. "I'm on my way out to the airport and could be at your place by eight." Guy listened in disbelief. What was she saying? It sounded as if she was saying no. No, she needed to be alone tonight. Was everyone going crazy? He couldn't argue with her in front of Mulholland. He put down the receiver and walked out into the street.

31

MAHELLY LAY BACK IN HER COOL BLUE SHEETS AND THOUGHT ABOUT Guy. He had been very attentive this morning, even though he had been distracted. It had been early, about six, when he left. He had kissed her, covered her up, and brought the jar of juice and a glass from her kitchen and put it by the bed. He'd put her *Gone with the Wind* tape on the VCR and the zapper on her night table so she could simply touch a button if she wanted to watch TV.

"Be good, Jo," he'd said. "Just lie around and sleep, will you? Stay home from work today." He'd gone to the windows and pulled the shades down against the morning sun. "I may stay over in Chicago tonight if the meeting runs late. If so, I'll see you tomorrow."

Mahelly hadn't gone back to sleep. He hadn't heard himself call her Jo. Jo for Joanne. Joanne Spencer. His ex-wife. How funny. I guess when a person is worn down to the bone, the truth is exposed. And this truth explained why Guy had gone all mushy this weekend after a month of sweet, nonromantic attention.

Guy had seemed so terribly weary. He said his weariness was because of his job, but it seemed more than that to her. More personal, deeper. He'd thrown himself into domesticity with a passion she'd never seen in him before. He'd wanted to be mothered and she had mothered him. And he'd wanted to be the head of the household, and he had provided for her. He'd been hiding. He'd been playing house as a way of avoiding something, and he'd sold himself on his own make-believe.

Mahelly thought about Guy telling her he loved her and then being impotent this morning. He didn't love her, *couldn't* love her. How could you love a person who could only dance on her tippy-toes because at any minute the other person would be gone? Guy knew her as a woman for a few short nights and a weekend. Was that love? Did *he* know she wrapped up her toenail parings before she threw them away? Or that she hung up her clothes by color? Washed her socks and panties in lavender water? Did he know that she was allergic to cantaloupe and cucumbers? They had never had a fight! It was believable that Guy thought for a few minutes he loved her, but it was an image of her he loved—an image of her as a caretaker when he was in need, a caretaker like his ex-wife, Joanne. He hadn't fooled his body. His body had known more than his mind had.

Mahelly sighed. How long could mutual parenting hold them together? Until he was feeling good again. Then his healthier self would gape in amazement that he had tied himself to her. It was interesting how her feelings for him and his feelings for her had sprung from the same source—a need to feel safe. Ultimately, that wouldn't be good enough for either of them. Her instincts had been right every time she recognized that she and Guy would have to part. They must stop this now. They were getting in each other's way.

Mahelly sipped grapefruit juice and fluffed her pillows. She hadn't thought about much beyond her relationship with Guy in weeks. That was crazy and self-destructive. She needed to think about the other parts of her life. Hook up with the world. She pulled the phone into her lap and made some calls. At last she put the phone down and closed her eyes. This was nice. Convalescence. She would do absolutely nothing today but rest.

Hanna felt lousy. She had slept on the plane coming back, gone into a coma actually, anything to block the feelings that she had absolutely lost Guy. The Guy she sat next to on the plane today wouldn't connect with her. True, he looked worried about the meeting he was going to, but really, Guy was so smart he could cope brilliantly with whatever he had to do. No, he just didn't care about her any more. He'd turned off. It was over.

She sat at the dining-room table and turned out onto its surface the contents of a cigar box she had labeled "miscellaneous notions." She moved grommets and studs and hooks and eyes into interesting patterns. That was a funny idea. Miscellaneous notions, by Hanna Coleman. First notion! Join the circus. Or she could paint the dining room black. Or buy a Saint Bernard. Write a cookbook called *Cooking with Parsnips*. Have her head shaved. Get married. That was no miscellaneous notion. That was a fervent desire. Guy. Guy, please come back. Could she kidnap him? Shanghai him to Las Vegas? Marry him there in a wedding mill chapel. Move all of his clothes down to her apartment? She knew she had a vast and colorful imagination, but she'd done her best on the plane today. If there was a way to get her lover back, she didn't know it. She wanted to talk with Mahelly. She wanted to talk to her best friend.

She dialed the phone. Mrs. Colucci was out this week, she was told by someone at the gym. She dialed Mahelly's apartment number.

"Mel. It's me. Hanna."

"Where are you?"

"Home. How are you feeling?"

"A little weak but fine. How about you?"

"Sick to my stomach."

"Flu?"

"Guy." Hanna paused. "I know you're the wrong person to talk to," she said with a self-conscious laugh, "but who is the right person?"

"Oh, Hanna. Come upstairs. Would that be OK?"

"I was praying for an invitation."

They could have been back in school. The two sat in Mahelly's bed, sharing the pillows and blankets.

"I don't believe it!" Mahelly said, horrified.

"I'm not making up a word. She stood there with her hand on his butt looking like a lizard watching a fly." Hanna covered her face with a pillow. "Arrgggh."

"What did you do?"

"All I could think of at first was getting out."

"Oh, Hanna," Mahelly said sympathetically.

"Then he followed me out into the hallway in his *bathrobe,* and the elevator man had gone to Peking for coffee or something, so we just stood there."

Mahelly gasped. "And . . ."

"And he started mindfucking me. You know. Hanna, you're being a baby. Miranda's not a lizard . . ."

"He didn't say that."

"No. But almost."

"Go on. What did you do."

"I let him have it. I told him he'd manipulated me into this man-sharing mess and that I knew him for what he was." Hanna paused, savoring the pictures.

Mahelly shook her arm. "Hanna, Hanna, that was wonderful. What did he do?"

"Nothing. Went inside, I suppose. Miranda probably flicked him a few times with her whip, but what else would happen? Nothing terrible ever happens to people like him."

"That cold-blooded bastard! But I'm really proud of you, Hanna."

"Yeah, thanks. I'm proud of myself."

There was silence. The word mansharing had brought the subject into existence. They both thought it. Mahelly spoke.

"You wanted to talk about Guy."

Hanna swallowed. She looked at Mahelly and then looked away. "He doesn't love me any more."

"He does."

Hanna shook her head, no. "I've been to Chicago and back this morning."

"What?"

"I got on the plane with him."

"Hanna." Mahelly laughed. She could imagine Hanna doing that. The one and only Hanna. "And . . ."

"And I asked him to marry me." She looked at Mahelly nervously. How was she taking this?

"What did he say?"

"He said, 'What happened, did David dump you?' "

"You *told him* about David?"

"Not what I told you. You won't tell him?"

Mahelly looked at Hanna with exasperation. "We're best friends, aren't we?"

"We are. No matter what."

The two touched hands.

"He looked terrible on the plane and I could tell he doesn't love me any more." The images assaulted her and her feelings followed. "I'm losing him," Hanna said as her face crumpled. "I feel helpless and it's killing me and I don't know what to do."

"Hey, Hanna, don't cry. It's going to be all right. Here." She handed Hanna a tissue and squeezed her arm. Hanna blew her nose hard and wiped her cheeks with the back of her hands.

"Han, we never talk about you, but he's very upset about something."

"What?"

"I don't know. I honestly don't. I think he's processing a lot of things. He looks worried all the time and he slept almost the whole weekend."

"What do you think I should do? Quit? Hang on?"

"Hang on. He's going to have one less thing to worry about soon."

"What? You?" Could she hope? Were Mahelly and Guy going to stop sleeping together?

"He doesn't love me, Han. We're just complicating each other's lives."

"You sound different, Mel."

"It's been a big month. I've learned a lot from Guy. I feel better about myself as a woman—you know? Sexy."

Hanna nodded.

"And having it out with Frank cleared up a lot of things. I've been so furious at him for falling in love with a little blond twenty-year-old and then angry at him for trying to make me stay that way. And then he went and left his little blond 'bird,' without even saying goodbye. I felt worthless. I needed Guy to make me feel worthwhile, but I don't need him for that any more. And he doesn't love me, Hanna." She let the words hang in the air. "More than anything, I need to be by myself. It's going to be very hard. But I have to do it—be a woman without a man. Find out who I am. Please myself. Do for myself. Then maybe I can find someone to love who's half as good as Guy."

"God, Mel. You hurt, don't you?"

"I think it's growth," she smiled weakly. She didn't want the sad look on her face. She didn't want to cry with Hanna—it wouldn't be fair. She forced her face into a different expression. "You know what else? I took the space. The loft on Mercer Street. I told the broker I'm sending her a check." Mahelly grinned.

"You did?" Hanna said, clapping her hands.

"I did. And I called Donna today. The woman I used to work with at Holiday Spas. She's coming to work for me managing the gym, and after I get her broken in I'm going to take three weeks off. I'm taking myself to the Caribbean—St. Martin, St. Bart's, Antigua. I'll be back in time for the closing."

"Great. How wonderful! And three weeks in the sun. That's what I need. Can I come with you?"

"Not this time. I need to be alone, remember?"

The two smiled at each other. Hanna plucked at the blanket. "I've been pretty mad at you," she said. "I wanted you to stop."

"I know you did. And I wanted to. I felt horrible, but I couldn't help myself, Hanna. I was having love feelings after so long without having them. They made me feel so *alive*. Tell me, how do you just turn those feelings off? They went beyond my will. It was chemical, you know. Biological."

"Oh, God. I know what you mean. I guess I created a few feelings for David without as much cause."

"That slime."

"Mel, that wasn't fair of me to blame you for being with Guy. It wasn't your fault. I'm sorry I put you through all this."

"I was going to go through something, Hanna. If it hadn't been Guy, it would have been someone."

"I'm sorry anyway."

"OK," said Mahelly, smiling bravely. "I'm sorry too."

"I missed you," the two said in unison.

"Jinx, you owe me a Coke," said Mahelly.

The two smiled and hugged.

"I'm going downstairs," said Hanna. "I want to go over the story I wrote a few times before I present it to the devil tomorrow."

"Call me later."

"I will. I love you."

"Me too."

As Mahelly closed the front door, the phone rang. "Hello? Guy? Something sounds wrong with the line. No, not tonight. I need to be by myself tonight. I need to be alone. See you tomorrow. 'Bye."

Guy leaned up against the plane window. It was cold out there and dark. Maybe the plane would crash. He wouldn't resist death. What was going on? How had his world turned so shitty in such a short span of time? Half of everything he was feeling could be found in the file labeled "Stupidity over Courtney." Boy, what a jerk he'd been. Those stories about her had been true. He could never imagine being as evil as she had been, or as vindictive. He had learned a big lesson today in a bad way. And now, Mahelly. What was that all about? She needed to be alone, she'd said. Christ, what timing! Here he was, blood streaming from every pore, and all he wanted was his wife to bandage him. Was that asking too much?

He stopped his thought. It resonated in his head. Wife. Mahelly wasn't his wife. With sudden clarity he understood the homey *déjà vu* feelings he'd had at the cabin. Being with Mel felt like when he and Joanne were first married. He was the provider being cared for by his helpmate. What a setup. And he did it to himself. She hadn't asked for a weekend with him. It was his idea. There on the rug in front of the fire, hadn't Mahelly tried to say good-bye? She had known it wasn't for real. He was confusing love and need, and there was a big difference between the two. He didn't love her. He loved how he felt with her—safe and necessary. This was undoubtedly the worst month he'd had in his life. Tomorrow was his night with Mahelly. They'd talk then. Right after he figured out how he was going to salvage his career.

Guy looked out the window and saw the blue lights of LaGuardia rising to meet the underbelly of the plane.

The message was blue and conspicuous and on her desk. It said, "See me. ASAP. D.S." She couldn't help it. She shivered.

"He'll be in a meeting until 11:00," Jillian said pleasantly. "And then he's got another meeting until lunch, and a meeting through lunch. I think he sometimes thinks everyone gets into the office at 7:30 as he does."

"Oh," said Hanna lamely, knowing it was somewhere near a quarter to ten. "Do you have any idea what he wants?"

"Well," said Jillian sweetly. "He may have been a trifle cheesed off that you missed the editorial meeting yesterday and no one knew where you were."

Yow! The editorial meeting. She'd forgotten. Well, she'd had a few things on her mind, hadn't she? She straightened her shoulders. Tough, she wanted to say. Too bad, but yesterday I decided to put my personal life above my career for once. And probably too late. "A sudden emergency," she said instead.

"Oh, is everything all right?"

"I hope so. Listen, Jillian, give this to David will you. He's been waiting for it. Thanks." She placed a clean white envelope in front of Jillian. It contained an eight-page manuscript and probably the shards of her relationship with Guy.

Her office was a mess. The sweaters from the shoot were stretching arms out of cartons. Garment bags lay in repose across her desk. Her file drawers, left open on Friday, gaped helplessly at the ceiling. Her rain boots peeked pathetically out from under her desk, and the coffee cup she'd left on her desk over the weekend had been overlooked by the cleaning people and had grown furry islands in a marbled sea.

She drew the door shut and went to work. On top of the mess was the box of slides from the shoot. Her mission was to clear off enough space for the light box so she could see the pictures.

There was a knock on the door. Hanna got out of her chair and walked two paces to the door. She opened it, acknowledged David with a look, turned and walked back to her chair. She sat, elbows propped on the desk, chin resting on her hands, staring at the wall in front of her. She didn't want to look at David's mismatched eyes. She'd once thought those ridiculous eyes were sexy. How had she thought so?

"It's good, Hanna," David said, tapping the manuscript on the edge of her desk. "Very good. It's better than I thought it would be. The angle changes everything." David sat in the chair beside her and kept talking. "First the sexy heading. The reader thinks, 'here's a new idea, something I can try,' but then as you reveal the consequences of sharing your man, it becomes apparent that despite the slick, hip appearance of our urban lives, some things—love, monogamy—are fundamental to our humanity. A return to conservative ethics in the eighties. That's hot stuff!" David stopped and looked at Hanna expectantly. Wouldn't she smile? He was happy with her writing. He was proud of her. He continued. "I won't change a word. I knew you could do it. Another story or two like this and you could get a promotion."

"Thanks," Hanna said, not looking at David at all, looking at the photos of a happy summer a million years ago. How little his praise meant to her now.

"I mean it," he said.

Hanna nodded.

There was a long silence. David cleared his throat. Hanna could feel the subject changing. "Will you have dinner with me tonight?" he asked. There was something softer in his voice than she had ever heard before, something pleading, something vulnerable. She didn't reply at first. She just shook her head, no. Her silky auburn hair fanned out and moved right and left, slapping her cheeks as she shook her head vigorously, no. Then she looked at him. "No. No more. Never again." She turned her face away again.

"Listen to me, Hanna. I know you are upset with me for, what did you say, bullying you, but look at the result! This story is marvelous."

Had he really read it? It was a story about how her reckless disregard for the bounds of two intimate relationships had shredded every part of her life. Did he only see the story? Couldn't he see what it had done to her? No. And she would not be able to explain it to him. Explaining this to David would be like reading poetry to her microwave oven.

"Hanna, please look at me. I wasn't trying to do something to you. My feelings for you are sincere. I'm sorry that I may have hurt you."

Hanna looked at him. His face was only a foot from hers and she could see every line, every pore absolutely clearly. There was no haze in front of her eyes now, no wine, no illusions of a tall, godly David Stein. "Hanna, I'm sorry," he said again.

Hanna blinked, sighed. "OK, David," she said. "OK. But I want you to do something for me."

"Anything," he said.

"I want you to call me 'Coleman' again. If you do that, I can still manage to work here."

David winced. There was something wrong with him, Hanna noticed. He was feeling something. Hurt? Insecurity? He cared about her! It didn't matter. She might some time in the future appreciate his editorial skill, respect his leadership, but she would never allow herself to be moved by him again. She stared into his eyes.

"Hanna, don't you believe me? I meant my apology."

"I'm not angry any more, David. I swear. I want to be alone. Do me a favor? Shut the door on your way out." She turned her face and stared at the wall. David stood, walked to the doorway and gazed sadly at her. He sighed, then tapped the envelope against the door jamb, slap, slap. Hanna turned. David cleared his throat. "You did a good job, Coleman. An excellent job. I wish *U.L.* had a few more writers like you." Then he closed the door and walked down the hall.

When David left Hanna's small office, she was blinking at the snapshots on her wall. She was looking at Guy. Her cheeks were wet. The membranes in her nose were swollen. She was having heartbreak and she didn't know how she was going to survive it.

Guy wrapped up the remains of the greasy corned-beef sandwich and threw the mustard-stained rubbish into the garbage can. The clock on the Newsweek Building, which he could see from his window, said it was quarter to eleven. He had been sitting in this chair for sixteen hours! He had told Mahelly he would be over at eight. At eight, he'd called her to tell her to eat without him, and then the hours and the paperwork absorbed him and now it was almost eleven o'clock. He riffled the stack of freshly read and annotated paper he had processed, and rejoiced. His belated crash study course of the brown sugar market had been a lot of work, but it had paid off. This one piece of paper, this one right here, was a beauty.

He picked up a page and kissed it. Courtney had misinterpreted a chart she had handed him on his first day at the new job. It was a client-produced graph, and on it some innocent number cruncher in Chicago had plotted the overall national trend. It was down. The numbers were so small, it was easy to see how, if a person were looking for a certain trend, say a down trend, she might overlook that a certain section of the population in the Northeast was using the hell out of brown sugar.

Today, Guy had called old Charlie Jackson who had delivered a big brown carton filled with last year's sales records and there it was— support for his findings. Brown sugar sales were down *overall* for everyone including Swanee, but, Swanee Old Fashioned Brown Sugar was gaining sales, not declining, in one important market where their advertising was running. If they concentrated their spending there, and cut their spending elsewhere, they'd bust the competition and own the whole Northeast. "You're absolutely right, Guy," Charlie had said scratching his head. "What a difference a little copy makes, lobbed into the right market. Someone's going to catch it for overlooking this one."

Guy leaned back in his chair and savored the feeling. This was going to be beautiful. He was still guilty of being a dumb unprepared asshole, but this would bring him up to even, maybe better. He was going to love to see Courtney's face when the error came to light. He would be very careful not to gloat when he showed the results of his work to Bitner. In fact, he'd excuse Courtney. She had bitten off quite a lot of responsibility all at once, he would say, and actually the error had happened out in Sugarland. Calling Carter Mulholland would be tricky though. Carter would hate being shown up. Hey, Carter, he might say. It could happen to anybody. If Mulholland would be a human being, it would be OK. Carter could take the news to his own management and be a hero. He'd suggest to Jack Bitner that it would be best to let Mulholland carry the news in Chicago. That should do it. What do you know? With the five million dollar budget restored, his bonus check might be pretty decent this year.

Guy squared up his pack of papers and locked them in his desk drawer. Christ. Eleven fifteen.

"I'm sorry it got so late," Guy said to Mahelly when she opened the door for him.

"I'm awake. Come into the living room."

Guy heaved himself onto the sofa. Christ, he was beat. He accepted a cold beer and looked into Mahelly's eyes. She looked sad and reserved. She usually flung herself upon him, dragged him off to bed. And here he was on the sofa, drinking a beer. He knew what was coming. "Melly, did I understand what you *didn't* say last night when you told me not to come over? You want to stop?"

"Guy. Yes. I do love you. And I need to be on my own now."

Guy nodded. He could see this wasn't easy for her. Her voice was high in her throat and it wobbled. He felt sadness, and he felt relief. Something heavy he'd been carrying spread its wings and flew away. And yet he would miss being with this dear, tender woman.

Mahelly moved closer to Guy and put her hand on his. "Thank you for everything, Guy. You've taught me so much. I'm not sure I know how to be on my own, but I have to try."

"I know, Mel. You're doing the right thing."

"You're not mad?"

"Mad? No. How could I be mad at you?" He put his arms around her and kissed the top of her head. "I'm going to miss you though." He stopped. "And I know what you're doing."

"What do you mean?"

"I know this is selfless of you." He breathed in her scent and moved his cheek against her soft hair. "You are a wonderful, precious person. I do love you. And I loved every minute. We didn't do this just for you."

"No?"

"No."

Mahelly swallowed and reached an arm around Guy's middle and laid her head on his chest. He held her tightly. They hugged and touched and listened to each other's breathing and then Mahelly pulled away. "Kiss me good-bye?"

"My breath stinks from corned beef and beer . . ."

"Kiss me."

Guy put his hand on her face and kissed her. It was a gentle kiss, a good-bye kiss. Then he held her face and looked at her. "Thank you for doing this, Mel."

She walked him to the foyer and without looking up at him, she opened the door, touched his back, and then closed the door behind him.

Guy pushed the elevator button. When the elevator car came, he rode it down to his floor. He went into his dark apartment, took off his clothes, showered, and got into his bed. The sheets were as cold as stainless steel. The shock of them lessened his relief at finally lying prone. He thought about Mahelly and how she had said good-bye to him. She was right, and he knew she was right. Sure, life with her would have been safe, uncomplicated, but that wasn't what he wanted forever. She had pushed him out, for her own reasons, for his, and for Hanna.

He thought of Hanna crying on the plane yesterday. Eight hundred miles to say I love you. Had he really thought he could do without that aggravating female? Poor Hanna. She had really been through hell. What must she be feeling now? Lonely? Sad? Abandoned? And what about his own feelings? The idea of not having that woman with him, sent a chill of fear to his midsection.

Fuck. That's what had been wrong with him all this time. He wanted a love relationship with a woman he could count on. Was there anything crazy about that? No. He was monogamous, always had been. And the woman he wanted was Hanna. He loved her, he loved every nutty thing about her. Here was a good question—why was he up here when she was practically right below his feet?

Guy dialed numbers in the dark. "Did you mean what you said on the plane? Did you mean 'forever'?" he asked.

Hanna, also in the dark, noddly silently. She gripped the receiver with both hands. Silent tears had started.

"Hanna? Words, please. Speak into the little holes."

"Yes. I meant it."

"You didn't mean forever unless you got an offer to work in the Soviet Union?"

"No."

"Or forever unless there's a crazy kind of sunset in Tahiti you have to see or an antimarriage movement . . ."

"No, no, no. Please, Guy. Don't tease. I meant it really, forever and ever and ever."

286

"I love you, Hanna," he said, and hung up the phone.

Guy made his way to his closet in the dark, found his robe and put it on. He got back into the elevator and pushed 12. When the door opened, he marched the long walk to Hanna's door and rang the bell until she opened it.

Hanna came out into the hallway. She was swaddled in a long flannel gown. She didn't say anything. She just looked at Guy and he looked at her.

They went into one another's arms. They stood swaying in the doorway for an indeterminate time. Then Hanna closed and chained the door and led Guy by the hand. Guy shucked his robe and stood at the foot of the bed, bearlike, furry and huge, licking his chops. "Come and get me," she said, plump in the middle of her bed, lush in the center of her satin goose-down comforter. And he sailed in. They wrestled and grappled and pulled one another's hair. Guy looked for long moments into Hanna's eyes, and she looked into his.

"I love you," he said again.

"I love you," she said.

They touched lips softly, barely and then bit into the other's mouth as if it were fruit. They gave and took and tried to consume flesh and essence. Then warm and soft and sleek and hard found all the right places, and they merged, stopping sometimes to revel in their love, separating completely, panting, and then pulling together, together, together until spent, they fell asleep, one inside the other, wrapped in each other's arms.

32

IN THE SPRING, MAHELLY SULLIVAN COLUCCI WAS IN MUTUAL FASCInation with an architect named Simon, who played the piano and made homemade pasta, and had the most beautiful face she had ever seen.

She hated to leave him alone for even a minute, but she did leave for just that minute so she could stand on the steps of the church for the photographer—she on Guy's left side, Hanna on his right, arms around one another in back, Hanna's and Mahelly's hands linked together, across Guy in the front.

Hanna would later frame this picture in sterling silver and place it on the night table so she and Guy would see it every morning and every night of their married life.